CLAPHAM LIGHTS

Tom Canty was born in Dartford, Kent in 1981 and attended Dartford Grammar School and the University of East Anglia. Clapham Lights is his first novel. He lives in London.

Find out more at www.tomcantywriter.com, on Twitter @tomcantywriter or #claphamlights or www.facebook.com/tomcantywriter.

CLAPHAM LIGHTS

Tom Canty

SILVERTAIL BOOKS • *London*

First published in 2013 by Silvertail Books
www.silvertailbooks.com

Copyright © Tom Canty 2013

The right of Tom Canty to be identified as the author
of this work has been asserted by him in accordance
with the Copyright, Design and Patents Act 1988

A catalogue record of this book is available
from the British Library

ISBN 978-1-909269-02-6

Typeset in Ehrhardt Monotype by Joanna MacGregor
Printed and bound in the UK by Biddles, part of the MPG
Books Group, Bodmin and King's Lynn

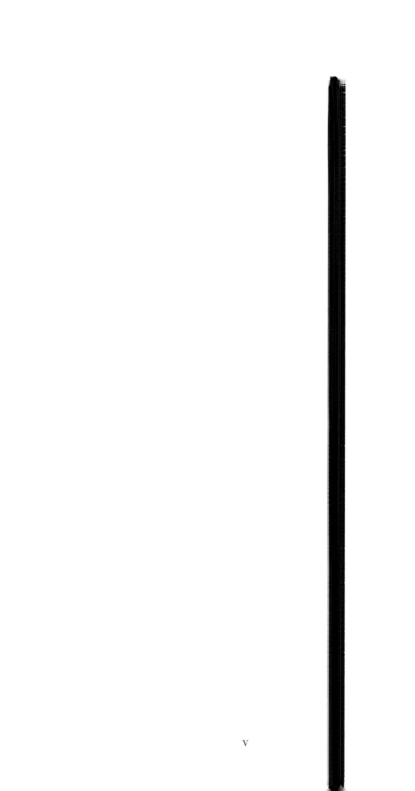

CHAPTER ONE

'Tennant, that couple over there want a four-bed,' says Christian D'Souza, manager of the Lavender Hill branch of Cinq Estates. He points at a pregnant woman and her husband waiting on a maroon sofa in reception. There is a continuous stream of house-hunters passing through the open-plan office and the phones are ringing incessantly. 'Take them to the gaff in Streatham I mentioned on Monday. You know the one, yeah?'

'Err, which one was that?' Craig Tennant is softly spoken with a Norfolk twang, and his suit hangs off his tall, lean frame. His brown hair is short and neat, and he has pale, stubble-free skin.

'Akabusi Street, off Tooting Bec Common. It's number sixty-three or sixty-five. Hannah's got the keys.'

'Right. How much is it on the market for?'

'It's not been valued yet.' Christian tweaks his oversized tie knot. He's wearing a sovereign ring and the office lights reflect off his gelled hair. 'If it's in good condition, say around five fifty. Tell *them* seven hundred. If it's top notch, push for eight hundred. Use your initiative. See what you can get away with.'

'OK.'

'Don't come back here until you've got them to make an offer. I want to shift it as quick as possible. They've obviously got a bit of wedge, so if they look interested knock a couple of grand off so they think they're getting a deal. Got it?'

'No problem.'

'Piece of advice: avoid saying Streatham and definitely don't mention Brixton. Drive there through Balham. In fact, tell them it's in Balham.'

'Right. What are their names?'

'No idea. You ask them. Oh and Craig, there's a thirty quid Next voucher in it for you if you can get rid of it.'

1

Craig retrieves his car keys and leather folder from his desk and introduces himself to the couple, who are flicking through a copy of *Maison d'Etre*, Cinq Estates' corporate magazine.

Paul and Jane are both in their early thirties. Jane's baby bump protrudes from beneath a white long-sleeved t-shirt and she has puffy eyes and blotchy skin. Paul has broad shoulders, a small scar below his right eye and is wearing a Hackett rugby shirt and jeans.

'Would you like a drink before we start?' Craig asks. 'We've got still or sparkling water, smoothies, beer, wine?'

'No, thanks,' Jane says, placing the magazine on the coffee table.

'So you're looking for a four-bedroom house, is that right?'

'Preferably three bedrooms,' Paul says, 'but we want a study, so possibly a four-bedroom house we could convert.'

Craig makes a note. 'We've got some great three and four-bedroom places at the moment. Are there any areas in particular you like?'

'Clapham Common or Old Town, and perhaps Balham,' Jane says.

'And we want to be close to transport, for work.'

'And we'd like a garden.'

Craig makes another note. 'OK. What kind of budget have you got?'

'Around six hundred and fifty thousand,' Paul says.

'Is that the upper limit? Or is there any room for-'

'That's the upper limit.'

Craig looks down at his pad and pinches his bottom lip. 'That's a good budget, definitely a good budget, but to get three bedrooms, a study and a garden you may have to widen your search slightly because there are a very limited number of properties like that on the market. Would you consider Tooting or Streatham?'

Paul and Jane glance at each other.

'I don't think so, no,' Jane says. 'Definitely not Streatham. We've been following the market around here for several months and we think our budget's generous considering how the market has plateaued.'

Craig looks puzzled by the word 'plateaued'. 'I know prices nationally haven't been rising, but the market always tends to slow between March and May. Some one-bedroom flats in Clapham have been selling for as much as five hundred thousand and a lot depends on the condition of the house. Would you consider somewhere that needed some work doing to it?'

'Only cosmetic work,' Paul says. 'We're not taking on any building projects.' He looks Craig in the eye. 'So do you think you can help us or not?'

'Yes, yes, of course I can.' Craig taps his pen on his leg. 'Actually, there is a four-bedroom house that's literally just become available in the last couple of days.'

'Where is it?'

'Balham. In the Balham–Clapham area. Do you know the area well?'

'Fairly well,' Paul says.

'Where do you live at the moment?'

'We're renting in Primrose Hill.'

'So you're not in a chain?'

'No.'

'That's good.' Craig writes that down. 'The house I want to show you is fantastic. I think it could be what you're looking for. One of my colleagues took a couple there earlier and they loved it. Are you pushed for time because I could drive you round there now?'

'Shall we have a look?' Paul asks his wife.

'I don't want to push you,' Craig says, 'but I think there may have already been one offer at the asking price.'

'OK,' Jane says, nodding.

'Great,' Craig says. 'I'll get the keys. I won't be two seconds.'

He hurries over to reception but has to wait for Hannah Fox, the new receptionist, to finish her phone conversation. She has a chestnut-brown bob, hazel eyes and perfect teeth. Beneath her desk are four glass fridges full of bottled drinks and a succession of luxury houses pass by on a plasma screen above her head. She looks slightly shaken as she takes off her headset.

'Hannah, are you OK? Is something wrong?'

'The man on the phone was shouting about being owed money and said that he had my name and was going to the police.'

'Oh, right. One of those. In future when you get a call like that, transfer it straight to Christian.'

'I tried to but he told me to deal with it.'

'Send it through to me next time then, and don't take it personally, it's not you they're angry with. If they start getting nasty just put the phone down. You'll be surprised how quickly you get used to it.'

3

'Thanks Craig,' she says with a smile.

Lavender Hill is bustling with shoppers as Craig leads Jane and Paul to a maroon and gold Mini Cooper parked in the side street adjacent to the office.

'We're not going in this are we?' Paul says. 'It looks like it's been vandalised.'

'Yes, sorry, we have to.' Craig releases the central locking. 'It's company policy to drive clients to viewings. The paintwork was done by a graffiti artist.'

'And what's this thing?' Paul asks, tapping on the Cinq-branded wooden box bolted to the roof.

'It's meant to be a house. I know it looks stupid, please just try to ignore it.'

Paul mutters something inaudible and helps his wife in.

'It is around here, I just need to find the road,' Craig says, as they pass Balham station for the third time. 'Do you mind if I stop and call the office? I was given the wrong directions.'

He pulls up in the entrance to Sainsbury's and gets out.

'Shall we just get out and go?' Paul asks his wife. 'He hasn't got a clue.'

'I don't want to walk anywhere, and the house can't be far away. You never know, it could be nice. I don't mind this area.'

'Your choice.'

'Could you move your seat forward a bit more, please?' Jane asks, fanning herself with an old copy of the *Metro* that was on the back seat. 'It's a bit claustrophobic.'

'I would if I could, darling,' Paul says, looking in the rear-view mirror, 'but if I moved forward any further I'd be sitting on the dashboard.'

Craig jumps back into the driver's seat and the car shakes, making Jane wince.

'Right, sorry about that. I know exactly where we're going.'

He speeds out of the car park and up Bedford Hill, almost running over a cyclist as he tries to overtake a bus.

'What's this called?' Jane asks, gazing at the parkland on either side of the road.

'Um, this is Balham Common.'

'It said Tooting Bec Common on the sign back there,' Paul says.

'Yes, it's um, both. Balham Common and Tooting Bec Common are the same place, on either side of the road. Clapham Common is just at the other end of the road. Really close.'

Craig turns off at the top of the common, takes a sharp right the wrong way down a one-way street and parks.

Akabusi Street is lined by terraced Victorian town houses. Some are in pristine condition, others have fallen into disrepair. It's steep and Jane struggles to keep up as Craig paces along the pavement.

'Couldn't you have parked outside?' Paul asks him.

'Sorry, I didn't think it was this far up. And down the road is a bit… safer.'

Jane has to lean on a wall for a moment to get her breath back.

Number 63 is a large three-storey property with a loft conversion, sash windows and a stained glass doorway. There are two wheelie bins hidden behind its overgrown hedge, one with a used nappy poking out of it.

'Not bad is it?' Craig says, taking off his flimsy aviators as he holds open the front door.

The hallway is bright with a black and white tiled floor and high ceiling. The first door on the left leads to the minimalist living room with a dark wood floor and cast iron fireplace. Paul and Jane appear impressed.

Craig leaves the couple and wanders up the hallway into the dining room, which looks out onto decking and a manicured lawn. He glances at himself in the mirror above the mantelpiece and then heads into the kitchen where Jane is opening and closing the glossy white cupboards.

'It's a new kitchen,' she says.

'It is. It's a lovely house. Perfect for starting a family. Have a look around. I'll leave you to it.'

Craig is sitting in the living room playing on his phone when he hears Paul and Jane coming back downstairs. He jumps up and straightens the cushions on the suede sofa.

'It's a great place isn't it?' he says as the couple walk in.

'It is nice,' Jane says, 'I can't deny that.'

Paul looks less happy. 'How much is it on for?'

'My manager said it's on at seven hundred thousand pounds but I'm sure the owners would take six hundred and seventy-five for a quick sale.'

Paul shakes his head. 'Seven hundred thousand?'

'That's a good price for this area.'

'It doesn't sound like one. And that's over our budget. Who owns it?'

'A couple with children. Grown-up children, they've moved out. That's why they're selling. They're moving to... somewhere else.'

'In London?' Jane asks.

Craig hesitates. 'They didn't say.'

Paul inspects the fireplace. 'What council tax bracket is this place in?'

'D, I think.'

Paul and Jane exchange doubtful looks and sit together on the edge of the sofa.

'What are the transport links like here?' Jane asks.

'Well, Balham station is just down the road. We drove past it earlier.'

'Yes, several times,' Paul says. 'That's the closest station is it?'

'Yes, but there are lots of buses. Every five minutes, from the top of the road.'

'What road is that?'

'That's Balham High Road.' Craig coughs and adjusts his belt.

Jane rubs her bump as Paul gets to his feet and gazes out of the window to the street. A group of young boys are kicking a football at a snarling pit bull terrier tethered to a gatepost. He takes his phone out of his pocket.

'They don't live around here.' Craig says, looking over Paul's shoulder.

'How do you know?' Paul says, concentrating on his phone. 'I've just put this address into Google maps and it comes up as Streatham *not* Balham.' He glares at Craig.

'Err... well... the address is Streatham, but the house is in Balham.' Craig backs towards the corner of the room.

'So it's in Balham *and* Streatham?' Jane says. 'How does that work? It can't be in two places at once.'

'It's on the border. It's south Balham. Maps are very... you can't always trust the computer maps as they've redrawn the borders recently. It gets a bit confusing.'

'It clearly does for you,' Paul says. 'Look Craig, I deal with bullshit-ters every day at work and you're not a very good one. You haven't got a clue, have you?'

'Yes,' he says, unconvincingly.

'Do you even know where we are?'

'Yes. South... Balham.'

'No, we're not, Craig. We're in Streatham.' Paul huffs and shows Jane the map.

'Craig, we're in the middle of nowhere,' she says. 'It's Streatham High Road, not Balham High Road, at the top of the street. We're nowhere near Clapham Common. We're nearer Brixton!'

'Yes, sorry, that's what I meant, Streatham High Road,' Craig says, smiling nervously. 'Clapham Common is just down the road. And so is Brixton. You just have to make sure you get on the right bus.'

'Everywhere is just down the road according to you,' Jane replies, raising her voice. 'I don't want to take a bus to Clapham Common, I want to live there. I specifically said we don't want to live in Streatham, so why did you bring us here?' Her cheeks are flushed.

'There's no way this place is worth seven hundred thousand either,' Paul says. 'Who valued it? That's about two hundred thousand too much. Do we look stupid to you?'

'No, you don't,' Craig mumbles. 'It's an up and coming area. We call it south Balham, but the name's not really caught on yet. I could try to get you a good deal. The owners might take six hundred and twenty-five thousand. That's under budget.'

'Have you actually ever spoken to the owners?'

'Not personally but I'm sure they'd take six hundred and twenty-five. Do you want to make an offer?'

'Are you joking?' Paul says. 'Do you really think we'd buy anything from you? You're a fucking idiot. How old are you anyway? Twelve?'

'I'm twenty-five,' Craig says, looking hurt.

'Paul, calm down,' Jane says, struggling to her feet, 'I would say take us back to Clapham, but judging by your sense of direction, Craig, it'd be quicker to walk.'

'Come on, we'll get a taxi.' Paul storms out into the hall. 'You look like you should be at school, not selling houses,' he calls back.

'Please, don't go,' Craig says.

They slam the door behind them and the sash windows rattle. Craig watches them stomp off arguing in the sunshine and then slumps down in an armchair.

'Tell me you made a sale,' Christian says, emerging from his office holding a calculator.

Craig swivels round and Christian pulls up a chair next to him. The office is closed to the public and all the other staff have gone home.

'Um, no, not quite, but they liked it,' Craig says, giving a small thumbs-up.

'What do you mean "no"? Craig, what's wrong with you?' Christian slams his calculator on the desk.

'I'm really sorry but they-'

'I'm not interested in excuses. What was the property like?'

'The house is great. Three storeys, four bedrooms, study, big kitchen and dining room, tiled hallway.'

'Big Victorian thing?'

'I think so.'

'How much did you say it was worth?'

'It was in good condition so I took your advice and said it was on at seven hundred.'

Christian crosses his left leg over his right, showing off his tasselled loafers and *Spider-Man* socks.

'But,' Craig continues, 'I told them the owner would take six hundred and seventy-five.'

'What did they say?'

'They thought it was too much.'

'Did you explain to them about the market?'

'I tried to but they still said it was too much so I said six hundred and twenty-five.'

'OK, that's better than nothing I suppose. You didn't drive along Streatham High Road did you?'

'No.'

'Good. Well at least you did one thing right. I think it was closed anyway; a bloke was shot dead at a bus stop there this morning. You didn't mention Streatham or Brixton did you?'

'Err, no. I told them south Balham.'

'Good. Phone that couple tomorrow and tell them you've spoken to the owner and they've dropped the price again and want a quick sale, yeah.'

'But tomorrow's Sunday.'

'Phone them and keep phoning until you get them to agree to buy the place. Threaten them if you need to.'

'I'm not going to threaten a pregnant woman.'

'Well find out where they live and go round there.'

'They live in Primrose Hill.'

'It's rough around there. No wonder they're moving.' Christian runs his hands through his gleaming hair. 'It's about time you put a big sale on the board,' he says, craning his neck to check the sales whiteboard hidden from public view in his office. Craig's column is empty. 'Think of all the lovely commission you'll make from a six hundred grand plus sale, Craig. You'll be rolling in cash.'

'Yeah, sixty quid,' he says flatly.

'And the Next vouchers. Don't tell anyone else about them by the way.'

Craig swivels back to his computer and brings an email up onto the screen. 'Christian, as you're here, could you have a quick look at this?' It is the length of an essay, full of exclamation marks, underlining and capital letters.

Christian peers at the screen and then sits back. 'I'm not reading all that, I haven't got time. Give me a summary.'

'I moved this man and his girlfriend into the gated flats near Brixton prison and they paid the deposit and the first month's rent but on the second night the girl was mugged and now they want to move out and want their deposit back.'

'What? Tell them to forget it. Not our problem. What does it say in the contract?'

'I gave them the option to leave after a month if they didn't like it.'

'What the hell did you do that for?'

'The place had been empty for over a year and I was trying anything to get them to move in.'

'Find that contract and tear it up. Tell them it's invalid because it isn't counter-signed by a senior manager and tell them that if they leave they're liable for six months' rent, a contract termination fee of four hundred quid, a two hundred quid viewing fee for every new person we show round the place... and a one hundred pound admin fee which will cover the cost of you having to read that email... and tell them they're not under any circumstances getting their deposit back.'

'OK, but he's said at the bottom that he's already been in touch with a solicitor and he's willing to take us to court.'

'He's probably lying. Don't under any circumstances give them anything back. Cheeky bastards.'

Craig starts to type out a reply.

'Craig, leave it, it's seven o'clock, do it Monday. Let's go for a beer. Oh, and one other thing,' Christian says as he walks away. 'Can you try and smile a bit more when you're with the customers? Look like you're enjoying yourself.'

CHAPTER TWO

M ark Hunter switches off his alarm and yawns. It's twenty-five past
five. He moves his head away from the wall, and his pillow – a
thick wad of quilted toilet paper – drops to the floor. A hand dryer whirrs
and the door to the bathroom thuds shut.

Mark picks up his hardback notepad, unlocks his cubicle and checks
he's alone. A leather document wallet and a folded *Financial Times* have
been left by the sinks.

Mark is six feet tall and has a wide, plump face. The trousers of his
pinstripe suit cling to his thighs and his jacket is stretched tight across
his shoulders. He drinks from a tap, straightens his tie in the mirror
and pats his double chin. There's a red mark on his temple from where
he's been sleeping which he unsuccessfully tries to cover by ruffling his
receding hair.

He takes the lift down to the in-house coffee shop, downs a double
espresso, and then travels back to the twelfth floor. He pushes through
the glass doors and wanders to his seat with his notepad tucked under
one arm and his eyes fixed on his BlackBerry.

MenDax Wealth Management's Scandinavian markets department
consists of just two banks of desks and Justin Fortesque's office. Mark
sits in the far corner, next to Amy Robertson. Behind them is a wall of
locked cabinets and discarded filing boxes. Beyond that, the vast space
is empty. The floor-to-ceiling windows provide a panoramic view of the
City of London and outside it's cloudy and spitting with rain. A new
office block is under construction in the shadow of the Gherkin, opposite
St Margaret's Church.

Justin, the head of department, and Julia Hayter, the senior account
manager, are at a meeting. Ian Butler, the other member of the team, is
on the telephone and chewing a biro whilst gazing down at Liverpool
Street station. He has a goatee beard and is wearing a sleeveless jumper
over his shirt and tie.

Mark rocks back in his chair to spy on Amy's computer screen. She is comparing the prices of flights to Dubai.

'Do you need some work to do?' he asks.

Amy ignores the question. She is the same age as Mark - twenty-six - and from Edinburgh. She has full cheeks and a freckly nose, her shoulder-length brown hair is pushed behind her ears and she isn't wearing make-up.

'Where have you been?' she asks.

'I had a conference call downstairs.'

'For four hours?'

'Yeah. It was boring. Justin's not been back has he?'

'No.'

Mark types some figures into a sprawling Excel spreadsheet, saves it, and deletes his only new email - a reminder that his subscription to *Men's Wealth* magazine is about to expire.

'I might go home,' he says, yawning.

'You should. You've had a busy day.'

Mark nods, seemingly oblivious to Amy's sarcasm. His cursor is lingering over the 'Turn Off' symbol when Justin bursts in followed by Julia, who towers over him. She has a gaunt, expressionless face and sunglasses perched on her head.

Justin places his briefcase on his desk and stands outside his office. His scalp is visible through his blond hair and he is wearing black brogues with built-up heels and a long red tie which curls over his stomach.

'Computers off,' he orders. 'We're celebrating. We've got a titanic investor coming on board, so it's drinky time, on me. No excuses.'

'Quality,' Mark says. He renames his spreadsheet *Growth and Prosperity Market Confidence Forecast: Winter '08 - Autumn '10* and re-saves it.

Ian starts to speak but Justin cuts him off:

'I'm not interested, Ian. See you all at The Receiver in fifteen. I've got a couple of calls to make.' He shuts his door and pulls down the blinds.

Mark calls his driving instructor to cancel his lesson and shuts down his computer.

'Come on Amy, let's go.'

The Receiver is a bar-restaurant-nightclub split over three floors in a former bank on Chamberlain Street. The rain has stopped and people are outside smoking in a cordoned off area on the pavement. Posters advertising pitchers of Pimms for £10 and 30% off champagne hang in the windows. Mark nods at one of the doormen and strolls in.

The spacious, neo-classical interior is full of suit-wearing office workers all drinking pints or white wine. There are only two staff behind the bar and a stocky man in a pink shirt thumps his wallet down when the woman next to him is served first.

Julia leads Mark, Amy and Ian downstairs. The lower ground level is dimly lit with a low ceiling and smells suffocatingly of air freshener. The floor is sticky and there's no music but a lot of noise filters down from upstairs.

Most of the booths around the perimeter of the room are occupied but Julia spots a spare table behind a pillar near the bar. There's a printed notice in the vacant area: *RESERVED FOR HARTMAN CLIFFORD LAMB FROM 6 PM* but she tears it to pieces and throws the bits on the floor. She takes a seat on one of the six faux leather chairs, and, after a brief look at the drinks menu, clicks her fingers at a waitress and orders four bottles of Pinot Grigio, six Asahis and two sharing platters. She starts a tab on her MenDax American Express card and tells the others that she's going upstairs for a cigarette.

The drinks arrive in four ice buckets. Mark smiles at the waitress, who ignores him, and pulls out two beers, dripping water all over the table.

'Who was your conference call with, Mark?' Amy asks. She sips her wine and grimaces.

'Just a contact from one of my other clients. I think it's a non-starter though. I was explaining the investment options to this bloke, but he didn't understand. The more simple I made it, the less he seemed to get it.'

'Perhaps it was you he didn't understand,' Amy says.

Mark doesn't react. Ian sniggers and picks at the label on his beer bottle:

'Any idea who Justin's big deal is with?'

Mark shrugs.

'I heard him say something to Julia about having to go to Beijing,'

Amy says, 'but I don't know any more than you two.'

At the foot of the stairs, two tall men are blocking Justin's path but he's so far below their eyeline they don't notice him until he squeezes between them and scurries across to the group.

'Hey, the main man!' Mark says.

'No need to panic, I'm here.' Justin climbs up onto a chair and takes a beer. 'Why are you down here? It's much better upstairs.'

'It was Julia's choice,' Amy says.

'Oh, fine.' Justin looks around the open floor. 'Anyway, the news: Julia and I have pulled off another massive coup. I can't say too much, but it's going to be huge for us.'

Mark edges forward.

'Who with?' Amy asks, underwhelmed.

'SomCop.'

'Who?'

'SomCop,' Justin repeats. 'The Somali Maritime Cooperative. They're in shipping.'

They all look blank.

'Shipping what exactly?' Ian asks.

'In their culture it's disrespectful to ask too many questions but I've got all the info at the office. I think one of them mentioned sugar, or it might have been textiles-'

'Or piracy,' Amy suggests.

'Possibly. That kind of industry anyway. All this is off the record of course until I make the announcement next week, so keep it to yourselves.'

Justin ogles the waitress as she slides two platters onto the table and rushes off. 'I haven't seen her before.'

'She's new,' Mark says, popping three cocktail sausages into his mouth. 'I think she's foreign.' He then gobbles a whole salmon skewer, pulls the stick out from between his teeth, swigs his beer and quietly burps. 'Are we having a big one, Justo?'

'Of course we are. Let's get ON IT! No one's going home before nine.'

By eleven thirty, the lower ground bar is packed. There's a DJ in the corner and a bouncer stands at the stairs leading to the basement night-club. It's hot and the air is thick with perfume. Near the MenDax table, three podgy City boys are all bellowing over the music trying to impress a woman in a low-cut top.

Mark and Ian are onto their ninth Asahis and Amy is trying to avoid the gaze of a drunk man on the next table. Julia is sitting with two men from MenDax's tax advisory department.

Ian is trying to tell Amy about the house he's buying with his girl-friend as Mark hums along to *Billie Jean* whilst watching a blonde girl at the bar. She catches Mark looking at her and turns her back.

'Have I told you about my new place?' Mark asks, interrupting.

'Only about a hundred times,' Amy says.

'The old school, right?' Ian says.

'It's a converted orphanage. It's massive.'

'How much are you paying?'

'Just over two grand a month. So not that much for Clapham.'

'That's nearly three times my mortgage.' Ian pushes his beer to one side and coughs.

'We got a good deal through my flatmate's property company. It's a lot because of the location, and because it's a penthouse... and it's mas-sive. I'm having a party soon. You should come over.'

Mark reaches for the wine bottles but they're all empty. A waitress brings over two more warm Pinot Grigios. He tells her to put them on the tab and fills his glass to the brim.

A man carrying five bottles of Corona stumbles straight into the back of a young woman, knocking beer all over her top. She swears at him but he laughs in her face.

Ian starts tapping on his iPhone. 'Kelly wants to know what time I'll be home.'

'Tell her you don't know,' Mark says. 'Doesn't she realise it's impor-tant for your career to be here?'

'Important how?'

'Well this is where you can network and do deals, isn't it.'

'You think people come here to *network*?' Amy says, looking across to a table where a man is asleep.

'You should always be on the lookout for new business opportuni-ties,' Mark says.

Amy rolls her eyes.

Justin is at the bar on tiptoes rubbing himself against a spotty girl wearing a short skirt. He tries to kiss her but she dodges him, fills her glass with his champagne and disappears down to the basement. He drinks from the bottle and staggers over to the group with his shirt half hanging out.

'Hey gang,' he says, putting an arm around Amy. 'We need more drinks. MORE DRINKS!' he shouts as *Yeah* by Usher reverberates around the room.

'Who's your new friend?' Amy asks, removing Justin's hand from her shoulder.

'I don't know,' he says. His head rolls from side to side. 'I'll get drinks. I'll get some shots. Shots. Wait here.'

Amy tells Ian and Mark that she's going. Mark tries to convince her to stay but she takes her bag and coat and slips out.

Justin re-emerges from the crowd with a busty girl in a tight white vest and tiny skirt. She's wearing a leather belt fitted with shot glasses and has holsters on each hip containing bottles of spirits. Justin pushes her towards the table and sits down opposite Mark and Ian, almost falling off his chair.

'Shots, shots, shots,' he says, grinning inanely.

The girl asks what they want. Justin wants to know how old she is and where she lives. She says that's none of his business, so he orders three sambucas and three tequilas. Ian looks apprehensive.

'Come on gay boys, down the hatch, one after the other,' Justin says, flashing his tab number. 'Cheers!'

He knocks back his drinks and collapses in his seat. Ian has his eyes screwed shut. Mark makes sure nobody is looking and pours his tequila on the floor. Suddenly, Justin jumps up and runs towards the toilets.

Half an hour later, Justin still hasn't reappeared. Mark nudges Ian:

'Come on, let's go downstairs,' he shouts over *American Boy*.

'No.' Ian is struggling to speak.

'I've seen some fit girls going down there.'

'I've got a girlfriend.'

'And? She's not here, is she? Let's go downstairs and see if we can whack it on some girls.'

'What?'

'Whack it on some girls. It means *pull*, Ian,' Mark says, making jerky head movements to the music.

'I can't. I'll miss the last train.' Ian is barely audible.

'Ian, you might be a bit of a social retard, but anyone can whack it on girls. It's all about tactics. Come on. I need a wingman.' Mark shoulder barges him.

'No. I can't move, I'll be sick. You go.' He points a limp arm towards the stairs.

'No, I'm not going on my own. It won't work.'

'Stay here then.'

Mark scowls and drinks clumsily from his bottle. 'I might get the shot girl over and give her some banter.'

'Go on then,' Ian says, cupping his hands over his mouth.

'Have you got a pen? I've got a foolproof whacking tactic.'

Ian produces a biro and Mark plucks a business card from his wallet.

'What are you going to do?' Ian asks. 'Flick ink in her eyes so she can't see your face?'

'No. I'm going to give her a few lines and then, as she's going, I'll slip her the card.'

'Why do you need a pen then?'

'That's the clever bit. On the back of the card I'll write a message. The dirtier the better.'

Ian looks sceptical and hiccups.

'I give her the card face up so she can't see it and then wait,' Mark says.

'Wait for what?'

'Wait for her to flip it over, obviously. It might take a minute but it always works. She'll either give me the nod at the end of the night or text me. I guarantee you.'

Mark stands up and scans the dark mass of bodies. The shot girl is talking to a barman. He sits back down, scribbles on the card and shows it to Ian, who struggles to focus.

'Why, why don't you write the f-word instead of suck?'

Mark shakes his head. 'You never use the f-word with a woman, Ian. I want her to think I'm a gentleman.' He wipes his oily nose with the sleeve of his shirt and flicks at his hair with his fingers. 'Watch this,' he says, jumping up from his seat and waving. The shot girl saunters over.

She asks if they're sure they need another drink. Mark says he's only just started and orders two double sambucas. She puts two glasses on the table and pours.

'So, what's your name?' Mark asks, lurching towards her.

'Um, Jenny,' she says, pushing her fringe away from her eyes.

'That's a good name. You've got a pretty face.'

'Thanks,' she says, dispassionately.

'Have you got a boyfriend?'

'No.' She avoids eye contact and slides the sambuca bottle back into its holster.

Mark picks up his card. 'Why don't you take-'

'That's eighteen pounds,' she cuts in, 'and I don't want your card.'

'I wasn't, I was just-'

'And you can stop looking down my top as well,' she snaps. 'Who's paying for these?'

Mark slips the card back into his wallet. 'It's your round, Ian. I'm going for a piss.' He picks up his jacket and barges his way to the toilets.

A loud west African man is perched on a stool beside the sinks hawking a collection of aftershaves and hair products.

'Freshunup boss? No Armani, no poonani. Chewing gum boss?' he says as Mark washes his hands.

'Yeah, cheers.' Mark helps himself to a stick of gum. 'How much?'

'Two quid boss.'

'Sorry, I haven't got any change.' He drops a £5 note onto the silver dish.

There is pathetic whimpering coming from behind a cubicle door:

'Someone call an ambulance. I think I've had a heart attack. Bog man, please, anyone.'

It's Justin. Mark peeks under the door but leaves him there.

Back in the bar, Ian is passed out on the table, his head amongst the bottles. Mark swerves past two drunk women screaming at each other, takes a wad of notes from his pocket and heads for the exit. Outside, he hails a black cab and tells the driver to take him back to Clapham.

CHAPTER THREE

T he electric gate's sensor isn't working so Craig has to get out of the car in the rain and type the entry code. When the gate slowly clunks into life, he edges forward into the car park of The Block, Wall Street, the converted Victorian orphanage where he and Mark share a flat. The building, advertised on a banner outside as 'a development of luxury 2, 3 and 4 bedroom modern urban living experiences', is illuminated by security lights and surrounded by tall railings.

Mark's Audi TT is in the flat's allocated space so Craig parks in a guest spot. He grabs his two Asda bags, locks the car and enters their block through a doorway which still has the original INFANTS stone pediment. He checks their post box in the communal hallway and takes the lift to the sixth floor.

Craig lets himself into the flat, kicks his shoes off on the polished wood floor and turns on the spotlights in the living room. A pile of unopened post has been left on the dining table and Mark has scrawled a note saying he's gone to Manchester on urgent business and won't be back until tomorrow.

A forty-inch flat screen television sits on a stand in the far right-hand corner facing two blue three-seater sofas arranged in an L-shape. French doors lead out onto a roof terrace which overlooks the gloomy streets of Battersea.

Craig switches on the television. Italy are beating France two–nil in the European Championships and the game is in injury time. He scans through the onscreen TV guide and deletes reminders for *Ross Kemp on Gangs* and *Getting Hard with Danny Dyer*.

He drapes his tie over the back of a chair and goes into his bedroom, which is off the hallway. He hangs up his suit and changes into a pair of bright red football shorts and an ill-fitting polo shirt that has 'University of Eastern England Cambridge, Tour of Ireland, 2005' stitched on the

19

chest and 'Tennant 11' printed on the back. His bed is immaculately made.

Craig's portable television, DVD player and midi hi-fi system sit on an Ikea desk to the right of his bed. On a shelf above the desk are CDs – Keane, Coldplay, The Killers, Snow Patrol – and DVDs – *The Godfather* box set, *American Pie*, *The Office*, *Van Wilder*, *Apocalypse Now*, *Anchorman*. All seven Harry Potter novels are lined up in chronological order on the bedside table, next to his radio alarm clock. He pulls the blind down over the wide rectangular window facing the bed, flicks off the light in his en suite shower room and goes into the kitchen, which adjoins the living room.

Craig wipes the marble work surfaces with a cloth from one of the two sinks and turns on the oven. The huge American fridge smells rancid. An uneaten bag of salad in Mark's half has turned to slush and there is mould growing on a lump of cheddar on the top shelf of the door. Craig throws them both in the bin and empties his shopping bags.

He puts a discounted spaghetti carbonara ready meal to one side and packs away the two half-price loaves of granary bread, and the Asda own-brand baked beans, frosted flakes, peanut butter, tomato soup and instant noodles.

He then unloads the dishwasher and eats the only thing in the fruit bowl - a bruised apple.

A distorted version of *Mr Brightside* starts playing in his room and he rushes to answer his mobile. It's his mum. He puts her on speaker and rips the ready meal out of its packaging. Janet Tennant has a strong Norfolk accent and complains that Craig sounds distant.

He punctures the cellophane top of the pasta tray with a fork and explains that he has just got back from work. His mum bombards him with questions: Is he OK? Has he been eating properly? Why is he working so late?

Craig says that he's fine, and that she knows why he has to work late because the only people with enough money to buy houses are at work during the day. He gets a blast of hot air in the face as he opens the oven door and slides in the pasta tray.

Craig asks if his dad is there, but he is out playing table tennis. He says he might have to borrow some more money until next month. There is silence on the other end of the line and Craig checks his mum is still there.

She asks how his job hunting is going. He says that he hasn't had any time to look. Janet says that it might look better on his CV if he waits a few extra months until he has done two years at Cinq. Craig says he doesn't want to work there for another week let alone three months. He pretends the oven's timer is buzzing and says he has to go. Janet says she loves him and asks when he is coming home next. He says he isn't sure.

After he finishes scraping the spaghetti carbonara's melted container off the inside of the oven, Craig makes himself a corned beef sandwich and sits down at the table with Mark's MacBook. After several failed attempts to get onto the internet, he goes to the *Guardian* Jobs website but gets stuck when he has to type something in the position wanted box. After five minutes of inactivity he clicks on the Norwich City FC website and then Facebook, where he searches for Hannah Fox. He pauses before requesting to become her friend and then looks at her pictures. In one photo she has her arms wrapped around a tall, handsome man on a beach. Craig scowls, goes back to her profile - where her relationship status isn't given - and logs off.

He takes the laptop back into Mark's room and pushes it under the pile of *GQ* and *Nuts* magazines on the desk. Next to the magazines are a red lever arch file marked 'Business', a copy of *Billionaire before Breakfast* and a scrunched KitKat wrapper.

Mark's duvet is in a heap in the middle of his king size bed and the pillows are crushed against the headboard, below a poster of Mohammed Ali. There are crumpled t-shirts and jeans strewn all over the place and a wet towel has been dumped on top of a navy and pink dressing gown by the en suite bathroom. The sliding doors of Mark's double wardrobes are open and the top drawer of the oak chest overflows with pairs of Calvin Klein boxer shorts and multi-coloured Paul Smith socks.

The right half of the wardrobe is chaotic. There are sloppily-hung stripy Jack Wills shirts, a mound of Diesel jeans - some still with their labels on - a mass of polo shirts, five dull v-neck All Saints jumpers, a mountain of hoodies - the top one of which has JW VARSITY REGATTA sewn on the front in oversized letters - and two Abercrombie and Fitch gilets. Craig slides the door open further and switches on the wardrobe's light.

The floor is covered with footwear: Adidas ballet shoes, synthetic split-toe Nikes, Paul Smith sneakers and Converse baseball shoes, as well as a pair of hi-top Nike Air Jordans. There are also three pairs of Havaianas flip-flops and some unworn Timberland boots.

Craig looks at the belts hanging inside the door. He tries on a blue plastic number, fixes it on the tightest setting and holds it around his waist like a hula hoop. There's a new mustard-coloured Burberry on its own hook - the Humphrey and Weston label says £225.

Craig moves the doors across and peers into the other side. Mark's collection of pinstripe suits takes up half the rail; the rest is stuffed with Windsor-collared work shirts. Craig pulls out a blue one with a bright white collar and cuffs, and laughs. There are four pairs of elongated dress shoes on the floor, one of which is snakeskin. Craig returns the doors to their starting positions.

The light on the television on the wall facing the bed is blinking so he presses the standby button on the control and it flickers into life. He takes two steps back and stands transfixed at the paused image on the screen: A pale, scrawny man with a ponytail is being ridden in a disabled toilet by a woman with one arm.

It's eleven p.m. Craig yawns as he switches off the lights in the hall and double locks the front door. He brushes his teeth and changes into tartan pyjama bottoms, which are too short for his legs, before selecting a shirt and tie and hanging them on his wardrobe door. The radio alarm is set for six fifty-five. He flops down onto his bed and reaches for *Harry Potter and the Prisoner of Azkaban*. He opens the hardcover, runs his finger over the author's signature and sniffs it.

Sunlight is pouring in through the blinds as the radio alarm clock starts buzzing and Craig's stunned face pops up from under the duvet. He has his book in one hand and a pocket torch in the other. He marks page 117, throws the torch on the floor and rolls out of bed.

'Oh my god, oh my god,' he keeps repeating as he shuffles around. He slips off his pyjama bottoms and stands under the power shower, leaning against the wall with his eyes closed and his chin resting on his chest. He pours Lynx Africa shower gel over his head, letting it slide down his face and body and when there are no more suds in his hair, he steps onto the bath mat and checks himself in the mirror. There are bags under his eyes and he has a glowing red spot below his bottom lip.

He covers his face in foam and shaves off his non-existent beard. He then dries his hair and face, pulls on a pair of boxer shorts and replaces the cream tie he had picked out with a sober navy one.

After brushing his teeth, he applies a small amount of wax to his hair and gives his work shoes a wipe with yesterday's socks.

In the kitchen he can barely keep his eyes open as he scoffs a bowl of Mark's Coco Pops and gulps down two cans of Red Bull. He checks his watch and traipses down to the car.

'Sorry I'm late, sorry I'm late,' Craig says as he charges into the Cinq team meeting. The rest of the twenty-two-strong sales team are sitting in a scattered semi-circle facing Christian D'Souza, who is standing at the back of the office holding a clipboard. He has his hair slicked back and is wearing a purple shirt and tie combination. Everyone stares at Craig.

'Craig, how the bollock can you be late? You only live five minutes away. Sit down.'

As Craig pulls up a chair at the back, Christian continues:

'As I was saying, I expect you to be booking in at least twenty-five viewings a day this week, minimum, *absolute minimum*. A new member of staff who shall remain nameless, *Danny*,' he says, looking at Danny, 'asked me what to do if you're asked a question you don't know the answer to. It's simple: make something up. Be creative. Selling houses isn't about what you know; it's about knowing what you don't know. If you don't know something, but can say something you don't know in a way that makes it sound like you know, the mug you're saying it to won't know whether you know or not. Always give the customer the answer you think they want to hear.

'Remember the golden rules of sales. One: never take no for an answer. And two: never, ever, stop talking. The more you talk, the better. It makes you sound intelligent and reassures the customers you're on the ball. It really doesn't matter what you say because most of the time they aren't listening anyway. As I say every week; everyone that walks in here has money to burn. It's your job to make them burn it.

'Moving on, team, I've got last week's sales figures. Some of you have done very well. Others have been piss poor.'

Christian makes each one of the sales team stand up in turn. If they've hit their target they get a round of applause and a Krispy Kreme doughnut. If they have fallen short, as Craig has, they're made to stand at the front whilst Christian makes the rest of the staff shout abuse and shower them with balls of paper. A new girl, Vicky, gets hit in the eye and runs to the toilets crying. Craig takes his punishment passively.

'I've emailed you all this week's Shit List,' Christian continues. 'For those new members of staff, these are the twenty worst properties on our books. Frankly they aren't fit for,' he pauses, 'they aren't fit for paedophiles, that's how rank they are. If by some magic you can let or sell one of them you'll get a twenty pound JD Sports voucher. That should focus your minds.' Christian checks his clipboard.

'Next item on the agenda; this week's starters and leavers. You've probably noticed a few new faces in the office already. I'd like you all to welcome Fraser, Ian, Kate, Jermaine, Anthony, Mishbah, Kirsten and sorry I've forgotten your name.' He points at a shy-looking girl with a straight fringe.

'Isabel,' she murmurs.

'And Isabel of course.' There is a muted round of applause. 'If anyone phones up and asks for Tim Spoons, Katherine Ward-Hart, Fu Chang, Sam Carmichael, Mo Akmal, Kirsty Levanthal or LeBron McTavish, they no longer work here, so tell whoever wants them to get lost, unless they want to buy a house. Right I think that's just about it.' Christian flips over the page. 'Oh sorry I forgot to say, the prize for this week's top sales person is an all-expenses paid trip for one to Legoland Windsor. A knockout prize. I can tell you'll all be competing hard for that.

'One last thing; as Craig was late this morning he has to buy a Starbucks for everyone, so leave your orders with him and he'll run off like a good boy and get them. Actually Craig, do you want to tell us what you were up to last night as you so rudely interrupted the meeting? You look like shit. Out on the lash were you?'

They're all looking at him again.

'No. I didn't get much sleep and it took me a while to get ready. Sorry.'

'Don't lie to us, Craig. I can smell the booze from here.'

'That must be coming from someone else.'

'Well what *were* you doing then?'

'I was… I was reading and lost track of time.'

There are sniggers and confused looks amongst the staff.

'*Reading*? Are you ill?'

Craig pays the £88.36 coffee bill on his credit card and trudges back to the office carrying the drinks in a cardboard box.

CHAPTER FOUR

Mark stands in the sunshine outside Pizza Galleria on Piccadilly and checks the venue on his BlackBerry. A long queue snakes out along the pavement. He peers up and down the line, pushes through the restaurant's doors and joins it at the front, ignoring complaints from the people behind him. A bearded waiter hands him a single-sheet menu and asks if it's a table for one.

Mark says there should be a booking for Harry Todd. The waiter consults the maître d' and Mark follows him down the spiral staircase.

Twenty tables have been crammed into the lower floor, most of them occupied by bloated tourists. The atmosphere is stuffy and opposite the stairs, three red-faced chefs are frantically sliding pizzas in and out of industrial-sized stainless steel ovens.

Mark takes off his suit jacket and loosens his silver tie. The waiter shuffles his way past a crying child whose highchair juts out into the gangway and points Mark to a table at the back where a morbidly obese, balding man in his fifties is mopping his brow with a serviette. He is wearing a blue short-sleeved shirt and a red tie.

'Harry?'

The man wipes the sweat out of his eyes and puts his tinted glasses back on.

'Hello. You must be Mark. Pleasure to meet you.'

His mountainous stomach gets trapped under the table as he rises from his seat, jolting the cutlery.

'Hi,' Mark says, wiping his hand after they have shaken. 'I'm a bit late. I took a cab from the office and the traffic was bad.'

'Oh that's no problem,' Harry says. 'I was delayed as well. Person under a train at Peckham Rye.'

'Oh.'

They sit down and Harry peruses the menu.

'It's hot in here,' Mark says, tugging at the collar of his shirt.

'It certainly is. I don't get on well with the heat. It's probably not so much of a problem for a fit young man like yourself.' ⸳

'It's a bit hot, even for me.' Mark sucks his stomach in.

'I hope you don't mind the restaurant. I know it's not exactly The Ritz. My secretary suggested it. You do like pizza don't you?'

'Yeah, I do. The Ritz is down the road for future reference.'

A loud American woman on the next table tells her friend to look in the guidebook and find out if Buckingham Palace was where Princess Diana lived.

An eastern European waitress asks Mark and Harry what they'd like to drink. Harry, with Mark's approval, orders a bottle of Chardonnay and a jug of iced tap water.

'So, Harry, let's talk business. Justin filled me in with a few details but obviously I'd rather hear it from you so I'm clear about how we can work together.'

The wine arrives as Harry begins to explain and he invites Mark to sample it. Mark swills it around in his mouth and swallows it.

'Yeah fine,' he says.

'You must drink a lot of wine, in your line of work,' Harry says. 'All the client lunches and what have you.'

'Drinking wine's an important part of the job. That and champagne.'

Two sideburns of sweat have formed beside Harry's ears. He chuckles and wipes them away with the back of his hairy hand.

'So, tell me more about the Kent and Sussex Agency,' Mark says, pressing.

'The Kent and East Sussex Regional Development Agency,' Harry corrects him. 'Well, the KESRDA is a government-sponsored public body which helps aid economic development and regeneration, develop business competitiveness and improve skills. That sort of thing.' He has a swig of water.

'How can we help you then?'

'Since we were set up nine years ago we've built up quite a surplus of public money, as it were, and we've decided that we should invest it rather than just letting it sit in the bank. Hopefully that's where you'll be able to help us.'

'And what's your job?'

'I'm the financial director.'

Mark gulps a large mouthful of wine. 'Whether we can help you or not depends on the amount of money we're talking about.'

Harry takes a pen out of his shirt pocket, writes a figure on a fresh serviette and pushes it across the table.

'FIFTY MILLION!' Mark shouts.

Conversations stop at the surrounding tables and diners turn to stare at them.

'No,' Harry says, pausing as the chatter resumes, 'you've added an extra naught. It's five million. Please keep your voice down.'

'I'm definitely the man to talk to,' Mark says, composing himself.

The waitress asks if they are ready to order. After much consideration, Harry plumps for a fifteen-inch American hot pizza, a side order of garlic dough balls and a Caesar salad. She reads back the order and turns to Mark.

'I'll have a green salad,' he says. 'I'm on a diet.'

'You don't need to diet,' Harry says, as the waitress darts back to the kitchen. 'But that's beside the point. Mark, this is obviously a substantial amount of money. We can't afford to take risks. I don't know how much experience you've got in dealing with sums of this size-'

'Lots,' Mark interjects. 'I've got lots of experience.'

'What we're looking for is really quite simple. We want our money to be safe, and to make decent returns. Nothing astronomical. Just better than we'd get with a bank. We don't want any undue risks.'

'Harry, we never take undue risks. We're Europe's leading wealth management company. We have decades of experience of managing enormous quantities of money. My department alone looks after over ten billion pounds of investments. You don't build up a reputation like ours without a solid track record.'

'I realise that. It was one of the reasons we approached you.' Harry drinks and licks his lips. 'How long have you worked for MenDax, Mark? You seem quite young, if you don't mind me saying. Not that that's a bad thing.'

'Four years. I joined straight from university.'

'Which university were you at?'

Mark stalls. 'Cambridge,' he says finally.

'Cambridge? I thought you seemed like a bright lad. What did you study?'

'Business. And economics. Business and economics.'

'My son was at university in Cambridge as well, but not real Cambridge. He was at UEEC - the University of Eastern England Cambridge. Have you heard of it?'

'Um, yes. What does he do now?'

'He's unemployed at the moment.'

Mark grunts and drinks a whole glass of water. There is a long silence.

'If we did choose to invest with you,' Harry says, 'what would you do with the money?'

'Invest it in Scandinavia – it's MenDax's specialist area.'

'And what's your role? Are you just the first contact or would you be managing our account?'

'Oh, I'd be personally managing your account. We don't send out salesmen to rope you in like some companies do. You deal with the decision makers from day one.'

'Good.'

'I'm an executive investment fund manager for Scandinavian markets, which means I only manage a small number of specialist accounts. Most investment companies have people managing up to a hundred accounts each. At MenDax, we manage no more than five so we can give them the time and attention the client deserves.'

'What other accounts do you look after?'

'I'm afraid I can't tell you. It's confidential.'

'I was hoping you'd say that,' Harry says. 'It's good to know we can trust you.'

'Trust is one of our key values. Everything we discuss is strictly confidential. With many of our competitors, you're just a name or number. With MenDax, I'll be available to you twenty-four seven, even at weekends. It's part of the our ethos to build personal relationships with our investors.'

'How do you do that?' Dark sweat patches have started to emerge from under the arms of Harry's shirt.

'Regular meetings, frequent investment reports, etcetera. Also with MenDax you can withdraw your money at a moment's notice. With many of our competitors you would have to give them up to six months.'

'That's certainly a plus.' Harry excuses himself and wipes his face with his monogrammed handkerchief. 'Would you invest the money *purely* in Scandinavia? What's the attraction?'

'The attraction is simple. Scandinavian banks have been deregulated and are able to offer far more attractive high-yield investment products than anywhere else in the world. It's called the iceberg economy, are you familiar with the term?'

'No. Why's it called that?'

'Because it's rock solid and far bigger than it appears on the surface.'

Harry grins and rubs the sweat patches below his breasts.

'We would look to invest your money in perhaps two or three products and we can absolutely guarantee excellent returns,' Mark adds.

'From my experience of investment, Mark, I thought it was important to have a diverse portfolio. We don't want all of our eggs in one or two baskets.'

'No, not at all, Harry. We build you a personal investment programme. We can put together an incredibly diverse portfolio; the only common denominator is that they are linked to the continued profitability of the Scandinavian economy.' Mark leans back in his chair. 'In the same way all English investment packages link back to the stability of the Bank of England.'

'Which banks do you invest with?'

'Loansbanki, that's the biggest in Iceland, and usually Glitchnir. Although it depends on who is giving the best returns at the time. I can email you when I've done an in-depth analysis.'

'Good. What type of returns are we talking about?' Harry tops up Mark's wine glass.

'In the current economic climate, you could reasonably expect twenty per cent per annum, before commission,' Mark says, holding Harry's gaze.

Harry looks astonished. 'Twenty per cent per annum? That's unbelievable. How?'

'I'm afraid how we do it is confidential until you become an investor. We have built a reputation around strategic investment excellence. We have to protect our,' Mark taps the side of his head, 'knowledge.'

'Of course. I understand.'

When the food arrives, there isn't enough room for everything Harry has ordered, so another table is pulled over. Somehow he manages to stuff a dough ball into his mouth before the waitress has put the plate down.

'Would you like to know more about MenDax?' Mark asks, breaking the silence. He undoes his cufflinks and rolls up his sleeves.

'OK. Fill me in.' Harry accidently spits a fleck of dough into the water jug and pops two more balls into his mouth even though he's still chewing the first one.

'The company was founded seven years ago by Steffen Men who was a futures trader on the DAX, hence MenDax. The DAX is like the German version of the FTSE 100.'

'I know what the DAX is, Mark.'

'Yes, of course. We deal with both big institutional investors and high-value private clients, and our HQ is in London but we've also got offices in Berlin, Zurich and New York. We're Europe's most profitable investment company per head per capita per annum. That's the important thing to remember. Last tax year we made more money than Monaco and-'

'Actually, Mark,' Harry says as he drops a sun-dried tomato onto his stomach, picks it up and eats it, 'why don't you send me that on an email?'

'Sure.'

'Good. Anyway, enough of all this business talk. Tuck in.'

Harry hacks away at his pizza with the blunt cutlery and shovels chunks into his mouth. He then pours his salad onto the remaining half of his pizza, folds it in two and devours it as Mark tries not to look.

'What time do they expect you back at the office?' Harry asks, picking food out of his teeth.

'I'm not going back until later. I've got another meeting this afternoon.'

'You're a busy man, clearly. I've told my team not to expect me back as I'm off to the Oval later to watch the cricket.'

'Actually, I'm sure we've got a box at the Oval... and that's another benefit of investing with us. Each year you'll get tickets for the internationals. In fact, if there's space for another corporate guest for the Test match, I'll definitely get you in. If you're serious about investing, of course.'

'Oh, I'm serious. Now I know what you mean by MenDax building strong personal relationships.'

'Good. Um, Harry,' Mark says, changing tone, 'I've left my watch in my gym bag, have you got the time?'

Harry lifts his glasses and checks his gold Casio. 'It's two forty-two.'

'Shit, I'm going to have to go. I won't have time for dessert. I've got to be somewhere before three. Harry, do you mind covering this? I'll pay for the next one.'

'It's a shame you have to rush off.'

'Yes, it's just that I've got another client to meet and he's only in the UK for one day a month.'

'You go, Mark.'

Mark unrolls his sleeves and adjusts his tie as Harry, whose shirt is a patchwork of damp stains, gets up to shake hands. Mark gives him a limp business card from the stack in his wallet, thanks him for lunch and hurries off.

He dodges through a group of French school children who have congregated outside the restaurant and rushes towards Green Park. The sun is burning down and he's breathing heavily. The clock on the spire of St James's Church says ten to three. He runs as far as the Royal Academy and stops again to catch his breath at a bus stop. Spotting a gap in the traffic, he lumbers across the road, narrowly avoiding a motorcycle courier, and hails a taxi.

'The Churchberry,' he pants.

'What, hang on mate, that's two hundred yards up the road, you can walk it,' the cabbie shouts out the passenger window.

'I can't. I'll give you a tenner.'

'Get in.'

Mark sits alone at a table on the edge of the dining room and, thanks to the air conditioning, has started to cool down. Crystal chandeliers hang from the ceiling and on the wall beside him is a portrait of King Charles II on horseback. At the next table along, three glamorous elderly ladies are sharing tea and scones.

A waiter with a slick side parting waltzes over.

'I'm not too late for lunch am I?' Mark asks.

The waiter studies his watch. 'We stop serving lunch at three p.m. You have two minutes to spare,' he answers with a hint of irritation.

'Good. Right. To start I'll have two portions of the deep fried white-bait-'

'Are you waiting for somebody to join you, sir?'

'No. For main I'll have the spit-roast duckling and the chicken, ham and leek pie.'

'And this is just for you, sir?'

'Yes.'

'Is that all, or would you like the dessert menu as well?'

'Err, no. But I want some drinks. Get me three bottles of the Gruner Veltliner Renner,' Mark's eyes turn to the champagne list, 'A bottle of the Bollinger Grande Annee... and a pint of diet Coke. Bring all of it over but only uncork one of the bottles of white for starters.'

'I'm sorry, we don't serve diet Coke.'

'Normal Coke?'

'No, sir.'

'What's that Italian stuff that's like orange Tango?'

'San Pellegrino?'

'Yep, a pint of that.'

'Are you sure that is all, sir?'

'Can I have some tomato ketchup as well?'

Mark scoops the last silver forkful of vegetables into his mouth and washes it down with half a glass of white wine. He slouches in his seat and undoes his belt buckle. He is taking short breaths and holding his chest.

'Are you feeling ill, sir?' the waiter asks unsympathetically. 'Perhaps you would like some fresh air?'

'I'm just a bit full.'

'Am I to assume that you do not want the additional bottle of wine or the Bollinger?'

'I'll take them home.'

'I'm sorry sir, but you cannot take them home. We are not a super-market.'

'Can't you make an exception? I'd be very grateful, if you get my meaning.'

The waiter says he'll have to check. He returns to the table with the two bottles and tells Mark to be discreet on the way out. The bill is £311. Mark hands over his MenDax American Express card, tells the waiter to take a £50 tip and asks for a receipt.

Tom Canty

As he stands up to leave, his BlackBerry vibrates. It's an email from Justin telling him to get back to the office immediately.

CHAPTER FIVE

Mark bursts into Craig's room and pulls back the duvet. It's ten o'clock on Sunday morning and Craig is asleep, face down. His *Simpsons* boxer shorts have slipped below his waist. Mark shakes him by the shoulders and he moans.

'Craig, get up.'

'Why?' he asks, his voice muffled by his pillow.

'I've got a surprise for you.'

'Show me later. I'm tired.'

'We're going out.'

'I'm not. I need to save money.'

Craig's eyes are red and there is a patch of dribble on his pillowcase. He turns to look up at Mark, wipes his mouth and has a drink from the glass of water by his bed.

'What are you dressed up for?'

'I'm taking you on a cultural day out,' Mark says. He's wearing jeans and a long-sleeved white Ralph Lauren polo with a blue silk scarf. 'I've got us two tickets to the *Critical Condition of England* exhibition at the Tate Modern.'

'What's that?'

'It's an art gallery.'

'I *know* it's an art gallery. What's the exhibition?'

'It's meant to be the coolest thing in London. The tickets were expensive so get up and get ready.'

'If the tickets were so expensive, why did you buy me one?'

'I told you, it's a treat.'

Craig yawns and turns onto his back. Mark stands there with his arms outstretched:

'Craig, come on, get up.'

'Isn't there anyone else you'd rather go with?'

'No. I'm asking you, and besides nobody else can make it. Now get up and have a shower. I want to leave in half an hour.'

The sun is shining but it's not warm so Craig pulls on his sweatshirt as they walk out of Mansion House underground station and along Queen Victoria Street. Mark has been wearing sunglasses since they left the flat. They reach Peter's Walk and Craig makes Mark wait so he can take a photo of St Paul's Cathedral. Mark complains that he's making them look like tourists.

As they cross the Millennium Bridge, weaving their way through an Italian tour party and stepping over a busker playing a didgeridoo, Mark hands Craig his ticket. It has COMPLIMENTARY printed where the price should be and Craig frowns as he slips it into his wallet.

The South Bank is swarming with tourists. A young female guide with a rolled-up golf umbrella is anxiously checking a map as the group of teenagers she is in charge of jostle each other and get in the way of joggers. There is a BBC crew filming outside the Globe Theatre and, just out of shot, a stall selling £8 hot dogs.

Outside the Tate, every step, ledge and grassy area is covered with people having lunch, all of them shaded by the colossal rectangular building and its towering chimney.

Mark leads Craig into the turbine hall and up the escalators to the fourth floor.

'It looks like a factory from the outside,' Craig says, peering up to the glass ceiling.

'It was a power station.'

'Oh right, I thought it was a bit of an odd design for an art gallery. Can't we have a look at some of the other stuff first?' Craig asks as they pass the entrance to the *Beauty of Disfigurement* collection.

'There's not much to see really mate, that's why the main bit's free. They keep all the good shit back for the exhibitions. Last time I came here there was some big metal slide in the main hall made from bits of scrap. I tried to go on it but it started shaking. It wasn't very good.'

A gangly man wearing an earpiece checks their tickets and hands Mark a slim visitors' booklet, from which he reads:

'*Critical Condition of England* is a ground-breaking new exhibition showcasing six of the country's most gifted young artists. Each was commissioned to produce an original artwork, in any form, which is a lucid reflection of modern English society. The result is a unique and captivating collection of mind-altering exhibits which examine the fragile nature of civilization and question the futility of existence in a culture obsessed with the dehumanisation of the nuclear family and the deification of celebrity iconoclasts.'

'What does that mean?' Craig asks.

'Hopefully we'll find out.'

They enter a square room with bright white walls, a high ceiling and a narrow doorway at the far end. There are only two other people in there; a pair of bald men in their fifties studying a painting on the furthest wall. To Mark and Craig's left there is a video installation, around six feet square, and facing it, a long white bench where they sit down. The piece, entitled *No Help Service*, is a short film about five nurses at Stockwell Hospital who set up a brothel in a disused ward. One of the nurses claims that working in the NHS is dangerous and degrading and that it's only by selling her body that she has regained her self-respect:

'I became a nurse because I wanted to ease pain and suffering but cleaning wounds and emptying bedpans was demoralising. Since I've been sleeping with men for money, I'm changing lives in a way that I never could in my job.'

As the film ends a disclaimer pops up on the screen stating that the nurses were played by actresses and that the story is based on interviews conducted with real medical professionals which have been discarded and re-written for the purposes of entertainment.

'So that was all completely made up then?' Craig says as they walk towards a series of black and white photographs.

'I don't know. Some bits of it might be true. But there can't be a brothel in the hospital surely? Can there?'

'Why don't you go to the A&E and find out?'

'But what will I say's wrong with me?'

'I don't know; say you've been having sexual problems and see if they take the hint.'

'But then they might think I'm being serious and start poking around.'

'Why don't I break your arm like they do to the goalkeeper in *Escape to Victory*?'

'Thanks for the offer mate, but I think I'll pass.'

The ten photographs they are now standing in front of are entitled *Husband v Wife. Hull. 2007.* They depict a boxing match in an underground car park between an overweight man wearing a vest and boxing gloves, and his equally overweight wife who is armed with a broken bottle. In the first shot, the wife jabs at her husband's face; in the second he is shown on his knees, bleeding. In the next four photographs he's on the floor covering his head as she attacks him with an iron bar. In the final three shots, she stamps on his head; stands over him victorious cheered on by the sparse crowd; and loads his unconscious body into a shopping trolley.

'This is just weird,' Mark says. 'In real life there's no way she'd beat him up. He'd punch her before she could get the bottle near him.'

'What part of this is art?' Craig asks.

'Let's have a look at that painting down the end.'

The third piece in the room shows a classroom of infants being taught to read using pornographic magazines.

'The brochure reckons this is *an attack on the levels of literacy in schools*,' Mark says in a loud, bored tone.

'It's not even a good painting,' Craig adds. 'The kids' faces are blurred and the perspective's not quite right. The whole thing looks a bit wonky.'

'Apparently their faces are blurred to protect their identities.'

'Why didn't the painter just change them?'

'No idea.'

Mark steps away and starts tapping on his iPhone. Craig turns to him and gestures that they should go through to the next room.

'What's that?' Craig says as they enter the second gallery.

In the centre of the room is a large blank canvas on an easel. Next to it, on a plinth, is a magnifying glass attached by a cord to the floor.

'Apparently there's a message on the canvas but it's invisible to the naked eye,' Mark says, reading the guide as they get closer. 'You've got to use the magnifying glass to find it.'

Neither Craig nor Mark are that interested in trying to find the hidden message and give up after a few seconds.

'What's that mark in the bottom corner?' Craig asks, taking the magnifying glass. 'Ha. I've found it.'

'What does it say?'

'It says, *Imagine.*'

'Imagine what?'

'That's all it says.'

Mark looks for himself. 'So instead of the artist actually painting, we're meant to imagine what he might have painted if he could have been bothered to do so.'

'I suppose so,' Craig says, sounding sleepy.

Mark checks the guide as they move on. 'Bloody hell, apparently someone's already bought it for ten grand.'

'Ten thousand for that? That must have taken about two minutes. Why can't anyone just do a nice painting any more?'

'A nice painting of what?'

'I don't know. Some fields with a river and some trees in the background.'

'What, a landscape?'

'Yeah.'

'But that's what they did in the old days, people like Constable and Turner and Keats. I suppose it's all been done.'

'Do you know who I think is a good artist?' Craig says, getting a side view of the exhibit.

'Umm… Rolf Harris?' Mark laughs at his own joke, and the two older men in the room glare at him.

'I knew you were going to say that. No, the bloke who did the *Angel of the North* and those statues on that beach.'

'And his name is?'

'I can't remember his name but I like the way he, oh, hang on-'

One of the two bald men is walking directly towards them looking stern, his tweed jacket flapping:

'My friend and I are trying to enjoy this exhibition and would rather do so without being subjected to your childish guffawing and asinine comments, so please keep quiet.'

Mark looks at Craig who is trying not to laugh and the complainer turns to walk away.

'Who do you think you're talking to?' Mark says, stopping him in his tracks.

'I'm sorry.'

'I said, who do you think you're talking to?'

'I was just asking–' he starts to counter.

'I don't care what you were just asking. Do you know who I am?'

'Um, no, I don't.'

'My name is Mark Hunter and I'm the managing director of MenDax.'

'MenDax?' the man says, puzzled.

'MenDax Wealth Management; the company paying for this exhibition. So we'll behave however we like and if you say another word, I'll get you banned from every art gallery in London.'

Mark glares at him and the man's double chin wobbles as he stands too shocked to speak.

'Come on Craig,' says Mark, 'I'm bored anyway. Let's go.'

On the way out they pass a display board thanking the principal sponsors: The UK Young Artists' Fund, MenDax Wealth Management and Spudson's Potato Waffles.

Craig is sitting at a table outside The Hamlet Tavern on the South Bank. Mark, who has indigestion after finishing off his fish and chips in less than two minutes, is at the bar getting a second jug of lager. The wind has dropped and it's warmer than it was earlier.

A half-full Thames Clipper cruises past and Craig leans against the railings and gazes down at the tea-coloured river as tiny waves break against the wall. In the distance, the dome of St Paul's dominates the skyline.

Mark shuffles back through the crowd with the refilled jug and drops back down at the table.

'Feeling any better?' Craig asks.

'Yeah a bit. Just trapped wind I think.' Mark fills their glasses and takes a huge glug. 'I like doing stuff on a Sunday. It gets a bit boring sitting around the house.'

'Normally you've got a hangover.'

'True. I was looking up reviews of the exhibition when I was sitting in the toilet.'

'What did it say?'

'The papers absolutely slated it. They basically said that a bunch of complete unknowns had been given a lot of money they didn't deserve and had produced a lot of rubbish. No wonder they had so many free tickets to give away at work. The whole thing's been a complete disaster apparently, apart from for the guy who sold the magnifying glass thing. You never know, that might turn out to be a bargain if he gets famous, although I doubt it. Did I tell you I'd invested in a couple of paintings?'

'No,' Craig says, surprised. 'What are they?'

'Abstracts, by a girl I met in a club back home. She was a student at the local art college and invited me along to her graduate show. They were five hundred quid, together, but they're pretty good. Here, I'll show you, I've got pictures on my phone.'

They are paintings of geometric circles. The first is one large over-lapping pattern within a square, predominantly blue and yellow, on a white background. The second is of twelve smaller circles, four rows of three, which are a variety of green, orange and pink.

'I quite like them actually,' Craig says. 'They look like those drawings you used to do with a Spirograph.'

'That's what she uses.'

'Really? You paid all that for two paintings done with a Spirograph?'

'Yeah, but she's a proper artist, that's the difference. And she was fit.'

'So that was the reason.'

'Yeah, but she said she had a boyfriend. I saw her in town last time I went home funnily enough.'

'What was she doing, selling her Spirograph prints to gullible people in a shopping centre?'

'No, she was in Café Nero. Working.'

Craig laughs. 'Her art career's really taken off then?'

'Mate, in twenty years those paintings could be worth millions.'

'Why don't you put them up in the flat? We could use a bit of colour on the walls.'

'I'd worry about them getting damaged. Anyway I can't remember where I've hidden them.'

A train crosses Blackfriars Railway Bridge and pulls into the station as Craig stares out across the river at City of London School.

'I'll be in Café Nero soon if work doesn't get any better,' he says.

'Still bad then?'

'It varies. Sometimes it's all right, but you never know how it's going to be from one day to the next. It's just hard to plan to do anything because you never know how much money you're going to be earning each month. It all depends on who walks through the door.'

'The market's taken a hit recently, hasn't it?'

'Yes, I suppose it has thinking about it.' Craig sips his beer and looks at Mark. 'There aren't any jobs going at your place are there?' he asks timidly.

'Jobs?' Mark puffs out his cheeks, tilts his head back and exhales.

'Yeah.'

'For you?'

'Yes.'

'I'm not sure really, mate. I could have a word in the post room.'

'Mark, I'm not working in the post room.'

'Why not? They get pretty well paid.'

'Isn't there anything else I could do?'

'The problem is, mate, you're not really qualified any more.'

'What do you mean I'm not qualified? I've got a better degree than you.'

'We've got the same degree.'

'I got a 2.1, remember?'

'Yeah, but I've got finance qualifications now.'

'Since when?'

'I've got two.'

'What are they then?'

'Just things I've been doing through work. Online mainly... and a couple of exams.'

'How comes I've not seen you studying?'

'I either do it at work or when I get home. You're always back from work so late it's no surprise you've never seen me. I'll show you the certificates if you don't believe me,' Mark says.

'No, no, I believe you, it's OK.'

'Anyway you haven't got any relevant experience either.'

'Nor had you when you started.'

'Well, yes, but...' Mark tops up Craig's glass. 'Look I'll tell you what, I'll have a word with my boss and if anything comes up I'll recommend you, OK? I can't do any more than that.'

'Thanks. That's all I'm asking for.'

'No problem.'

Mark guzzles down the rest of his pint and burps quietly into his fist.

'I'm not sure how much longer I'll be at the London office for anyway,' he says.

'How come?'

'I'm thinking of going abroad.'

'When?'

'In a year or so, perhaps.'

'Oh, OK. I thought you were going to tell me you were moving out.'

'No, not for a while. Don't worry; I'll give you plenty of notice.' Mark pours himself another full pint. 'My plan is to stay in London for the next year or two and then get a transfer to one of the other MenDax offices abroad.'

'Where were you thinking?'

'Well, preferably New York or my second choice would be Sydney, to help set up the new office there. I don't want to go to Europe or the Middle East.'

'Why not?'

'I want to go somewhere they can speak my language and where there'll be loads of fit women I can marry.'

'If you want to marry more than one woman you'll have to go to the Middle East.'

'You know what I mean. Australian girls are all fit because they go to the beach every day so they have to keep in shape, and everyone says women in New York will sleep with anyone with an English accent.'

'I'm sure they'd make an exception for you.'

'Yes, ha ha.' Mark yawns and scratches his chin. 'It might all change but that's the plan anyway. I'll see where I am at the end of this year, but as long I'm earning more than a hundred grand, I'm content to stay with MenDax. If not, I'll have to assess my options.'

'*A hundred grand?*' Craig says, his mouth hanging open.

'That's not that much mate, it's actually less than I'm worth. For someone like me, at this stage in my career, I've got to be earning over a certain salary, it's as simple as that. In fact, let me have a little bet with you. If I'm not earning over a hundred thousand by the end of the year, I'll pay your rent in January.'

'I'm not interested in betting, Mark.'

'You haven't got to give me anything. And I will pay it you know.'

'Mark, I don't care.'

'Fair enough. But I'm still going to do it. It'll give me a bit of extra motivation. What's wrong with you anyway? You've been very boring recently.'

'I've just been tired, mate. I've not exactly had a lot of time to have fun.'

The boys look on as a tall young man in an Imperial College Rowing Club hoody walks past.

'Do you ever wish we were back at university?' Craig asks.

'No, definitely not. Do you?'

'Umm, well, yes. When I'm at work I do.'

'I don't miss it *at all*.'

'Not even being able to go and get smashed and get up whenever you want?'

'I probably go out and get smashed more now. In fact I enjoy it more now because only the hardened drinkers stay out late.'

'But don't you miss being able to do pretty much whatever you wanted?'

'I still do whatever I want.'

'No you don't. You're contracted to turn up to work five days a week.'

'Yeah, but I'd rather do that and have plenty of money than sit around all day doing nothing, worrying about how to pay for stuff.'

'I thought your parents paid for everything?'

'They weren't paying for my drinks. At least they thought they weren't. I've honestly never been more bored in my entire life than I was at uni. Nothing happened. Ever. I know it was a bit different for you because you had the football team and all your other mates but I didn't have any of that. I think they make the drinks cheap in uni bars because alcohol's the only thing stopping most students from topping themselves.'

'That kid in halls in the first year did, didn't he?'

'He'd probably run out of money to get drunk and couldn't see the point any more. I don't blame him.'

'You don't mean that.'

'Perhaps not,' Mark says, shrugging. 'I think people that miss being students are either lazy or scared of the real world, or a mixture of the two.'

'Yeah, but I'm not lazy or scared of the real world; I just don't like my job.'

'That's three reasons then. Anyone who spends their lives on a university campus is just trying to avoid life, and that's impossible.'

'But you can try different things and meet interesting people. You don't have a boss breathing down your neck the whole time.'

'Do you know how many interesting people I met at uni? None.'

'I'm sorry I'm not more interesting,' Craig says half-offended.

'I don't mean you, obviously. I mean other people. Everyone goes on about university this or university that, but I don't understand it. If my only ambition was to do nothing apart from drink and sit watching DVDs all day then I'd probably miss it loads, but since we left I've never once thought "Oh I'd love to be a student again". The only time I think about it is when I have a day off sick and I sit around the house on my own watching TV, and all that reminds me of is how fucking dull it was.'

'You didn't seem to dislike it that much at the time.'

'True, but I never knew what it was like to have a good job.'

'I still don't.' Craig looks up at the sky. 'But at least we had some freedom, and the feeling we could do literally anything or go anywhere.'

'Yes, but we never had enough money to do anything good. It's not like we could have just hopped on a plane to Rio. You can have as much freedom as you like but without money it's meaningless. You might as well be locked up. Anyway mate, enough of this depressing chat, have I told you I'm going on a date with a model this week?'

CHAPTER SIX

C raig sits in his car with Kiss FM on and the windows shut. The dashboard display says that it's 11.42 a.m. and 19°c. He is parked on the forecourt of a dilapidated Edwardian house next to a C-registration Vauxhall Cavalier which has both front wheels missing. Steps up from the pavement lead to a numberless front door. The building's paintwork is peeling badly and iron bars cover the windows on all floors. There is a blue plaque on the wall marking the spot where a policeman was shot dead in 1981. The houses either side are both in the process of being demolished.

Craig reclines his seat and shuts his eyes. Seconds later there is a knock on the window. He panics and activates the central locking. On the other side of the glass is a skinny girl with spiky blonde hair. She has neon yellow sunglasses perched on her nose and is wearing a long vest with a silver skull printed down one side and short denim shorts.

'Hello, are you Holly?' Craig says, relaxing as he gets out of the car.

'No, I'm Crystal,' the girl says, 'that's Holly.' She points at a tall girl with bright red hair, sucking on an orange lolly. She is dressed in skinny stonewashed jeans and a black and white striped t-shirt with red dots over it.

Craig waves. 'I'm Craig,' he says, locking the car and checking the boot. 'Did you find your way here OK?'

'We got a bit lost. It's longer than five minutes from the tube.'

'It all depends on which way you walk. If you take the short cut through the estate, it's much quicker.'

He leads the girls up the crumbling steps and puts a key in the lock which is bent around the edges and surrounded by deep dents. The door sticks so he shoulder barges his way in. Post and flyers litter the hallway and an old BMX bike without a saddle rests up against the dirty wall. The place smells damp. Craig kicks the post into a pile and holds the door open for the girls, who step tentatively inside.

'Girls, I know what you're thinking, but this place has just been bought by a new landlord and he hasn't started work on the communal areas yet. All he's done so far is the top two flats, but by the time he's done, this whole place will look ace.'

Craig climbs the stairs. There are stains all over the landing carpet. He tries to turn a light on but it doesn't work so he opens the roll blind covering the window at the end of the hallway. It kicks up dust into his face and makes him cough. The window provides an excellent view of a building site and a tower block and the windowsill is thick with dust and dead flies. He rolls the blind back down.

There is a dead mouse in front of flat 4. Craig manoeuvres it between his feet, shows the girls in and then kicks it behind a bin bag outside flat 3.

Inside, the flat has been refurbished to a basic standard. A narrow hallway divides it in two: on the right are the two identical unfurnished bedrooms painted magnolia with cheap laminate wood floors and ill-fitting sash windows with shutters. The rooms are no bigger than ten feet by eight. Craig describes them as 'generous'.

The kitchen has, as Craig reads from the spec, '*Rear aspect sash window, Formica worktop with tiled splash backs, stainless steel sink and drainer unit with chrome mixer tap, four ring electric hob with extractor hood over with oven and grill under, space and plumbing for washing machine, wall mounted and low level storage units, fridge/freezer, ceiling lighting.*'

'It's OK, I suppose,' Holly says, finishing her lolly. 'Where's the bin?'

Craig opens every cupboard door. 'Err, don't worry, I'll take that,' he says reaching for her stick and putting it in his pocket. 'The kitchen's all brand new.'

'Is there going to be a washing machine put in?' Crystal asks.

'Yes, definitely. A washer and tumble dryer. That's what the owner said when I spoke to him the other day. Of course the biggest advantage about this place is the fact that there's no furniture. That's means you can bring all your own stuff in and you haven't got to have sofas or beds you don't like.'

'Who owns the house?' Holly asks, taking off her sunglasses to reveal eyes covered in glittering make-up.

Craig walks over to the window. 'The owner's a great bloke.' He pauses and looks down onto the street. A man wearing Adidas tracksuit bottoms and a basketball vest runs past his car. 'He's a property developer and businessman but he used to be an athlete. I can't remember his name but he comes from Brixton and he's putting money back into the community. Urban regeneration projects...'

The girls follow Craig into the empty living room.

'Just think of what a cracking room this would be when you get all of your stuff into it, girls. Big TV on the wall, stereo, and... and all those other things you've got. This would be great for a party, or just having your mates over. Are you girls working in London or students or...?'

'We're at the London College of Fashion,' Crystal says.

'Cool, I love fashion. And you're both... fashionable, obviously.'

Holly leans against a wall and plays with her nose piercing. Crystal looks out at the estate opposite.

'Have you got any questions?' Craig asks.

'Yes,' Crystal says spinning to face him. 'What's the rent again?'

'It's three hundred pounds a week. And that's a snip for around here, particularly for a flat as good as this. Although I could probably get it down to just over a thousand a month if you can move in straight away.'

Holly makes a note with an eyeliner pencil on the back of her hand. 'What are the tube and bus links like?'

'Brilliant. Brixton's really central. It's easy to get anywhere from here. There's buses, the tube, overland train at Loughborough Junction just up the road. Where's the London College of Fashion?'

'Oxford Circus.'

'That's easy from here on the tube. Jump on the Victoria line at Brixton, change for the Northern line at Stockwell, then change for the, um, Central line and that goes to Oxford Circus.'

'Or you could just stay on the Victoria line the whole way there,' Holly says.

'Um, yes, you could, you're right. Another great thing about Brixton,' Craig continues, 'is the bars and clubs on your doorstep, and the late-night funky house places all the way up Coldblood Lane. There are also loads of great restaurants too: curry, Thai, Italian, Jamaican, Moroccan, Rwandan, and there's a massive KFC and McDonald's. It's got pretty much everything you could want.'

Crystal is chewing gum and stands with her hands on her hips. 'Isn't it a bit, kind of like, dodgy around here though?'

'I looked up Coldblood Lane on the internet and it said it was one of the most violent streets in the country,' Holly adds.

'I thought you'd ask about this,' Craig says, shifting his weight from one foot to the other and then back. 'Most of the stuff on the internet is out of date. A few years ago this place was full of crack dealers and gangs of prostitutes but now it's one of the safest areas in London. You can't walk down the street without seeing an armed policeman or hearing a siren.'

'How come it's changed?' Crystal asks.

'It just has really. People have been doing stuff in the community and... and the police changed the law so you could deal on the streets and when they did that, there were less shootings.'

'Is there a gun problem around here?' Crystal asks.

'No, not at all. There used to be, a bit, but virtually all the criminals are now in prison.'

'Are we near the prison?' Holly asks.

'Yes, but living near a prison is very safe. All the criminals are in one place.'

'Ummm. My pops was worried when I said we were coming to Brixton,' Crystal says.

Craig looks concerned and says, 'You can't trust your parents' opinions. They wouldn't like Brixton, but they probably don't like clubbing either. Brixton's a vibrant area for young people and families. If it was really dangerous nobody would bring their kids up here. The majority of people have proper jobs and live here because it's cool. The important thing is to appreciate the local culture, like rap music and smoking weed and.... Chicken Cottage.'

Crystal starts giggling.

'What's funny?'

'Aren't you meant to be selling this place to us rather than making it sound scummy?'

'I am selling it to you. I was just trying to give you some honest advice.'

'Is it easy to buy weed around here?' Crystal asks, twiddling the beads that hang over her boney chest.

'Yes, massively. Dead easy.'

'Can you leave me and Hols to talk for a couple of minutes?'

Craig goes into the kitchen and sits up on the worktop swinging his legs. The girls are laughing in the next room. They call him back in.

'What do you think then, girls?'

'It's not bad,' Holly says, her smile revealing crooked front teeth.

'I could get you a top deal. I could even talk to your parents to put their minds at rest if you're worried about them.'

'We're interested,' Crystal says, 'but we'd like you to do something for us first.'

Craig's eyes widen. 'Yeah, sure, anything.'

The girls hold hands.

'We know it's a bit cheeky, but could you buy some weed for us?' Holly asks, fluttering her eyelashes.

Craig looks a little deflated and his tone becomes more serious. 'If I buy you some weed, will you definitely move in?'

The girls check each other. 'It depends how much you can get us,' Crystal says sauntering up to Craig and turning over the end of his tie to reveal a Burton label.

'How much money have you got?' he asks.

'Eighty quid between us. How much could we get for that?' she asks, taking a step back.

'Umm, quite a lot. About a pound.'

'A pound?' Holly says. 'Don't you mean an ounce?'

'Yeah, sorry, an ounce. I don't smoke much weed any more. The price has gone up a lot recently. And if I do this, you'll definitely one hundred per cent take this place? No backing out?'

Craig stops on double-yellow lines outside the Ritzy cinema and tells the girls to wait in the car. He puts on his aviators and crosses the road, stepping between two women pushing buggies loaded with Iceland bags in the direction of St Matthew's Church.

Brixton is warm and bustling but the air is thick with exhaust fumes as roadworks have caused the traffic to clog at the bottom of Brixton Hill. A line of buses to Streatham and Thornton Heath wait at the lights.

Craig stands at the crossroads outside KFC for several minutes watching people pass by. An old man with long dreadlocks and huge felt hat in the colours of the Jamaican flag is preaching about Jesus. Nothing happens. Then Craig follows the flow down to the tube past a busy Woolworths and JD Sports, where he stops to look at trainers.

Outside the cavernous entrance to the underground, a woman with a toned stomach is handing out flyers promoting yoga classes and down on the concourse, police are manning a metal detector that all commuters have to pass through on their way out.

Craig walks into Jammers, a record shop opposite the tube. He's the only customer. He hums along to the Sean Paul track that is being broadcast to the street and pretends to be looking at Chaka Demus and Pliers CDs. Behind the counter, a white Rastafarian is thumbing through a box of old vinyl.

'If there's anything you're looking for mate, give us a shout,' he says over the music.

'Um, there is actually.' Craig approaches the counter and pauses. 'Do you where can I buy some weed?' he asks uneasily.

'Are you taking the piss?'

Craig sprints out of the shop up towards McDonald's, dodging pedestrians and weaving in and out of barriers where the pavement is being dug up. He glances up at the clock on Brixton Town Hall. He's been almost twenty minutes.

He crosses back over the road and stands outside KFC again, looking desperate. Holly and Crystal are watching him from the car and beads of sweat have formed on his top lip. A traffic warden is having a cigarette outside the cinema, staring directly at Craig's Mini and making notes on her electronic pad. 'Bollocks,' he says to himself.

A black man in a New York Yankees baseball cap sidles up to him. 'Weed, coke, crack?' he says nonchalantly in a West Indian accent. He's covered in gold jewellery.

'Yeah,' Craig mumbles.

The dealer points Craig up Coldblood Lane and they stop in the shade of a public phone box outside a Wetherspoons' pub.

'What daya want?' he asks.

'Weed,' Craig says, his legs shaking.

'How much?'

'A pound.'

The dealer laughs. 'Man, you crazy?'

'An ounce. Sorry. How much is that?'

'A ton.'

'What's that?'

'You fuckin' serious man? A hundred quid.'

'I've only got eighty.'

The dealer sticks his hand inside his tracksuit top and then suddenly grabs Craig by the wrist, twisting his arm behind his back and slamming his face against the phone box, splitting his lip.

'ARRRRRRGH, ARRRRRRGH,' Craig cries. A group of schoolboys stop to watch and three old blokes have gathered at the pub window. The dealer snaps Craig into handcuffs, shoves him in the back and two other plain-clothes policemen surround him and force him to his knees.

'You are being arrested for the attempted purchase of a prohibited substance,' the undercover officer says, dropping the accent. 'You have the right to remain silent, but it may harm your defence if you do not say when questioned, something you later rely on in court. Do you understand?'

'But I wasn't! I wasn't!!' Craig pleads, a thin trail of blood trickling from his mouth.

CHAPTER SEVEN

'See you later,' Amy says, picking up her handbag and a pile of documents from her desk.

'Where are you off to?' Mark doesn't look up from his computer.

'I'm meeting Tom Carter from STA Shaw.'

'It's a bit late for a meeting isn't it?'

'We're having dinner.'

Mark swivels round. 'Dinner? What, so is it a meeting or a date?'

'A meeting.'

'How old is he?'

'I'm not sure, thirty-five?'

'Is he married?'

'Why does it matter if he's married?'

'I don't know. I'm going on a date tonight by the way,' Mark adds.

'That's nice,' Amy says patronisingly. 'Enjoy yourself. I've got to rush, if anyone rings could you take a message and tell them I'll get back to them in the morning, or get them to send me an email. I'll see you tomorrow.'

Mark waits for Amy to leave and leans back in his chair with his hands behind his head. He's alone in the office. He types two more seven-digit numbers into a spreadsheet, adds a pie chart and saves it as *Potential_Invest_Yield_Forecast_Sweden_2011* in his 'Forecasts' folder.

Mark turns to look down onto Liverpool Street. A man in a bright yellow jacket is handing out copies of the *London Late* to the stream of commuters on their way into the station. It's a blustery early-evening and most people are wearing jumpers or jackets.

Amy's phone rings but Mark ignores it. He browses the BBC Business homepage and then searches 'mendax waelth managment' on Google. There are 21,243 results. He clicks on a link to the MenDax website but instantly closes it.

After staring out of the window for a few more minutes, Mark double-clicks on Krazy Golf from his list of favourites and logs in.

He gets to hole eighteen on level par but takes five strokes on the last after his ball falls down a mine shaft. He beats his mouse on the desk in frustration.

A new message from harry.todd@kesrda.gov.uk appears in his Outlook inbox. The subject line is blank but there's an attachment. *Thanks for the business card. Want to suck them do you? Well here they are.* Mark looks confused and clicks on the paperclip icon. A photograph pops up.

'HUURRGGHH!'

It's Harry Todd, naked, except for a copy of the *Sevenoaks Chronicle* leisure supplement which covers his genitals. He is reclining on a double bed with one arm outstretched and his right leg cocked. His stomach spills down over his groin and he is cupping an enormous hairy breast with his other hand. Next to him on the peach bedspread are his tinted glasses, some furry handcuffs and a book about the Battle of Britain.

Mark scrambles to close the photo. He deletes the email and then empties his deleted items. He shuts down the computer and stares at the black screen.

Chernobyl vodka bar is dark, even though it is still bright outside, and Mark is one of only three customers. He examines the drinks list whilst the three female bar staff - all wearing tight shirts embossed with the chain's radioactive logo - talk amongst themselves.

He orders two pints of Glasnost and three caramel double vodkas. As the barmaid searches among the hundreds of bottles of spirits along the mirrored back wall, Mark checks his delicately sculpted hair and undoes another button of his sleek black shirt. It reveals pasty skin and sparse chest hair and he quickly does it back up.

Mark refuses the offer of a tray but after a failed attempt to carry all of the drinks, he downs one pint of Glasnost and necks one of the double shots, which makes him splutter.

He sits in a booth in the middle of a row parallel to the bar and reads the food menu. His finger lingers over the 'St Petersburger' but he puts it down and stares at the mural of Yuri Gagarin on the ceiling.

'Hello,' says a squat, muscular woman in a low-cut black top.

'Hi,' Mark says, half-ignoring her.

'How are you?'

'I'm fine.'

'Can I sit down?' the woman asks, her jaw flexing.

'Sorry, I'm expecting somebody,' Mark says bluntly.

'Mark, it's me. Claire.' She points to her face which glows with fake tan and is covered in an uneven layer of shimmering blusher. She has short brown hair and a long fringe swept over the right side of her face, partially covering her eye.

'Claire. I knew it was you,' Mark bumbles. 'I was joking. How are you?'

'Good thank you. How are you?'

'Yeah, fine.'

She flattens her skirt over her powerful thighs and shuffles onto her seat. Her chest is solid muscle and a silver pendant dangles from her neck.

'Have you been here long?' she asks, looking at his two empty shot glasses and half-drunk pint.

'I got here a bit early. I only live up the road. Did it take you long to get here?'

'No, it's only two stops on the train from Balham.'

'You live in Balham? Oh yeah, I remember you saying now.' His tone is flat and he keeps looking away.

'I remember you trying to invite yourself back there on Saturday night,' she says, smiling.

'Yeah, I was very pissed.'

'It was funny. I don't think I've ever been chatted up in a kebab house before.'

Mark takes the drinks menu.

'I love Clapham,' Claire says. 'There's always something going on, it's really fun.'

'Yeah it's all right. But you get a lot of twats around here as well. Do you want a drink? I'll get them.'

'Oh, could I have a cocktail?'

Mark drinks his last shot, shudders, and places the sixth empty back on the wooden wheel.

'I *love* Russian Roulettes,' Claire says. 'Let's do another one.'

'No, no I can't. I've got to be at work early in the morning.'

'Lightweight. Finish your pint. I'm one ahead of you now. My rugby team would drink you under the table.' Claire glugs her beer and bangs the glass down on the table. 'You never told me what you do, Mark.'

'My job? Finance - in the City. I'm an investor relations chief executive. I...' He doesn't elaborate. 'How about you?'

'I'm a PA at Mutual Equitable, the insurance company.'

'Really,' Mark says, uninterested. 'How long have you been there?'

Claire rolls her eyes. 'Too long. Since I moved to London, in 1990.'

'1990? *Eighteen years?*'

'I *am* thirty-nine, Mark.'

'*Thirty-nine?*' he says in disbelief. 'You don't look that old.'

'Thanks, I'll take that as a compliment. I did tell you this the other night.'

'Did you?' he mutters, checking his watch.

Claire takes her mobile from her Fitness First rucksack and reads a text. 'It's my son.'

'You've got a kid as well? Is he with a babysitter?'

'Babysitter?' Claire says, laughing. 'He's a bit old for that. He's at university.'

'What?' Mark says, his face contorting.

It's quarter past ten and Chernobyl is now full of young professionals either wearing suits or distressed jeans and t-shirts.

Claire leans in and licks her lips. 'Why don't we finish these and then head back to yours?'

'Umm, it's still early. Let's have another drink. I'll get table service,' Mark says, drunkenly looking around for a waitress.

The music goes up several decibels and Mark drums his fingers on the table.

'Who are all those men?' Claire says, scanning the murals on the walls.

'That bloke above the bar in the cap is Lenin,' Mark says. 'He was President of Russia during the First World War. The guy with the moustache is Stalin,' he says pointing to the man in military uniform painted over the fire exit. 'The bloke with the grey afro and beard is Karl Marx. He invented communism and wanted everyone to be poor. And the bloke with the long hair and long beard, next to the toilets, is Rasputin. He was King of Russia in eighteen ninety-something, but they killed him, because they wanted to get rid of the royal family.'

'You're so clever. Did you do history at uni?'

'No. I did business. I know all that from GCSE.'

Claire looks over to the toilets. 'Rasputin looks scary.'

'He was. He killed loads of people. He had a massive cock as well. I've seen it on the internet.'

'I hope he's not the only one,' she says, reaching under the table.

Mark flinches. 'No, he's not,' he says, grabbing Claire's hand as she claws at his trousers.

Mark pays the taxi driver and thumps the entry system's keypad. The gate won't open so he gives up and buzzes the flat. Craig lets them in.

'This place is amazing,' Claire says as they cross the car park.

'Suusssssshhhhh! Keep your voice down.' Mark leans on her to keep himself upright.

They get out of the lift at the sixth floor.

'I thought you said you lived in a penthouse?'

'Keep your voice down,' Mark whispers. 'It is a penthouse.'

'But it's not on the whole top floor.'

'Yes it is. Now, wait here,' he says pointing behind a pillar in the corridor. 'When I give you the sign, come in.'

'What? Why?' Claire asks, unzipping her knee-high boots.

'Just wait here.'

Mark lets himself in after trying three different keys. Craig is on the sofa in his dressing gown reading Chris Ryan's *Zero Option*.

'You're hammered aren't you?' Craig says.

'No.' Mark almost walks into the wall on his way into the kitchen. 'Cheers for letting me in.'

He drinks Tropicana straight from the carton, hiding behind the fridge door.

'Where have you been anyway?' Craig asks. 'You're wearing your pulling shirt. Have you been on a date?'

'No. Work do at Chernobyl. Someone's birthday.'

'Cheers for the invite.'

'It was work people only. You wouldn't have liked it. Shouldn't you be getting to bed? It's quite late,' Mark says, chewing a mouthful of wholemeal bread.

'I want to finish this chapter.'

'But that means I can't watch TV.'

'Can't you go to your room?'

'Can't you go to *your* room?'

Mark turns the TV on.

'OK, I'll go if you're going to be a twat,' Craig says, huffing. He slams the book shut. 'See you in the morning. Drink plenty of water.'

Mark waits until Craig's bedroom door closes and creeps out to Claire.

'I've been out here ages. What are you doing?' she asks.

'I had to get rid of my mate. Please be quiet,' he says, focussing on the tattoo of barbed wire around her left bicep.

Mark locks the front door as quietly as he can, which isn't quietly at all, and pushes Claire into his room. He kicks a pile of wet towels under his bed and dims the lights.

'Nice place,' Claire says. 'Can I turn the TV on?'

'No!' He grabs the remote control out of her hands. 'I'm just going to get ready for bed,' he says, gesturing towards the en suite. 'Make yourself comfortable.'

Claire sits on the unmade bed and sucks on a mint from her purse. After waiting five minutes, she sneaks out into the moonlit living room. The fridge is humming and she follows the sound and flicks on the kitchen lights.

'Who are you?' Craig says, shocked, as he wanders in. He's wearing pyjama bottoms and holding an empty mug.

'I'm Claire. I'm with Mark. You must be Craig,' she says eying his nimble body.

Craig stares at her and grins. 'Sorry, I didn't know anyone was here. You surprised me.'

'I didn't mean to frighten you.'

'That's OK.'

'So, you're Mark's flatmate?'

'Yes,' Craig says, making a lemon cordial.

'And you run your own property company now, Mark was saying.'

'Err, not exactly.'

Mark has been in the bathroom almost twenty minutes and Claire is back sitting on the bed.

'I thought you might have gone,' he says, poking his head around the door before re-emerging still in his clothes. 'I couldn't hear you.' He has started to sober up.

'No. I was waiting. I went to get a drink. I met your flatmate.'

'Why did you do that? I told you to stay here.'

'I was thirsty. He said he doesn't run a property company.'

'He's just being modest, ignore him.'

'Come here,' Claire says, patting the space beside her on the bed.

Mark sits down cautiously and she forces herself on him, holding his head in a tight grip and kissing him violently. He tumbles back onto the duvet and she pulls her skirt up to her waist and straddles him. Mark lets out a grunt as she brings her full weight down on him and forces her chest into his face.

'Please, please get off me,' he begs. 'I'm going to be sick.'

Mark thrusts with his legs and flips Claire sideways. She topples over and he hauls himself out from under her and runs into the en suite.

'Like to play rough do you? I'll be waiting for you big boy,' she says in a husky voice, unzipping her skirt.

Mark leans over the toilet bowl gasping for breath and then washes his sweaty face in the sink. There is no sound from the bedroom.

He opens the bathroom door to see Claire standing naked on the bed, flexing her triceps. She has her name tattooed in gothic script on her abdomen.

'Claire, fucking hell, what are you–'

'Come on, Mark, strip for me,' she says leaping towards him. 'I want your body.' She yanks at his belt, managing to undo it as he tries to fend her off.

'No, no, please don't hurt me.'

Claire drops to her knees and wrestles him to the floor, knocking over a pile of DVDs as she tugs at his trousers. 'I love a fighter.'

'Please, get off!'

Mark twists onto his front and gets his right foot trapped under the chest of drawers. She gets both hands around his belt and wrenches his trousers and boxer shorts down as he thrashes about on the floor.

'Fucking get off!'

'Come on, show me what you've got,' she growls, her face and chest slamming against Mark's lower back.

'Arrrrrrgh! Arrrrrrgh! Get off me! CRAIG, HELP ME!!'

Claire grabs his shoulders, grunts, and brutally flips him over, exposing Mark's naked body as he howls in pain and desperately tries to cover himself.

CHAPTER EIGHT

The Land Rover Defender stops at a gate along a deserted country road and the nine members of the Cinq Estates team – Christian, Craig, Danny, Ibrahim, Paul, Suresh, Adam, Bradley and Jamaal – are told to take off their blindfolds and get out. As soon as the door is shut, the driver speeds off. There is nothing but woodland and fields for miles.

'Where are we?' Danny asks.

'Surrey,' Christian says. 'That's all you need to know.'

The team are dressed in army fatigues and everyone is carrying a rucksack. Craig is leaning against the gate, yawning. It is warm but overcast, and muddy underfoot. One of the new boys, Jamaal, has wrapped his shirt around his waist to reveal a Chicago Bulls basketball vest which almost comes down to his knees.

There's a rustling in the bushes and then suddenly a savage howling as a huge figure in combat dress and a balaclava charges towards them firing a pistol over their heads. The Cinq team throw themselves on the floor, apart from Bradley, who sprints off down the road. The gunman flings himself over the gate, pulls his balaclava off and laughs manically. He is well over six feet tall and heavily built with a bent, scarred nose and a thick brown moustache. He has black and green war paint smeared over his cheeks and forehead.

'Sorry ladies, did I frighten you?' he barks. 'Get to your feet and line up in front of me.'

They follow his orders. Suresh, a timid teenager who only joined the company yesterday, is shaking. Craig and Christian stand at opposite ends. He points at Jamaal and without having to say anything Jamaal puts his shirt back on.

'My name is Griff Hammerson and I'll be leading you today.' He's Welsh and his tone is cold and intimidating. 'I am a retired Royal Marine commando and I served this country for almost three decades in some of the most violent and bloody conflicts in our history.

'I've killed men in the Falklands, Northern Ireland, Iraq, Afghanistan, the former Yugoslavia, Libya and Sierra Leone... and Germany, although that was an accident. I am a trained killing machine.' He walks towards Craig. 'If I wanted to, I could kill all of you with my bare hands, dismember your bodies and bury you in these woods, but luckily for you I'm in a good mood today.' He pulls a manic, teeth-baring smile. 'That was a joke. You are allowed to laugh.'

The team exchange nervous looks and eventually manage fake grins.

'Good,' Griff continues. 'You now look a little less like frightened rabbits. Now, you may be wondering why I surprised you like I did. It was *not* to frighten you, or purely to give myself a good laugh, even though I did find it rather amusing, it was to assess how, as a team, you react in a high-pressure situation. The aim of today's session is to build confidence and teach you how to think clearly under pressure.

'Now, your reactions told me you are a team low on self-confidence and lacking leadership. The fact that one of your team scarpered at the first sign of trouble told me everything. What was his name?'

'Bradley. He's new,' Christian answers, frowning.

'Has anyone got his mobile phone number so we can get him back?'

'He hasn't got a mobile at the moment. Some kids mugged him on a night bus.'

'Jesus Christ. He's as good as useless then. Forget him. He can find his own way home,' Griff says, shaking his head. 'As for the rest of you, why did nobody stand up and try to disarm me? Where was the leadership? Who was going to put themselves on the line for the sake of the team? Well?'

'We thought you might shoot us,' Danny says.

'If I'd have been firing real bullets rather than blanks, I would have shot all of you. It was one against nine, yet your first reaction was to protect yourselves which made you all equally vulnerable. It would have taken only two of you to wrestle me to the floor and disarm me. I accept that it takes a brave man to tackle a guy with a gun, but you have to be brave in whatever you do, be it fighting wars or selling houses. One, or at worst two of you may have been wounded but with the threat neutralized you have seven or eight other guys who you'd be able to rely on to treat your wounds and call for medical assistance... unless of course you'd taken a bullet to the head from close range, in which case you'd be dead as fuck.'

Griff takes a pen and paper from the pocket of his combat trousers. 'Which one of you lot is Christian?'

Christian steps forwards. Griff makes a note.

'Right, Christian, who's your number two?'

'I haven't got one. It's just me.'

Griff looks annoyed. 'Well who's the second most experienced one of you?'

'Err, Craig I suppose.'

Griff makes Christian and Craig stand either side of him and divides the others into two teams. He then asks them to come up with a team name for their opponents.

It's Christian's Crusaders vs. Bitch Boy Squadron.

*

Craig blows his nose and then pours a cold and flu remedy into a mug of boiling water. His eyes look sore and he keeps feeling his face and forehead with the back of his hand.

The Monday morning meeting has been cancelled as Christian has emailed to say he's at a branch managers' conference and won't be back until tomorrow.

Craig makes a rasping, dry coughing sound and blows his nose again. He leaves his drink to cool on the worktop and goes to the bathroom to get some more tissues.

When he gets back, Hannah is there making herself a hot chocolate. She's wearing glasses and her hair is tied back. She looks over her shoulder and when she sees it's him she turns and smiles.

'Don't come too close, Han. I think I've got a cold.'

She looks slightly aghast as he nears her. 'Craig, you look really poorly. Have you got a temperature?'

'I'm not sure. My head feels hot but I keep shivering.'

'Craig you might have flu. You should be at home in bed.'

'I can't afford a day in bed. I'll be OK. I feel a bit better than I did earlier and once I drink this I'm sure it'll go off,' he says, pointing at his mug.

'Yes, but if it doesn't go off you should go home. I don't think anyone's going to want to be shown round a house by someone who's coughing all over them.'

Craig sneezes into a tissue and apologises.

Hannah takes half a step back. 'And you might be passing your germs on to other people.'

'Sorry, Han,' he says again.

'Did this start on the teambuilding weekend?'

'I started feeling ill on the way home but I thought that might have been lack of sleep.'

'Didn't you stay in a hotel?'

'Everyone else did but me and Danny had to sleep under a tarpaulin in the woods all night and it poured with rain. We got soaking wet.'

'You slept in the woods? Why did you have to do that?' Hannah throws her spoon in the sink.

'It was a forfeit for being on the losing team. There were four of us at the start but one guy almost drowned when our raft fell apart and was taken to hospital and then Jamaal – do you know him?'

'Is that the kid who talks all *gangsta*?'

'Yes - even though his real name's Malcolm and he's from High Wycombe - well, he got us lost on the orienteering because he wouldn't go near any dark areas on the map because he thought that meant they were muddy and he didn't want to get his trainers dirty.'

Hannah is smiling. 'Are you joking?'

'I wish I was. He stormed off when me and Danny had a go at him and then Danny twisted his ankle, which is why he's not in today.'

'But didn't they give you a tent or something and a sleeping bag?'

'The bloke running it, this mad ex-army guy, gave us a tent but it didn't have enough ropes or pegs so we had to hang it between two trees, which didn't really work.'

'And you were out there all night in the rain?'

'It didn't rain *all night*, just for a few hours. And there were cars going up and down the track at all hours. They told us in the morning that we'd pitched up close to a well-known dogging site.'

Hannah laughs.

'It didn't seem that funny at the time. Anything could have happened.'

'You could have joined in. At least you would have kept warm.'

'Are you being serious?'

'No, of course not! Imagine what kind of old freaks you might bump into.'

'Err, yeah. Anyway, how was your weekend? How was the spa?'

Hannah raises her eyebrows. 'My weekend was awful. And it wasn't a spa; it was a hotel in the middle of nowhere that turned out to be a retreat for women with drug and alcohol issues. We should have realised when they insisted on going through our bags when we checked in. There were all these positive thinking posters everywhere and when one of the girls asked what there was to do, the receptionist recommended counselling sessions.'

'That's ridiculous, what did you do?'

'We stayed for a few hours and had a bike ride around the forest… the place was actually really nice but there was no spa, or bar, for obvious reasons, so at around seven we all got taxis back to the station and got the train home.'

'Who organised it?'

'No idea. Someone in head office I suppose. The people at the hotel couldn't understand why we were there either. That was only the start of things though.'

'What do you mean?'

Hannah sips her hot chocolate and then has a deep intake of breath. 'I didn't tell Marcus, my boyfriend, that I was coming home on Saturday as I knew he was having a night out with his mates and I thought it'd be a nice surprise for him, for me to be there when he got back, but he came in about four in the morning and he'd brought a group of people with him.'

'What, for a party?'

'Sort of, but that wasn't the issue. They were being a bit loud and I recognised Marcus's mates' voices but then there were some voices I didn't recognise. And it turned out that,' Hannah's tone hardens, 'Marcus had invited a few girls back to the flat.'

'Oh,' Craig says. He has to blow his nose again. 'But you never know there could be a reason-'

'Craig, one of them was sitting on his lap with her arms around him when I walked into the living room.'

'Oh, right. What did you say?'

'I didn't say anything. I just stood there. He jumped up and threw everyone out and then we had a huge row.'

'Shit. Have you sorted things out now?'

'No. I don't know. I've not spoken to him since Sunday morning. He kept telling me that he'd done nothing wrong but I don't believe him. I stayed at a friend's house last night, which is why I look so rough.'

'Hannah, you don't look rough, not at all. *I* look rough. I'm sorry about… everything, but I'm sure you'll work things out.'

'Anyway, sorry, you don't want to listen to me moaning.'

'It's OK.'

'At least I didn't have to sleep in the woods.'

Craig finishes off his remedy drink. 'I'd rather hear about your boyfriend than have Christian going on at me.' Craig starts to sway a little. 'Is he really at a conference - Christian?'

'I don't think so. I got a call from one of the other branch managers this morning wanting to talk to him, and there's nothing in the diary. Craig are you OK? You've gone a bit red.'

'Yeah, I feel a bit light-headed. I think I might need to sit down. I thought these drinks were meant to make you feel better.'

'How many have you had?'

'This morning or in total?' he asks as they wander back to their desks.

'This morning.'

'Eight.'

CHAPTER NINE

A new Golf GTi screeches to a halt in the middle of the farmyard and Mark lets out two blasts on the car's horn. A grey mare in the stable block rears up on her hind legs and whinnies, and a child-sized man dressed in wellingtons, faded jodhpurs and a green rollneck jumper runs out from the end bay and taps on the driver's window. Mark lowers it fractionally using a button on the steering wheel.

'You can't use your horn in the yard,' the stable hand says. 'It scares the horses.' He's Irish, has a pallid, drawn face and only his head is visible from inside the car.

'Yeah, I noticed that, mate,' Mark says.

'You can't park here either. We've got the hay delivery coming in a minute.'

'I'm looking for Jenny.'

'And you are?'

'Mark.'

'Ah, so you're Mark.' His eyes narrow. 'I'm Eoin. I think Jenny's up in the top field with Augustus.'

'Who's he?'

'A horse,' Eoin says, picking at one of his dirty fingernails.

'Where's the top field?'

'You walk up that road there. It's not far.' Eoin points up a muddy track running between a fenced-off show jumping area and an overgrown copse. 'You can park at the back of the house.'

'I'll drive it. I'm not walking, I'll ruin my shoes,' Mark says pointing down at his Timberlands.

'It's a bit bumpy up there. If I were-'

Mark closes the window with Eoin mid-sentence and drives off with a loud wheel-spin.

The narrow track is littered with horse manure and water-filled potholes. Mark drives carefully up the incline, slowed by his wheels sinking into the soft mud, until he's forced to stop to let through a scowling, ruddy-faced old woman on a horse.

He waits until she is out of sight and presses hard on the accelerator. The wheels send mud shooting into the air and over the rear of the car, which goes nowhere. He jerks the steering wheel left and puts his foot down again. The car shoots across the track straight into a wooden post, knocking it flat and causing the barbed wire fence to sag. Mark swears, reverses and ploughs on.

The further he drives, the firmer the ground becomes. He reaches the brow of the hill and the track stops abruptly. In the distance, a huge figure with a long copper-coloured mane is nosing around in the mud. Mark lowers the passenger window and leans over the seat.

'JENNY! JENNY!' he shouts, his face splattered by drizzle.

Jenny gets to her feet and marches across the field. Her riding boots and jodhpurs are muddy and her gilet is soaking. She removes her riding hat, scrapes her hair off her rosy face and clambers over a stile. She bends down into the car window and kisses Mark on the cheek.

'What are you doing here?' she asks, happy to see him.

'Hello, babe. I thought I'd surprise you,' Mark says, wiping off the wet lip marks.

'What a lovely surprise. How did you find me?'

'The kid in the yard told me.'

'Which kid?'

'The Irish one'

'Eoin? He's older than you. He works here.' Jenny coughs and takes a blackcurrant lozenge from her pocket. 'How did you drive all the way up here? I'm surprised you didn't get stuck.'

'It was fine.'

Jenny eyes Mark's clothes. 'Since when have you had a Barbour?' she asks, referring to the green quilted coat he's wearing.

'I've had it ages. Where's the horse?'

'He's being used for a riding lesson.' Jenny rummages in her pocket. 'I was looking for my earring, one of the special ones you bought me for my fifteenth birthday. Do you remember?'

'No.'

'I've found it now anyway,' she says, showing him a miniature silver teddy bear on a hook. 'Can I have a lift back?'

'Jen, no way. You're covered in mud.'

'So is the car. *Please* can I have a lift? Haven't you got anything I can sit on?'

'No, walk. It'll be good exercise. Or you can go in the boot.'

'Mark, I'm not going in the boot.'

He reverses back down the track and Jenny follows on foot, stopping briefly to inspect the broken fencepost.

Eoin is spraying the yard with a power hose. Mark parks beside the stables, checks if there is any damage to the front bumper and looks back up the track. Jenny is about fifty yards away.

'Mate, you couldn't just give the car a quick once over with the hose could you?' Mark calls out to Eoin.

'There's another hose round the back, you can use that.'

'I'd rather you do it. I'll pay you.'

Jenny waves at Eoin and Mark follows her into a portakabin which is the staff changing rooms and kitchen. There are posters of horses on the walls and riding paraphernalia litters the floor: hats, crops, stirrups, rugs covered in horse hair, and old saddles. It smells of animals and chemicals. Mark sits on a plastic chair which strains under his weight and plays with his iPhone as Jenny hangs up her riding gear and goes off to have a shower. Weak sunshine creeps in through the meshed windows.

Eoin jogs up the steps and removes his boots at the door. 'I sprayed your car,' he says. Standing up, he's only at Mark's eye level.

'Cheers mate. You're a legend. Do you want some money?' Mark asks, taking a handful of change from his jeans.

'No, don't worry about it. It only took a minute.'

Mark accepts Eoin's offer of a cup of tea but then changes his mind after seeing the grubby kettle.

'Jenny said you work in London,' Eoin says.

'Yeah, I'm in investment. In the City.'

'Do you enjoy it?'

'I can't complain,' he says, cleaning his phone. 'It's long hours.'

'Is that why you don't come back very often?'

'Yeah.'

Eoin pulls off his jodhpurs and stands in front of Mark in a pair of bulging y-fronts.

Tom Canty

*

Wokafellas is a vast, canteen-style Japanese restaurant on Epsom High Street. After queuing outside for five minutes, Jenny holds the door open and Mark ducks under the arm of her baggy polo shirt. Another brief wait ensues before a waiter leads them to benches at a faux pine table near the windows.

Jenny squeezes onto the bench causing the people either side to shift along as the waiter scribbles their drink orders on the paper place mats.

Two teenage goths on the end of the table pay and leave so the couple to their right slide along, giving Jenny enough space to move her arms. She reaches into her bag for a two-for-one voucher as Mark accidentally snaps his chopsticks.

Mark tugs at his Abercrombie t-shirt which clings to his paunch.

'Chicken katsu curry?' a teenage waitress asks, checking the scrawls on their mats.

'That's mine,' Mark says, finishing off his last duck gyoza.

'And chilli chicken ramen.' She places the bowl of noodles in front of Jenny and picks up the empty starter plates.

'No. That's mine too.' Mark slides the bowl over to his side. 'We should have some kind of salad coming as well.' He stuffs two spoonfuls of rice into mouth and attacks his noodles with a fork.

'Don't eat too quickly,' Jenny warns, sniffing her wine.

'I won't,' Mark says as he chews.

'How's work been this week?'

'Really good.' Grains of rice fall from his mouth back onto his plate. 'Made loads of commission.'

'Well done. You should be promoted soon with the amount of hours you've been working.'

'Yeah I know. I haven't left the office before ten thirty any night for the last few weeks. That's why I haven't been able to answer my phone, babe. If you're caught on a private phone call, Justin goes ballistic.'

'I'd hate to work somewhere like that.'

'It's just the culture at MenDax, babe. I can't change that.' Mark sips his beer. 'What's been going on at the farm?'

'Oh, we had quite an interesting week. Remember I told you that we

70

were getting a new horsebox?'

'No,' Mark says with his mouth full.

'Well, it arrived this week. It's amazing. It's so luxurious inside. You could have a party in there. It's about twice the size of that horrible old thing we used to drive around. It's got a really good shower and the beds are bigger. And do you remember in the last one the saddle racks kept breaking? Well in this one, they're metal instead of plastic. And it's got a microwave so we can actually heat food up rather than having to use those horrible little gas stoves. And there's more room for the horses as well. It was so exciting when it arrived that-'

'It sounds it, babe,' Mark butts in. 'Is there any chance we can save the rest of this story until later? It's just a bit boring.'

The Golf mounts the pavement and screeches to a halt outside Jenny's parents' large semi-detached cottage. She undoes her seat belt.

'Cheers, babe. I'll give you a ring tomorrow,' Mark says.

'Aren't you coming in?' Jenny turns her body to face Mark and the car wobbles.

'I've had a really tiring week, babe. I just want to go back to my own bed and sleep.'

'I'll come back to yours then.'

'No, babe. I just need a good night's sleep on my own. You know what it's like at mine. There's barely enough room for us both in my double. It'll keep me awake. I can't afford to be tired all week.'

Jenny's mouth drops.

'What's up?' he asks.

'We haven't seen each other for weeks. All I want you to do is come in. We hardly ever... I thought that...' Her lips start to tremble. 'I miss you when you're not here. We're meant to be a couple, Mark.' A tear runs down her cheek.

'We *are*.'

'It doesn't feel like it.'

'It's just work, babe. It's been manic the last few weeks. I'm at the office pretty much non-stop. When it slows down we can see a lot more of each other. I miss you too.'

'You're just saying that.'

'No, I'm not. You mean the world to me.'

Jenny mops her tears with her fleece. 'The last ten years with you have been the happiest time of my life. But now, I just, I just feel like we're growing apart.'

'Don't be silly, babe. I won't be in London forever. I know how much you love the farm, and of course we don't see each other as much as we'd like, but it's only short-term. Look, with a bit of luck I might be promoted to director level in the next few months. When that happens I'll be on far more money and perhaps we can look at getting a place together, around here somewhere.'

'Do you really mean that?' Jenny asks, sniffing.

'Of course I do, babe.'

'I love you, Mark,' Jenny says, putting her arms around him.

'I love you too.'

They kiss briefly. Jenny says she'll come over to Mark's for lunch tomorrow and heaves herself out of the car. She blows Mark a kiss from the front door and crouches down so she doesn't hit her head as she lets herself in.

*

The Hunter house is silent. Mark rolls out of bed and opens his curtains. There are no cars on the driveway and the gates are open. Mark's parents' detached mock-Tudor house is on King Road, one of the main routes into Epsom. Cars and 4x4s zip past as Mark looks out across the fields to the driving range at Epsom Hills golf club.

He opens his antique wardrobe. All it contains are three coats covered in plastic from the dry cleaners and his old school blazer. He digs around in the matching chest of drawers, puts on a tight pair of tracksuit bottoms and an old England rugby shirt and goes downstairs.

Mark sits at the breakfast bar in the spotless kitchen and gazes out into the garden. It's raining again and the lawns need cutting. Someone has left the door to the summer house open and the cover hasn't been put over the gas barbecue.

The fridge is fully stocked. Mark claps his hands, puts two griddle pans on the range and turns on the grill. 'Where's the George Foreman?' he asks himself as he searches the cupboards. He pours oil into a pan and loads it with three Cumberland sausages and four rashers of bacon. He chops a tomato in half and places it under the grill next to a portobello mushroom. He then microwaves a can of baked beans and drops two slices of granary bread into the toaster.

He stands over the crackling pans, rolling the sausages and flipping the bacon before messily cracking an egg. Large fragments of shell are lodged in the white but he only makes a half-attempt to pick them out. He turns the heat up and holds the pans at arms' length as fat spits all over the wall and the slate-tiled floor.

He loads his breakfast onto a serving plate and backs into the living room through the double-doors which stick in the thick carpet. Three oatmeal-coloured sofas are arranged in a U-shape around a circular coffee table. Mark lowers his plate onto unread copies of the *News of the World* and *Mail on Sunday* and turns on the giant plasma television which doubles as a mirror above the fireplace.

He demolishes the breakfast. After forcing down the last forkful of beans, he burps fiercely and lays down flat on the middle sofa holding his stomach. He flicks through the Sky channels, stopping at *My Super Sexy Sixteenth* on MTV. A spoilt girl from Hampstead has organised a disastrous diamond-themed birthday party. The rappers she booked - Stabbing Crew - haven't turned up, the hotel has to be evacuated after a fire alarm, and she bursts into tears when a spotty boy called Ryan says he thought her parents were going to buy her a helicopter. When the credits roll, Mark turns down the volume and closes his eyes.

The front door slams and moments later his name is shouted from the kitchen. Mark's mum, Patricia, bursts into the living room wearing a white tennis tracksuit and trainers. She is slim and her damp, dyed-brown hair is brushed back. She has a large nose and small dark bags under her eyes. 'Mark, what have you been doing in the kitchen? Get up now and clean it up.'

'I'll do it in a minute. I'll put it all in the dishwasher.'

She kisses him on the forehead. 'Why did you cook breakfast anyway? I'm doing lunch at two o'clock. Have you had a shower yet?'

'No, I'll have one in a minute. Where have you been?'

'Tennis.'

'Where's Dad?'

'He and John have gone to see Grandad. He thought you might have wanted to come, but you were still in bed.' Patricia pulls *You* magazine from the *Mail*. 'Have you phoned Jenny?'

'Can you do it please? I'll sort the kitchen out.'

'Oh, and there's another thing I was going to ask you, Mark Hunter,' she stops to say as she is leaving the room. 'Why is there a dent on the bumper of my car?'

'No idea. Why do you always assume it's my fault?'

Jenny excuses herself and leaves the dining table. She and Mark are sitting opposite Uncle John, with Patricia and Mark's dad, Graham, at either end. Patricia has prepared a roast banquet.

John smirks and waits until the bathroom door shuts in the hall. Patricia, who has changed into a sparkly black jumper and jeans, warns him not to say a word.

'What does she normally eat for lunch? Human growth hormones?' John says, reaching for one of the cans of Stella by his feet. 'She's like one of those East German hammer throwers from the Seventies. How tall is she these days?'

'John, keep your voice down and don't be so bloody rude,' Patricia says.

'Sorry, Pat, but honestly, look at the poor girl. What is she Mark, your bird or your bodyguard?'

'We don't really see that much of each other any more,' Mark says, glancing through the bay windows at John's Mercedes M-Class.

'Mark, that's your girlfriend you're talking about. I know she's a bit *big*, but she can't help it,' his mum whispers.

John helps himself to more potatoes. His stomach swells beneath his Ralph Lauren shirt and there are broken veins all over his bulbous nose. His cropped hair is badly receding and he has a small bald patch. 'Lost your appetite, Mark?'

'No, I'm just not that hungry,' he says, looking down at the untouched vegetables on his plate.

'Don't eat it if you don't want to,' his mum says.

'I'm just a bit full. I've just been trying to cut down a bit recently, trying to get fit. I'm thinking about entering a triathlon.'

Graham brings in a second bottle of white wine from the kitchen. He has grey hair, worn in a side parting, a grey moustache and glasses. He is far slimmer than his younger brother and has a fresh, healthy complexion.

'How was Grandad?' Mark asks.

'No better.' Graham's speech is more formal and softer than John's. 'There's no way he can go home at the moment. The doctor said he might have to be transferred to a care home.'

'All he needs is a few more days of rest and he'll perk up,' John interjects. 'There's no need to start thinking about care homes. You know what he's like, he'll be up and walking by the end of the week and probably discharging himself.' He shuffles in his chair and scratches his head. Gravy drips down his chin as he chews another chunk of beef. 'How's work going, Mark?'

'Pretty good.'

'Justin said that he might get promoted,' Jenny says. She has put on a baggy v-neck jumper.

'I think that Justin's a pompous little dwarf,' John says. 'He swans around like he owns the place. I hope you don't take any shit from him.'

'John, do you always have to swear?' Patricia asks.

'Sorry.'

'No, I don't,' Mark assures him. 'Justin leaves me to get on with things. He's not in the office most of the time.'

'Is that Jane girl with the fake cans still there?'

Patricia glares at him.

'Julia? Yes, she's still there.'

'I tell you what,' John says, 'I'm surprised you haven't had a go Mark. I would have done by now.'

Mark cringes.

'Well Mark's not like you,' Jenny says defiantly.

'No, sorry Jen, you're right, of course he not... not that I'd blame him. She's a pretty girl-'

'John, for god's sake,' Patricia says.

Jenny looks to Mark, but he keeps quiet. Her bottom lip starts to tremble. Patricia asks if she could help her out in the kitchen and glares at John as they leave.

'I've told you to watch what you say around Jenny. She can be very sensitive,' Graham warns him.

'Sorry, I know. Sorry, Mark,' John says, emptying another can of lager.

'It's not him you should be apologising to. Mark, don't you think you should go and talk to her?'

'No. She prefers Mum. Can I have another drink?'

John passes Mark a can. 'What do you reckon your bonus will be this year?'

'Umm, I'm not sure. We're doing pretty well, so I'm hoping for better than last year.'

'What did you get last year?'

'Twenty grand.'

'It wasn't anyway near that much was it?' his dad says, with a baffled look.

'Yeah, it was.'

'When do you find out?' John asks, rubbing his stomach.

'Second week of August.'

Graham starts piling up the plates in the middle of the table as the gold carriage clock on the mantelpiece chimes.

'How long have you been there now? Three years?' John asks.

'Yeah.'

'With your experience you should be earning about... ummm... four times what you were when you joined. If they try to fob you off with anything less, I'd threaten to leave. It's all a game of bluff, mate.'

'Yeah, I know.'

'Remember to tell them you're underpaid and ask for ten grand more than you think's reasonable. That way they'll meet you halfway and they'll think they're getting a good deal and everyone's a winner. There are a lot of golden tits at your place, Mark. You've just got to make sure you're sucking on the right one.'

'I'd be very careful about making extravagant demands,' Graham says. 'The last thing you want is to price yourself out of a job. There are plenty of other young men out there with your qualifications who'd happily work there for what you're earning, so don't talk yourself into redundancy.'

John waits until Graham leaves the room.

'Don't take a blind bit of notice,' he says. 'You don't get anywhere by playing it safe. That's fair enough if you're an accountant, but to make the big money you've got to take a risk. If they won't pay you what you're worth then walk out and find someone who will.'

'That's what I was planning to do anyway.'

'How much holiday do you get at the moment?'

'Thirty-five days.'

'Thirty-five? That's nothing. Ask for at least sixty. You've got to cash in while you can.' John slugs more beer and adjusts the waist of his navy chinos. 'Try to get a car out of them, and ask about doing an MBA or something like that. A lot of companies are willing to pay for it these days. Do some research, and throw a few suggestions at them. It makes you look ambitious. A bloke I know did a three-year business course at Harvard, paid for by his company and they kept him on full salary. You'd be set up for life if you can get that sort of deal out of them.' He farts and apologises. 'You couldn't pop to the living room and get me the *News of the World* could you mate?'

Everyone bar Graham is back at the table. Patricia picks at fluff on her jumper. Jenny's eyes are red and she is quiet. John is flicking through the paper.

'Sorry if I upset you earlier, Jen. I didn't mean anything by it,' he says. 'I was just-'

Jenny sniffs. 'No, it's fine. Lunch was lovely,' she says looking to Patricia.

'Thank you.'

'Yeah, it was great. Cheers, Pat,' John says.

Graham brings in a trifle and scoops generous portions into porcelain bowls. Mark devours his first helping before his dad has even sat down. He then helps himself to more and is onto his third spoonful when he suddenly turns bright pink and runs to the bathroom.

He turns the cold tap on full-blast and hacks up his undigested dessert. He pulls at the collar of his t-shirt, holds his chest and washes his mouth in the bidet. Reaching out for a hand towel, he wipes dribble from his chin and uses the other side of it to dry his forehead.

'Are you all right, Mark?' Jenny calls from behind the door.

'Yes, I'm fine. I'm just a bit hot. I'll be out in a sec, babe.'

Mark stuffs a recycling bag into his back pocket, unplugs the shredder and carries it into his room, locking the door behind him. He separates the post on his desk into two piles: 1) Barclays, NatWest, Virgin, Egg and Capital One correspondence. 2) Catalogues and anything else.

He feeds the unopened bank statements, credit card bills and letters into the shredder's metal teeth. It jams repeatedly and when it can't digest what Mark is trying to feed it, he tears the envelopes apart with his hands.

He empties the waste paper unit into the recycling bag for a third time and brushes the few loose strands of paper on the desk onto the floor. He then thumbs through catalogues from Ferrari, Jack Wills and Bang and Olufsen and slides them into his leather holdall.

There's a knock at the door.

'Hang on,' Mark says, stashing the recycling bag under his bed.

'Why did you lock the door?' Graham asks as Mark lets him in.

'I was getting changed.'

'Into the same clothes?'

Graham sits on the edge of the bed, with his hands on the knees of his corduroy trousers. 'You said you wanted to talk to me?'

'Umm, yes.' Mark sits down on his old yellow computer chair. 'I wondered if you could do me a favour.'

'Go on.'

'I wondered if you'd be able to give me a slight increase in my allowance.'

Graham stands up. 'Well this is going to be a short conversation isn't it? The answer is no. You shouldn't even be getting an allowance. I cannot believe that you can't survive on your wages, what are you spending the money on?'

'It's the flat, Dad. Since Craig made us move I'm paying out twice as much in rent and bills. I'm actually a lot worse off. The place is costing an absolute fortune. General living expenses are much more as well.'

'Mark, you're talking to me like I don't know how much running a house costs. I think you might have a bit more cash if you didn't go out getting drunk every night of the week. And despite your protestations I don't believe for a second that you're at work until eleven every night. You look hungover every time I see you.'

'Because I'm not getting any sleep because I'm working so hard.'

Graham looks quizzically at the shredder. 'If your flat is too expensive you shouldn't have moved there in the first place. The rent's not gone up has it?'

'Dad, please this is a one off. I need eight hundred to tie me over until pay day.'

'Eight hundred pounds? What for? You get paid on Friday don't you?'

'It's for bills.'

Graham shakes his head and folds his arms. Mark looks at him expectantly.

'Promise me you haven't been using any of your inheritance money.'

'Dad, of course not. It's all in a high interest account.'

'Promise. Because if you've been-'

'I wouldn't.'

'Good. Look, I'll give you the money as a *loan*, and you'll pay that back the minute you get paid. I'll check my account on Friday night and if that money isn't in there I'll be straight on the phone to you to find out why not. Is that clear?'

'Yes. Thanks.'

'If you can't live on your salary then something is seriously wrong.'

Mark says nothing and lunges forward, wrapping up his dad in an uneasy hug.

CHAPTER TEN

'Make yourselves at home, boys,' Craig says.

Adam and Tony dump their bags in Craig's room and saunter into the warm, sunny living room as Craig hooks back the French doors. A thin layer of dust is visible on the dining table and television.

'This place is sweet, mate,' Tony says. He has a stronger Norfolk accent than Craig and is slight, clean-shaven and has a spiky brown quiff. His short-sleeved check shirt, cargo shorts and bright white trainers all look new.

'Very nice,' Adam says, stepping out onto the roof terrace. He shields his eyes from the sun with his hand even though he has sunglasses hanging from his v-neck t-shirt. He is taller than Craig with a more athletic and hairier physique, short blond hair and a confident demeanour.

Craig gets three Coronas from the fridge and squeezes chunks of lime into the necks of the bottles.

'Cheers,' Adam says, taking a swig. 'Where's your flatmate?'

'Mark? I'm not sure. He was in bed when I left this morning. Probably shopping.'

Tony joins them outside. He's already drunk most of his beer.

'Mate, this is awesome. How long you been here now?' he asks, looking out over the houses.

'Almost five months.'

'It's so much better than that last place you lived in. How much rent you paying?'

'A lot.' Craig pauses. 'Over a grand a month.'

'That's a bargain mate.'

'It's a grand a month *each*.'

'I hope you're selling plenty of houses,' Adam says.

'That'd pay for ten weeks in my place,' says Tony.

'Yes, but it's London, not Norwich.'

Craig removes his tie and drinks his beer.

'What's the plan then?' Adam asks.

'We'll have a walk up to the common and go to the pub. There are usually loads of girls there sunbathing when the weather's nice. I'll go and get changed.'

Craig returns in a white polo shirt, camouflage combat shorts and Havaianas flip-flops. He messes up his hair and puts on his sunglasses.

Adam and Tony are sitting on the sofas, drinking.

'Have you had a makeover?' Adam says, standing up to have a closer look at Craig's clothes. 'When did *you* start buying Abercrombie?'

'I've only got one. You should have a look in Mark's wardrobe. He's got hundreds.'

Tony polishes off his bottle. 'Let's get going then.'

Clapham Common is teeming with activity. As well as the sunbathers and joggers, there are refereed games of eleven-a-side football and touch rugby, and a large group of shirtless men are having an Aussie rules training session. A gang of teenage boys are cruising around on BMX bikes, their faces shaded by baseball caps, and there are a number of professional dog walkers being pulled along by packs of spaniels and Labradors. A young girl's birthday party is taking place in the shade of trees on the edge of the common and even the surrounding roads are busy with cars and buses.

'Tony, stop staring, or at least put your sunglasses on,' Adam says as he kicks a ball back to a fat child wearing an Arsenal shirt.

'Mate, it's hard not to. Look over there.' Tony points at two olive-skinned girls in bikinis, stretched out on beach towels. One of them is reading *Heat*.

The boys wind their way towards the pub. Tony suggests getting some beers from a shop and sitting on the common, but Craig overrules him.

Three young women in Lycra shorts and bra tops bounce past and Tony follows them with his eyes.

As they get closer to the pub, Adam, squinting, reads the sign:

'The Whore on the Common? What kind of a name is that?'

'I don't know. It used to be called The Thornton Arms.'

The pub is a two-storey Georgian hotel and bar which sits alone on the edge of the common. Its name is displayed in golden letters high along the width of the building. A huge wrought iron lantern protrudes from the wall above the main door.

Outside, young drinkers are crowded around the wooden picnic tables. Four blonde girls in tiny shorts and big sunglasses are sharing a jug of Pimms next to a group of boys wearing low-cut t-shirts and smoking Marlboro Lights. To the right of the door, a chef is cooking on a barbeque made from an oil drum. The burgers are £12 each but the queue is over thirty people long.

Inside, it is shady and cool and none of the tables are occupied. The dull red walls are covered in old photographs of the common. The back half of the building is a restaurant with tables set for dining.

Tony orders three pints of Peroni, hands over a £10 note and is shocked when the barman asks for another three pounds eighty.

Outside, Adam and Craig pounce on a vacated table just ahead of a man in a South Africa rugby shirt. Tony carries the drinks over.

'Four-sixty a pint, these are!'

'It's not cheap anywhere around here, mate,' Craig says.

The boys toast Craig's flat and all the girls they've just seen in bikinis.

'How's work going?' Adam asks Craig.

Craig frowns. 'I need the market to pick up. It's been very quiet the last few months.'

'Are you still doing stupid hours?'

'At the moment I'm starting at eight-ish and usually finish about nine.'

'Your dad said you were working a lot,' Tony says.

'It's not like I can stop at six because I have to do as many viewings as possible in the evenings. Without any viewings, I can't sell anything and I need the money.'

'Are you still looking for other jobs?' Adam asks.

'Yeah, a bit, but I don't get much time. I might just wait until I've done two years, then go. How's everything at the school going?' he asks Adam, changing the subject.

'Mark's just text me. He's on his way here,' Craig says.

'Great,' Tony says sarcastically. 'Last time I came down here, he spent about an hour telling me about how much money he was earning.'

'Have I met him?' Adam asks.

'Yes, you must have done, when we were at uni. He was in my halls in the first year. About five-eleven, brown hair, quite fat now.'

'Was he the bloke at your birthday last year that kept going on about how he was going to buy a racehorse?'

'That sounds like him.'

A black cab pulls up and Mark jumps out. He is decked out in a straw boater, white shirt, red shorts, and navy shoes. He waves over to the boys, hands the cab driver a £20 note and tells him to keep the change.

'Where's he come from, Monte Carlo?' Adam says as Mark bowls over.

'All right boys,' Mark says, shaking hands with Adam and Tony. 'Good to see you again. I was going to come down earlier but I got stuck in the office. What time did you get here?'

'A couple of hours ago,' Craig says.

'It's a quality boozer isn't it,' Mark says rhetorically. 'How many beers have you had?' He looks at the collection of empty plastic pints that are stacked up in the middle of the table.

'Not many. Three each,' Craig says.

Mark says he'll get a round in and returns from the bar carrying eight beers on a tray.

It's eight o'clock and the evening sun is filtering through the trees. Most of the afternoon drinkers have dispersed and been replaced by people dressed up for a night out. The buzz of chatter drowns out the traffic and inside there's a deep queue at the bar.

'Do you work in Norwich?' Mark asks Adam.

'Just outside. I teach PE and English at Walsham College.'

'What's that? Comprehensive?'

'No, it's private.'

'Is that where you three went?'

'No,' Craig says. 'We went to the Lord Nelson. Walsham were our rivals.'

'PE teaching must be easy,' Mark says, 'all you've got to do is show a few kids how to play rugby.'

'Well, it's a bit more than that. I don't teach rugby anyway.'

'It's a private school that plays *football*?' Mark says, incredulous.

'No, we play both. I teach football though. We have specialist coaches for all sports.'

'Adam played for Norwich when we were younger,' Craig says.

'How come you don't still play? Mark asks.

'I broke my leg in two places in a reserve match.' Adam points to three long scars on his left shin.

'That's unlucky mate. Did you ever play in the first team?'

'No.'

'I think being a footballer's overrated though,' Mark says. 'If you're playing for Chelsea or Man United I could understand it, but not in the lower leagues. And your career's over by thirty-five. Even if you were getting ten grand a week, that's not enough to retire on.'

Adam raises his eyebrows at Craig.

Mark's watch twinkles in the fading sun. 'Where are we going tonight?'

'Can we go to Hoxton or Shoreditch?' Tony says. 'I read about them in a magazine'

'No. They're full of cocks in skinny jeans,' Mark says.

'It's five past eight,' Craig says. 'I reckon head back in a minute and get changed.'

'What time is that girl and her mates meeting us?' Adam asks.

'Who's that?' Mark asks.

'Hannah,' Craig says. 'We're not meeting them any more. She's gone home for the weekend.'

'But you said-' Tony starts.

'Yeah, sorry. There are loads of other girls around here. It's no big deal.'

'What are the plans then?' Mark asks impatiently.

'Drink at the Railway or Chernobyl, then Fire Bombs?' Craig suggests.

'Craig, you can't invite your mates down here and take them to Fire Bombs.'

'What's Fire Bombs?' Tony asks.

'It's a shit club down the road from here,' Mark says. 'It's like a student union, but with fat old women instead of fit students, and the drinks are watered down. It's where you go if nowhere else will let you in.'

'Where do you want to go then?' Craig asks.

Clapham Lights

'I'll show you boys a proper London night out. Let me make a call.'

The black cab turns onto Piccadilly and Mark tells the driver to take the right after The Churchberry. He tells Mark he knows where he's going.

They stop outside The Clarion, a dark, overcrowded pub. Most of its customers are standing out on the pavement, drinking and smoking. The boys split the fare equally.

'Let's get a beer here first,' Mark says, slamming the taxi door behind him. He adjusts his powder blue Paul Smith trilby and leads the way in. The pub has an uneven wooden floor and old gas lamps hanging from the ceiling. He orders four Magners from the Kiwi barmaid, asks Craig to wait with him and tells the other two boys to find somewhere to stand outside.

'Is this it?' Craig says, flattening the lapels on his shirt.

'Of course this isn't it.'

'Please tell me we're not going to Mankini.'

'Got it in one,' Mark says with an exaggerated grin.

'Mark, how are we meant to afford a night in there? It's insanely expensive.'

'It's not that bad, I went there a couple of weeks ago. I've booked a table.'

'How?'

'I know a guy who works there.'

'How much does it cost to get in?'

'Nothing, I've booked. Look, I know it's not cheap but it'll be fine. I'll just stick the drinks on my credit card and you can pay me back.'

'Mark, you know I haven't got any money.'

'It doesn't matter. Pay me back when you can.'

They carry the drinks out to Adam and Tony who are standing beside three older men in black tie who are smoking cigars.

'Is that Mankini down there?' Tony asks, pointing to a doorway down the road where two giant bouncers are standing beside flaming Roman torches. A blonde hostess with a clipboard waits between them.

'Where do you think we're going?' Mark says.

'Are you being serious?' Tony says.

'I've sorted it. Special treat for you boys. We've got a table reserved.'

'I thought you were going to take us to a strip club, not some celeb hangout,' Adam says.

'You'll love it,' Mark says, pouring cider into his glass. 'It's the home of the rich, the famous, and tonight, you three. Mark my words, the girls are amazing. Even better than the birds you get in Clapham.'

Tony looks anxious and keeps pressing an area on his chin. 'I think I've got a spot coming. It might put the ladies off. Is there a dress code?'

'No. It's relaxed. Everyone wears stuff like this really,' Mark says referring to his white and navy striped polo shirt, ripped jeans and white plimsolls. 'You can't wear trainers though. They might say something about your t-shirt not having a collar, Adam, but if they kick up a fuss, let me handle it.'

'I'm glad I brought a proper shirt and shoes with me,' Tony says. 'God, I actually feel nervous.'

'It's only a bloody nightclub, Tony. Don't be such a tit,' Adam says.

'Yeah, probably better if you don't start chatting to the bouncers on the way in, Tone,' Craig says. 'And try not to talk to anyone when we're in there either.'

Mark strolls past the queue of floppy-haired boys, and the other three follow him.

'Mark Hunter. I've got a table,' he says to the girl with the clipboard.

Tony and Adam look up at the luminous orange sign.

The bigger of the two bouncers puts his hand on Mark's chest as he tries to follow the girl through the doors. 'No trainers.'

'These aren't trainers, they're deck shoes. Ralph Lauren.'

The bouncer takes his arm away and Mark ushers the boys in. They are taken down a pitch-black staircase which resounds with the sound of rhythmical drumming and squawking animals.

The compact nightclub is themed to resemble a tropical island and is almost as hot. The walls are decorated with palms, rows of exotic flowers and menacing tribal figures, including one with an excessively large phallus. Stuffed parrots and other birds are suspended from the ceiling. The centre of the club is dominated by a giant circular tank where fluorescent fish swim amongst coral reef and miniature shipwrecks as *Atomic* booms out.

A group of big-haired girls are drinking cocktails at a table designed to look like a giant drum. They ignore the boys as they walk in. Nobody is at the bar, the dance floor is empty and one of the Hawaiian-shirted staff is having a beer.

The boys are shown to a semi-circular booth in a dark corner away from the dance floor. There is a small palm tree planted in the middle of the table. A waitress wearing a revealing orchid-print dress hands out drinks menus.

'I'll do the ordering boys,' Mark says, over the music. 'We'll have two Dead Man's Chests.'

'Blackbeard or Bluebeard?' The waitress has bright white teeth.

'What's the difference?'

'Blackbeard is made with Cristal, the Bluebeard with Moet.'

'What would Dr Dre order?'

'How the hell am I meant to know?'

'Cristal then, please.'

The waitress notes down the order and glides over to the bar.

'She's so fit,' Tony says.

'That's what you get in London boys,' says Mark.

'Mark, what did you order?' Craig asks, concerned.

'Don't worry. My treat.'

'Some of those chests were five hundred quid each.'

'Yeah I know. I've got it covered.'

Sympathy for the Devil is playing and the club is starting to fill up. Four horsey-looking girls in blazers are led to the next booth along. Bouncers appear with a rope barrier and cordon off an area in the opposite corner.

'Someone famous is coming,' Mark says, pointing over to the rope. 'Last time I was here I saw Girls Aloud.'

'What did they look like in real life?' Tony asks.

'Not that amazing.'

A pair of waiters dump two gold-plated treasure chests on the table. They flip open the lids and pour magnums of Cristal into the icy cocktail.

'This is unbelievable,' Tony says, sucking the champagne through a straw. 'We're going to be hammered.'

'How are we paying for this?' Adam asks.

'Ad, don't worry,' Mark says, 'I've covered it. Now let's get smashed.'

He takes off his trilby, which leaves a line running around the circumference of his head, and puts two straws in his mouth. The girls in the next booth are watching as the four suck away, their heads bobbing up as they stop for breath.

Craig puts his straw down and leans back in his seat. Tony stops drinking as well. Adam and Mark continue sucking. Mark keeps glancing at Adam who is still going. Eventually Mark gives up and rocks back, his arms outstretched.

Adam bends his straw over the front of the chest he's sharing with Tony and exhales. 'Not bad,' he says, smiling. He makes eye contact with at a girl at the next table who has flowing dark hair.

Mark nudges Craig and they attack the chest again. Adam and Tony watch as they finish off the last few millimetres.

'Killed it,' Mark says, triumphant. 'Right, let's get some more drinks in.'

'No rush mate,' Craig says, looking colourless.

Mark calls the waitress over and orders four Long John Silver Legs o'Lash.

Four hollowed out wooden legs are brought to the table. They are each two feet long and filled with coconut rum, Bacardi, pineapple juice, strawberry liqueur, passion fruit, lime, guava, grenadine, ginger beer and absinthe.

'How are we meant to drink this?' Tony asks.

'We've all got to stand up and down it in one. It's the rules. Come on,' Mark shouts. 'It's all in the technique. Lift it slowly and then open your throat.'

The boys get to their feet, and on Mark's count of three, lift the legs to their mouths and drink. People turn to watch. Craig lasts five seconds before having to stop, and stands his leg on the table. Tony has his eyes shut and drinks as best he can whilst Mark chugs away, holding the limb using an unorthodox backhand grip. Adam drinks with his knees bent, head tilted back and demolishes it in less than ten seconds.

He raises both hands above his head, shouts 'WOOOO HA!' over Duran Duran's *Save a Prayer* and holds the leg upside down to prove it's empty. The crowd clap and cheer and a tall, wiry young man with ginger hair and a flushed, familiar face jumps over the VIP rope. He's wearing a pink striped shirt and faded jeans, and everybody stares at him as he bounds over to the table and gives Adam a high five.

'Hey, buddy, that was awesome. That's the quickest I've *ever* seen. What's your secret?' he asks in an overconfident, aristocratic manner.

The other three boys lowered their lash legs and gawp in astonishment, Mark spilling drink all down his front.

'There's no secret mate, I just drink it,' Adam says, unflustered.

'Hey come over and have a drink with us later, yah. You'll have to race Hugo. What's your name?'

'Adam. And you are?' he asks.

He laughs. 'You're joking right? Come over and say hello. We're over there behind the rope. I'll tell my man. Nice work.'

'Cheers,' Adam says.

Mark tugs at the Prince's arm as he turns to leave. 'Your Majesty. Hi there, Mark Hunter. Pleasure to meet you. I'll be over in a minute.'

He looks at Mark with disdain. 'Who invited you, you fat fuck?'

Mark is presented with a bill for £1,500. The waitress slots his Barclaycard into a chip and pin machine but it's refused. A look of panic spreads across his face and he hands over his MenDax American Express card, which works.

'Are you all right, mate?' Craig asks. 'You look a bit pale.'

'I'm quality, mate. Let's get some more drinks.'

Mark tries to get the attention of a waitress, but the woman with the clipboard reappears at their table.

'You'll have to vacate this area. We're got Delicious from *X Factor* and two girls from *Big Brother* coming.'

'What? I've paid a fortune to sit here,' Mark says.

'Management decision. You'll have to find somewhere else. Now move or we'll move you.'

It's three a.m. and the desert island disco is in full swing. Tony and Craig are on the sweltering dance floor jumping around to *Message in a Bottle*. Adam is pinned against the fish tank by a girl with platinum-blonde hair, next to two Middle Eastern girls dancing with a man in white jeans. Mark is at the bar drinking cocktails with a Russian woman who wants him to buy her a diamond bracelet.

CHAPTER ELEVEN

J ustin is in his office, on the phone. Unusually, the blinds are up and the door is open.

'He keeps looking at me,' Mark says.

'Really?' Amy replies, uninterested.

Mark opens an Excel document he's called *KESRDA Retroactive Quarterly Revenue Accruement July 2008 to July 2018*. The spreadsheet is divided into forty rows which Mark has split into quarterly periods starting from July 08, and thirty columns starting at 10%, increasing in denominations of 0.5 up to 25%. The vertical columns are alternately coloured navy and pink with the text in white. He has filled in as far as October 2014. Mark grabs his Casio calculator, which has 'Hunter 11H' written on the case in Tipp-Ex, and continues to pump eight-figure numbers into the empty cells.

'Who do you think he's talking to?' Amy asks about Justin.

'No idea.'

'I wish he'd stop laughing so loudly. It's really annoying me. I can't concentrate.'

'What's wrong?'

Amy sighs. 'I'm dealing with Robert Finch from Crumb Renfia and he keeps emailing me asking the same questions, which I've already answered, over and over again.'

'Big player?'

'Not really.'

'I wouldn't even bother replying. You've got it easy. You should try making sense of these figures,' Mark says, slurping his pint of apple juice and pointing at his screen.

'What are they?'

'Forecasts for the Kent Development Agency.'

'Why's it all coloured in?'

'It's coloured coded. Makes it easier to read.'

Justin strolls out of his office and straight over to Mark. His tan stands out against his white shirt.

'Right Marky Mark,' he says, leaning on a filing cabinet, 'have you got any meetings planned this afternoon?'

Mark checks his Outlook diary, which is blank. 'No, someone cancelled on me yesterday.'

'Good. Have you got a valid passport?'

'Yes.'

'Excellent. You're going on a special mission for me.'

'OK.' He smiles. 'Where?'

'I was meant to be meeting Henk Van Gilder from Dutch UT in Amsterdam at four o'clock, but I've got a cricket match for Old Wilstonians in Richmond so I can't go. That's where you come in. What do you know about DUT's portfolio?'

'I'm fairly familiar with it. I'll take another look now though.'

'Good idea. You're booked on the ten past one flight from Heathrow and there'll be someone to meet you at the other end. All you've got to do is turn up, shake hands and tell Henk everything's hunky-dory. He mentioned something about a new product he's looking at, but if he lets on he's got more to invest, direct him through the usual Icelandic options. Normally he doesn't ask too many questions. Last time I went out there, I was only in his office for about twenty minutes and then he took me out to a-' Justin glances over at Amy, 'straight to a restaurant and then we went out and got bladdered. He's a great bloke, you'll love him.'

'Sounds quality,' Mark says.

'You're coming back on the twenty past ten. BA business class both ways of course. Sorry it's not later, but the late flight was fully booked.' Justin checks his watch and walks backwards towards his office. 'You better get moving actually. Book a cab and charge it to our account. Enjoy yourself.'

'No worries, Justo.' Mark saves and closes his spreadsheet and shuts down his computer.

'Thanks Justin,' Amy says sarcastically as he shuts his door. 'Why do *you* get to go to Amsterdam?'

'That's business for you. Don't be jealous, Amy. Why don't you go and complain to your new boyfriend?'

'I haven't got a boyfriend, Mark. As you well know.'

'Good. Anyway, I'm better at meetings than you are.'

'What? How do you work that out?'

'I just am. I'm a natural businessman. And businessmen like meeting other businessmen, not moaning women.'

'Go and get your flight, Mark.'

'It's because it's Amsterdam as well. You can't send a woman there; it's unethical. The only women in business over there stand in shop windows in their underwear.' Mark laughs to himself as he zips his pencil case and walks out.

There is nobody using the self-service check-in, but Mark can't get the machine to scan his passport so he joins the back of the queue at the executive check-in desk. In front of Mark is a tall man with long straggly hair, wearing jeans and a crew-neck jumper. Mark taps him on the shoulder:

'Sorry mate, but you do know this is business class,' he says.

The man, who's slim and in his forties, looks back at Mark. 'I'm fully aware of where I am thank you.'

'I just thought-'

'You just thought wrong,' the man replies sharply, wheeling his case to the now-empty desk.

Mark checks his own passport photo and the lady at the desk calls him forward. Her hair is tied back and she has a blue and white neckscarf tucked into her shirt. Mark hands over his passport and e-ticket. She checks them and types on her keyboard.

'Are you checking in any luggage, sir?'

'No. Business trip.'

She gives back his passport and prints a boarding pass. 'As a Club Europe passenger, you may proceed through to the lounge area where you can relax before your flight and enjoy complimentary food and drinks,' she says mechanically.

'Sorry, I'm not a Club Europe passenger, I'm flying business class.'

'Club Europe is our business class service, sir.'

'Oh, good.'

Mark struts into the near-empty lounge. It's drafty and unexceptional but has an excellent view of the runways, where a Virgin Atlantic aeroplane is coming in to land. There are a handful of people dotted around on high-backed armchairs reading newspapers or typing away on laptops.

Mark orders a beer, helps himself to a turkey club sandwich and sits on a sofa facing the runways. He takes a copy of the *Financial Times* from the newspaper rack and squints at the sun. After swallowing his sandwich, he studies the wine list and checks the lounge's departures board which hangs from cables in the ceiling. His flight is still not boarding. He scurries back to the bar and orders a bottle of Merlot.

Five minutes later, passengers for BA flight 0447 to Amsterdam are called. Mark tries to drink a second glass of wine, but can't and leaves it there.

Club Europe passengers are directed left as they board the Boeing 737. Mark looks at the economy class seats before he turns through the curtains and a smiling BA stewardess with long curly blonde hair directs him to a padded leather window seat. There are six rows of six seats, divided by the gangway, with the middle seat of each trio kept free. Mark sits in the front row on the right and fastens his seatbelt.

The long-haired man from the check-in queue stops at the front and checks his ticket. He places his laptop on the seat one away from Mark and pushes his bag into the overhead locker.

A slim male steward stands at the head of the cabin for the safety briefing, which Mark listens to attentively. Expected time of arrival in Amsterdam is fifteen thirty.

The captain tells the cabin crew to prepare the aircraft for take-off. Mark wipes his hands on his trousers and shivers. He has a packet of mint imperials in his pocket and drops four into his mouth. He's asked to pull up his window cover, against his wishes.

The aeroplane accelerates along the runway and ascends smoothly into the sky but Mark sits pinned to his seat with his head pressed into his right shoulder and his hands locked around the arm rests. His face is screwed into such a tight ball that the tendons in his neck stand out.

When they reach cruising altitude, he gradually turns his head forward and opens his eyes. The 'ding' to acknowledge that seatbelts can be undone sounds but Mark keeps his buckled.

An older stewardess with large glossy lips asks him if he would like any refreshments. He orders a glass of white wine and starts a game of

Monopoly against his BlackBerry. The long-haired man asks if he could turn the sounds effects off as he is trying to work.

Mark is soon £800 up and decides to build two houses. 'Houses on Park Lane, baby. That's the way I roll,' he mutters. He then rolls a four which takes him to Old Kent Road and collects £200 for passing 'Go'. The computer's dog is sitting outside Fenchurch Street station. He rolls a one: Community Chest. A card pops up: *You have been caught having an affair with your 14-year-old daughter's best friend. Your wife has divorced you and has been awarded sole ownership of your bank account and any houses you own. Go straight to Jail.* 'Bitch,' he says.

An hour later, Mark is £3,000 behind the computer. He picks at the penne pasta in the bowl on his lap and drinks his sixth glass of wine. There is a pasta stain on his shirt which he hasn't noticed.

Suddenly the plane shakes violently. He spills his drink over his trousers and drops his BlackBerry. An announcement comes over the intercom:

'Ladies and gentlemen, this is your captain speaking. You will have noticed that the seatbelt sign has been switched back on. There are currently storms over northern Europe and we may encounter some turbulence as we prepare to land. Please return to your seats and ensure all overhead lockers are safely fastened.'

The plane jolts right and Mark shuts his eyes as glasses rattle in the galley. The aircraft dips, throwing passengers forward and he lets out a small squeal. A baby is crying several rows back. The stewardesses do their best to look calm. The plane stabilises but then the cabin lights dim and it lurches left. Somewhere near the cockpit, there's a loud thud. Mark thrusts out his hand and reaches across the empty seat to the man next to him, who swats him away.

The plane continues to judder and Mark pushes his head back into the seat and closes his eyes. The captain's voice again sounds over the intercom:

'Cabin crew, please prepare for emergency landing.'

There is a commotion in economy class where at least one woman is screaming. The young blonde stewardess at the front of the cabin undoes her seatbelt and rushes through the curtain, passing the male steward who heads to the cockpit.

'No, no,' Mark mumbles, digging his nails into his leg.

The aircraft starts to lose altitude. There are gasps and shrieks every time they hit turbulence. Mark's eyes are squeezed shut as the pilots adjust the plane's position. Thunder cracks, and flashes of lightning illuminate the dark afternoon sky, further frightening the passengers.

The aircraft begins its final swift descent and lands with three huge bumps on the rain-lashed runway at Schiphol airport.

'Hurrrgh, hurrrgh,' Mark groans.

'We've landed for Christ's sake,' the man next to him says.

'Thank god. Thank god.'

The captain apologises for the turbulent end to the journey and the heavy landing. He explains that they'd encountered a flash storm and thanks everyone for remaining calm in challenging flying conditions. A spontaneous round of applause brakes out. Mark tentatively looks out of the window and cranes his neck to see the tarmac.

The seatbelt sign is turned off and there is a flurry of activity as the passengers retrieve their belongings. He takes a moment to gather himself.

'Are you feeling better now?' the blonde stewardess asks as he passes her at the exit.

'Yes, thanks.' He stops as if to say something else, but then walks on.

'What's your reason for coming to Holland?' asks the moustachioed immigration officer.

'Business,' Mark says, snatching back his passport.

He walks into the arrivals hall and scans the crowd of taxi drivers and people waiting for friends and relatives who mainly try to avoid eye contact with him. He searches for his name on the drivers' boards. There is a 'Mr Davis', a 'Sarah Holt', a 'Peter Merton- DVGV Ltd', a 'Sanderson', but no 'Mark Hunter' or 'MenDax'.

He walks confidently back towards the arrivals gate against the flow of passengers calling out, 'Mark Hunter, Mark Hunter, Mark Hunter? Mark Hunter. Mark Hunter? Mark Hunter, Mark Hunter. MARK HUNTER! MARK HUNTER!!'

A man wearing a chauffeur's hat appears at the end of the line holding a square of white card with 'Mike Huntley' printed on it. Mark rushes up to him.

'Almost mate. Mark Hunter. Which way's the car?'

The driver looks confused. 'Noo, noo. Mike Huntley,' he says in a heavy Dutch accent.

'Never mind the pronunciation mate, let's get moving. Henk's expecting me.'

Someone taps Mark on the shoulder.

'What are you up to?' It's the man from the flight. 'What's going on, Wim?' he asks the driver.

'I don't know who this is,' the driver replies.

'Let's go.' He turns to Mark. 'There's a cab rank outside if you need to get somewhere. Now, *oprotten*.'

Mike Huntley and his driver chuckle and head off to the short stay car park.

Mark stands at the gate until he is the only person left. He tries to call the office on his BlackBerry but the battery has died. 'Shit,' he hisses.

He follows the signs to the information desk and pushes in front of two women in burkas.

'You need to make an announcement,' he says to the dumpy Dutch woman working there. 'Do you speak English?'

'Yes, I do. Can I help you?' She is wearing orange mascara.

'Driver to meet Mark Hunter, from London. Make an announcement. I'm late.'

She repeats Mark's words back to him and holds down the button on the silver microphone on the desk. The airport's public address system bongs:

'Could Mark Hunter from London please report to the information desk opposite Café Rembrandt on the ground floor. Your driver is waiting for you.'

'No, no, I'm Mark Hunter,' Mark says, exasperated. 'I've got a very important meeting in Amsterdam and I need a driver.'

'There is a taxi station at the front of the terminal.'

'No, no. I'm expecting a driver. I'm Mark Hunter and I'm meeting a driver, for Mark Hunter. *Mark Hunter*,' he says, patronisingly.

The PA system bongs again:

'Could the driver Mark Hunter for Mark Hunter please come to the information desk opposite Café Rembrandt on the ground floor where

96

Mark Hunter is waiting for you. Thank you.'

Mark leans on the desk and brings both his hands up to his head in frustration. '*I* am Mark Hunter. My meeting is... Oh forget it. You're bloody useless.'

He tries to turn his BlackBerry back on but it's dead.

Mark is €255 down at the airport casino. He puts his last twenty on red 7 and watches the bored young croupier spin the wheel. The ball stops on black 8. He groans as his chips are gathered up.

'I'm afraid it is seven thirty, sir. The casino is closing.'

Behind Mark are two vacant blackjack tables and over a hundred unused slot machines. He picks his jacket off his stool and leaves as a KLM aircraft takes off in the rain outside.

He withdraws €50 from an ATM, treats himself to a large Whopper meal at Burger King and spends some of the change playing a sit-down Formula One driving game in the children's arcade. After coming seventeenth at Monaco he stays in his seat until well after the race has finished.

The airport's plaza is quiet and all of the shops have closed so Mark wanders aimlessly until he reaches the Café Rembrandt. The information desk has its shutter pulled down.

Six pints of Amstel later it is time to check in.

*

Justin calls Mark into his office and tells him to sit down. Mark fiddles with his tie as Justin types an email.

'What the fuck happened yesterday?' Justin asks.

'Justin please don't get angry. I'd just arrived at the airport and-'

'I am angry! Bloody angry. What a liberty. He can't just cancel a meeting at an hour's notice when you've flown over specially to meet him. Did you reply to his email?'

'No.'

'Good, I hoped that you hadn't. Let me deal with it. What an excuse as well. It's not our fault his son's in trouble at school. Where's his wife?'

'Exactly what I thought,' Mark says, relaxing. 'Can I still charge him for the hours?'

'Yes, of course.' Justin clicks the top of his pen and starts grinning.

'So I trust you managed to keep yourself entertained, shall we say.' He winks.

'Yes. That wasn't a problem.'

'Did you, did you go to the, um, I think you know what I'm getting at,' he says, raising his eyebrows.

Mark doesn't say anything.

'Don't play the innocent with me, Hunter. I know you too well. Your silence speaks volumes. Where did you go?'

'Just out into town. Had a look around, few beers.'

'See anything you liked?'

Mark smiles. 'I don't kiss and tell.'

'They let you kiss?' Justin says, 'Since when has that been allowed?'

CHAPTER TWELVE

T he reception of JSA Recruitment is a cramped, bare box room and Craig waits on a stained sofa next to a dusty plastic pot plant.

Through the glass door are the recruitment consultants' desks, crammed into a scruffy office. A man with flat, shapeless hair is shouting down the phone. Next to him is a girl with braces who has a purple-haired troll on top of her computer screen. Piles of paper and Post-It notes are scattered on top of filing cabinets and over the floor, and an old grubby photocopier has been shoved into an opening next to the staff kitchen where mugs are piled high in the sink.

A wide-hipped woman wearing jeans and a striped shirt backs through the door holding a coffee in one hand and a buff-coloured file in the other. She has bulging eyes and long, lank hair.

'Craig?' she says in a cheery Scouse accent.

He stands up. 'Hi.'

'I'm Emma, nice to meet you. Can I get you a drink?'

'Yes, can I have some water please?'

Emma puts her drink and file down on the ring-marked coffee table and makes her way back into the office. She reappears with a full cup barely bigger than a shot glass.

She takes Craig upstairs to a meeting room which is a tiny white cell with two beige bucket chairs and a view of a brick wall.

Emma skim reads a copy of Craig's CV, places it on top of her file and crosses her legs.

Craig waits for her to say something.

'Craig, I've had a look at your CV and got an idea of your experience, but I think the best thing for us to do is for me to ask you some questions. I'll make some notes and then I'll tell you if I think we have any positions that you would be suited to. Does that sound like a good idea?'

'Yes, OK,' he says.

'Good. You currently work as a sales negotiator at Cinq Estates estate agents, is that right?'

'Yes, I've been there since I moved down to London, in 2006.'

'You've been there almost two years?'

'Yes.'

'You're a sales negotiator. You negotiate sales?'

'I'm one of the team of estate agents. When people come into the office, or phone, they tell me what they're looking for and I try to find them a house or a flat, or whatever it is they need. I then take them on viewings and try to convince them to buy or rent one of the places I've shown them.'

'But now you want to leave?'

'Yes.'

'Why's that?'

'I don't enjoy working there. I've been doing the same job since I started and there's no prospect of promotion, even though I was told when I joined that I'd be up for promotion within eight months. I work twelve-hour days, and almost every Saturday and some Sundays. I feel like all I'm doing is working which is why I'm thinking of changing careers.'

Emma makes notes. 'Is working long hours a problem for you?'

'I don't mind long hours, but I'm working nearly eighty hours most weeks. And because our salary is sales based, sometimes you can make literally nothing.'

'So in any new role you would want to work less but for more money?'

'Err... yes.'

'How much money are you earning at the moment?'

'It varies and it depends on if you get lucky and sell some houses. For the last three months I've earned about seventeen hundred pounds after tax.'

'That's a decent salary.'

'That's for the last three months in total.'

Emma writes the figure down. 'Why did you join the company? Had you always wanted to be an estate agent?'

'I'd just come down from Norwich and needed a job. I saw an advert and applied. I went on a training course with nine others and I got it. We'd apparently been selected from over a thousand graduates; that's what they told us anyway.'

'Prior to that you worked for,' she checks his CV, 'Tennant Haulage Limited in Norwich. What was your role there?'

'I was an account manager, in the sales team. I dealt with new business. We'd transport goods and animals throughout the UK and Europe.'

'How long did you work there for?'

'From when I was sixteen until the year after I left university.'

'So you left school at sixteen? It doesn't say that on your CV.'

'No, I worked there part-time when I was at school and university. It's my parents' business.'

'So the estate agents is the only real job you've had when you haven't been working for your mum and dad?'

'I was a member of staff like anyone else.'

'But you never had an interview?'

'Not a formal one, no.'

'I'd avoid talking about that when you go for interviews. Don't mention that your parents own the company.'

'But it's called Tennant. Don't you think people might guess?'

'If anyone asks, just say it's a coincidence. Why did you decide to leave and move to London?'

'I wanted a new challenge and to move away from home. I'd been to university and then went to work for my parents again. It felt like a step back. Also I wanted to use my degree.'

'You got a 2.1 in business and sociology from the University of Eastern England Cambridge.'

'Yes.'

'Where's that?'

'Cambridge.'

'Oh, right. I've never heard of it. Did it used to be a polytechnic?'

'I'm not sure. Maybe. It's usually in the top fifty in the rankings.'

'I doubt it. A 2.1 from an unknown university is not going to open many doors unfortunately, Craig.'

'Did you go to university?' Craig asks, irritated.

'Yes. I studied media at the University of Wakefield... for a term.'

Craig frowns whilst Emma makes more notes.

'Have you got any other qualifications that you could perhaps put on your CV instead of your degree?'

'No. Like what?'

'What did you get at A-level?'

'Three Bs. It says on my CV.'

'Have you thought about doing an MA or any other qualifications? Further education impresses employers.'

'I might consider it but I don't have the time.'

'You've not had a gap year either, have you?'

'No.'

Emma taps her pen on her knee. 'Your experience is only in sales. Do you enjoy sales?'

'Some of the time.'

'When?'

'When people know what they want and want to buy it. I don't like having to lie or pressurise people...'

'So selling is a weakness of yours?'

'No, I can sell. I do sell.'

'But you have problem communicating with people?'

'No.'

'So you like selling, but you don't like having to sell,' she says to herself. 'Would you say that you're not target driven?'

'What do you mean?'

'That you're not motivated by being set specific targets.'

'No, I am.'

'But you don't like the idea of having to meet sales targets. That's why you want to leave your current job?'

'No. I want to leave because I want to do something different. I want to work for a different company.'

'Can I just warn you that it does not reflect well on a candidate if you make negative comments about your current employer. You may come across as a problem employee. What *does* motivate you?' she asks, giving Craig a stern look.

'Umm, I'm not sure. I just want to do a decent job and get paid a reasonable salary.'

'What would you consider a reasonable salary?'

'Around twenty-five thousand.'

Emma writes the figure down on her pad with three exclamation marks after it. Craig watches her and grits his teeth.

'Is money a key motivation for you?' she asks.

'No.'

'You say "no", but the impression I'm getting is that you're looking to leave your current role because you don't think you're paid enough, but your salary is only a reflection of your inept sales skills. If you're not hitting your targets, Craig, no employers, apart from your own parents, will ever offer you a job.' Emma pauses. 'What would you say your strengths and weaknesses are?'

'I'm a hard worker.'

'I think we've established that isn't true.'

'I am a hard worker,' he insists. 'I'm very conscientious, and well organised. I can build a good rapport with people. I work well under pressure.'

'Craig, let me stop you there. It sounds as if you're repeating this from memory. What are your weaknesses?'

'I wouldn't say that I have too many obvious weaknesses, but I think sometimes I don't stand up for myself like I should. I'm more likely to keep quiet.'

'You're not assertive enough?'

'Perhaps, yes.'

'What you're saying is you'd like to speak your mind more often, you'd like to be a troublemaker, but you don't have the guts?'

'No, that's not what I mean.'

'What *do* you mean? You say you don't have a problem communicating and then you tell me that you do. Which is it?'

'I don't have a problem communicating.'

She pauses. 'You said you work well under pressure, but you're in a high-pressure job at the moment, you don't enjoy it and you're clearly not flourishing. What kind of relationship do you like to have with your boss? Do you need managing or are you a self-starter?'

'What's a self-starter?'

'Someone that can just turn up and get on with the job.'

'I can get on with my work. I don't need to be told what to do. I can manage myself.'

'So you don't like taking orders?'

'No, it doesn't make any difference to me. If I'm given orders I'll carry them out. If I'm left on my own, I'll get on with the job.'

'Which would you prefer?'

Craig takes a few seconds to reply. 'I'd prefer to manage myself.'

'How would you add value to a company?'

'By working hard and trying hard.'

'But how would you add value? What you've just said is doing your job.'

'I'd add value by... umm... by...'

'How have you added value in your current job?'

'I'm not really sure.'

'So you haven't, is what you're saying.'

'No, I have, I just can't explain.'

Emma writes something on her pad and underlines it, twice. 'What are your personal goals and career aspirations?'

'Umm, career aspirations? I'm not really sure. I was hoping to see what other jobs I could do.'

'Where do you see yourself in five years' time?'

'I'm not sure.'

'Craig, if you give employers these answers in an interview they'll throw your CV straight in the bin the minute you leave the room. You should have your life and career mapped out. Most of the candidates I speak to tell me that in five years they want to be at director level or be a marketing manager or will have made over a million pounds of sales. If you don't have these ambitions people won't take you seriously.'

Craig scratches his chin with his thumb and looks out of the window at the wall. 'Are there any jobs that you think I would be suitable for?'

Emma takes a deep breath and bites her pen. 'When I saw your CV I thought you might be a candidate to move into a recruitment position, but even at the most junior level I don't see that being an option. You just don't have the drive or intellectual capacity.' Emma flicks through a wad of A4 sheets from her file. 'What do you know about mobile technology?'

'What do you mean? Mobile phones?'

'Yes.'

'Quite a bit.'

'Great, because IM-Mobile, the mobile communications company, are recruiting for members of their sales advisory team. Would that interest you?'

'What would I be doing?'

'You'd take incoming calls from customers and explain the benefits of IM-Mobile's products and services. They're an excellent company to work for. I've placed a number of candidates there and they all love it. The office is based in Chelmsford, east London. Where do you live?'

'Clapham.'

'It's about fifteen minutes from Clapham Junction on the train.'

'Chelmsford's in Essex isn't it?'

'It's on the Essex/east London border. It's a great place to work. Excellent benefits.'

'I'd be taking phone calls and talking to customers all day?'

'Yes. I know that you have communication issues, but they have an exceptional training programme which will help you develop.'

'Is it a call centre?'

'No, definitely not. It's a customer support centre, it's completely different.'

'How?'

'In a call centre you'd be making hundreds of outgoing calls. In a customer support centre you'd be taking calls. Do you make a lot of calls in your current job?'

'Yes, we have to make over four hours of outgoing calls a day.'

'Excellent. I'll get onto my contact and we'll see if we can arrange an interview.'

'Hold on, I'm not sure about this. I want some time to think it over.'

'Craig, you can't afford to turn opportunities like this down.'

'I'm not sure I want to work that far away. Aren't there other jobs?'

Emma huffs and pulls another job spec from her pile. 'Would you be willing to relocate?' she asks, drawing a big question mark.

'Where to?'

'Inverness.'

'What, Scotland? No.'

The tiny room is getting warm. Emma makes more suggestions: travelling pharmaceuticals salesman, Sky dish installer, driving instructor, IT manager, freelance fishmonger. Craig dismisses them all. He likes a 'sports marketing' position until it turns out to be another cold-calling role selling corporate hospitality.

Emma tucks her papers back into the file and drops them on the floor at her feet. 'Let's get this straight, Craig. You want me to help you find a job which pays a minimum of twenty-five thousand pounds, where there's no pressure, you won't have to work long hours, you won't have to meet targets, you won't do sales, you won't have to communicate with anyone, you'd be closely managed but would be your own boss, you wouldn't need to add value and you wouldn't need a good degree. You'd also need motivating on a daily basis, a generous bonus scheme and prospects of promotion.'

'No, not exactly like that,' he says. 'I just want to do something different. Not sales.'

'I've tried to explain that you don't have very many options. You need to be realistic. Do you think you're too good to work in a call centre? If you do, you're wrong.'

'No, it's not that.'

There is a buzzing noise coming from Emma's pocket. She types out a text whilst Craig carries on trying to explain what he is looking for.

'Look Craig,' she cuts in, 'I don't think there's anything I can do for you at the moment.' She gets to her feet. 'Keep checking our website. If you do see anything you like, or you have second thoughts about the IM-Mobile job, get in touch.'

She leaves the room and trots backs downstairs. It takes Craig a couple of minutes to realise she's not coming back, so he lets himself out.

It's muggy on Clapham High Street. There are extensive roadworks and large swathes of the pavement are cordoned off meaning pedestrians have to walk between plastic barriers that curve out into the road. Buses, cars and vans crawl along and the traffic grinds to a halt every few seconds. A deep hole outside of Boots containing a damaged pipe is filling up with water but the workmen in high-visibility vests don't seem concerned. An old women and a greasy teenage girl in a tracksuit have stopped in the middle of the pavement for a chat, oblivious to the people trying to get past.

Craig buys himself a Lucozade from Somerfield and then waits at a bus stop on Clapham Common next to a hunched man in a tweed flat cap who is grumbling to himself. He calls two other recruitment agencies and cancels his appointments.

A number 345 bus arrives but he hasn't got enough money on his Oyster to travel so he's forced to get off. He throws his empty plastic bottle in the bin and trudges home.

Clapham Lights

The wireless Xbox controller has run out of batteries. After minutes of fruitless searching, Craig takes the batteries out of the remote control to his television. He kicks off his running trainers and resumes England v Holland in the World Cup semi-final on *Pro Evolution Soccer*.

The sun starts shining directly onto the screen, so he pauses the game and lowers the blinds. Then the wireless controller stops working again. 'For fuck's sake,' he says, turning the Xbox off.

He flicks on a Keane CD and goes into the kitchen where he takes his last two slices of bread from the freezer and drops them into the toaster. There is no butter in the fridge and no spreads in the cupboards so he has to eat them dry.

He goes to his room and counts the 1p and 2p coins he collects in a jar. It comes to £1.24. He loads them into his pocket, puts his trainers back on and walks to Asda.

CHAPTER THIRTEEN

' I ordered for you, Mark. I hope you don't mind,' Harry Todd says. 'I thought you might not come.'

'No,' Mark says, slipping his suit jacket over the back of the cow hide-covered seat. 'Why would you think that?'

'You are almost an hour and a half late.'

'I got stuck in the office and the tubes were delayed. I got lost on the way here as well.'

'I thought you would know this area well.'

'Why would I know Kensington?'

'I thought it's where the young and wealthy go partying, at least it used to be.'

'No. We all go out in the City or Soho.'

Harry pours Mark a glass of wine. The restaurant, an Argentine Abattoir steakhouse, is air-conditioned and dark. The tinted windows let in almost no light and the interior décor is all black. Framed cow hides hang on the walls near the open kitchen, which is the only part of the restaurant fully illuminated. Thirty candle-lit tables are well spread across the floor, and all occupied.

Despite the cool atmosphere, Harry is still sweaty. He is wearing a starched white shirt and blue silk tie. The hair he has remaining around the sides and back of his head has been neatly trimmed and he is wearing a new, more modern pair of frameless glasses.

'You do like steaks don't you?' he asks.

'Who doesn't?'

'Well, vegetarians,' Harry says, pouring the remains of the white wine into his own glass. 'I like this restaurant. I brought my wife here after we'd been to the open-air opera in Holland Park. Have you ever been to the opera, Mark?'

'I went once, on a trip with work. To be honest, I didn't enjoy it.'

'What did you see?'

'Umm, I can't remember what it was called. *Der Fieldmouse*, or something like that.'

'*Die Fledermaus?*'

'Yeah, that's it.'

'I'm not a fan either.'

Harry excuses himself to go to the bathroom. He has lost weight since their last meeting and has less trouble getting up.

Two plates of oysters and crab cakes are delivered to the table. Mark orders another bottle of Harry's choice of wine, examines an oyster and puts it back into the ice.

Harry drops back down onto his seat and arranges his napkin. Mark says that he'd rather just eat the crab cakes as he doesn't particularly like seafood. Harry offers to order him something else but Mark declines.

They polish off a second bottle of wine as Harry gives Mark an insight into the bitter rivalry that exists between the Kent and East Sussex branches of the Kent and East Sussex Regional Development Agency, and lectures him about the campaign for his home town, Maidstone, to become European Capital of Culture 2019. Mark doesn't attempt to conceal his boredom.

The main courses arrive: two huge fillet steaks with peppercorn and mustard sauces, and three side orders.

'I'm trying to watch what I eat,' Harry says, pouring mustard sauce over his mixed salad. 'I went to see the doctor the other day and my cholesterol reading was forty-eight.'

'What should it be?'

'About five.'

'Oh.'

'The doctor said that there's a real chance my heart could give in at any moment, unless I change. I'm to avoid stressful situations and intense physical activity.'

'Shouldn't be that hard,' Mark says, chewing on a hunk of medium-rare steak.

'It's harder than you think, Mark. Talking of stressful situations, isn't your appraisal coming up soon?'

Mark stops cutting his meat. 'Yes. It's next Friday. How do you know?'

'I was sent an email by Justin Fortesque.'

'Oh,' Mark says, concern spreading over his face. 'What did he say?'

'He asked for some feedback on your performance.'

'Harry, let me explain.'

'No, let me finish, Mark,' he says putting his cutlery down. 'Justin said there was a big bonus pool this year and that my feedback would be important when deciding what slice of the pie ends up in your back pocket.'

'Harry, look, I think it's important to realise that although you may not think I've been–'

'Mark, relax, relax.' Harry twists round in his seat and produces two sheets of A4 from his suit. 'What I've done is drafted a couple of emails to Justin. Let me read them to you while you get on with your meal. Here's the first one,' Harry says, lowering his glasses:

'Dear Justin, thanks for your email, I'd be more than happy to provide some feedback on Mark.

'I cannot speak highly enough of the young man. He is a credit to your company. Mark has made investing with MenDax, which I expected to be complex and stressful, an absolute pleasure. His encyclopaedic knowledge of foreign investment markets has helped KESRDA reap returns in the first quarter which I didn't think possible.

'I had met with a number of representatives of companies similar to your own but Mark's enthusiasm and professionalism really stood out and were decisive factors when it came to deciding who to invest with. Whenever I have a question or query, Mark is always on hand with an answer which is testament to his exemplary work ethic.

'He has done a magnificent job for KESRDA and deserves to be rewarded handsomely for his efforts. It has been a privilege to have such an intelligent and capable young man as Mark working on our behalf. Regards, Harry.'

'That's perfect Harry, thanks,' Mark says, exhaling. 'I was a bit worried for a minute there. Shall we get some more drinks?' He looks around for a waiter.

'I think you may like to hear version two first, Mark.'

'Look, Harry, it doesn't really matter, I'm not fussed about the wording. The first one is perfect, so just send that.'

Harry stares at him. 'I think you should hear the other email.'

'OK, if you insist,' Mark says, glugging down more wine. 'The steak is beautiful. Don't let yours get cold.'

'*Dear Justin,*' Harry reads, '*thanks for your email, I'd be more than happy to provide some feedback on Mark.*

'*Since I first met Mark in May I have been astonished by his work ethic and professionalism.*'

'Harry, I told you, just send whatever.'

'Mark, let me finish,' he continues, not looking up from the paper in front of him. '*I have been astonished by his work ethic and professionalism because they are both non-existent. Initially I was impressed with Mark. He seemed to have a detailed knowledge of the investment markets and spoke at length about MenDax. KESRDA made the decision to invest with MenDax in good faith, encouraged by the close relationship that MenDax likes to harbour with its investors and promises of regular meetings and performance updates.*

'*However, since we officially invested on 2ⁿᵈ June this year, Mark has not been in contact with me once, despite my repeated phone calls and emails. All the KESRDA has received is a one-line email from your accounts department to acknowledge that our money has been received. Having invested such a vast amount I am appalled by the utter disrespect that both I and the KESRDA have been treated with, and as our supposed investment portfolio manager I hold Mark Hunter solely responsible. I have absolutely no idea where our money has gone, whether it has actually been invested as promised, or if it's just sitting in MenDax's petty cash. As an FD, this is a completely unacceptable situation and if we are not fully informed within seven days of exactly what has happened to our money we will have no option but to start legal proceedings to recover it.*'

'Woooaah, whooaah, hang on. It's been invested like I said,' Mark counters.

'Really? And you know that do you?'

'Yes.'

'Let me finish. *Mark promised that we could withdraw our money instantly but having studied the investor information on your website, I discovered that MenDax require twelve months' notice if you wish to withdraw investments of over one million pounds. Incidentally, Mark also told me that MenDax have a corporate box at the Oval cricket ground which I, as a client, may be invited to use. I telephoned the Oval out of curiosity and no such box exists.*'

'I didn't mean the Oval, I meant Lord's.'

'I've not finished yet. *Mark Hunter is without doubt the most unprofessional, duplicitous and clueless individual I have had the misfortune to deal with during my long career. How he manages to keep his job is a complete mystery to me and can only be the result of a severe managerial oversight. The thought of Mark making any financial gains from the KESRDA investment, into which he has put in a grand total of just over an hour's work at a pizza restaurant, is totally abhorrent to me. Whatever you decide to award Mark, he won't have earned a penny of it, if my experience is anything to go by. Regards, Harry Todd.*'

Mark sits back in his chair and runs his hands down his face.

'So, Mark, tell me which would you rather me send?'

'You can't send the second one.'

'Why wouldn't I?'

'Because if you do, I'll show everyone that picture you sent me. What would your wife say? What would they say at work?'

'I don't think you're in a position to make threats, Mark. Besides my wife and my colleagues know I'm bisexual. You started this. You tried to seduce me. You gave me a business card saying you wanted to suck my tits.'

'That business card was a mistake. It wasn't meant for you.'

'Come on, Mark. I saw you looking at them all the way through that lunch.'

'Only because they were bursting out of your shirt. It was hard to miss.'

'You like them, Mark, don't you?' Harry says, subtly cupping his left breast.

'No, I don't like them,' he says angrily. 'Not at all.'

A waiter breaks the tension by asking if they are enjoying their meals. Mark doesn't say anything.

Harry spoons some more new potatoes onto his plate. 'Do you want your bonus, Mark?'

'Yes, of course.'

'Do you need it?'

'Yes.'

'I mean *really* need it.'

'Yes, I really need it.'

'How much?'

'Desperately.'

'It would be a real shame if I sent the second email to Justin, wouldn't it?'

'Please don't. I need that money. If I don't get it, I'm in serious trouble. It makes no difference to you. Do you know how much money I earn?' Mark says, stabbing his fork into his last piece of steak. 'Forty grand. Forty grand! How am I meant to survive on that? I need my bonus to live. Do you want me out on the streets, eating out of dustbins? Would it make you happy if I was begging outside a tube station with people throwing coins into my Paul Smith trilby? If I don't get this bonus I'm finished, Harry, finished. I've got responsibilities. I want to put down a deposit on a flat in Imperial Wharf and I've got to pay for next year's ski trip to Meribel. You can send the email if you want, but you'll have to live for the rest of your life with me on your conscience.'

'Don't be so dramatic. It's quite simple, Mark. I'll send Justin a glowing report, but you have to fulfil your end of the bargain. You be a good lad and you'll get your bonus.'

'I'll do whatever you want. We'll have a weekly meeting, in whichever restaurant you want, on me. I'll send daily investment updates, close of play every day. I'll give you forecasts for the next ten years. I'll get tickets for the Test match at the Oval. I'll pay for them myself.'

'That's very generous of you, Mark, but I don't want any of those things. Let's get another drink first.'

Harry orders two bottles of Domingo Molina 2008 and proposes a toast.

'It's this way,' Harry says, pointing down Phillimore Walk. It has gone ten o'clock but the night sky is bright.

Mark drags his feet and hiccups. Harry holds him under his arm and leads him towards Holland Park, which is less than a hundred yards away. An elderly man walking two Dalmatians eyes Mark with contempt as he passes. Mark looks back over his shoulder and walks straight into a metal bollard, hitting his knee. Harry rubs it for him when they stop for a rest at the gate.

The pathway is well lit, but tall, groaning trees shroud the central areas in darkness. Harry takes Mark along a path away from the noise of traffic on Kensington High Street and the pair stagger deeper into the park. They cross into an ornamental garden and stop behind a hedge which shields them from potential onlookers.

'I feel sick,' Mark says, hands on knees and spitting at the ground.

'Get it up,' Harry says, patting him on the back.

'It's not coming.' Mark stands up straight. 'I need some water.'

'You can have some water afterwards. Let's get this over with. Come on, quick.'

A car alarm is going off in the distance and a dog is barking. Harry takes his tie off and stuffs it in his pocket, then pulls his shirt out of his trousers and unbuttons it. It flaps open in the breeze exposing his colossal stomach which sags down over his beltline. Mark stands side-on to him, leaning against the hedge.

Harry licks his index fingers and rubs his big pink nipples, closes his eyes and starts shuddering.

'Come here, come here,' he says, holding out his arm. 'Come here.'

'Don't make me do it. Don't make me do it,' Mark pleads.

Harry yanks him by the shoulder. 'You'll do this because you want the money. Now stop messing around and get on with it before somebody sees us.'

He opens the left half of his shirt and jangles his breast. The scent of Old Spice wafts into the air. His chest is thick with hair and his nipples are erect. 'Come here, Mark, come here.'

Mark leans in and Harry clamps his hand on the back of Mark's head, drawing it forcefully to his bosom. Mark's protests are muted by flesh.

'Suck them, Mark, suck them. Like you said you wanted to. Don't just put your face there. I want to feel your lips.' Harry holds him in a headlock. 'That's it, that's it. Like a piglet.'

Mark beats Harry's chest. 'I can't breathe, I can't breathe,' he cries.

'Keep your voice down.'

Mark gasps for breath. 'Can I go now?'

'Go? No. We've only just started. You've not even touched the right one, he's lonely.' Harry pinches his other nipple between his thumb and forefinger. 'Now earn your money. And put some heart into it.'

Mark spits on the ground, licks his lips and attacks it with his tongue.

'You dirty boy,' Harry says as he gazes up at the stars.

'Do you want a cigarette?' Harry asks.

Mark ignores him and sits at the foot of a tree, staring at his feet.

'How are you getting home?'

'Tube.'

'Which station are you going to?'

'High Street Ken. Can we stop this chatting? I want to go home. I feel sick.'

'That'll be all the wine you had.'

'It was that to start with.'

'Don't be like that, Mark. I hope we can still be friends,' Harry says, doing up his tie.

'No.'

'Just think of the money.'

'I don't care about the money. Send that email in the morning and blind copy me in. I feel violated.'

A teenager in a Chelsea shirt is arguing that he has been short-changed so the girl behind the counter of McDonald's is told to give him 20p by her manager. At the next till, Mark orders two hamburgers and a large milkshake and pays on card.

He sits on his own at a table by the window and watches as a black cab motors up Kensington High Street and drops three underdressed teenage girls outside a nightclub.

Mark finishes his drink and keeps licking his teeth. He spits into his cup and leaves it there.

A miserable-eyed homeless man with a matted beard is sat outside High Street Kensington station with a sleeping bag over his knees. Mark empties a pocketful of change into his lap and walks down to the tube.

CHAPTER FOURTEEN

C raig sits on his bed in the dark with Mark's MacBook open on the duvet next to him. It's 1.56 a.m. and he's on his account summary page on the HSBC website. His current account balance is -£3979.44. Available funds are £20.56. His HSBC credit card balance is -£1998.60. His limit is £2000. There are eleven days until the end of the month.

Craig logs out and minimises the web page. The screen wallpaper is a shot of Daniel Craig as James Bond walking out of the sea in *Casino Royale* with Mark's head photoshopped on. He flicks on his bedside lamp and gets a pen and paper from his desk.

On gumtree.co.uk, Craig clicks on the London jobs section. There are 9,509 permanent jobs and 2,012 temporary positions. He selects temporary and slowly runs the cursor down the list of categories until he reaches *Part-time, Casual and Weekend* and scours the first few adverts:

Party Promoters required for top West End Nightclubs – central London
Life have no meaning? Join Al-Qaeda – Worldwide
Become a model and get unbelievably rich - Clapham
Senior executive positions, Lloyds TSB (20 hrs p/w + bonus) – City of London

Craig clicks on the ad wanting models, which has been viewed 7,460 times, and skim reads the blurb:

Top London model agency is looking for new models (age 16-35) for fashion shoots, music videos and TV commercials. No experience necessary, you just have to be hot.

Pay ranges from £500 - £4000 a day for modelling, £800 - £3000 a day for music videos and £450 - £950 a day for film extra work.

Please email three pictures of yourself (they don't have to be professional but we require one face shot, one topless and one full frontal naked.)

We will get back to you within 48 hours if you are successful. STRICTLY NO MEN.

Clapham Lights

Email mhuntermodels@hotmail.co.uk

He doesn't seem to notice the email address and goes back to the jobs list. There are vacancies for part-time telesales executives, beauty therapists, charity fundraisers, German-speaking bicycle tour guides, sous chefs and walkers for dangerous dogs but he doesn't look at anything until he gets to:

Earn £150 this Sunday – Wandsworth
Someone reliable required to clear a garage. Call Chris on 02099833212.

He makes a note of the number on his phone, turns off the laptop and gets ready for bed.

*

Pleasant Street is terraced with smart two-up, two-down houses and lined with cars. It is only a short walk from Wandsworth Town station and the railway line runs across the top of the street. Craig checks a text which tells him to wait outside the double garage beside number 58 - the final house on the left. The house looks freshly painted in a pale pink but there are no curtains up and the rooms are empty. The garage doors have been boarded up and tagged with spray paint and an empty skip sits outside in the road.

It's a warm day and Craig's wearing cargo shorts and an old grey t-shirt that has a small tear around the neck. He notices an elderly lady watching him from an upstairs window opposite. The stillness of the street is interrupted every couple of minutes by passing trains.

A short, round man in his thirties walks purposefully towards Craig. He has a shaved head and is wearing a green polo shirt which is too big for him. As he gets closer he wipes his forehead with the palm of his hand.

'You must be Craig,' he says. He sounds local. 'I'm Chris, good to meet you.'

'Hi.'

'Got your overalls?'

'Overalls? I've got a jumper in my bag.'

'It's pretty messy in there,' he says pointing at the garages. 'You might want to get yourself something to cover your clothes with and a face mask. Get one from the hardware place at the bottom of the road – you'll need to go down there anyway to pick up the stuff you'll need. I'll give you some cash.'

'OK, sure.'

117

'What I need you to do is dead simple; just open the garages up and chuck all of the shit into the skip and then wash the whole place down - thoroughly. It might take you a few hours, but just make sure you do a proper job. This place goes on the market next week and it's got to look top drawer.'

'No problem. I will.'

'Good. Here's a list of the stuff that'll be waiting for you at the shop, and here's a tenner to get a protective suit and a face mask, I'm not having your clothes getting ruined. You might need to get some thicker gloves as well.'

'OK, cheers.'

'You're going to need a claw hammer to get the boards off the doors, so I'll get one from inside the house and I'll leave it behind the front wall. I'll probably be gone by the time you get back from the shop but I'll be back at four to inspect and give you your money. That all right with you?'

'That's fine.'

'If you finish any earlier then give me a bell. The shop's bottom of the road and right. It's called Darren's Hardware, you can't miss it. I've told them you're coming. If you get hungry there's a Sainsbury's just along from that. Any questions?'

'Um, no I don't think so.'

'Good. I'll attach the hose in the back garden and leave it behind the gate for you. I'll leave the gate unlocked. All right?'

'Yep, that sounds fine.'

'Good stuff. I'll see you later then,' he says, moving towards the house. 'Good luck.'

It takes Craig - now dressed in a white hooded coversuit - almost an hour to yank the boards off the garage doors. He chucks them in the skip and has a rest against the front wall. He has twelve litres of white spirit, a pair of sponges, industrial gloves, plastic goggles and a dust mask in a bag by his feet. He catches the woman over the road watching him again and stands up, applies the gloves and hangs the mask and goggles around his neck. He picks at the paint peeling off the left-hand door and tugs at the handle. The door opens with a high-pitched metallic squeal.

Craig jumps back, splutters and says, 'Oh my fucking god.' He slips the mask over his nose and mouth, swats away flies from his face and rushes to get the goggles on. Once he's done this, he steps forward and flicks the light switch.

Despite having two doors, the interior is a single space with a light bulb hanging from a central beam. The sun is coming from behind the house so it's gloomy inside. There are six filthy mattresses spread across the floor amongst rotting newspapers, crushed cider cans and cigarette butts. In one corner is a gas stove surrounded by shards of glass from a smashed mirror. It reeks of urine.

Craig steps tentatively inside and something cracks underneath his feet. It's a syringe. He kicks it away and bolts out into the street to check it hasn't pierced the sole of his trainers.

He delves inside his suit for his mobile phone and starts to write a message to Chris telling him that he's not going back in there because it's dangerous, but then, after some consideration, deletes it and opens the gate into the back garden.

The shed is unlocked so Craig takes a shovel and a broom and then unfurls the hose. He sprays the soles of his trainers and covers them with the empty bags from Sainsbury's and the hardware store, tying them in triple knots at the ankle.

The other garage door opens smoothly, letting in more light and exposing the full horrific state of the inside. The mattresses are covered in brown stains and mildew, and there are piles of what looks like hardened vomit as well as shredded, blood-splattered toilet paper. There are a number of burnt spoons by the stove, empty cigarette packets, and a couple of buckets full of some form of liquid waste which have fat flies circling above them. Craig doesn't even look at what's in the buckets; he picks them both up, struggles outside and launches them into the skip.

He takes a minute to compose himself and heads back inside. Something is stuck under the mattress closest to the doors, making it harder for Craig to pull out. He yanks it to one side and out roll two decomposing rats, writhing with maggots. He scoops them up with the shovel, keeping as far away from them as possible, and adds them to the skip.

Disposing of the mattresses takes almost two hours and leaves Craig covered in indistinguishable smears. Each one he shifts exposes more piles of filth: mushy mould-ridden bread, used razor blades, a grimy leather belt, a broken mug full of mouse droppings.

Tom Canty

There are trails of liquid running from the garage to the skip and once Craig has dragged the last mattress out, he has a fifteen-minute break but doesn't go near the sandwiches or crisps he bought for lunch. After finishing a bottle of Tango he begins shovelling away the debris littering the floor. Amongst the scraps of paper and glass are a tiny stained blanket and a baby's dummy which Craig picks out with his gloves for closer inspection.

It takes him another hour to clear the floor. The last thing he gets rid of is an old radio-cassette player with a snapped aerial, which was plugged into the wall. Craig heads back outside, looks at the disgusting pile of waste in the skip and then sits on the front wall. He removes his goggles and mask, which leave red rings around his eyes, nose and mouth, and checks the time. Chris is due back in two hours.

The power hose has a long reel, allowing Craig to get into the furthest corners of the garage and to spray away the old spiders' webs that hang from the beams. He works in a slow, methodical manner, giving each area of the breeze-blocked wall and concrete floor a high-pressure soaking. The dirt slowly ebbs away and although a few puddles form, most of the dirty water flows down into the drain outside. On the back wall someone has scratched the word 'death'.

After the initial blast, he takes the bottles of white spirit and splashes them over the dark patches on the walls which helps neutralise the smell. Craig then gives the whole place another thorough hose down, including the fronts and backs of the doors, empties the last two-litre bottle of white spirit into the skip and covers it with a blue tarpaulin as the dreadful stench is being intensified by the heat of the sun. The only things he hasn't touched are the sponges so he rubs them roughly against the walls until they look well used and slips them into the skip.

Craig turns off the light as the sun is now shining directly inside and stands back to admire his work. The transformation is remarkable. He hoses his hands and feet down, throws away his coversuit and the bags protecting his trainers and hangs the goggles and mask on the gate. After rolling up the hose and replacing the shovel, he eats his sandwich and drinks his bottle of water.

The elderly lady who was watching him earlier crosses the road with a cup of tea and a custard tart.

'I thought you might like this,' she says. 'That must have been hard work.' She has a grey perm and is wearing a cardigan despite the temperature.

'Thank you, that's very kind.' Craig eats the tart in three bites. 'It's really nice. Thanks.'

'It's about time someone cleaned that out. They've done a nice job with the house, but after what happened I'm not surprised nobody wanted to go in there.'

'After *what* happened?'

'Drugs,' she says in a hushed voice.

'I thought so.'

'There was a group of them squatting in the house, but when they were evicted they moved into the garage. We'd hear the doors go and we thought something was up but it wasn't until the police turned up one morning that we found out something was wrong.'

'What was wrong?'

'One of the neighbours had complained about the whiff coming from inside there and nobody could trace the owner so the police opened the place up and there were six of them in there. All dead from drugs,' she says, wide-eyed.

'What? Six dead bodies?' Craig looks horrified. 'I've just cleaned a place where six people died?'

'I assumed you knew that part, I thought you wanted to know why.'

Craig shudders. 'That's disgusting. It's making me feel sick.'

'I thought you might have read about it in the newspaper. They'd been dead weeks before they were found. One of the girls in there even had a baby, but it was taken away by the social services when she went to hospital.'

'No, I had no idea. There's no way I'd have gone in there if I'd known that.'

'You've done a splendid job though. It's good to see a young man not afraid of some hard work. Are you finished with the mug?'

Craig thanks her for the tea, and after looking at it long and hard, gives the garage a final sweep. The sun has dried most of the floor.

When Chris turns up at exactly four o'clock, Craig is killing time by sweeping the area outside the front of the house. He's impressed with Craig's efforts and pays him £150 in cash:

'Hats off to you mate. Cracking job. We had a bit of a problem with a couple of junkies using it you see,' he explains, 'that's why it was boarded up.'

'I heard it was a bit more than a problem.'

'What did you hear?'

'That there were six dead bodies found in there.'

Chris half-turns away from Craig and looks at the spotless interior. 'Look, I won't lie to you,' he says in a more serious tone, 'I've had a few blokes down here before who've walked off after two minutes and professional cleaning companies wouldn't touch it because of what they read about the place, so I'm very grateful. I know it wasn't a pretty job, I didn't want to go near the place personally, so look, how about I give you this.' He takes another £50 note from his wallet. 'I don't think I can say fairer than that.'

Craig takes the money. 'You do know there were syringes on the floor and stuff covered in blood. If I'd have cut myself on anything I could have–'

'All right, all right, I get you.' Chris takes three £20 notes from his wallet and hands them over. 'How's that.'

Craig nods in appreciation. 'Thanks.'

'Good. Thank you, even if you have cost me a bloody fortune.'

Chris locks the garage doors whilst Craig takes the broom back to the shed. When he gets back out the front, Chris is waiting for him:

'Craig, if you want any more casual work, doing similar stuff, give us a ring OK? I might have a couple of house clearances coming up if you're interested.'

'Yeah, cheers I'll let you know,' Craig says with a distinct lack of enthusiasm. He looks through the front window of the house. 'So do you own the house?' he asks.

'Yeah, me and a mate buy places at auction, do them up and sell them on. This'll go on the market next week.'

'Oh, really. Do you sell it privately or–'

'No we use an agent. Cinq Estates, have you heard of them?'

'Um, yes I have. Which office do you use out of interest?'

'East Putney mainly. Why?'

'Oh, I've got a mate that works there, that's all.'

'He must have a few quid. The amount of money the estate agents make around here is unbelievable. They're all as bent as you like. I honestly don't know how some of them get away with it. Nice work if you can get it though, eh.'

CHAPTER FIFTEEN

Julia stalks out of Justin's office holding a brown envelope. Instead of returning to her desk, she walks straight out and disappears round the corner.

'Do you know what I love about Julia?' Amy says to Mark.

'No,' he replies, hammering away at his calculator.

'It's that she's had so much Botox that you can't tell if she's thrilled to bits or suicidal.'

Mark grunts and carries on typing numbers into a new spreadsheet he's called *GDA Portfolio Accelerated Standard Depreciation March 2010– March 2050*. The vertical columns are alternately coloured green and white.

Justin pops his head around the door and tells Mark that he'll have to reschedule for this afternoon. Mark says that's fine and starts composing an email.

'Mark, is something up?' Amy asks. 'You're a bit jumpy. Are you worried about your appraisal?'

'Don't be stupid, Amy. I've just got to get this finished.'

'Your go,' Justin says, handing Mark the putter.

Mark bends over and threads the luminous orange golf ball between the stapler and the coffee mug but it comes up inches short of the putting machine sitting five metres away on the carpet. He knocks the ball back to Justin and hands him the club.

'Justo's go,' Justin says. He rolls the ball way past the machine. It pings off a wall panel and rolls under the printer. Mark fishes it out with a ruler.

'Last putt, Mark,' Justin says, 'to win the Ryder Cup. Get this in and I'll add a grand to your bonus.'

'Really?' Mark says, standing up in his stance.

'You've got to get it in first.'

Mark tucks his tie into his shirt and strikes the ball powerfully. It clips the mug and rockets into the Puttmaster, stopping dead.

'GET IN! OH YEAH!' Mark shouts, dropping to one knee and wagging his finger.

'Mark! Quiet! People will wonder what's going on in here.'

'If anyone asks what's going on I'll tell them I've just won a grand off you!'

'Not me, actually. Ian. I've got a strict budget to work to. I'll have to knock a thousand off his bonus. Don't say a word, OK?'

Justin kicks the Puttmaster under his desk, stashes the putter and ball in a cupboard and jumps up onto his chair. 'Right I suppose we need to get on with this.' He takes an envelope from his drawer and places it on the desk.

Mark sits opposite, still beaming from his golfing triumph.

'Now, Mark,' Justin begins, 'I was meant to send you a list of questions and boxes to fill in about your personal and professional goals, and whether you feel valued and all that rubbish, but I think it's just an exercise to keep HR busy, so I haven't bothered. Is that a problem with you?'

'Not at all. I hate all that as well. Completely pointless,' he says, shifting in his chair.

'Good, I'm glad you agree. There's only one goal here: make money. We're not a counselling service. If people don't like it here they should go somewhere else. Filling in a sodding questionnaire never helped anybody.'

'That's HR though, isn't it? It's all about ticking boxes and not upsetting anyone.'

'Either you can do the job or you can't. Either you like the job or you don't. I'm fed up with hearing about equal opportunities and discrimination. Who looks out for the privately-educated upper-middle class white male these days?' Justin chuckles.

The phone rings. Justin excuses himself and answers. He has a hushed conversation, turning away from Mark and giving only one or two-word answers. Mark bites his thumbnail and shifts onto his left side.

'Sorry,' says Justin, swinging back. 'That was Julia. She's having a bit of difficulty with a new contract.'

'Is it a big deal?'

'No, nothing important. Forget I said anything.' He leans forward with his elbows on the desk. 'I won't lie, Mark, I've been really unbelievably impressed with you this year.'

'Thanks.' Mark sits up but his movements are jerky.

'I remember we sat here this time last year and you told me how you wanted more responsibility and wanted to be given more freedom to take on new clients. At the time, I wondered whether you had it in you to get the big investments in such a competitive environment. But, as usual, my hunch proved right.'

Justin has a sip of water. 'I'm very instinctive, Mark, and I was confident you were doing an excellent job, but, and I hope you don't think I was going behind your back here, I got some feedback from your clients. I picked a couple of them and asked them what they thought of you, if they were happy with us and if they had any other comments.'

'Who did you email?' Mark asks, feigning confidence.

Justin clicks his mouse and concentrates on his laptop. 'I emailed Harry Todd from the KESRDA, and Steven Clarke from Hamilton Stewart Hamilton.' He looks back at Mark. 'I chose those two as they're obviously a long-term client and a relatively new one. It's easy to continue a successful relationship but not so easy to start one. The more established accounts pretty much manage themselves, wouldn't you agree?'

'Yes, definitely,' Mark says, nodding.

'Steven Clarke didn't reply by the way.'

'Oh, he's been on sabbatical, that's why he didn't get back to you.'

'His out of office said he left the company in February.'

'Yes, that's right, to go travelling.'

'Hasn't he got three young children?'

'I deal with his boss anyway. He was the number two.'

'Who's his boss?'

'A guy called… Craig. Craig House.'

'I think I've heard of him. Did you update the client records?'

'No. I should have done that, I know.'

'It doesn't matter. The point is, I expected good feedback from Hamilton Stewart Hamilton. What I didn't expect was what I got sent by the guy from the development agency.'

Mark bites his thumb. 'Really?'

'I know how tough it is to make that initial contact and then bring in the money. So for you to seal the KESRDA investment so quickly is exceptional. Harry Todd's feedback is superb.'

Justin opens Harry's email and reads: '*Mark's enthusiasm and professionalism really stood out and were deciding factors when it came to deciding who to invest with…* You have an *exemplary work ethic… It has been a privilege to have such an intelligent and capable young man as Mark working on our behalf.* Brilliant, Mark.'

'Cheers.'

'If you can get five mil out of this guy after a couple of meetings, and he likes you, there's bound to be much more to come. What approach did you use?'

'Direct. I used my business instinct. I could sense it was going to be substantial investment so I went in for the kill.'

'The direct approach always pays. No point pussyfooting around.'

'I take my deals seriously, Justo. If the clients don't think you're a serious businessman, they won't invest, that's my view.'

Justin turns on his rotating desk fan. 'Do you know what I like about you, Mark? I can rely on you. I know that I can leave you to get on with the job and you won't let me down. Between you and me there are other people in our team who I wouldn't trust as far as I could throw them. I like to know what they're up to, who they're meeting, what they're planning, but with you it's different. I've not checked on the progress of your accounts for months and months because I know that you'll tell me if there's anything I need to know.'

'Which there's not.'

'Just as I thought.' Justin focuses on his laptop. 'I'm just bringing up your client list. Here we go. How are the other accounts going? Any problems?'

'No. None.'

'How's Philip Giles from Carter Dunce?'

'Fine.'

'That's good to hear. His cancer's in remission then?'

'Umm….'

'When did you last talk to Samantha Harvey from Hunts Brothers?'

'Last week. She had an issue, but I sorted it.'

'Excellent. Is she still seeing that idiot from ZTN?'

'I think so.'

Mark drums his fingers on the arm of his chair whilst Justin types. This lasts almost ten minutes.

'Sorry, Mark. Just talking to one of my old school chums on MSN.'

'Don't worry, I haven't got any meetings this afternoon.'

'I'll tell him to bugger off. Bugger-off-Simmo-some-of-us-have-important-work-to-do,' he says as he types, emphatically hammering the return key to end the conversation. He picks up the envelope. 'Your bonus,' he says, handing it over. 'Open it.'

Mark tears it open and reads the letter inside. He smiles, then frowns and folds it into his trouser pocket.

'You're not happy?' Justin asks, surprised.

Mark hesitates. 'It's less than I was expecting.'

'I'm sorry you feel that way, Mark, but I have to work within the confines of the budget. Obviously I can't go into details about what the others have been given, but rest assured that you have done very well in comparison. And don't forget at the end of October you'll start getting commission payments from the KESRDA deal, which will be another five thousand or so.'

'I know that you have restraints,' Mark says, adopting a more serious tone, 'but I don't really feel that my contribution has been recognised. I spend more hours at my desk than anyone else and I have more meetings. I was here until seven o'clock three nights last week.'

'Mark, please don't think that your hard work hasn't been noticed. I would like to give you all more, but my hands are tied. If it's any consolation, my bonus wasn't quite what I was expecting either.'

'But hasn't the department been performing well?'

'I couldn't give you exact figures but everything I've seen indicates to me that we're doing very well.'

'Why aren't we being given a bigger bonus pool then?'

'The money's being swallowed up by the senior management. I know it's not fair that has repercussions for us, but what *you* have to do is continue to work hard so that one day you'll be the senior manager taking home the seven or eight-figure bonus.'

'But I've got to think about my career. There are other people my age with my experience earning twice as much at our rivals. I don't want to have to leave, but unless I'm given greater incentives I'll have to start looking for another job. I get three or four calls a week from headhunters as it is. What's my motivation to work here if I'm not getting top dollar?'

Justin scratches his shaving rash-covered neck and grabs a pencil from his drawer. 'What's your basic salary at the moment?'

'Thirty... three.'

'How long has it been since you've had a pay rise?'

'Six months.'

'I'm sorry, that's an oversight on my part.' Justin reaches for his calculator. 'I'll tell you what I'll do. I'll raise your basic to thirty-six as of next month. That with your bonus will push you through the forty-four K mark. How does that sound?'

Mark's eyes widen. 'Good. Thank you.' He pauses for a moment. 'Can you do anything about my holiday allowance?'

'How many days do you get currently?'

'Only twenty-nine.'

'Right, you can have thirty-five. Does that sound reasonable?'

'Yes. That's good. Thanks, Justin,' he says, smiling.

'Good. I feel like we're making some progress. Are there any other issues you'd like to raise while you're here?'

Mark rubs his nose. 'If I'm going to be taking on more clients, I think I'll need a car.'

'You can have a car, of course,' Justin says, 'but you might not want it.'

'Why, what is it?'

'Some horrible eco-friendly hybrid.'

'Forget that then. Am I going to get the grand from the putt as well?'

'Yes. I'll adjust it with accounts. Don't tell anyone about that. I'll say it was an admin error.' He makes a note on his pad. 'I'm glad we've had this chat, Mark. I don't like to think of you sitting there working your backside off, unhappy. I've got big plans for you this year and there are big plans for this department, so my advice would be sit tight and don't do anything hasty.'

'That depends on what the big plans are.'

'I'm going to let you into a secret. There's going to be some restructuring of MenDax in the near future.'

'Restructuring how?'

'Strictly between us, it's likely that the Asian arm of the business will be sold off and that MenDax will be streamlined. Apparently the Berlin office will be closed and the whole operation will be based in London. I think they're looking at new offices at the moment. We are also in takeover talks with two of our competitors.'

'Who?'

'I can't say,' Justin says, licking his lips. 'Mark, have you got any shares in MenDax?'

'No.'

'None at all?'

'No.'

'I would strongly advise that you buy some in the next month or two.'

'OK. How do I do that?'

'I've got a friend who's a broker who'll sort it out for you.'

'How much money would I need?'

'I'd recommend putting in as much as you can afford. Have you thought about what to do with your bonus? If the takeovers go ahead, you'll double or treble your money within six months. Do you know Mike Lierberwitz, the financial director?'

'Yes. Beard and glasses.'

'That's him. I was talking to him in The Receiver last week and he said he'd pretty much invested his life savings.'

'And this is a sure thing is it?'

'Mark, this is big business, but worst case scenario - we don't complete the two takeovers - you'll still have the shares in a FTSE nine hundred company. It's a no-lose situation.'

Mark glances at the door and back to Justin. 'I'll think about it. What will happen to us, our department, if we do buy the companies?'

'We'll grow, expand. We'll take over the running of the investment departments. These could be very exciting times for you, Mark. I'll need you by my side to help train the new members of staff. There will be promotions and pay rises, and of course, we'll have a greater number of clients. More responsibility. If everything goes ahead, it wouldn't be unreasonable for someone of your talents to expect your salary to treble. What do you think about that?'

'Brilliant,' Mark says, open-mouthed. 'And if everything goes to plan, when will the takeovers happen?'

'Sooner rather than later judging by what I've heard. By Christmas, you could have fifty staff under you.'

'Are you being serious?'

'Completely serious, Mark. So don't go running off to the first company which offers you a pay rise because you'd be shooting yourself in the foot.'

'No, I won't, don't worry. I'm not going anywhere now.'

'In the short-term we're going to take on five or six junior fund managers who we can train ahead of any prospective takeovers.'

'Who are you looking for?'

'Anyone really. All they'll have to do is shake a few hands and learn the ropes on the smaller accounts. A child could do it. They won't get paid all that much, probably start them off on twenty-two grand, see how they go. You don't know anyone who'd be interested do you?'

'No, I don't think so. None of my mates would work for that,' Mark scoffs. 'Stick an advert in the *FT*. Hopefully we'll get some fit girls applying.'

Justin laughs, jumps down from his chair and yanks up the blinds. He stands with his back to Mark, studying the portrait he's commissioned of himself. He's is sitting in an armchair in the middle of a vast library with an aloof, scholarly expression on his face and has been flatteringly depicted as taller, thinner and less tanned. He tells Mark it cost twelve thousand pounds. Mark says it's a masterpiece.

Out on the floor, Amy is on the phone and Ian is staring at a spreadsheet and scratching his head.

'What do you think of Amy, Mark?' Justin asks.

'What do you mean?'

'Professionally.'

'Umm...' He considers his response. 'I don't want to say anything bad about her, because she's a great girl, but I don't think she'd be difficult to replace if she left.'

'Why do you say that?'

'Most of the time I look at her computer she's shopping on the internet.'

'The feedback from all of her clients was very good though.'

'I'm not saying she's doing a bad job, but I don't really know what she's doing a lot of the time. She's always out of the office as well.'

'She has a lot of clients. She's always at meetings.'

'It's a similar situation with Ian.'

'In what sense?'

'He's a nice bloke, but he's never going to be able to run the department. He hasn't got the charisma to bring in the big deals. You've got to take the clients out, impress them. Nobody's going to be won over by Ian. He's too... ordinary.'

Amy puts the phone down and catches Justin looking at her. She gets up and goes to talk to Ian.

There are dark clouds outside and the office is murky. Justin locks his desk drawer and plucks his MenDax golf umbrella from its stand. He plays an uncoordinated cover drive, thanks Mark for the meeting and hurries off to catch the 16.21 train home to Tunbridge Wells.

CHAPTER SIXTEEN

'Get out of my way you foreign retards,' Mark mutters as he barges past a group of American tourists who are blocking the exit at Victoria underground station. He races up the stairs, leaving Craig trailing behind, weaves through the crowds and waits outside Marks and Spencer.

At street level, it is warm but drizzling. Craig bobs in and out of a cluster of Chinese students and apologises to Mark for being slow. He says he was stuck behind a man who was trying to get through the ticket barriers by thumping the Oyster reader with his fist.

Mark says he is going to get a sandwich and asks if Craig wants anything, but he doesn't. Craig waits outside, watching the incessant stream of people, taxis and buses. A *Big Issue* seller wearing a frayed woolly hat lights a roll-up in the bus terminal as an eastern European teenager with rotting teeth tries to sell Craig a travelcard.

'Are we getting a bus from here?' Craig asks, as Mark reappears munching a chicken sandwich.

'Craig, you don't get the bus to Humphrey & Weston. It sets the wrong tone. We'll get a cab. It's much quicker.'

Twenty minutes later they are still in the taxi queue.

There are roadworks from Hyde Park Corner all the way down Knightsbridge and their taxi sits motionless outside the French embassy.

An ambulance with its siren blaring negotiates its way through the traffic behind them and the cabbie jolts up onto the kerb to let it past. He says that Humphrey & Weston is only down the road and suggests that the boys should walk. Mark insists that he wants to be dropped outside the main doors and says that he has a bad foot. The cabbie looks in the rear-view mirror and raps his fingers on the steering wheel.

Humphrey & Weston is London's most exclusive department store,

133

situated in an immense Edwardian building on the corner of Knights-bridge and Ermine Street.

The traffic eases and the boys jump out. A concierge in a top hat opens the gold-plated doors and welcomes them in.

'It's a bit posh in here,' Craig says as they enter the bright lights of the beauty department.

'It's Humphrey and Weston, you gimp. Of course it's posh.'

They wander through the labyrinth of make-up and perfume counters and Craig grins at a graceful young sales assistant dressed in a sparkling white skirt and tunic. Her hair and make-up are immaculate.

Mark strolls down the stairs to menswear, following the neon signs. He tells a gawky French sales assistant that he wants a personal shopper. The young man, dressed in a cream shirt and tie, makes a phone call.

They are fully booked. Mark says he has a very important awards ceremony next week and needs assistance to choose an outfit, regardless of how much it costs. The assistant makes another phone call as Mark inspects a rail of velvet lounge jackets. He is asked to wait on the sofa near the changing rooms and assured that he will be seen shortly.

A muscular man with a diamond-encrusted cross swinging from his neck is being led around by his tiny girlfriend who is wearing a pink tracksuit and baseball cap. Two round-faced Indian men with shaved heads and pencil beards are holding Armani t-shirts to their chests.

'What are you doing?' Craig asks, spotting Mark stretched out on the sofa.

'Waiting for my personal shopper,' he replies nonchalantly.

'Personal shopper? What do you need that for?'

'Because I want to get some new clothes and the personal shoppers are always fit girls. If a fit girl picks out stuff that she thinks looks good on me, then other girls will think it looks good as well. Tactics, mate.' Mark looks past Craig at a petite blonde girl in figure-hugging black trousers who is approaching. 'This is probably her. I'll be about an hour. Go and look at the clothes.'

Craig turns blind and crashes straight into the girl, catching her on the nose with his elbow. She cries out and Craig grabs her by the shoulders to stop her tumbling over.

'I'm really sorry,' he says. 'Are you OK?'

She holds her nose in her hands. 'Yes, I'm fine,' she says, her eyes watering. 'Are you Mark?'

'No, I'm Mark,' Mark says, ushering Craig out of the way. 'Are you the personal shopper?'

Craig backs away and slips into the shoe department.

'Hello, Mark. I'm Charlie.' She checks her ringed fingers for blood from her nostrils. 'Shall we sit down?'

Charlie sits and Mark flumps down next to her. She is in her mid-twenties, has a high-pitched voice and a tattoo of a rose on her wrist. She brushes her long streaked hair away from her face and tells Mark that she only has an hour as she has another appointment at three. Mark says that he doesn't have much time either and pinches at his skin-tight Led Zeppelin t-shirt. He says he has an awards ceremony on Tuesday and is 'just looking for a new suit, shirt, tie and shoes, a new pair of jeans, a few new t-shirts and a belt'.

'Slim fit suits are in this season. It looks great.'

Mark turns sideways. He can't do up the grey jacket and the trousers stick to his legs all the way to the ankle. 'I'm not sure,' he says.

'You could of course opt for something a little more traditional, but this is very stylish,' Charlie assures him.

They are in a windowless private changing suite, no bigger than twelve feet square with full-length mirrors along the walls. Mark's clothes are slung over a cushioned chair behind a curtain which protrudes from the back wall. Charlie is sitting on a chaise longue next to a pile of clothes she has selected.

Mark's face is turning red. He undoes the collar of the shirt and loosens the skinny tie. 'Are these trousers definitely a thirty-eight?' he says, tugging at the waist.

'Yes. I don't think we have any in a forty, but I could ask.'

'No, don't worry.' He tries to lift his right hand to his mouth to mimic drinking but the tightness of the jacket makes it impossible. 'Are you sure it's not too tight?'

'That's just the cut. It's not tight.'

'What would you think if you saw me on a night out?'

'I'd think you were wearing a very cool suit.'

'How much is it?'

'That one is nine hundred.'

Mark gives himself one last look in the mirrors and sucks his stomach and cheeks in. 'I'll take the suit, but not the shirt and tie.'

'Excellent,' Charlie says, checking the time on her Swatch. 'When are your awards?'

'Tuesday. I've been nominated for Young Entrepreneur of the Year.'

'Do you own your own business?'

'Yeah,' he says, retreating behind the curtain. 'Foreign investments.' His arm thrusts out holding the suit which Charlie takes and places neatly on a hanger.

Craig pops his head around the door. 'Hi, is Mark in here?

'I'm trying stuff on,' he calls out from behind the curtain. 'Go and look at the clothes.'

'I have been.'

'You can wait here if you like,' Charlie says, clearing a load of discarded t-shirts off a chair.

'Thanks,' Craig says. 'Sorry about earlier. Is your nose all right?'

'It's fine thank you. No lasting damage.' She starts folding the t-shirts into a neat stack. 'Have you not seen anything you like?'

'No, not really. I was looking at some jeans, but they're all a bit–'

'Expensive!' Mark shouts.

'No. Not really my style,' Craig says, looking down at his scuffed trainers.

Mark pulls back the curtain. 'What do you reckon?' The right leg of the jeans he is trying on is so shredded it's practically missing. A white belt with orange studs hangs around his waist because it is too big to fit through the loops. On his top half he is wearing a shapeless Oligarch's Oil Club t-shirt. It's too short - so exposes his fat stomach - and has a giant silver handgun sewn across the shoulders.

'I like it. Very, very cool,' Charlie says.

Craig suppresses a laugh. 'Very nice, mate. I like the t-shirt.'

'The jeans are quality. They're Emperors,' Mark says, sticking out a leg to admire them.

'Have you tried the jacket on?' Charlie asks.

'Yeah, it's quality. Check this out, Craig.' Mark gets the jacket from behind the curtain, slips it on with his back turned and zips it up to the neck.

'Look at this.' He turns round with his arms outstretched. The leather biker jacket is designed to look like a tuxedo with a shirt and silver bow tie beneath.

'It's different,' Craig says. 'Who's it made by?'

'It's a new brand called Money and Sense,' Charlie says. 'It's a really exclusive piece. They've only made ten thousand. Each one is individually numbered with gold thread on the label.'

'I love it. I'm having it,' Mark says.

'It definitely completes the look,' Craig says.

'Mark, I've got to rush off,' Charlie says. 'I'll put your purchases behind the counter. 'Next time you come in, ask for me by name.'

Mark jumps back behind the curtain and quickly puts his own clothes back on. 'Charlie,' he says quietly, signalling at her to come over. 'Yes?'

Mark glances over at Craig, who is playing on his phone. 'I was wondering whether you might like to have a drink sometime, or dinner?'

'Sorry,' she says flatly. 'Having relationships with customers is strictly forbidden I'm afraid.'

'I completely understand.'

'Is there anything else I can do before I go?'

'I did want some shoes, actually. What would you recommend?'

'Talk to Greg in shoes, tall guy with the goatee, and ask for the new Onslow Wongboppers in whale skin. They're hot at the moment.'

Charlie thanks Mark and wiggles out of the dressing room. She leaves the door open and Craig watches as she makes a comment to the man behind the till who starts laughing.

'Pretty fit, don't you think?' Mark says.

'Not bad. You kept staring at her. Your eyes were burning a hole in her top.'

'I wish they had done,' he says, tying up his plimsolls. 'I just want to get some new shoes and I'm done.'

Mark and Craig browse the Wongbopper range. Mark picks up a grey whale skin winklepicker and asked for them in a six. The sales assistant tells him that the range starts at size seven and suggests he should check the children's department. Craig sniggers and Mark shoves the shoe into the sales assistant's chest:

'Put it back. I don't like them anyway.'

He paces over to the cash desk, picking up a Dunhill man bag on the way, and pays the £1,982 bill whilst Craig fingers pairs of Paul Smith socks.

Craig yawns as they sit in the window of Bean, a coffee shop on Knightsbridge. 'I might have a look in Exit. I need to get a new suit. Mine's falling apart.'

Mark puts down his mocha and picks chocolate muffin crumbs off his plate. 'You are *not* under any circumstances buying a suit from Exit. If you buy a new suit from Exit, I'll take it out of your wardrobe and burn it the first opportunity I get.'

'Why are you being an idiot?'

'It's a shop designed for fat middle-aged men with no dress sense. An Exit suit is fine if you're a forty-year-old door-to-door salesman from somewhere up north. No wonder you don't sell many houses.'

'What's that got to do with anything?'

'People can tell if you're wearing an Exit suit.'

'What? No they can't. There's nothing wrong with Exit suits.'

'It sends the wrong message.'

'It doesn't send any message.'

'It does. Do you think successful businessmen wear Exit suits?'

'Yes.'

'Give me one example.'

Craig shrugs. 'I bet the bloke who started Exit wears an Exit suit.'

'I bet he doesn't for that exact reason. An Exit suit says "I can't afford a more expensive suit because I don't earn very much money, because I'm not very good at my job". If you looked a bit more successful, people would buy more houses.'

'Why?'

'Craig, isn't it obvious? What's that saying about the clothes maketh the man?'

'I don't know.'

'People like associating themselves with successful people. If you have the choice between buying a house from someone who looks like they sell lots of houses or buying a house from somebody who looks like they sell no houses, you'll choose the successful guy every time.'

'You could wear a suit made from pure gold and you still wouldn't have a chance of selling some of the dives I have to.'

'You'd have more of a chance.' Mark slurps his mocha. 'The key to having lots of money is looking and acting like you have lots of money. Once you do that, the money will follow. How much money you actually have is irrelevant.'

'That's rubbish.'

'Mate, it's not. The more money people think you have, the more they want to give you *their* money. It's like when a footballer or a celebrity goes to a nightclub. How many drinks do you think they buy? I'll tell you how many - none. People are bending over backwards to buy them drinks because they're hoping that success will somehow... rub off on them. If you turn up to a viewing wearing a top-of-the-range suit, people will be biting your hands off to buy the place. Why do people shop at Harrods? It's not because they think they're getting a bargain.'

'Why do *you* shop at Humphrey and Weston?'

'For the fit personal shoppers. Stop changing the subject. Buying a good suit is a business investment. I guarantee that if you buy a better suit you'll sell more properties. It's business sense.'

Mark pays for the coffees and his muffin and takes Craig over the road to Jacob Perville.

They are up on the mezzanine level overlooking the rest of the stark, minimalist shop. The air conditioning is making Craig's eyes water. He dries them and takes a long, considered look at the dark grey suit in the mirror. It fits well and has been reduced to £290.

Mark is sitting on a pouffe with his bags at his feet. He tells Craig he should buy it. Craig doesn't respond so he tells him it's an absolute bargain and an investment. The Swedish sales assistant keeps quiet.

'OK. I'll take it,' Craig says decisively.

At the till, he pushes his Norwich and Peterborough Building Society debit card into the machine. There is an air conditioning unit right above the counter and tears are streaming down his face as he enters his pin.

'How many days do I have to return this?' he asks as he takes the receipt.

'You have twenty-eight days from the day of purchase to return the items.'

'And what time do you open on Monday morning?'

Tom Canty

'Ten a.m.'

'Thanks.'

Mark is looking at women's handbags by the front door.

'Ready to go?' Craig asks.

'Yes, mate. You must be pleased,' he says checking out the suit carrier in Craig's hand. 'I was tempted to get one myself.'

'I don't think they had your size,' Craig says. 'Look mate, I might head home. I need some sleep if we're going out later.'

Knightsbridge is now damp and chilly. Most of the shoppers and tourists have disappeared down into the tube station or off on buses, and the traffic has eased. Two black Mercedes and a Lexus wait at the temporary traffic lights. The workmen digging up the road have gone, leaving piles of smashed tarmac cordoned off behind mesh fences.

Mark stops outside Vision Electrical and says he wants to have a look at a new television for the living room. Craig says he'll meet him back at the flat and makes him promise that he won't buy anything without running it by him first. Mark talks him into taking a couple of his bags home because they are digging into his hands.

A security guard informs Mark that the shop will be closing in ten minutes so he whizzes around the displays of stereos and laptops and gets to the televisions.

An entire wall of the store is covered from the floor to the ceiling by flat screen and plasma televisions ranging from twenty inches in size upwards, all HD ready. They simultaneously broadcast BBC News, Sky Sports News or a promotional video for Sky played on loop. Mark stands in awe. Behind him a row of smaller televisions are all playing *Aladdin*. He turns and watches it for a few seconds before spinning back to the larger screens.

He walks to the far end of the display, spellbound. In front of him is a colossal Humomi C-Max with a laminated sheet of A4 stuck on the top left corner advertising a '*Managers Special. Was £1,599, Now £1,199. Free Blu-Ray disc player. 1080p true high definition. 32p Tru Cinema technology. Virtual Dolby® Surround and BDE ViV9 sound*'. He takes two steps back and studies it intently.

*

The queue outside Fire Bombs stretches up Clapham High Street as far as NatWest bank. A group of drunk girls in high heels totter their way along the pavement behind three shaven-headed boys wearing FCUK t-shirts and drinking Stella. As they join the back of the line, one of the boys walks into a girl with glasses, knocking her against the window of Snappy Snaps. Another ten people are let in. At the front are a group of twenty or so rugby players dressed identically in embroidered club shirts, navy ties and jeans.

Two fake-tanned girls with obvious hair extensions get out of a taxi and go straight past the bouncers and in through the red and black doors.

'I'm not waiting here,' Mark says. He steps over the barrier and walks to the front with Craig in tow. Two bouncers - one with a gold tooth and the other with corn rows - stand between them and the doors. Mark tells the one with corn rows that he and Craig are VIPs and shakes his hand, sliding a £20 note into his palm. The bouncer takes the money and lets them pass.

The pair pay the £10 entrance fee to a woman sitting in a perspex booth and walk up to another set of bouncers who stab their tickets onto spikes and search them. Mark winces as gloved hands run over his white Armani shirt and up and down his new jeans.

The club smells of Red Bull and disinfectant and has a dull red glow emanating from the lights over the bars which line the main room. *Shut Up* by the Black Eyed Peas is pumping out and Mark leads Craig to a bar overlooking the mass of bobbing heads on the dance floor.

He orders two pints of lager, four bottles of Smirnoff Ice and two double Aftershocks from a moody barmaid who doesn't speak much English. They down the Aftershocks, which make Craig shiver, and stand at a table facing the bar. Mark glugs his first Smirnoff Ice and points to a girl whose boobs are almost falling out of her top.

'Come on, let's get spastic,' he says, throwing the empty plastic bottle on the floor. 'Turbo shandy.' He downs half his pint and refills it with his other Smirnoff Ice.

Craig does the same and forces the drink down, beating Mark by a couple of seconds.

Mark pushes his way past a hen party wearing matching bunny ears and dancing to *Rehab* and joins the queue outside the toilet. He leans against the wall and tries to keep his eyes open. It is almost one a.m. A bouncer forces his way out of the toilets dragging a semi-conscious teenager by the head. The skinny youth's dragon motif shirt is covered in sick and he has blood streaming from his ear. Mark says 'twat' under his breath.

The toilet is claustrophobic and reeks of sick. Mark spits into the urinal when he has finished and washes his hands. There are the usual range of aftershaves, chewing gums and mouthwashes next to the sink, but no attendant sitting on the stool. He has a quick glance behind him and takes two sticks of chewing gum and an orange lolly. He drops £1 onto the coin tray and takes £3 change.

The deep bass of the music makes the dance floor vibrate as Mark crosses it half-pretending to dance. He stumbles into one of the rugby team, who glares at him, and is then slapped on the bottom by a woman with a nose ring. He fends her off and shuffles back towards Craig, who is talking to a girl.

Mark takes a diversion to the bar and orders a bottle of champagne and four glasses. The barman uncorks a 2007 Ron Perpignan.

Mark puts the bottle in his mouth, picks up the glasses and charges over to the table. Craig takes the bottle and rolls his eyes at Hannah.

'Mark, this is Hannah,' he says. 'From work.'

Mark dives in and kisses her on the cheek. Her thickly-mascaraed eyes are bright and piercing. She is wearing red patent shoes, skinny jeans and a tight black vest top.

'Would you like some champagne? Me and Craig are celebrating,' Mark says, overfilling the first glass so it spills over the table.

'No, thanks,' Hannah replies, backing away from him. 'My friends are at the bar.'

She taps Craig on the chest with her clutch bag, gives him a lingering kiss on the cheek and tells him to come and find her later.

The boys watch her melt into the dark throng on the dance floor.

'She's fit,' Mark says, drinking more champagne. 'Why didn't you tell me about her?'

'I have told you about her. She's just broken up with her boyfriend.'

'What are you waiting for then?'

'I don't know.'

Craig is approached by a girl with a long narrow face, black curly hair and oversized gums:

'I've been watching you all night. I think you're hot.'

'Are you joking?' Craig mumbles, drowned out by music. His mouth is hanging open and he's spilling his WKD on the floor. 'What's your name?'

'Amanda,' she says in his ear.

'Mander. I like your make-up,' he says, referring to the mauve smudges around her eyes.

'Thanks.' She reaches for his hand. 'Do you live around here?'

'Clapham Junction.'

'Is that your housemate?' she asks, pointing at Mark who is with her friend at the bar.

'Yeah it is.'

'Have you had a lot to drink?'

'Loads. I don't feel very well.'

'How are you getting home?'

'Dunno.' He closes his eyes and breathes slowly.

Mark comes over and pats Craig on the back. 'Your mate just slapped me in the face,' he slurs at Amanda.

'What did you do?' Craig holds onto the table for balance.

'I told her she had a beard.' Mark bursts out laughing, trips over his own feet and cracks his head on a chair. He sits on the floor rubbing his bump and Craig helps him up.

He convulses and holds an empty pint glass to his mouth. He brings up a mouthful of watery bile and runs towards the exit, bursting through a group of girls dressed as policewomen.

'Do you want to go after your mate?' Amanda asks Craig, running her hand over his groin.

'No.'

'Shall we go back to mine?'

'I think I need to go home.'

'You can come back to mine, it's close.' Amanda brings her face to his and kisses him.

'I really need some water,' he says, wiping his mouth.

Craig sees Hannah approaching over Amanda's shoulder and steps away from her, taking her hands from his chest.

'Are you OK?' Amanda asks.

She turns and gazes straight at Hannah who stops dead and looks dumbfounded. Craig lurches towards her, his feet dragging:

'Han, please, don't walk off,' he pleads.

'I just came to say I'm going. How much have you had to drink, Craig?'

'Please don't go, Han, I wanttatalktoyou–'

'Craig, I can't understand what you're saying. Your friend's staring at us. You can't leave her on her own.'

'She's not my friend. I'm sorry. I didn't mean to–'

'What are you apologising for? See you on Monday.'

Craig leans in for a kiss, but Hannah sways back.

'I don't think so, Craig.'

'Sorry, Han I–'

'I'm going home.'

Mark clasps his McDonald's bag to his chest and stumbles along the edge of Clapham Common. It is a mild night and after trying to hail a bus, he sits down on a bench next to a tree.

'I'm not a gay,' he shouts to nobody. 'Don't try and be gay with me or I'll fight you.'

A black cab with its light on drives past and Mark shouts 'OIIIII-IIAAAAHHHHHH' at the top of his voice and then says 'I hope you crash,' when it doesn't stop. He tears open the bag and spreads his haul over the bench.

He eats the two hamburgers first and then the nine nuggets and large fries, sucking on a large chocolate milkshake as he goes. Once he's finished, he screws the bag up and throws it in the bin next to him. He sits with his head between his legs and then twists into the foetal position on the bench. Seconds later he lifts his head and vomits thick lumps of undigested burger, nugget and brown milkshake all over the footpath. He spits out thick strands of mucus and then coughs up more sick.

A fox skips up to the bench and starts nosing around the bin. It sniffs Mark's vomit, gives it a lick and scampers off across the road in the direction of Clapham Old Town. Mark gets to his feet and apologises for the mess.

The clock on Mark's iPhone says 3.57 a.m. and the sky is getting lighter. It has been a few minutes since a car last passed along Lavender Hill.

Mark tries to break into Planet Pizza by kicking the door but ends up in a heap on the pavement holding his foot.

He limps along to the phone box at the top of his road and picks off a collection of prostitutes' calling cards. He discards a couple immediately and calls 'Roxy' who is dressed as a schoolgirl. There's no answer. Next he rings 'Angel' who is dressed in leather and practices 'BDSM 4 U'. Again, no answer. The last card he tries is 'Black Beauty' who is a massive brown backside in a G-string.

'Hello, can I have sex with you, please?' he says in a slow, infantile voice.

'I can. How much does it cost?' he waits for the answer.

'That's good value. Cheaper than Asda. You've got good business sense.

'Sorry,' Mark says, spitting on the floor, again, 'I had the taste of sick in my mouth.

'Sorry, did you say you're in Battersea?

'Do I have to come to yours? Can't you come over?

'I've got a really cool flat.

'Don't get angry... Yes I am serious. If I come over will you cook me something to eat afterwards? Have you got pizza?

'Can I order a pizza and get it delivered?

'I can. What's your address?' Mark pats his pockets.

'Sorry I haven't got a pen. I'm in the street. Can you text it to me? My number is,' he slumps forward with his head pressed against the box's glass side, 'I think it's... I can't remember, sorry. I've been drinking. I've got an iPhone. Are you on Facebook? My name's Mark Hunter. Facebook me the address and I'll... hello... hello...'

*

The curtains open and Craig tugs the duvet towards his head.

'Would you like some water?'

He groans and takes a fleeting look at Amanda, who's sitting topless on the edge of the bed. She has small breasts with puffy nipples and pale, bony shoulders. Her straggly hair is tied back and her eye make-up is even more smeared.

'Yes, can I have some water please? My mouth's so dry,' he says, shielding his eyes from the sun.

145

She strokes his face. 'Have you got a headache?'

'Yes, terrible.'

Amanda covers herself with a dressing gown and leaves Craig in the tiny bedroom. There's an ashtray full of cigarette butts on the bedside table and Slipknot posters everywhere. He sprawls out of bed and pulls the curtains shut. He then fishes his boxer shorts off the floor and slips them on.

Amanda comes back holding a glass of water and a box of paracetamol. Craig thanks her and they sit there in silence whilst he swallows two tablets and finishes off his drink.

She then removes her dressing gown and gets back into bed. 'Do you feel too ill to stay for a little while longer?'

Craig sneezes. 'Err... I need to go home, quickly,' he says, gathering up his jeans and t-shirt. 'My parents are coming over.'

Amanda looks disappointed and takes her hands out of her pyjama bottoms. 'Are you doing anything later? I'm going to the pub with my friends.'

'I'm with my parents, I'm afraid.'

'Are you doing anything later this week?'

'I'm pretty busy with work this week, sorry,' he says, not looking at her.

'Where do you work?'

'On Lavender Hill. What do you do?'

'I work for BP. On Balham High Road.'

'I didn't know BP had an office in Balham.'

'Oh, no, it's not an office. It's the petrol station. I work in the Wild Bean Café.'

'I thought I recognised you from somewhere.' Craig tucks his t-shirt into his jeans and ties up his trainers.

'I'll text you,' Amanda says, as Craig looks longingly at the open door.

'Yeah, sure. Sorry, but I've really got to go.'

The entry system is buzzing. Craig runs out of his bedroom soaking wet with a towel around his waist and picks up the receiver. He gives instructions about how to get in and goes back to his room to get dressed.

There's a commotion in the hallway and when Craig opens the front door he sees two bulky men struggling to carry a giant rectangular box from the stairwell.

'Mark Hunter?' the nearest one asks, a vein bulging from his fore-head.

'No, I'm his flatmate,' Craig says, standing in the doorway. 'What's this?'

'His new TV. Give us a hand would you?'

Craig supports the huge box in the middle as the delivery men care-fully manoeuvre into the flat, taking tiny stuttering steps. The box is laid down in the middle of the living room, taking up most of the floor.

'Sorry, but are you sure you've brought the right TV?'

The man with the bulging vein wipes his hands on his yellow t-shirt and takes a delivery note from his cargo trousers. 'Mark Hunter, yeah?'

'Yes.'

'One hundred and six-inch Humomi C-Max. Next day delivery and installation.' He passes the sheet of paper. 'We don't normally do Sun-days mate, but this was an emergency apparently. You'll need to sign that for us once we're done.'

Craig sighs. 'OK.'

'Good,' the delivery man says. 'I'm fucking glad it weren't the wrong one because there's no way I'm lugging this thing back down the stairs.'

The other man, who is wearing black boots and has a beard, slices open the box with a pocket knife. 'Where's it going?'

'I suppose where the TV is at the moment,' Craig says looking over to the corner of the room where the current screen sits.

'It won't fit in that corner, mate. It'll come too far out into the room. I'll tell you what we'll do. We'll set it up and leave it against the double doors and you can move it wherever you like.'

'Err, yeah, sure,' Craig says. 'What's happening to the old TV?'

'That's nothing to do with us, mate. You'll need to move it though so we have space to work in. We'll be done in about half an hour. You've got Sky haven't you?'

'Sky Plus.'

'We'll sort it all out for you. Any chance of a cup of tea?'

Craig signs the note and tells the men the exit code for the gate. He closes the door and stomps back into the living room. The new television is stationed in front of the French doors, blocking out most of the natu-ral light and casting a shadow across the room. He turns it off and sweeps up the fragments of cardboard and polystyrene that litter the floor. He brushes the mess into the bin and throws the dustpan and brush into the cleaning cupboard.

The front door slams and Mark bounces into the living room carrying three Selfridges bags. 'It's here. Quality.' He picks up the remote controls and turns on MTV Base.

'Ah, I'm glad you're back,' Craig calls sarcastically from the kitchen.

'Hello, mate. I didn't know you were here.'

'It's a good job I was.' He stands next to Mark who is flicking through the Sky Sports channels. 'I'm not happy.'

'Not happy? Why? What's wrong?'

'What do you think?'

'You don't like the TV I take it. What's wrong with it?'

'Mate, look at it. It's far too big for the room. It looks stupid.'

'No it doesn't. It looks great. You're just grumpy because you've got a hangover.'

'No I'm not. How are we meant to get onto the terrace?'

'We'll move it.'

'Where? It can't go in the corners because of the sloping ceiling and it can't stay where it is because it blocks the doors.'

'We'll put it there,' Mark says, pointing to the side wall. 'Perfect.'

'It'll stand out miles, and it blocks a window. And we'll have to move the sofas right back.'

'Why?'

'Why? Because you can't sit six feet away from a one hundred-inch screen!'

'One hundred and six-inch actually,' Mark corrects him.

'You'll have a headache in two minutes!' Craig throws his hands out and huffs. 'I don't want it in here.'

'It's an investment, for us,' Mark says, turning to Nickelodeon.

'What do you mean "for us"? This is yours.'

'I thought we could go halves?'

'How much was it?'

'It was a manager's special.'

'How much?'

'It's a Humomi C-Max. Comes with a free blu-ray disc player.'

'I don't care. How much was it?'

'Twelve hundred.'

'What? And you expect me to pay for half of it? No way. If you can't pay for it you'll have to take it back.'

'It can't go back. I did a special deal. No returns. Don't worry about the money. I'll lend it to you.'

'I don't want you to lend it to me.' Craig has his hands on his hips and looks at the floor in anger.

'Can I have the cash then?'

'*No, Mark.* You know I haven't got any money as it is. I can't afford it and I'm not paying.'

'It was a bargain. A fifty-inch will cost fifteen hundred, at least. You think so small. What's wrong with having a big television? There's nothing wrong with wanting nice things, Craig.'

'Even if you buy them and then expect someone else to foot the bill?'

'Half the bill.'

'Why didn't you mention this last night?'

'I did, you were drunk, you must have forgotten.'

'That's just a lie.'

'It's not.'

'Did you ever think that it might be a special deal because nobody in their right mind would ever buy such a massive fucking TV unless they lived in a fucking castle? Look at it! It's mental!' Craig storms to his room and slams the door. Small fragments of plaster from the doorframe fall to the floor.

'It's not my fault if you don't appreciate beauty, YOU NORFOLK FUCKTARD!' Mark shouts. He switches back to MTV Base. *Nutters* by Dezzie Rapist is playing so he turns the volume up as loud as it goes and dances around the room firing imaginary gunshots with his fingers.

CHAPTER SEVENTEEN

' M ate, why are you dressed in black?' Mark asks as he fills the cafetiere. He keeps sneezing, causing his loosely-tied dressing gown to flap open, exposing his boxer shorts.

'I'm helping out a friend.' Craig is sitting at the table eating honey on toast and his hair is neatly styled.

'What friend?'

'It's a friend of my parents'.'

'What is he, an undertaker?'

'No.'

'Well what are you doing then?'

'A friend of my parents' runs a business providing staff for posh events and they needed some more people to work at something they've got on today and they asked if I wanted to help out and I said yes. Satisfied now?' Craig wipes the crumbs from the table onto his plate and gets up.

'Where's that happening?'

'Fulham.'

Mark grins. 'What, the polo?'

'Yes,' Craig says, cautiously. 'How do you know about that?'

'Where do you think I'm going this afternoon?' Mark's grin has become a smirk. 'You might be working in the MenDax marquee! You can be my personal waiter. I'll ring a little bell and you can bring me glasses of Pimms, and strawberries and cream!'

Craig lets out a deep sigh. 'I'm not working in your bit thankfully so you'll have to get your own drinks.'

'Where are you working then?'

'I'm not telling you,' Craig says as he loads his plate and glass into the dishwasher.

'Why not? Don't be a dick. What time do you finish? I'll get you into the MenDax VIP area and we can have a few drinks.'

'I start before the polo starts and finish after it ends.'

'You must get some kind of break though?'

'I don't know.'

'Well ring me then and I'll come and find you.'

'I will if I have time. Just as long as you don't…'

'Just as long as I don't what?'

'Just don't get pissed and embarrass me and start asking for loads of free drinks or something.'

Mark tries to feign innocence but can't. 'As if I would do that.' He ruffles Craig's hair and tries to give him a hug.

'Mark, piss off,' Craig says, pushing him away, 'I'm late anyway. I've got to be there for nine thirty. I'll see you later.'

Craig is directed to the Grutlinger champagne bar, a small but pristine white open-fronted tent looking out over the polo field, sandwiched between the enormous Humphrey and Weston food court marquee and the Mankini cocktail garden. Each company's area is marked out with a miniature white picket fence and has neat stacks of white metal tables and chairs and piles of branded table umbrellas waiting to be put out.

There is nobody at the Grutlinger bar, and apart from a man on a sit-down mower giving the polo field a last cut, Craig is alone. There are voices coming from inside the Humphrey and Weston marquee but he decides to sit in a Grutlinger deck chair which has been left propped up in front of the bar and enjoy the morning sun.

The polo field is bordered by advertising hoardings for De Beers, Mercedes, Veuve Clicquot, and Etihad Airways, and surrounded on three sides by tented bars and sponsors' marquees. On the far side is the temporary grandstand, sixty rows high and running the entire length of the field. All of its green seats are empty and above it, through the trees, it is just possible to make out three blocks of council flats.

A van pulls up on the grass behind the Grutlinger tent. The driver walks through the flap at the back, stopping when he reaches the four tall glass fridges. Craig jumps up and the driver asks him where he wants the champagne. After some hesitation, Craig tells him to bring them through and offers to help.

He signs the delivery note for 120 cases of champagne and then stands there looking at them. There's not much room to move so he loads as many bottles as he can into the fridges and leaves the flattened boxes in a tidy pile.

A woman in an ivory-coloured suit enters the tent unannounced. She is at least ten years older than Craig and slim with shoulder-length blonde hair. Her wedding ring sparkles in the sunlight.

'Hi, I'm Antonia,' she says in a friendly and cheerful manner. 'Sorry I'm late but the journey from Clapham is a nightmare. Well done for making a start.'

Craig introduces himself and she tells him that she's the new head of Grutlinger's outdoor promotions, but has only been in the job two weeks. She leaves him with three price lists to hang up by the bar and some laminated information about the company which he's to leave on the picnic tables when he's finished laying them out. She says she has a daughter of one of the company's partners coming along to help, but that she won't be here for about an hour so he'll have to finish setting up on his own. She asks him not to serve anyone who's had too many because having people pass out is bad for the brand, gives him a cash box full of change and tells him that she'll be back at the end of the day to count the takings and pay him.

There are more people milling about now and almost all of the marquees and bars have people preparing them for when the gates open at midday. Once Craig has finished arranging the tables and chairs, and put up the mauve Grutlinger umbrellas, he slides a few more bottles into the fridges and counts the change in the box. There is £155.20. He locks the box and hides it under the bar. Glasses of Grutlinger are £8 each.

Some of the players are taking their horses for a gallop across the field and there are a team of people placing bins at regular intervals along the grassy thoroughfares.

Craig takes delivery of 2000 plastic champagne flutes which he piles around the back of the tent and then has a read of the company's promotional material. Grutlinger is from the champagne region of Bulgaria rather than France.

A confident teenage girl in a black shirt, very short skirt and sunglasses saunters up to the bar at one minute to midday. She is tall and tanned with long brown hair.

'I'm Pippa,' she announces. 'Who are you?'

'Craig.'

She looks unimpressed and walks around the back. Craig starts to explain where everything is but she stops him and says, 'I know how a champagne bar works, Craig. My dad owns the company.'

Their first customer is a man in a straw panama. Craig makes a complete mess of opening a bottle and half of it ends up over the bar. The customer laughs it off as a 'lively one' but Pippa looks at Craig with complete contempt.

'Have you never opened a bottle of champagne before?' she says as Craig mops up. 'You turn the cork not the bottle. How *don't* you know this?' She demonstrates and opens one perfectly. 'And make sure you tilt the glass more when you pour it.'

'Sorry. I'll get the hang of it.'

Pippa pours herself one but doesn't offer Craig any. 'Aren't you a bit old to be working behind a bar?'

'Why am I too old?'

She doesn't offer a reason. 'Why haven't you got a proper job then?'

'I've got a proper job as well.'

Pippa laughs. 'You've got two jobs?'

'Why's that funny?'

'It just is.'

'I take it you don't have a job.'

'What, no way. It's the holidays. I'm only working here because my dad is trying to punish me.'

'What did you do?'

'I slapped my step-mum and called her a bitch at her fiftieth birthday party.'

For the next five hours Pippa does nothing but hand out free drinks to her friends, leaving Craig to serve everyone else. There is a constant flow of customers, the vast majority of whom had been put off by the queue at the Veuve Clicquot tent. Judging by the initial facial expressions of the drinkers, Grutlinger is an acquired taste, but by the eighth or ninth glass, most people appear to be enjoying it.

The park is now packed and Craig is constantly distracted by the glamorous girls passing by, although the crowds make it impossible for him to see any of the polo. Mark sends him a text saying, '*Ths place is unbelievable. Never seen so many things I've wanted to ride and I dnt mean the horses!! May be pissed. Where r u?'*

'Excuse me. Sorry, excuse me.' There is a girl holding a Louis Vuitton purse leaning over the bar. She has deep brown eyes, flawless skin and is wearing a low-cut floral chiffon dress.

Craig looks up from the cash box and stares. 'Sorry. What would you like?'

'Some champagne,' she says pouting.

'OK.'

'I'm not sure if I'll like it though. Can I try some and if I like it, I'll buy some? I promise.'

Craig takes extra care pouring her a glass. She takes it, blows him a kiss and walks off.

'Craig, could you be any more gullible?' Pippa says. 'She's probably been getting free drinks at every bar here.'

There is a pool of water in the middle of the MenDax marquee which used to be an ice sculpture of a horse.

'Three grand that cost,' Justin says. 'And it lasted less than an hour.' He sips his mineral water. 'Having said that a few years ago I paid three grand for something that lasted less than two minutes,' he says with a hollow laugh.

Mark is drunk and finds his boss's joke hilarious. He is very red-faced after several hours drinking free cocktails in the sun and is sporting an all-white outfit: white deck shoes, white shorts with white belt, white shirt with the sleeves rolled up, and a white jumper tied around his waist. Justin is in pale chinos, a pink shirt and Ray Bans.

A waitress brings round another tray of oysters but Justin sends her away. The marquee is clammy and crowded, and very few of the people enjoying the free bar appear to have MenDax hospitality passes.

'Hey, Marky, you know who that is there don't you?' Justin says subtly nodding towards a group to his left.

'No. Which one are you talking about?'

'Don't you know how to whisper? The bloke in the red trousers, with the glasses and short hair.'

Mark looks across and catches the man's eye. 'No. Who is he?'

'That's Steffen Men.'

'What, really? The main man? He doesn't look quite as rich as I thought he would.'

'What were you expecting, someone wearing a crown?'

'No, but...'

'You should go over and say hello.'

'Really, are you sure?'

'Why not? I had a word with him earlier and mentioned your name and he told me to tell you to say hello. You don't have to stand there and chat to him for ages, just introduce yourself. He likes to put names to faces. Just don't suck up to him too much and don't say anything stupid.'

'What should I say then? Can't you come over there with me?'

'Don't be stupid. Why don't you mention his daughter, he was going on to me about what a good horse rider she was. He's always talking about his kids. Look, he's on his own. Go over.'

'OK. How do I look?'

'Wipe your face so you don't look quite as hot.'

Mark rubs his face with the sleeve of his jumper, takes a cosmopolitan from a passing waiter and heads straight for the MenDax founder.

'Steffen,' he says offering his hand.

'Hello,' Steffen replies, looking a bit confused as he shakes with Mark. 'Sorry, have we met before?' He has a strong German accent.

'No, we haven't. I'm Mark Hunter and I work in the London office.'

'Oh. Pleasure to meet you Mark,' he pauses as if he expects Mark to say something, but he doesn't. 'You have caught the sun today?'

'Yes, I have... I should have put some sun cream on and, and the drinks...' he blathers. 'Do you like polo?'

'Umm, I am not so keen, but it's a good sponsorship opportunity. Are you a polo player?'

'No, I'm more of a... I've never played polo.'

Steffen acknowledges someone over Mark's shoulder. 'Enjoy your afternoon, Mark,' he says, starting to move away.

'Your daughter is a really good rider, I'm told,' Mark suddenly blurts.

In an instant, Steffen's face turns from friendly to ferocious. 'What did you say?'

Sweat forms on Mark's forehead and he mumbles, 'Your daughter's a really good horse rider. I-'

'You think you're funny, you fat English clown?' he snarls.

'No,' Mark says, a look of terror spreading across his burnt face. 'I was just-'

'You were just what?'

'I was just saying...'

Steffen gets to within an inch of Mark and hisses, 'Five years ago my daughter fell off her horse at a gymkhana and was paralysed from the head down. She breathes through a ventilator and requires twenty-four-hour care. You think this is funny do you?'

Mark makes a frightened whimpering noise and Steffen charges past him and out of the marquee.

The tournament is won by Team Buenos Aires who beat BAE Team Tripoli in the final with a goal late on in the fifth chukka. The captain of Team Buenos Aires, a shaggy-haired Argentinian called Hector Marcelo, appears surprised when he mounts the podium to receive the winners' trophy and realises that apart from members of his own team, nobody is remotely interested.

The MC, a man in his fifties in a gold-buttoned double-breasted jacket who has provided an incessant, droning commentary throughout the day, manages to get everyone's attention by announcing that it's time to draw the raffle. Mark, who has bought five tickets at £10 each, reaches into his pocket for his strip. He watches on from the opposite side of the field to the MenDax area slurping lemonade as the prizes are distributed.

'Now, we're down to the final two prizes,' the MC bleats. 'Second prize is a luxury hamper from Humphrey and Weston which has been donated by MenDax Wealth Management, one of our principal sponsors. If I could invite,' he checks his sheet, 'Steffen Men, the founder and chairman of MenDax to draw the ticket and present the prize.'

Steffen Men climbs the three steps up to the podium, shakes the MC's hand and draws a ticket from a drum. The MC sticks the microphone under his nose and Steffen declares that the winner is 'Blue ticket... number one zero three nine.'

The ticket belongs to Mark. 'Shit,' he murmurs.

'Blue ticket, one zero three nine. One thousand and thirty-nine if you will,' the MC repeats. 'Any takers? It's a fantastic prize; I'm just looking inside it now if you can't see me. We've got several bottles of vintage champagne, port, cognac, some caviar, foie gras... and some delicious cheese. I don't know exactly how much it would cost to buy in the shops, but suffice to say, a lot,' he says, chuckling. 'Last call or we'll have to re-draw. Blue ticket number one zero three nine.'

'HERE!' Mark shouts, shoving his way through the throng, knocking drinks out of several hands.

'We have a winner,' the MC declares in triumph.

Mark reaches the foot of the podium, glances up at Steffen Men and tentatively joins him. Steffen congratulates him with an aggressive handshake and whispers, 'Enjoy it while you can.' Mark is sweating profusely.

'How do you feel?' the MC asks him as he exchanges the winning ticket for the suitcase-sized wicker hamper.

'Sorry,' Mark says into the microphone. 'I'm sorry,' he repeats, looking at Steffen Men.

'Um, right, OK, well done. I'm not sure how you can be sorry to win such a terrific prize, but there you go, it takes all sorts I suppose. Enjoy it,' the MC says, as Mark struggles down the steps with his winnings.

The Grutlinger tent has finished serving and Antonia is counting up the takings as Craig and Pippa - doing her first work of the day - wipe over the tables and chairs. Almost all the spectators have left the park.

Antonia taps her pen on the bar and locks the four piles of banknotes in the cash box. 'Can I talk to the two of you please?' she calls out.

Craig collects up four more discarded glasses on the way and slots them into the box on the floor.

'I've counted up the takings and I've counted how many bottles of champagne we have left,' Antonia says. 'Would one of you two like to explain to me what's going on?'

'What do you mean?' Craig asks.

Pippa says nothing.

'We're around eight hundred pounds short.'

'We can't be,' Craig says.

'We are. I've checked and double checked... and I've allowed for a lot of spillage and only five glasses to a bottle. So either one or both of you has been giving away free drinks, or you've been helping yourself to the takings. Which is it?'

'I've done exactly what you asked me to do,' Craig says. His hands are twitching and he's talking quicker than usual. 'I've charged eight pounds for every single glass and put the money in the box.'

'I caught Craig giving away free drink,' Pippa says.

Antonia stares at him. 'Is this true?'

Craig shakes his head. 'No,' he says emphatically. 'Yes, but it was one drink and I was tricked by a girl who said she wanted a taste. It only happened once. One drink doesn't explain eight hundred pounds.'

'I only caught you once,' Pippa says. 'You could have been doing that all afternoon. I was too busy collecting the glasses and loading the fridges. My shoulder really hurts,' she says giving it a rub and grimacing.

'That's absolute rubbish,' Craig says, irate. He turns to Pippa. 'You did absolutely nothing all day apart from sit out here with your friends. In fact I don't remember one of your mates ever paying for a drink, you were taking bottles from the fridges straight to their table.'

Pippa swings towards him with both hands on hips. 'Why would I do that? They paid for all their drinks. I never let anyone have a free drink. My dad owns the company. You were giving free drinks to your friends.'

'None of *my* friends were here!'

'Yes they were, I saw them!'

As she says this, a freshly-drunk Mark bursts through the back of the tent carrying four bottles of Grutlinger.

'Hey Craigos, I've finally found you mate. I've helped myself to few bottles like you said I could,' he says, winking. 'What's going on here?'

Antonia glares at Mark and then back at Craig who has his hands over his face in despair. 'I think you should go. And no, before you ask, you're not getting paid.'

Craig refuses to sit next to Mark on the tube, but Mark follows him down the half-empty carriage lugging his hamper until there's nowhere else to go.

'Sorry mate,' Mark says.

'I'm not talking to you.' Craig is slumped with his head against the window.

'What can I do to make it up to you?'

Craig doesn't answer.

'What's the problem?'

'I spent all day working to earn some extra cash and, if you include the tube fare, it's ended up *costing* me money.'

'Mate, you know I'll always help you out if you need anything. Here,' Mark says, handing him a bottle of vintage port and a 500g potted Stilton.

'And what am I meant to do with these?'

'You can sell them on the black market. They're worth a lot more money than you would have earned today.'

Craig glowers at Mark scoffing chocolate-dipped orange slices. 'Thanks mate,' he says with angry sarcasm, 'a bottle of port and some cheese, that's all my problems solved. Why didn't I think of this before? I should become a black market luxury goods salesman. Mark, do you pride yourself on being *completely fucking useless?*'

CHAPTER EIGHTEEN

M ark is dining with Helen Nightingale, the *London Late*'s dating columnist, in the cosy members' room at Stove, the exclusive Soho restaurant. There are just six round tables, each with a dedicated waiter. The view of Greek Street is obscured by multi-coloured stained glass windows and the wood-panelled walls are covered in bright abstract paintings. The diners avoid eye contact with everyone except their companions and waiting staff. On the table next to Mark and Helen, a couple are discussing how long it will be before Tristan's divorce settlement is finalised.

'I come here at least once a week,' Mark says, tucking into his scallops. 'I like the privacy. You don't get people hassling you.'

'Does that happen a lot?' Helen asks. She is slim with large ears, straight blonde hair and glasses. Her pitted skin is covered in concealer and she's dressed in a black blazer and white dress with a black chevron across the chest.

'Sometimes,' Mark says. 'You get quite a few celebrities in here. I saw Gandalf from *Lord of the Rings* having dinner with the bald guy from *Star Trek* last week.' He points over his shoulder with his knife at a table where four young men with diamond earrings are eating. 'They're footballers,' he says quietly.

'I don't recognise them,' Helen says. 'Who do they play for?'

'I don't know.' Mark glugs his wine. 'You must get bored of seeing celebs don't you?'

'It depends who it is. When I've been at press conferences with Brad Pitt or Madonna it's been exciting, but usually I'm writing about *Big Brother* or *Celebrity Ambulance Driving*, or who's fallen over outside Mankini.'

'Do you go to Mankini?'

'Yeah, but I don't like it. Full of posh kids showing off.'

'No, I don't like it either. My flatmate likes it though.'

'Who, Craig? Are you still living with him?'

'Yeah, he rents from me. But he's not the one who goes to Mankini though. He can't afford it. That's my other flatmate, Justin.'

Helen adjusts her glasses. 'I used to quite fancy Craig. We all thought he had something about him.'

'He's got a girlfriend now.'

Mark orders another bottle of Australian Chardonnay. 'Do you get recognised sometimes from the column?'

'No, never. The picture of me is hideous. I get a lot of emails from people saying I'm a slag, but a lot of blokes ask me out on dates as well,' she says.

'Who calls you a slag?'

'Jealous women, mainly. They don't seem to realise that most of it is completely made up.'

'Is it?'

'Yes! Mark, I haven't spent the last year sleeping with a different bloke every week.'

'Oh.'

'It's not always complete fiction though. We might take a story one of us has heard from a friend or something like that, change the names and add in a few spicy details to make it more interesting. I don't think the readers would like it too much if I wrote about my nights in watching DVDs. You can't believe anything you read in the newspapers.'

'But you are single?'

'Yes. Of course. If I had a boyfriend I'd have to give the column up.' She runs her fingers down the stem of her wine glass. 'How about you?'

Mark tops up Helen's drink and shrugs. 'I'm playing the field. I was seeing a girl from work for a while, but we broke up.'

'What happened? If you don't mind me asking.'

'Oh, it's complicated. We were working in the same department and then I got promoted over her. She was angry I think. She's left the company now.'

Helen eats her last watermelon ball and places her cutlery on the rim of the plate. 'It's a shame when that happens. It's hard to maintain a relationship with someone at work, especially in London. What's the name of the company you work for?'

'MenDax. Europe's biggest wealth managers.'

'I can't say I've heard of them. What do you do there?'

'I'm the investment portfolio chief executive.'

'Rich City boy then?'

Mark smiles. 'Yeah, pretty much. I run a team looking after investor portfolios. It's high-pressure and long hours but the money's good.'

'Did you go there straight from uni?'

'Yeah. I was headhunted.'

'At university? How?'

'One of the tutors must have recommended me.'

A waiter collects their plates.

'How did you start at *London Late*?' Mark asks as he glances at his BlackBerry.

'I went there on work experience and they took me on after that. I'd worked at the *Canvey Island Echo* in the holidays at uni and the editor there wrote a really persuasive letter on my behalf. And I had all the work I'd done on the university newspaper as well, which was really important.'

'What, all those stories about student loans and stuff?'

'Yes, I know it wasn't very glamorous, but it shows you can write and you're committed, which is the important thing.'

'Not as cool as what you're doing now though.'

'It's not that different in some ways. It's all writing.'

'Do you get loads of free stuff and go to VIP parties?'

'Not as much as you'd think. We get a few bits sent to us from PR companies but nothing that great. We get invited to product launches and events, but all these companies want their products, or bar, or whatever it is, mentioned in the newspaper. The novelty soon wears off. It's a job like any other in many ways.'

The waiter arrives back at the table with a shoulder of lamb for Mark and Helen's salmon fillet.

'This looks lovely,' Helen says.

Mark fills both of their glasses. 'Don't forget to drink your wine.'

'I won't.' She raises her glass to her lips but doesn't drink. 'I'm looking for something new at the moment. Working at the *Late* is fun, but I want more of a challenge.'

Mark shovels a bowl of carrots and green beans onto his plate. 'Are you going to quit journalism? You don't get paid very much do you?'

'No, I'm not quitting journalism, obviously. I've got a friend working at *The Guardian* and I'm trying to get in there. Ideally I'd like to write
features for one of the broadsheets, but it's hard to get in.'

'Why's it hard?'

'Because it's very competitive. There are *so* many journalists.'

'But why do so many people want to do it?'

'If you work for one of the big broadsheets you get to meet interesting people and go to interesting places. Not everyone can wear a suit and
sit in front of a computer screen staring at numbers for ten hours a day.'

'No, you're right. Most people couldn't.'

Helen picks at a small piece of salmon with her fork. 'Where's Craig
working?'

Mark snorts. 'Cinq Estates. He has to drive one of those stupid cars.
Do you know the ones I mean?'

'Yes. Oh dear. Poor Craig. I always thought he'd do really well.'

'The car is an embarrassment. I refuse to go in it. I offered to buy
him a new one so we wouldn't have that thing parked outside of the flat,
but he has to drive it.'

Mark's forehead is shiny and he loosens his collar.

'Do you remember Clara who lived with me in the third year? The
small one,' Helen asks.

'Did she have a bit of a funny lip?'

'No, that was Ruth. Clara played Hockey.'

Mark looks blank. 'Umm, no, I don't.'

'Well, she rented a flat through Cinq Estates in Stockwell and when
she moved out they refused to give her deposit back and tried to charge
her a thousand pounds for not giving them more notice.'

'What did she do?'

'She took them to a small claims court. She eventually got the money
back but she warned me *never* to rent through them.'

'It was probably Craig. He's a bit of a money-grabber nowadays.'
Mark drains the rest of his wine. 'Come on, drink more,' he urges.

She has a large sip and fans her face with her hand. The two spots on
her cheek have reddened.

'A drink will cool you down.'

'Are you trying to get me drunk, Mark?'

'No, it's just that they've put a couple of new wines on the menu and

I want to try them.' Mark waves his arm at a waiter. He orders a bottle of Riesling and then stabs at his lamb.

'I was surprised you emailed me,' Helen says, digging into her crème brulee.

'Why?' Mark forces a huge spoonful of chocolate pudding into his mouth.

'Well, we never really spoke to each other in the last year at uni.'

He makes Helen wait for a reply as he eats. 'I just thought it'd be good to get back in contact, have a nice meal. A lot has changed since uni. We're grown up now, successful.'

'Would you have emailed me if I didn't have a newspaper column?'

'Yes,' Mark says unconvincingly. 'I think about you a lot. I always thought there could have been more between us, but it never really happened for one reason or another, did it?'

'Perhaps because the one night you came back to mine you were ill in my bed and left me to clear it up?'

'That didn't help, no.' Mark smiles and licks chocolate sauce off his lips. 'I'd read your column a few times and I thought it'd be good to have a meal. To network. It must be better than having some loser taking you to a *Lord of the Rings* convention.'

'Nobody really took me on a date to a *Lord of the Rings* convention, Mark. That was made up.'

'Well, anyway. I thought it'd be good to see you again, to catch up. Do you want some more wine?'

*

Mark has the doors to the terrace open and there's a warm breeze. He's on the sofa in tracksuit bottoms and a t-shirt in the shadow of the new television playing *Terror Cell: Bradford* on the Xbox. He picks dry skin from behind his ear and wipes his fingers on the armrest.

The front door opens and Craig walks in holding a copy of *London Late*. 'I'm glad we're getting value for money from the TV,' he says, throwing the free newspaper on the sofa. 'No need to buy curtains to keep the sun out.'

'There's hardly any sun.'

'How was work?' Craig asks, as he searches in the fridge.

'I came home at three.'

Craig undoes his tie and kicks off his shoes. According to his socks it is Sunday and Thursday. 'Why did you come home at three?'

'I was meant to be at a meeting but it got cancelled.'

'Don't they expect you to go back to the office?'

'I don't have to tell someone where I am every minute of the day. We're trusted to get on with our work.'

'But you don't do any work.'

'They don't know that.' Mark puts his hand up his t-shirt and scratches his stomach. 'How come you're back so early anyway?'

'I'm still meant to be at work, but I haven't got any viewings so I'm not waiting around in the office.'

'Sell any houses today?'

'No. I thought I had a buyer for a four-bedroom place near Wandsworth Common but they pulled out.'

'Why?'

'There was a programme about us on TV last night apparently, exposing a few of the agents' tricks. They saw it and didn't want to deal with us any more. It's all anyone's been talking about.'

'Didn't you see it?'

'No. It was on at the same time as *The Bourne Identity*.'

'Best of seven?' Mark suggests, as his Barcelona side slump to a third successive defeat to Norwich City on *Pro Evolution Soccer*.

'No, mate. I'm hungry. Perhaps later. I might make some dinner.'

'What are you having?'

'Tuna sandwich, I think. I'm too tired to cook.'

Mark flicks down through the television channels until he gets to BBC One. He watches footage from a police helicopter of a man in a stolen car crashing into a chip shop, and switches to *Channel 4 News*. The European Central Bank has pumped a further €108.7 billion into the banking market to try to improve liquidity. He turns over to *Dog the Bounty Hunter* on Bravo.

The flat is really hot. Craig pours himself a glass of water from the cooler in the fridge, downs it, and pours himself another to take into the living room with his sandwich. He checks the radiators - which are all on. He tuts, looks at Mark, and goes to the boiler to turn the heating off.

Mark is stretched out with his feet up watching Dog arrest 'a small-time drug dealing punk' who has skipped bail.

Craig puts his plate down and opens the *London Late*. He skim reads an article about a fourteen-year-old who has been given an ASBO for stabbing a shopkeeper to death, and carries on eating. He flips through pages of celebrity photographs and a story about profligacy at City Hall but stops at the *Getting Laid in London* column. Next to the text is a full-length picture of Helen Nightingale wearing a long red dress and pouting. Her complexion has been airbrushed and she isn't wearing glasses.

'What are you laughing at?' Mark asks.

'This bloke's taking a pasting,' Craig replies, reading on.

'What is it?'

'It's the column by that Helen girl we were at uni with. The one about her sleeping around.' Craig has another bite of sandwich. 'Didn't you sleep with her in the second year?'

'I can't remember.'

'Yeah, right you can't remember. I'm sure you did.'

'I think I might have done one night after Liquid.'

'Of course you slept with so many girls it must have been hard to keep track. How many was it, three?'

'Three? It was twelve. At least.'

'That's a lie. One of them might have been twelve, but there weren't twelve in total.'

'Most of them were in the first year before we really knew each other.'

Craig turns back to the newspaper. 'You should read this mate, it's funny. She's gone on a date with some bloke from uni. He sounds like a complete twat.' He laughs again. 'What an idiot.'

'Chuck it over,' Mark says, sitting up. There is a white stain on the waistband of his tracksuit bottoms which he assures Craig is yogurt.

When he finishes reading, Craig throws the newspaper over. It hits Mark in the chest and drops into his lap. He flattens it out on the coffee table:

MY NIGHT OF HELL WITH OLD FLAME

When an ex invited me for dinner, I hoped he'd changed. He had – for the worse!

I'd pulled Mike after a drunken night out in my last year at university. He wasn't my type as I normally go for pretty boys or sporty types but I mistakenly thought he was hot and he came back to mine. I spent the rest of the night on my hands and knees, but I wasn't getting any steamy action, I was cleaning the floor after he vomited all over my room. Hardly Prince Charming!

A month ago, Mike got back in touch. After exchanging emails he invited me to dinner at Stove, and, judging by his email signature, now had a senior finance job in the City. I'm not one to turn down a free meal at one of London's best restaurants so I accepted, hoping my vomiting ugly duckling had blossomed into a beautiful (and rich!) swan.

I topped up my fake tan and bought a new outfit for the big night but my dreams of a new and improved Mike were dashed.

He arrived late, a fatter and more arrogant version of the boy who'd been sick in my room. His hair had receded and he was wearing a horrid double-breasted pinstripe suit.

He was rude to the waiters, mispronounced the dishes, and talked endlessly about his job and how much money he was earning. We'd finished the main course before he even asked me a question!

Mike plied me with white wine and implausible stories, like how he'd just broken up with his girlfriend who was a stripper at Peppermint Pussy Cat, and when it came to time to pay, he made a fool of himself by having two credit cards refused and started an argument with one of the waiters about service charge. I wanted to hide under the table!

Outside, he hailed a taxi and told the driver to head to Clapham, where we both live. As I was falling into a wine-induced trance, he slid his hand up my skirt and tried to pull down my knickers.

I woke up two hours later naked on a double bed with the room spinning. Mike then rolled me onto my back and mounted me like an over-amorous hippo, slobbering wine-laced gob all over my face.

He climaxed within a minute and whispered 'You love it!' in my ear. It was the most disgusting sexual experience of my life – even worse than last week's threesome at a homeless hostel.

I woke up at dawn and sneaked out suffering the hangover from hell. Thankfully it was a short walk of shame as I only live a couple of streets away (hopefully he won't remember where).

Tom Canty

When I got home, I left a message on my editor's answerphone saying that I wouldn't be in as I was suffering from post-traumatic stress disorder and that if she hadn't heard anything by Friday I'd either become a nun or committed suicide.

When it comes to dating rich City boys it's always the same – the size of their bonus is inversely proportional to the size of their penis. And as for Mike turning into Prince Charming – well, there are some things money can't buy!

Mark throws the newspaper to the floor.

'Who do you reckon it is?' Craig says, grinning.

'I don't know. It's probably all made up anyway.'

'I think you do know who it is,' Craig says, laughing. 'I think I know. It's obvious.'

'Who?'

'Think about it: he lives around here, works in the City and he's got really fat.' Craig holds his arms out in expectation that Mark will provide the answer, but he doesn't. 'It's Mike Davidson. Must be.'

CHAPTER NINETEEN

A haggard old man shelters from the driving rain under a broken umbrella and pretends to browse the houses in Cinq Estates' window. Craig and Danny watch as he swigs from a two-litre bottle of White Lightning in a plastic bag, spilling some down his tracksuit.

Christian runs outside, shakes the man's hand and tries to usher him into the office. He pushes Christian away, coughs up some black phlegm and staggers off.

Christian jogs back inside. The rain has marked his suit and flattened his hair. 'Why didn't one of you get out there and talk to him?' he yells at Craig and Danny.

'Because he was a tramp,' Craig says.

'Never, ever, judge a person by what they're wearing. He might have been a millionaire, but you'd never find out because you sat there on your arses rather than getting out there and selling.' Christian slams his office door.

Hannah tries not to laugh and looks over at Craig.

'Yes, of course, millionaires usually wear tracksuits and drink cider from plastic bags,' he says.

Danny giggles, lowering his head behind his computer so Christian can't see him.

It's the 20th August and there is only one entry on the sales board. Bradley has sold a bedsit in Tooting Bec for £67,500.

Christian opens his door and calls Craig over.

Craig closes his inbox and rolls his eyes at Danny.

Christian sits behind his desk, his fists clenched. Craig shuts the door and stands in front of him. He's told to sit down.

'What do you want to see me about?'

Christian rocks back in his chair and orchestrates a long, uncomfortable silence. 'Why are you and Danny sitting around out there messing about like a pair of kids?'

'We're not.'

'I've been watching you. Don't lie to me.'

'We were just having a joke, that's all,' Craig says quietly.

'You aren't here to have a joke; you're here to sell houses. Explain this to me, right: You haven't sold a single house for two months and yet you're sitting around in the office, browsing the internet like you haven't got a care in the world whilst everyone else is out there on the streets trying their arses off to sell some houses!'

Craig glances at the sales board. 'I've made all of my calls. I've called everyone on the database at least three times in the last week. I've spent on average five hours a day on the phone, but nobody is interested.'

'That's bollocks. Those monkeys at Crouch and Giles sold seven houses in SW11 alone last week and a five-bed in Wimbledon for two million. How do you explain that if nobody is buying? People are buying. You aren't selling. How many viewings have you done this week?'

'Six.'

'Six? Craig, you should be doing fifteen a day.' Christian picks up a biro and jabs it into his desk. 'No wonder we aren't selling anything!'

'Who am I meant to show around?'

'People. Find people.'

'Where? Please tell me where, I'd love to know. We've not had anyone walk through the door for two days.'

'Go out in your car and look for them.'

'What just drive around the streets asking people if they want to buy a house?'

'That's what everyone else here is doing, so why don't you?'

'That's not what everyone else is doing. Do you want to know where the rest of your team are?'

'I know where they are.'

'So you know that they're all at the McDonald's off Wandsworth Bridge?'

'That's bollocks. I spoke to Yado a few minutes ago and he said he was on a viewing on Bedford Hill.'

'Who's Yado?'

'Big guy, started a few weeks ago. I think his name's Yado. Or is it Wado?' Christian checks the sales board. It's Yado. 'Making up lies about your colleagues isn't going to get you anywhere, Craig. There's no room for liars in this office. My team are out on the streets selling, all apart from you and Danny. I think I'd know if they weren't.' He bites his bottom lip. 'You're skating on very thin ice. The ice is so thin that you're on the verge of falling in and drowning. And there aren't lifeguards on duty. Do you get me?'

'Yes.'

'You're lucky you've still got a job after the sales figures you've posted recently.' Christian runs his fingers down his pink tie. 'I don't know where this arrogant attitude of yours has come from, but let me tell you, it stops now. I don't want some loose cannon in this office, going off whenever and wherever he feels like it. *Selling* is the key to our success, Craig. If I don't feel that you can get out there and sell, then you might as well leave now.'

'I can sell.'

'And how can people working here trust you if you tell me that they're all in McDonald's?'

'I was being honest.'

'Craig, you say that like it's a good thing. The key to honesty is knowing when to be honest.' Christian takes something from the bottom drawer of the mini filing cabinet beneath his desk. 'Look, I like you Craig. You remind me a bit of me when I was younger, and I know that deep down there's a top salesman in you, but you've gone to shit recently. It would be the easy way out to fire you, but I'm not gonna. I've invested a lot of time and money into developing you and I'm not giving up, even if you are. I'll level with you. When I joined here from school in 2004, I struggled. I wasn't making the sales. My boss at the time was Ben Rossiter, you've probably seen his photo in the magazine, he's now national sales manager. He called me into his office and gave me such a massive bollocking I thought I was going to get the chop. I'm not ashamed to admit it, I was almost in tears, begging him not to sack me. But he told me that he thought I had potential and gave me something that would change my life forever.'

'What was it?'

'This.' Christian reaches down and places a twenty-inch steel saw on the desk.

Craig looks baffled. 'He gave you a saw?'

'Yes, Craig. He gave me a saw. He gave me this saw, told me to get in my car and wherever there was a 'For Sale' sign of another agent, I had to cut it down and burn it. It was a test, Craig. A test of commitment.'

'What did you do?'

'What do you think I did? I got out there and sawed down signs until my hands bled. Do you know how many I did?'

'No.'

'Guess.'

'Twenty?'

'Nowhere near.' A smug grin spreads across Christian's face. 'One hundred and three. It's a record.'

'And you want me to do the same.'

'Yeah, I do.' Christian pushes the saw towards him. 'I don't expect you to do as many as me. Let's say fifty.'

'Fifty?'

'Yeah. Minimum. Print off the list of houses for sale from the registry, go home, get changed and get sawing. Oh, and don't park too near where you're doing it, for obvious reasons.'

'What do I say if anyone asks what I'm doing?'

'Say that the company is being rebranded and there'll be a new sign put up tomorrow. Make sure you make a note of where you're cutting the signs down and then email it to the signage department immediately. Are you up for this or what?'

'Err...Yes. I suppose.'

'That's what I hoped you'd say.'

A Swann Estates 'For Sale' sign stands in the garden of a smart semi-detached house on the corner of Smith Street and Fairfax Road in Balham. There isn't anybody around so Craig sneaks in through the gate. He hides behind a bush and starts sawing the sign a third of the way up.

He's only made a small incision in the post when he has to stop to get his breath back. He looks at his red right hand and wrings it. It starts raining again and Craig brushes his damp hair off his forehead and takes a sip from a bottle of water he's placed at his feet in the flowerbed.

A car stops outside the house. Craig drops the saw, crouches into a ball and waits. Footsteps pace off down the street, so he continues sawing frenetically. The wood splinters and the sign breaks in two.

The front door opens and a man with a walking frame edges out into the porch as Craig tucks the two halves of the sign under his arm. He has liver spots over his face and hands and is wearing a long brown coat.

'Excuse me,' he says, his voice trembling. 'Excuse me. Where are you going with that?'

'Umm, sorry, I've been told to take it down. There'll be a new sign going up tomorrow.'

'Have they sold my house?'

'Sorry, I don't know. I'm just doing the sign.'

'They come over here at all hours. I don't know who's here. They just turn up and let themselves in. You're not bringing people over are you?'

'No, I'm not. I'm just taking the sign down. Some men will come tomorrow and put a new sign up.'

'You haven't been treading on the roses?'

Craig checks his footprints in the soil. 'No, I've avoided them.'

A set of keys drop on the doormat between the old man's slippers. He shakily attempts to bend over and looks to Craig in desperation. Craig leaves the sign on the lawn and passes the keys into his brittle hands.

'Please, if people are going to call,' he says, 'could you ask them to telephone me first? It's such a nuisance having people walking through the house, it's really quite a worry.'

Craig tells him that he is sorry but he only does the signs. He apologises for being in the garden without permission and carries the broken bits off to his car.

The two pieces are added to the collection he is building on the back seat. He sits in the driver's seat with the engine running and phones Swann Estates to tell them that one of their signs had been vandalised by kids. He scans down the list of seven addresses he's compiled and scribbles out 41 Smith Street.

Craig parks and looks up at the grimy low-rise council flats which surround him on three sides. Their exterior walkways overlook a main courtyard where there are industrial-sized wheelie bins. Some flats have washing hanging up outside and most have lights shining out of their small front windows. Somewhere, a child is screaming.

He pokes the blister on his hand with his pen and gets out of the car. The rain is hammering down. He quickly flips down the front seat and starts throwing the sawn-up 'For Sale' and 'To Let' signs beside the bins where there's already a heap of old furniture, toys and a couple of hefty old televisions.

An overweight woman wearing a yellow plastic mac waddles towards him, carrying shopping bags. Craig frets, gathers the rest of broken signs up in his arms and throws them onto the rubbish. Most of them slide off onto a pile of bin bags. He jumps back into his car and speeds off, clipping the wing mirror of a blacked out BMW as he turns out of the estate in the direction of Clapham Junction.

The Cinq office is still open even though it has gone nine o'clock. Christian is standing over a young girl at a computer. He notices Craig, backs away and tells the girl she should go home.

'Who's that?' Craig asks, walking into Christian's office.

'Naomi, I think.' Christian takes his suit jacket from a hanger on the back of his door.

'How long's she worked here?'

'A few months.'

'Really?'

'Or I might be confusing her with Nadia.'

'Hasn't she left?'

'Yeah, that's right. Nadia was meant to be tying up a deal for a place on Wordsworth Road but she called in saying her mother was ill and she needed a week off so I had to let her go. How many boards did you cut down?'

'Thirty-eight.'

'Why not fifty?'

'It took longer than I thought in the horrible weather. The saw kept slipping. I almost sawed my hand off a couple of times. I decided to focus on more expensive houses. I did a lot of places around the common and the bigger semis in Balham.' He takes the list from the pocket of his waterproof coat and hands it over.

'Have you emailed the signage department the list?' Christian asks.

'Yes.'

'Excellent. They'll have our boards up overnight. I'll find out who owns these places and give them a call tomorrow. Have you got the saw?'

'It's in the car.'

'Where did you dump the signs?'

'On that estate around the back of Clapham Junction.'

'Good thinking. You've done well, Craig. Have you got any plans tonight?'

'No.'

'Why don't you go home and change and we'll have a beer somewhere?'

Craig stands inside the main door of The Temperance. The pub is split across two floors and the mezzanine level restaurant is closed so he wanders downstairs. The bar runs all the way along the left-hand side and there are dark-stained tables around the edge of the room with four sunken Chesterfield sofas arranged in pairs in the centre. Large standard lamps are dotted along the walls, some almost touching the low ceiling. There are plenty of places to sit.

Christian is at a table by the bar. He's still in his work clothes and doesn't have a drink. He calls over to Craig, who has changed into jeans and a black sweatshirt, and tells him to buy him a pint of Staropramen.

There doesn't appear to be anyone serving. A man in a suit stands alongside Craig and pulls a £20 note from his wallet. The trapdoor to the cellar opens and a man with tattoo-covered arms climbs his way out. He asks who is next and the man in the suit orders three bottles of Leffe and a small glass of white wine.

Craig pays for his two pints on card and carries them over to Christian.

'Do you know what I think you lack Craig?' Christian says, after sampling his beer, 'Assertiveness. Killer instinct. You get pushed around too much. I told you to buy me a beer and you just did it without questioning. I was here first; I should have got the first round in. I was watching you at the bar and that bloke just pushed in right in front of you and you said nothing. It's what's holding you back, Craig. If you were a bit more ruthless, you'd make ten times as much money.'

Craig drinks. 'It's not really my style to be pushy though.'

'Make it your style. If you don't ask, you don't get. Some people are shepherds and some people are sheep. You've got to be a shepherd. People like being told what to do. They may not realise it, but they do. If you tell someone to buy a house or a flat, more often than not they'll follow your instructions. People don't like thinking for themselves, they don't like making decisions. They much prefer to be told what to think. Great men don't sit around waiting for someone to ask them to become leaders, they go out there and get it. You've got to take the same approach.'

'OK.'

'The point is, Craig, you need to assert yourself more. You've got to fight for every last deal out there. It's a competitive market and you've got to have a winner's attitude. A winner doesn't sit in the office on the internet. A winner gets out there and sells.' Christian takes another gulp. 'You're not here to make friends, Craig. If you upset a few people along the way, it don't matter. If you see someone from Crouch and Giles, or Swann, or Griegsons, remember these people are your enemies. Every house they sell is money out of your pocket. If people are stalling on you, or not showing up at viewings, phone them up and have a go at them. They are costing you money.'

Craig looks at the photograph hanging on the wall between them. It is the pub from the time it was a temperance hall. 'I'm trying my best and doing as much as I can,' he says.

'I'm not interested in you trying your best. I'm interested in you putting sales on the board. I'd much rather you didn't try at all and sold ten houses a week.' Christian sniffs and rubs his nose. 'The art of selling is making someone buy something they don't want. Some people say that it's convincing people to buy something they never knew they wanted, but I don't agree. The great salesmen sell people things they know they don't want but still buy anyway. That's the approach you need to take. It's a battle of wills. You've got to wear people down. Selling is an art form, a science. I've got books at home. You can buy them off me.'

Christian finishes his third pint. 'The more you sell the more money you make. If you don't sell then everyone suffers. You do like money don't you?'

'Of course.'

'If you don't have money, you can't buy, and if you can't buy, you can't live. You're stuck.' Christian's eyes are glazed. 'Cinq gives you the opportunity to make big money, not many other companies do. I keep a list of things I want to buy in my desk drawer and I work out how many houses we need to sell to buy them.'

'So do I,' Craig says. 'DVDs and CDs and stuff like that.'

'No, Craig. Big things.'

'Christian, is there any chance we can talk about something other than selling?'

He sniffs. 'Did I tell you I'm buying a place in Battersea Beach?'

'No. What's that?'

'The new places overlooking the river.'

'There? Aren't they expensive?'

'Expensive, but worth the money. I've been able to get a one hundred and fifty per cent mortgage. At my age I couldn't afford to leave it much longer before getting on the property ladder. It's so important to own your own house. Renting's just pouring money down the drain. If I were you I'd buy as soon as you can.'

'But I haven't got the money.'

'You don't need money. You just need a job and you've got one. The more houses you sell, the quicker you can pay the mortgage off. That should be your motivation.'

'One more beer, come on,' Christian says, as the bell rings for last orders. He gets off his seat and walks carefully over to the bar. He pushes in between two women and brandishes his credit card. The barman serves the women either side of him first and then takes his order.

'I got a couple of shots,' he says coming back and passing Craig his drinks.

Craig downs his tequila, licks a line of salt off his hand and sucks on a lemon slice. 'Thanks,' he growls, quickly taking a huge mouthful of beer.

Christian accidently sprays lemon in his own eye. 'Ahh, pain, pain,' he says, rubbing it vigorously with a napkin. It's bloodshot.

'Are you all right?'

'I'm fine.'

Only Christian, Craig and two women finishing off a bottle of red wine are left in the pub. A South African guy collects their glasses and tells them that it's time to drink up. Christian dismisses him.

'Craig, I've an assertiveness test for you. Go over to those two girls and invite them back to mine. Don't take no for an answer.'

'They're not even fit.'

'I don't care. Go and do it. Now.'

'I don't want to.'

'I don't care.'

Craig's seat scrapes on the wooden floor as he reluctantly gets up and approaches the girls. He speaks to the one who has a lopsided jaw and she shakes her head. Her friend, who has a chubby face, glances over at Christian, who is still rubbing his eye. Craig walks back to him.

'What did they say?' Christian asks.

'They said they had boyfriends and that you looked like you'd been crying.'

'What? Why didn't you tell them I hadn't been?'

'They weren't fit, in any way.'

'So what? You were only over there for ten seconds. You allowed yourself to get stepped on, again. If I'd have gone over, we'd be in there by now.'

'Maybe.'

'Definitely. You'd try harder if it was Hannah.'

'No I wouldn't. Anyway I'm friends with Hannah. They were just randoms.'

Christian swirls the beer in his glass. 'I've seen the way you look at Hannah, Craig. Don't think I haven't noticed. She's very vulnerable and I don't want you taking advantage of her. It's unprofessional.'

'There's nothing going on.'

'I know there's not because she's coming out on a date with me next week.'

'What? Really?'

'Yes. So you're to steer well clear of her. Do you get me? If I catch you even talking to her, then I'm going to have to discipline you.'

'What? But I have to talk to her. We work together.'

'If you need to talk to her, you come and check it with me first. Clear?'

'Are you serious?'

Christian sneezes and accidently knocks the rest of his pint over the table into Craig's lap.

CHAPTER TWENTY

C raig rolls out of bed to answer the entry phone. Mark's room is open and his bed hasn't been slept in.

'Hello.

'I'm sorry, he's not here.

'You're what?

'Umm, OK. Push the gate. It's number... oh, you know which number it is.'

He presses a button to release the gate, runs to his bedroom and makes a call on his mobile:

'Mark, it's me,' he says, agitated. 'Where are you? Some girl called Jenny's turned up here saying you're expecting her. I've let her in, but I'm not sure if I should have or not. Who is she and what's going on? Ring me back ASAP.'

He pulls on a pair of Norwich City football shorts and a creased t-shirt, quickly brushes his teeth and tries to style his bed hair. There is a thump on the front door.

He opens it and steps back. His mouth moves as if to speak but nothing comes out.

'Hello. You must be Craig,' says Jenny. She is friendly but serious.

'Yes,' he says, staring at her. 'Do you want to come in?' he asks finally.

She ducks in under the door frame. 'Has Mark popped out?'

'I'm not sure. I've only just got up.'

Craig presses himself against the wall as Jenny plods past and follows in her shadow.

'Mark said you'd bought a new television,' she says, sitting down on a sofa and un-popping her gilet, which she wears over a red lumberjack shirt. 'Isn't it a bit big?'

'It was Mark's choice.'

'That doesn't surprise me. It blocks out the light.'

'Yes, I know.' Craig goes into the kitchen and puts the kettle on. 'Would you like a cup of tea?' he asks, pulling up the blinds. 'Please. A small amount of milk and no sugar, thanks.' Jenny digs her mobile out of her pocket. 'Mark's phone's going straight to voicemail. He's probably at the gym.' Craig sniggers. 'At the gym? What gym?' 'The one he usually goes to I suppose. I don't know what it's called.' Craig hands Jenny her tea and sits with her. The coffee table is covered with old *London Lates*, a copy of *Nuts* and two old curled *Esquires*. He tidies them into a neat pile, hiding *Nuts* - which has a topless woman on the front cover - at the bottom.

'Are you just down here for the day?' he asks.

'Yes, just the day. I've got to talk to Mark about-' she hesitates, 'something.' Her eyes are sunken and dull and she feigns a smile. 'I've got to be back at the farm later.'

'Do you live on a farm?'

'No, I just work there. I thought Mark might have mentioned it?' Craig shakes his head. 'Umm, no. He's not said. He's never explained how you two know each other, actually.'

'We were family friends for a long time first and then we started seeing each other properly when we were fifteen.'

Craig nods, bemused. 'You and Mark were going out when you were fifteen?'

'People are always surprised when they find out how long it's been.'

'How long it's been? It was quite a while ago.'

Craig sips his tea as Jenny picks a long wiry hair off her jeans.

'Are you still working for the estate agents?'

'Yes, I am.'

'Mark showed me your office last time I was down. Are you still at the one up the road?'

'Mark showed you my office? So you've been here before?'

'Yes, quite a few times now. We obviously keep missing each other. I think you've either been back at home or at work when I've stayed.'

'It looks that way. Where did you sleep when you stayed here?'

Jenny looks puzzled. 'Mark's bed obviously. Where do you expect me to sleep?'

'Mark's room, of course. Yeah, sorry. I don't know why I asked that.'

'Craig, if you want to get ready or need to go out, I don't mind waiting here. I can entertain myself. I'll watch TV and wait for Mark.'

'I've got no plans. I'll just wait here with you if you don't mind.'

There is a key in the front door and Craig rushes up the hall. Mark stumbles in. His eyes are barely open, he stinks of alcohol and he's shivering. Craig drags him to his room and shuts the door.

'Mate, please don't push me I think I'm going to be sick,' Mark says.

'Did you get my message?'

'No, I've lost my phone. I think I may have left it in a taxi.' Mark sits on the edge of his bed with his hands over his eyes.

'There's a girl called Jenny sitting out there.' Craig thumbs towards the living room. 'She seems to think she's your girlfriend. What's she talking about?'

'Is she massive with ginger hair? Smells like horses?'

'Err, yeah.'

'Jenny,' Mark mumbles. 'Girlfriend, sort of.' He falls back onto the bed.

'What? Your girlfriend? Have you gone mental?'

'Please, I've got a terrible headache. I thought I'd told you about her.'

'No, you haven't told me anything and you know you haven't. You're *unbelievable*. She says you've been going out since you were fifteen.'

'We have... on and off.'

'And you were going out all the way through uni as well?'

'Yes. Mate, please can we talk about this later. I'm dying here.'

Craig stares at Mark's prostrate body in disbelief. 'Where have you been anyway?'

'Some girl's house. She was fit. Looked like that one from *Dr Who*.'

Craig paces around the room. 'You smell disgusting. Get out there and talk to her.'

'All right, all right. Stop having a go at me.'

He drags Mark to his feet and pushes him out into the hall. Mark almost falls over. Craig stands in the doorway and watches with his mouth gaping as Mark tells Jenny that she's early and kisses her on the top of the head.

She gets to her feet. 'Where have you been? You were meant to be meeting me at the station.'

'Sorry, babe. I stayed at Justin's. We were celebrating. I don't feel

very well. Do you want something to eat? I might have a bacon sandwich.' He wanders out into the kitchen and takes a large frying pan off
the rack on the wall and lights the gas.

'Mark, we need to talk,' she says.

'Babe, just let me have something to eat then I'll have a shower and
I'll treat you to lunch somewhere.'

'Mark, you smell really awful. Have you been sick?'

'Not in the last hour.'

The bathroom is steamy as the shower has been running the whole time
Mark has been sitting on the toilet and his pasty, spotty body glistens
with sweat. He slides off the seat and kneels on the floor with his head
drooping into the toilet bowl. He wipes the droplets from his brow and
then, after throwing up, wipes his mouth with his arm. He flushes the
chain and gets into the shower.

'Sorry I've been a while, babe,' Mark says, emerging from the steam of
the en suite with a fluffy blue towel wrapped around his bulging stomach.

Jenny has tidied his room. The bed is made, towels have been hung
over radiators and there is no sign of the cups and plates that had been
stacked on the bedside table. There aren't even any clothes on the floor.

Mark picks up his red 'Business' file. 'You haven't been reading this
have you?'

'No, I've been clearing up.'

'You haven't chucked anything away?'

'No.'

He lets his towel drop to his feet and scratches himself. He quickly
dresses and goes back into the bathroom to brush his teeth.

Jenny is perched on the bed watching an old episode of *Friends*. Mark
puts some gum into his hair and styles it meticulously in the mirror.

'Shall we go out then, babe?' he says, slipping his keys into the
pocket of his jeans.

'Mark, I'm not hungry. Can we just stay here for a little while?'

'Stay here? No. Come on, let's go out. I need a proper lunch. We'll
go to the pub and get a roast.' Mark turns the television off. He has a
large, bloody spot on his nose.

'I was watching that,' Jenny says.

'What do you want to do then, babe? Do you want to go to Battersea Park Children's Zoo again?'

Jenny tells Mark that she needs a serious talk with him and tells him to sit down. He tells her to make it quick because he wants to get a good table and sits facing her on his desk chair.

'Mark,' she says. 'Mark.' She bursts into tears.

'What's wrong, babe? Has one of the horses died?' Mark gets up and pats her on the head.

'No,' Jenny says, dabbing her eyes with a tissue. 'I've done something very bad, Mark. Very bad. And I'm so sorry.'

'What have you done? I'm sure it's not that bad,' he says, now sitting next to her on the bed.

'I've been seeing someone else.'

'Sorry, *what*?' Mark says, as if he's misheard.

'I'm so sorry. I've been seeing someone else,' she says, snorting.

'You've been cheating on me?' he says, his face screwed up in bewilderment. He shuffles away from her. 'Are you sure?'

'I've been seeing someone else.'

'*You've* been seeing someone else? Are you sure you're sure? You're not just having a period or something and going a bit mental?'

'No. I'm so, so sorry.' She reaches out to touch his hand, but he flinches and folds his arms.

'A bloke?' he asks.

'Yes.'

'Who?'

'It doesn't matter.'

'Yes it does. It matters to me.'

'Eoin.'

'Who?'

'The Irish jockey from the stables.'

'The midget bloke? You've been seeing a fucking Irish dwarf behind my back? Have you completely lost it? You've been cheating on me, *me*, with him! After all I've done for you.' Mark won't look at her. 'How long's this been going on?'

'It doesn't matter,' Jenny says, snorting again.

'How long?'

She starts sobbing again. 'Two years.'

183

'You've been shagging him behind my back for *two years*? Jesus Christ.'

'Yes. I'm sorry, I'm sorry,' she blubs, burying her face in the duvet. 'I never meant to hurt you.'

'Well you didn't seem to be thinking about me when you were doing it in the bloody hay barn or wherever you went.'

'It wasn't like that.'

'Well what was it like?'

'It just happened. I don't know. I was lonely. You were down here and I was upset. I didn't know what I was doing. I was confused.'

'You don't sound confused.'

'I kept meaning for it to stop but it just didn't. It's over, Mark.'

'I couldn't give a fuck. I'm not having you back. Not after this.'

'No, that's not what I meant. It's over between us. You and me,' she says talking to the side of his head.

'What? You can't break up with me.'

'I have to. Me and Eoin are moving in together.'

'You're moving in together? What am I meant to do? I was going to buy us a house. I can't believe this.'

Jenny gets some tissue from the bathroom and blows her nose. Mark ruffles his hair.

'I'm just thinking about all those things we've done whilst the whole time you've been with him,' he says.

'Come on, Mark. It's not been working between us for a long time. We barely see each other.'

'That's because I'm working every hour I possibly can to save for our future. I was making so many sacrifices for you, and this is how you repay me.'

'I didn't think you thought we had a future. You never call me, you never invite me down. We haven't had sex in eighteen months.'

'Do you blame me? You were getting it from someone else. I thought you smelt different.'

'I think that might have been a new type of feed we were giving the animals.' Jenny's nose is running. 'You're ashamed of me, aren't you?'

'No.'

'Don't lie, Mark. I know you are. That's why you kept me hidden.' She dabs her eyes. 'When I came down this morning, Craig didn't even seem to know who I was. Do people even know you've got a girlfriend, or doesn't that fit in with your London life?'

'Everyone knows.'

'Craig didn't.'

'I've told you before, he's a bit simple.'

'You're ashamed of me. You never once invited me to see you at university and your family laugh at me.'

'That's not true.'

'I heard your uncle say I looked like a man in a big ginger wig. How do you think that made me feel?' she sobs.

'It was just a joke. He didn't mean it. My mum loves you. She'll be very angry when I tell her what you've been up to.'

'She knows.'

'What? What do you mean she knows?'

'I needed someone to talk to.'

'Why didn't you talk to your own mum?'

'My dad had an affair once and Mum never recovered. She'd throw me out if she found out. Your mum told me to come down and talk to you. She was very kind.'

Mark stares out of the window at the overcast sky with his back to Jenny. 'Betrayed by my girlfriend *and* my own mother. I feel... I feel like I've been stabbed in the heart. I hope you can live with yourself.'

'I just want to be treated properly. Eoin treats me like a woman.'

'What?' Mark says, turning round. 'Are you saying I didn't treat you well? The amount of presents I bought for you. The holidays.'

'Your parents paid for the holidays.'

'I paid for the food, which cost a lot more, by the way.'

'I just wanted you to respect me, not lock me away like a dirty secret whilst you saw other girls behind my back.'

'I hardly think you should be lecturing me.'

'Mark, I know you've been seeing other girls.'

'Who told you that? I haven't done anything. I've been devoted to you.'

'I went on your Facebook account.'

'How?'

'You forgot to sign out one day at my house. I saw your emails.'

'What emails?'

Tom Canty

'The ones where you had been inviting other girls out for drinks.'

'They were client lunches.'

'No they weren't, Mark. I'm not stupid. Some of them were my old school friends.'

'I never did anything.'

'You tried to.'

'But I never did anything. Because I've got too much... love. Because of my love for you.'

'I think I should go,' Jenny says.

'Is this how it's going to end, is it? You just walking out?' Mark turns and lays face down on the bed, away from her.

'I didn't want it to end like this. I loved you, Mark.'

Jenny tries to give him a kiss on the cheek, but he tells her not to touch him. She leaves the bedroom and walks into the living room where Craig is playing *War Wounds III* on the Xbox. He asks her if everything is all right. She says Mark is a bit upset and picks up her handbag. Craig gives her the exit code for the gate and she says it has been nice to meet him.

Mark slams his bedroom door and there are a succession of thuds and crashes, then some hammering on the wall and muffled wailing. Craig calls out to Mark and puts his ear to the door.

'Mark. Are you all right, mate? You haven't hurt yourself have you?'

There is no response. Craig turns the door handle.

'Leave me alone,' Mark says, his voice trembling.

'If you want to talk, I'm right outside.' Craig puts his ear to the door again. Mark is crying. Craig waits until it stops.

'I heard what happened, mate,' Craig calls out. He slides down the wall and sits cross-legged on the floor. 'I'm really sorry. Nobody wants that to happen to them. I didn't even know you had a girlfriend. She was quite big wasn't she? But not in a bad way, I mean. Sorry, I probably shouldn't have said that.' There is silence.

'I had my heart broken once you know, back at home,' Craig says. He sighs. 'It was a girl called Roxanne. Like the song. Roxanne Clarke. I met her at my cousin's wedding reception at the Marriot Hotel in Spixworth.

'It was during the lower sixth summer holiday. I had a bad headache because the ceremony was outside and I'd been out in the sun all day. It was about half ten and the disco was going but I felt terrible because I'd been drinking all day so I went outside to get some fresh air, and Roxanne was standing there. She was waiting for a taxi because she had to get up early for a netball match. She was the most beautiful girl I'd ever seen. Long dark hair. Amazing legs. Really pretty face. She looked a bit like Hannah actually.

'We got talking and she gave me some headache tablets. It turned out that she was the daughter of my cousin's boss. We text each other a few times and then went to see *American Pie 2* at the Riverside. That was the first time I kissed her. It was the best date ever. All my mates were really jealous.

'We did loads of stuff together that summer; went on a trip to the Broads, spent a day in Cromer, went to the Norfolk Show. We were just hanging out and being together really.

'All her mates and my mates would meet up and go and get pissed down Prince of Wales Road. We even met each other's families.

'I would have done anything for her. But she was a year older than me and she'd just finished Caister St Edmunds Ladies' College. She was going off to study history at De Montfort University. She said that she loved me and that we wouldn't break up but it was never the same after she went. I went to see her a couple of times but she was different. She had her new friends and her new life and I suppose I was just a schoolboy.' Craig rests his head against the wall.

'One day I was in Castle Mall and I saw her arm-in-arm with a massive bloke in a De Montford rugby top. I remember I was in Superdrug buying some blister plasters. I just dropped them on the floor and ran out. I walked the streets for hours. It was like being in a nightmare. Next thing I knew, I was in Jarrold's balling my eyes out. I had to phone my mum to come and pick me up because I was too upset to drive. I honestly felt like I wanted to die at the time. Seems stupid now.

'I've seen her around a few times since but, I couldn't talk to her. We never even officially broke up.' Craig swallows hard. 'So, if you want to talk, I've been there mate. I know what it's like.'

He stretches out his legs and clears his throat.

Mark's bedroom door opens. He has changed into a Jack Wills hoody and has his iPod headphones in.

'Why are you sitting down there?' he asks.

'I was talking to you, checking that you were all right.'

'Yeah, sorry. I was in the bathroom. I thought you were on the phone,' Mark says, stepping over Craig. 'I'm OK. Thanks. It was just a bit of a shock.' He rattles his keys and bites his lip. 'I'm off to that girl's house to see if my phone's there and then I'm going to Asda to get a pizza. Do you want anything?'

CHAPTER TWENTY-ONE

E bony, a curvy stripper in fishnet stockings and high heels, is gyrating to N.E.R.D.'s *Lapdance*.

Justin has booked a table at the foot of the Peppermint Pussy Cat's main stage - a long straight runway with a semi-circular head. The club has leopard-print furniture and oversized plastic chandeliers that hardly emit any light. Every table has the gold silhouette of a naked woman stencilled on it and the same image is on the velvet curtain at the back of the stage.

Justin orders another round of drinks from a waitress in a French maid's outfit and adjusts the two cushions on his chair. He nudges Mark and discreetly tells him that he, Lex and Horatio are going to the bathroom and asks if he wants to join them. Justin taps his nose. Mark tells Craig he'll be back in a minute but Craig doesn't take his eyes off the entertainment.

Lex and Horatio are old school friends of Justin's and both work in banking. Lex is overweight, balding and wearing a navy pinstripe suit with a red shirt which has a white collar and cuffs. He's spent the last twenty minutes telling Amy about his ex-wife who is a 'stupid brainless bitch with a fat arse' who comes from a 'the poor part of Kensington'. Horatio is overweight, balding and wearing a navy pinstripe suite, glasses and a giant Cartier watch. The four men stroll off to the toilets leaving Amy, Ian, Craig and Julia.

Ebony turns her back to the table, bends over and blows Ian a kiss through her legs. He tries not to look embarrassed.

'Slut,' Julia says, watching Ebony's huge breasts jangling just a few inches away.

'She likes you mate,' Craig says to Ian.

'Strippers like anyone who they think they can milk money out of,' he replies.

'Or anyone who gawps at them,' Amy adds.

'You've been to strip clubs before?' Craig says, surprised.

'Too many. It's Justin's idea of team building. At least it's a bit more comfortable here,' Amy says, scanning the tables of businessmen. 'He used to take us to The Muffin. Have you been there?'

'No.'

'It's in Shoreditch. You put pound coins in a pint glass and some grotty old woman strips. It's disgusting.'

'The only strip club I've been to is the Byzantium Pleasure Rooms,' Craig says.

'Where's that?'

'Great Yarmouth. It was my old football team's end of season night out. It was a bit different to this. One of the dancers went to my primary school.'

'I don't think most of these girls even know what a school is.'

'Haven't a lot of them got normal jobs and do it to earn a bit of extra money?' Ian says after sipping his beer.

'That's what they'd like you to think,' Julia says. 'I don't think you'd find them that alluring if you found out they were single mothers who were doing it to fund their crack habit. Look at her,' she says with a glance to the stage, 'she's clearly drugged up... and she's got cellulite.'

Ebony picks up her knickers and disappears offstage to a smattering of applause. Many of the men at other tables leave their seats and Julia pours herself another glass of Bollinger.

Justin and the three others return to the table. Lex rubs his nose whilst Horatio talks incessantly about asset management.

'What were you doing?' Craig asks Mark, who plonks down next to him.

'Having a word with Justin,' Mark says, reaching for another beer from the collection in the middle of the table.

Julia says she's going for a cigarette. Horatio watches her tall, slim figure as she strides off. He brushes wispy strands of hair away from his eyes and scratches his armpit.

'Justo, what's Julia's situation? Boyfriend?' he asks.

'No, binned him a few weeks ago. He lost his job. Lehman Brothers.'

'Bad luck,' he says, laughing.

'You'd need a couple of mil just to keep her interested.'

'Not a problemo,' Horatio says with a wink.

'Have you had a go?' Lex asks Justin.

'No,' he says, pointing at his wedding ring.

'She turned you down then?' Horatio says, guffawing. 'I'll tell you what, put a word in. I'd go right through that.'

'Bit thin,' Lex says. 'Be like shagging a stick.'

Amy shakes her head.

Girls on Film starts playing and the lights are lowered. Carly, a tall blonde with bad roots takes to the stage dressed in a black bustier and G-string.

'Now that's a real woman,' Horatio says, getting a wad of cash out of his pocket.

Horatio polishes off his drink and turns to Amy:

'Do you know what I like about the girls here? They're professional. You pay top dollar but you're getting the best, not some rough old dog.' He scans the menu. 'Are you hungry?' he asks, checking nobody else is listening.

'Not really.'

'Why don't the two of us head to Coq d'Argent for some supper?'

'No thanks.'

'Are you sure?'

'Yes.'

'Come on, my treat.'

'I'm not hungry, thanks.'

'Not even for a hundred quid?'

'What?' she says, irritated.

'Two hundred?'

'You're serious, aren't you?'

Mark, Craig and Ian are watching them.

'Well, yes,' Horatio says, smiling.

'Jesus, you're like a fucking child,' Amy says, getting up from her seat and taking her jacket.

'What the problem?' Justin asks.

'Your idiot friend seems to think I'm for hire as well,' Amy snaps. 'I'm going.'

Mark grabs her by the arm as she tries to leave. 'Don't go, don't go.

We're sorry. He's only messing around.'

People at other tables are looking at them and a bouncer gets up from his stool at the bar. Amy gives Mark a fiery glare and storms out, passing Julia on the way. Ian and Craig stare at the table.

'Justo, you need to have a word with her,' Horatio says. 'She's out of control.'

'We should get more drinks,' Lex suggests.

'Boys,' Justin says, addressing Mark, Craig and Ian, 'take this and have some fun.' He throws a rolled up bundle of notes at Mark. 'Enjoy yourselves.' His eyes are unfocussed.

'I need to get my train,' Ian says.

'Where's your team spirit?' Justin says. 'Forget your girlfriend. Look at some fit girls instead. I'm paying. What's wrong with you?'

'Kelly just text me saying that if I don't come home immediately, she's locking me out.'

'Tell her to fuck off,' Lex says, laughing.

Ian leaves.

'What an ungrateful bastard,' Justin says. He turns to Mark and Craig. 'I'm counting on you now. You're staying with me. If you try and go home, I'll sack you both.'

Craig looks confused. 'But I don't work for you.'

'Justo, would I let you down?' Mark says.

'I know you wouldn't. That's why you're my main man,' he says, spilling his beer. 'Now take that money, take your boyfriend and go see some naked women. Go on, fuck off.'

Mark leads Craig over to the bar where some of the strippers are drinking cocktails. Mark orders two bottles of Spanish lager and pays out of Justin's money. He tells Craig to choose whichever girl he wants. Craig says he isn't sure who to go for. A tall brunette wearing knee-high boots and a voluptuous 'schoolgirl' with dyed blonde hair ask them if they'd like a private dance.

'Do you lez up?' Mark asks.

The brunette wants to know how much money they've got. Mark flashes the heap in his pocket.

'Let's go,' she says, taking the pair to a small private lounge. A huge bouncer with three gold hoop earrings smiles at the girls as they go in and ignores the boys.

Clapham Lights

Mark and Craig sit a couple of feet away from each other on a curved sofa. There are purple drapes hanging from the walls and the lights are dimmed.

'Is there anything in particular you'd like us to do gentlemen?' the 'schoolgirl' asks as her friend selects a track on the CD player.

'I want the other one to strip for me,' Mark says, pointing at the brunette. 'You can strip for my mate, and when you're both completely naked, and I mean completely naked, everything off, I want you to wrestle on that,' Mark points to the shagpile rug on the floor, 'and kiss each other, *everywhere.*'

Back in Black by AC/DC blasts out and the girls begin gyrating. Craig's stripper pulls on his tie and opens his jacket. She tells him she finds men in Jacob Perville suits a real turn on and takes a large red lollipop from her skirt. She sucks on it, rolls it around on her tongue and then pops it into Craig's open mouth.

'What's your name?' she asks, blowing into Craig's ear.

'Craig,' he says. 'What's yours?'

'Lara.' She's unbuttoning her shirt to reveal a lacy red bra.

'Like the cricketer.'

'What?' she says, swaying into him.

'Like Brian Lara.'

'Who's that, handsome?'

'Don't worry,' he says as Lara puts her left foot on the sofa and seductively lifts her skirt over her smooth legs to reveal a silky garter.

'You're a bit shy aren't you, Craig?' Lara says, undoing the clasp on her bra and slipping it off.

'No,' he mumbles, transfixed by her chest.

'Tell me, do you like schoolgirls?' she whispers in his ear.

'Umm, yes.'

'Do you like me, Craig?' Lara says, standing over him with her nipples only millimetres from his lips.

'Yes.'

'Do you know how old I am?'

'Thirty-five?'

'No, you cheeky bastard,' she says, slipping out of character. 'I'm sixteen. I'm a sixteen-year-old virgin looking for a hunky man like you to teach me about sex. Can you do that for me?' she asks, hovering above his lap.

'I'll try. You're not sixteen though are you?'

'I'm whatever age you want me to be.' She licks her index fingers and runs them over her nipples.

'But you're not sixteen though, are you? Or a virgin?'

'I am a virgin, Craig,' she says, licking her lips.

'Really, and you're a stripper?'

Suddenly she pins his shoulders to the sofa. 'It's role play,' she says softly. 'I'm just going to dance and you can watch and enjoy. I think it's better if we don't talk.'

Mark is laid back on the sofa, nodding his head to the music. His semi-naked stripper dances in front of him, teasing him that she's about to remove her G-string. She has a large butterfly tattoo on her lower back and a pierced left nipple.

'Take them off,' Mark demands. 'I want to see the lot.'

She straddles him and he pokes a few £20 notes into her waistband. She jumps to her feet, turns her back on him and tantalisingly slides her underwear over her tanned bottom.

'That's the shizzle!' Mark says. 'Turn around, turn around.'

She wiggles her hips, pushes her breasts into his face and he growls.

The door flies open and a massive bouncer with gold front teeth and a knife tattooed on his neck tears in and hauls Mark off the floor by his throat. He elbows Mark in the chest and then punches him on the side of the head sending him flying onto the sofa. Someone turns the lights up.

'Don't hurt me, don't hurt me,' Mark begs, holding his face.

The bouncer holds him by the collar and asks the girls if they are all right.

'We're OK,' the brunette says, hurriedly putting her clothes back on. 'He could have broken my back the fat prick,' she says, pointing at Mark.

'What did he do?' the bouncer asks, putting his knee onto Mark's chest.

'We were wrestling on the floor and the fucking twat dived on us.'

'It was a flying elbow drop,' Mark moans. 'I was getting into-'

'Shut up, you,' the bouncer snarls. 'Have you been paid, girls?'

Mark takes a bundle of notes from his pocket.

'That should cover it,' the bouncer says, grabbing the wad out of Mark's hand.

'But that's all my money.'

The bouncer digs his fist into Mark's neck and pulls him to his feet, tearing the arm of his suit. He's marched out through the club with Craig in tow.

Justin, Lex and Horatio are sprawled over the table. They give Mark a drunken ovation.

As they reach the entrance, the bouncer slams Mark against a wall, tells him not to come back until he's learned to behave, and throws him out onto Oxford Street. He thanks Craig and says that he'd be welcome back without his friend.

A pair of drunken women in trouser suits stagger arm-in-arm towards Tottenham Court Road as Mark rests up against a closed mobile phone shop and inspects his torn sleeve. He also has a small bump over his left eye. There is a homeless person asleep under a pile of blankets in the shop's doorway.

Mark checks his iPhone. He has seven missed calls from 'Home', three text messages and four new voicemails. He deletes all of them.

Craig asks him if he wants anything and is sent over the road to get chicken chow mein and a drink from the Nice Wok Chinese buffet.

They sit on the steps of an HSBC bank eating from foil containers.

'I want another drink,' Mark says, forking more greasy noodles into his mouth.

'Mark, we need to go home.'

'No, come on, don't be boring. I'm not at work tomorrow. You can pull a sickie.'

Mark holds the container up to his mouth and the last few noodles slither in. He then hails a taxi, tells the driver to take him to Embassy and shouts at Craig to forget his food and get in.

*

Mark opens one eye and lets out a long, sorry moan. His iPhone keeps vibrating. It's 9.16 a.m. and 'Home' has called fourteen times.

He reaches out to the bedside table and accidently knocks a pint of water over the business section of *The Sunday Times*. He mops the water up with a hand towel and picks up his watch. Yesterday's suit and shirt are on the floor.

'Shit, shit,' he says to himself, falling out of bed. He runs into the bathroom and drops to his knees in front of the toilet, forcing his fingers down his throat, but nothing comes up. He spits into the bowl and has a freezing two-minute shower which makes him shiver uncontrollably. His phone is vibrating again. This time he answers it:

'Mum, I can explain,' he splutters. 'I've literally just left a meeting. There's been an absolute meltdown at work. My biggest client called threatening to withdraw their money. I've been locked in negotiations with them since three yesterday. We worked all through the night. I've not even been to bed.

'I couldn't. I had to be there. If I'd lost that account, I'd have lost my job.

'I didn't have any time. I was fighting to keep the client. I've not even had anything to eat.

'I'm in a taxi now.

'Work are paying. It's driving me straight to the church. Can you text me the address please?'

Mark opens his wardrobe with his spare hand and throws a suit and a white shirt onto the bed. He thumbs through his tie collection. 'I need to borrow a black tie. Has Dad got one? I couldn't find mine.

'Yes, I'm sure he is, but tell him it couldn't be helped.

'I'll see you there. If the traffic's bad, I'll ring you and you can delay them.

'Just tell them to do another lap of the block or something.

'It starts at eleven, yeah?

'I'll see you later... oh and by the way, I'm still not talking to you.

'You know why.'

Mark chucks his towel on the floor and stands over the toilet, shaking. He then goes back into the bedroom, dresses and leaves Craig an abusive voicemail for not waking him up.

'That's £239.40,' the taxi driver says as he stops next to a hearse outside St Christopher's. The village church – which is commemorating its three hundred and fiftieth anniversary - has scaffolding erected over the spire and is surrounded by rows of crooked headstones. The graveyard is immaculate, with trimmed grass and well-pruned bushes.

'Do you need the money now or can you send an invoice to my office?' Mark asks.

'I need the cash now, mate. You need to book in advance and tell us which account to charge it to if you're going to do that.'

'Can't you find out for me?'

Mark convinces the driver to call his head office and ask for the fare to be charged to the MenDax Wealth Management account.

The driver laughs and thanks the person on the other end of the line. 'You haven't got an account with us any more,' he says. 'Cancelled it in March. I'll have to have the cash.'

Mark huffs, hands over the exact money and asks for a receipt. He slams the taxi door, runs through the churchyard and slips in between the weathered oak doors. The service is already in progress.

The vicar, a tall, slender man with a bushy white beard, is standing at the alter reading from the Bible. Behind him is a coffin, draped in a Union Jack. Mark's family are sitting at the front.

The majority of the mourners are elderly and the pews are full. The rest of the congregation stand four-deep at the back.

Mark joins the standees and perches on the base of the stone font to get a better view. He gazes up at the beams which criss-cross the ceiling and at the vast stained glass windows that depict scenes from the Old Testament. A wooden statue of Christ on the cross is nailed high above the vicar's head.

The congregation are asked to turn to page two of the order of service for the hymn *Abide with Me*. Mark doesn't have one so peers over the shoulder of the woman in front of him.

At the conclusion of the hymn, a frail old man with a walking stick and Brylcreemed hair moves to the lectern. He picks a folded sheet of paper from his silver-buttoned blazer and puts on thick reading glasses. He coughs into a handkerchief and begins in a slow, melancholy tone:

'Victor Archibald Hunter was born to George and May Hunter in Hastings in June 1921. Tragically his mother died during the birth, leaving his father to raise Victor and his elder sister Doris alone.

'At the age of eleven, Victor won a scholarship to Hastings Royal Grammar School, where we first became friends. He excelled at school and shone on the athletics field but unfortunately his academic career was cut short after his father suffered a farming accident in which he lost both legs, forcing Vic to give up his scholarship aged thirteen to take a job as a delivery boy to feed the family.

'He had worked his way up to the position of clerk by the outbreak of the war and was conscripted into the 6ᵗʰ Battalion of the Royal Wessex Regiment. When Singapore fell to the Japanese in February 1942, Victor, along with thousands of other Allied prisoners, was transported to Tamarkan prison camp in Thailand, where he spent three years working on the deadly Burma–Siam Railway.

'Despite enduring cruelty that would be unimaginable to many people here today, when Victor spoke about his wartime experiences he said he always considered himself one of the lucky ones as so many of his friends never made it home.

'He returned to Hastings in late 1945, and after time spent in hospital recovering from cholera, he married Frances in January 1946. A year later, Frances gave birth to their first son, Graham, who was followed by John in 1949.

'Victor worked at Baxter's department store in Hastings until his retirement in 1986 by which time he had risen to the position of director and he is very fondly remembered by everybody he worked with.

'After the untimely death of Frances in 2002, Victor's health sadly started to deteriorate and the trips to the pub that myself and our long-standing friends enjoyed became fewer and further between.'

The woman next to Mark wearing a large black hat starts crying.

'Victor was a very loyal friend; a warm and generous man with a kind heart. He never had a bad word to say about anybody and I was proud to call him my friend and my best man. He will be sorely missed.'

He folds his eulogy back into his blazer and walks unsteadily back to his seat. There is a round of applause. The vicar asks everyone to stand to sing *Jerusalem*.

The crowd at the back of the church parts and the Hunter family file out. Mark shoves his way between two teenage boys and joins the sombre procession.

As they turn into the graveyard, the sun comes out and Mark jogs to the front to be alongside his parents. He taps his dad on the shoulder:

'Have you got my tie?'

Patricia gives Mark a withering glance and hands him a black tie from her handbag.

'Nice of you to turn up,' Graham says, not looking at his son.

'I had a meeting. Didn't Mum tell you? I haven't been to bed.'

'Why don't I believe you?'

Mark fastens the tie as they follow the vicar over the dewy grass to the first of a line of open graves at the back of the churchyard, which adjoins acres of barley fields. The vicar gives Graham and Pat a brief explanation of the burial ceremony as Mark shuffles away and stands next to Uncle John, who is dressed entirely in black.

'Where were you last night?' John asks.

'Peppermint Pussy Cat. Work drinks. Don't say anything.'

'Don't worry I won't. I wish I'd been with you. I had to sit listening to your dad being miserable. What time did you get in?'

'About five, I think. I feel terrible.'

John gives Mark a packet of mints. 'Have a few of these. You reek of drink.'

Mark empties all of them into his mouth.

The four pall bearers align themselves on the green synthetic turf surrounding the grave and delicately lower Victor Hunter into his final resting place. The head of the group throws a handful of soil onto the coffin and steps away, head bowed.

There is another Bible reading and a prayer. The vicar then invites the family to scatter some earth. Graham, John and Mark's older sister Annie, all edge forward, followed by Mark. He takes a handful of mud from the dug up pile, bends down and drops it into the hole. It lands with a hollow thump.

As he lifts his head, his face turns white and his cheeks inflate as he tries to swallow. He squeals, scampers past the vicar and flings himself onto his hands and knees on the edge of an adjacent hole. He makes a strained yelp and vomits ferociously. He growls again and more transparent liquid gushes from his mouth as he convulses. Patricia forcibly restrains Graham and the rest of the mourners look on in a mixture of horror and revulsion. Mark glances over his shoulder, his eyes streaming, and wipes his mouth with his tie.

Mark changes out of his muddy and sick-stained clothes and puts on a pair of jeans and a shirt he finds in his dad's bag in his grandparents' old spare room. The house smells of lemon air freshener. He breathes in and rises onto tiptoes as he tries to do the trousers up but the waist is two inches too small. The shirt is on the verge of bursting.

The wake is in progress downstairs and there is the sound of cups and saucers chinking and restrained chatter. Annie, Mark's sister, comes up the stairs carrying a pile of coats which she dumps in her grandad's old room. She is slight with bright eyes, brown highlighted hair, and a deep sun tan. There is a silver piercing at the top of her left ear and she has beads around her wrists.

'Why are you putting them in there?' Mark asks, following her in.

'Mum told me to. I wouldn't start causing a fuss if I was you. Why weren't you here last night?'

'I had important business. You wouldn't understand.'

'Is that why you threw up?'

'I must have a virus or something.'

'You're a twat, Mark.'

He trots down the stairs into the living room where Patricia is distributing cups of tea. Someone has moved the dining room chairs into the living room so more people can sit down. She asks Mark to help her. He says that he shouldn't after what she's done but he'll make an exception today. She tells him to stop being so pathetic.

Uncle John opens the drinks cabinet. He pours a generous drop of whiskey into his coffee and sidles up to Mark:

'Keep out of your dad's way. He's on the warpath after your performance in the churchyard.'

'I couldn't help it.'

'It was a bloody stupid thing to do.'

'I'm ill.'

'You didn't have to get on your hands and knees. Someone behind me thought you were praying. They were burying someone in that hole this afternoon. I don't think anyone wants their relative laid to rest in a pool of your sick. Wipe that smile off your face, Mark. Show some bloody respect.' John drinks his coffee. 'Your dad said he could smell alcohol on you. Why don't you go and have a beer?'

'I can't. I'll be sick again.'

'Don't be a girl, Mark. If you don't have a beer, it'll look odd. He'll be expecting you to have a few drinks. If you don't, he'll know that you got shit-faced last night.'

'Can't you go and have a word with him for me? Tell him I'm working so hard it's making me ill.'

'Mark, he's not stupid. I'm in his bad books as well. He said I haven't given him any help with the funeral arrangements, even though your mum's done most of it.' He drinks more coffee. 'And he wants me to say a few words about Dad, but I told him I'm not going to.'

'Why not?'

'I'm not keen on public speaking. What am I meant to say about him anyway? Tell everyone what a great father he was?'

'I'm going to get some buffet,' Mark says. 'This is making me feel worse.'

The kitchen is full of elderly people wanting more to eat or their glasses refilled. Someone has dropped a sandwich on the lino. Mark is standing by the fridge with his sister, pouring a can of lager into a tankard.

'When did you get back?' he asks.

'Yesterday. I flew in to Heathrow and got the train here. I got back about nine.'

'Why didn't you get picked up?'

'Because I thought Mum and Dad would be busy organising everything for today, not that it would have occurred to you.'

'How's everything in Sydney?'

'Pretty good. I've moved to a new hospital.'

'Mum said something about that, but I wasn't really listening. When do you think you'll come home?' Mark asks.

'I was saying to Mum and Dad last night that my contract runs until March, so I'll see how I feel then. I was thinking about going somewhere else for a year.'

'Like where?'

'South Africa perhaps.'

'Why do you want to go there?' Mark says with a mouthful of cake. 'Hasn't everyone got Aids?'

Annie sighs. 'No Mark, not everyone. I'm going to go and talk to the adults next door if you're incapable of having a sensible conversation.'

'You can't walk off. I'll have to talk to one of these old people,' he whispers. 'Anyway you haven't asked me about what I'm up to.'

'I don't need to. I know exactly what you do. You sit in an office all day twiddling your thumbs and at night you go out and get pissed and annoy people.'

A man asks Annie where the toilet is. Mark helps himself to a mini pork pie and a few crisps from the kitchen table, stands by the window and stares out into the garden, where the vicar is having a cigarette.

'Lastly, I'd like to thank Reverend Dawkins for conducting the service, which barring one hiccup went very well.' Graham looks straight at Mark, who is cowering beside a bookcase. 'So thank you. It was exactly what Dad wanted. There's plenty more food and drink to be got through, so please help yourselves and you're all welcome to stay as long as you like.'

Uncle John, holding a tumbler two-thirds full of whiskey, staggers into the room and stands next to Graham. He's taken off his tie and is holding an unlit cigar.

'I just want to say a few words,' he whispers.

Graham glances at Patricia who mouths that Graham should let him. Graham steps away and stands next to his wife and daughter.

John puts down his drink and composes himself. There's a nervous tension in the room.

'As my brother has said,' John begins in a strained voice, 'thank you all for coming today.

'I know there's been a lot said about Dad, but I'd like to say a few words about the dad I knew. My dad.' He takes a large swig of whiskey.

'Dad wasn't a very emotional man. He wouldn't tell you that he loved you or put his arm around you. It just wasn't his way.

'He had a tough upbringing, which he always reminded us, and that made him a tough man. He was used to life being hard. He used to say to us that a few hard knocks made a man of you.

'He thought that hard work was the key to life. If you worked hard you got your rewards. If you didn't work hard then woe betide you.'

John sways and rubs his eyes. 'When I was eleven I used to have two paper rounds. It took me three hours every morning. Dad made me do an extra one as a punishment for not getting into grammar school like Graham did. One morning, it was well over thirty degrees, and I had chicken pox. I did the rounds as usual and when I got home I went straight upstairs to bed. Dad came storming into my room, dragged me out of bed by my hair and kicked me down the stairs into the back garden.

'He screamed in my face wanting to know why I was still in bed and I tried to tell him that I'd finished my paper rounds and I was ill. He said he didn't care and told me I was a lazy little bastard and would be punished.

'He made me stand out in the burning sun in just a pair of pants for hours and hours. It must have been at least seven hours.' John has another sip of his drink. 'He sat in the kitchen watching me and if I started to slouch, he'd run out and beat me with a length of cane he used to grow runner beans up at the allotment.

'I was crying my eyes out and he told me that unless I stopped crying he'd get really angry because no son of his would be a cry baby, and the noise I was making was interrupting him reading his newspaper. I was trying to stop but I couldn't because I felt so ill and sun burnt.

'I remember he came outside and pushed me on the lawn, and then ran into the shed and got a watering can and a tea towel. He tied my hands and feet with garden wire, pinned me to the ground with tent pegs and then filled the watering can up from the tap. Then he put the tea towel over my face and he started pouring the water over me.' John clears his throat and his hands start to shake. His eyes are glassy. 'I couldn't breathe, but the tea towel kept slipping off.

'I heard noise coming from the kitchen and suddenly Mum came running out, going mad at Dad. "What are you doing? What are you doing?" she screamed. She told him he was doing it all wrong and that he should have… he should have used a bath towel, not a tea towel, so she ran back inside and got him one from the airing cupboard. She held it tight over my face and Dad kept pouring and pouring until I passed out.

'When I came round in hospital a couple of days later, Dad told me that he'd taught me an important lesson. I'm not sure what the lesson was, but he could be a bit cryptic sometimes. It was hard to know what he was thinking. He wasn't a very emotional man, but that day he said he was almost proud of me.'

Tears are rolling down his face.

'I'd like a toast,' John says, his voice trembling, 'to Victor.' He sinks the rest of his drink and rushes out of the room.

Tom Canty

The last of the guests have left. Mark sits in the living room watching a documentary on Channel Five about a woman with two heads whilst his mum clears up the last plates and glasses. There is a cake smear on the old leather sofa which he hides under a cushion.

Above the fireplace are two framed photographs: Graham and Patricia's wedding day and a shot of Mark's late grandmother on a beach. The drinks cabinet has been left open. Next to it is another glass cabinet housing a collection of classic toy cars.

Annie wanders in with a sandwich and slice of Battenberg. 'Can we watch something else?' she says, curling into an armchair.

'There's nothing on. Grandad didn't have Sky.' Mark throws her the remote control. 'Where's Dad?'

'Driving John to the station so he can humiliate himself somewhere else.'

'He wasn't that bad.'

'Not that bad? He was drinking pints of whiskey by the end. Trust you to defend him.'

Mark types a text message as Annie eats her cake.

'Has Dad spoken to you about the will?' he asks.

'No. Do you really think Grandad would have left you anything?'

'I spent loads of time with him when I was younger. He used to love playing swingball with me.'

'That was about twenty years ago. When did you last visit him?'

'Umm, when you last came back.'

'You've not seen him since last summer? In fact you didn't even come down then, it was just me and Mum. You were taking Jenny to Chessington World of Adventures.'

Graham goes straight into the kitchen where Patricia is washing up and tells her that John passed out in the car and had to be carried onto the train. He pours himself a glass of red wine and joins his children.

'You've upset me today, Mark,' Graham says. He looks tired. 'We had enough to think about without your performance.'

'I'm sorry. I couldn't help it. Mum told you I was stuck in negotiations. I haven't been to bed for almost two days. No wonder I was ill.'

'Mark, you stank of alcohol.'

'We had some champagne when we'd renegotiated. One glass, that's all I had.'

'Mark, I know what you look like when you've been drinking. There's no point in lying to me. You should have been here with us last night. I don't like you ignoring my phone calls either. It's not on.'

'There was nothing I could do,' Mark says. He glances at Annie. 'Do you know if Grandad left me his medals, Dad?'

'I don't know.'

'Can I have a quick look at the will if it's around?'

'Mark, give it a rest will you, for God's sake!' Graham says, turning the news on.

Mark sits on the toilet with the tap running and his iPhone pressed to his ear:

'Craig, it's me. I'm still annoyed with you, but I need you to do something. I own part of a house in Worthing and I need you to get it valued, tomorrow if possible. I assume you've got an office down here or somewhere near.

'The address is 12 Merit Street, Worthing, Sussex, BN14 7TY. It's a three-bedroom semi with a large garden and a garage. It's in good condition. We must be talking four hundred grand at least. Ring me when you get this.'

CHAPTER TWENTY-TWO

V alerie Simpson, a surly woman in her late forties with a thin, tight face and long auburn hair, tells Craig that her daughter, Ophelia, is running late. She leaves Craig at the gates to The Block, Wall Street and sits back in her BMW convertible which is parked outside the terraced houses across the road.

Ophelia, a freckly girl with a mass of wavy bleached hair bounces down the street. Despite it being an autumnal afternoon, she's wearing shorts and flip-flops and has a long seashell necklace hanging down to her waist. She has full, round features and long, fluttering eyelashes. Valerie gets out of the car and gives her daughter a passionless hug.

'How do I look, petal?' she asks, posing in her jeans and knee-length cashmere cardigan in the middle of the street.

'Beautiful, Mummy.'

Craig introduces himself to Ophelia, who gives him a beaming smile, and opens the gate. Valerie says that she's heard that this is a violent area and Craig tries to reassure her that the streets around Clapham Junction are very safe compared to other parts of south London.

'This building is so amazing,' Ophelia says, tilting her head back to take in the towering walls.

'I can't say I like it, petal. It looks like a ghastly factory.'

'It was an orphanage for Victorian children until the Seventies,' Craig says. 'It's still got lots of original features, but it's totally new inside. It's one of the most desirable properties in London.'

'That doesn't say much for the rest of London.'

'*Mum*,' Ophelia says.

'No, it's fine.' Craig leads them into his block. 'I am biased though. I've got an apartment on the same floor as the one we're going to. I've seen lots of new developments in this area and this is definitely the best. A lot of places are renovated on the cheap to move people in as soon as possible. These have been finished to a much higher standard. They're very popular with lawyers and executives and people who work in the City.'

'And estate agents,' Valerie says.

'Yes and estate agents.' Craig presses the lift button. 'It's got a lift.'

'We can see that.'

There's a screwed up KFC box in the corner and Valerie stands as far from it as possible, pinching her nose the entire way up. The doors ping and open. The motion-sensitive lights blink into life as Craig leads the mother and daughter along the corridor to a front door two away from his own.

'The house is owned by a lovely woman called Abigail who lives here with her two children,' Craig says, letting them in. 'I'm not sure how tidy it will be, but I'm sure you'll be able to see through any mess.'

The laminate floor shines when Craig turns on the hall spotlights. The interior is pristine and decorated with a stylish minimalism. The living area is bigger than in Craig's flat and comes furnished with a long black dining table, chaise longue and sofa, and stumpy coffee table. A flat screen television and a stereo system hang on the wall.

'This place is amazing,' Ophelia says, walking into the kitchen. 'It's *so* cool.'

'I thought you'd like it,' Craig says. 'Have a look in the bedrooms. They're both en suite.'

Valerie stands in front of the mirrored wardrobes in the master bedroom, opens one of the doors and has a close look at the shoe collection.

Ophelia breezes into the second bedroom and sits on one of the two children's beds. Craig follows her.

'This room is so cute,' she says. 'Look at their little clothes.' She picks up an 'I Love Mummy' t-shirt from a pile of clean washing that sits in a basket by the girl's bed.

The children's toys have been neatly piled into the corners or hidden in boxes on top of the wardrobes. There are small round marks on the walls where posters have been taken down.

'It is cute isn't it,' Craig says, opening up the bathroom. 'I love the kids, they're so funny. The little boy is always running up and down outside, shouting his head off. I play football with him in the corridor sometimes.'

Ophelia grins. A tiny roll of her tanned stomach pokes out from between her shorts and her yellow t-shirt.

'Is it just the three of them who live here?'

'Yes, it is.'

'No Daddy?'

'I don't know,' Craig says. 'Abigail has never mentioned him. I think he might have... died, sadly. There are a couple of photographs of a man in the bedroom.'

Ophelia's face drops. 'Oh my god, that's so terrible. Those poor children. Why are they moving?'

'Abigail said that she doesn't really want to bring the children up in London. They're moving down to Hove. I think that's where her parents live.' Craig sits down on the bed opposite. 'Have you just come back from holiday?'

'I've been in Bali.'

'Oh right. Where's that?'

'Indonesia,' she says, smiling. 'A friend of mine from university has got a house out there. We were celebrating graduating.'

'Where did you go?'

'Newcastle. I did art history.'

'Oh, right. Do you work near here?'

'No, not yet. I'm doing some work experience at a gallery for a few weeks but I'm not sure after that. I'd like to do something arty but I've not really decided yet. I just want to move up here first and settle in. Then I'll start job hunting.'

'Where are you living at the moment?'

'With my parents, in Kent.'

Ophelia looks around the gleaming en suite and goes back into the living room to join her mother.

'What do you think, petal?'

'I absolutely love it. Did you see the balcony? It's perfect.'

'It hasn't got much character.'

'It's got style though, Mummy. And it's safe, which you said was one of the most important things.'

Valerie takes a seat on the chaise longue and calls for Craig, who comes scurrying from the bedroom.

'What do you think Mrs Simpson? Amazing flat isn't it? It's got everything. It's a great location. Excellent transport links,' he says.

'I like it,' she says impassively.

'Have you been out to the roof terrace?' Craig asks, opening one of the doors which lets in a blast of cold air.

'I can see it through the window, thank you.' She gestures that Craig should close the door.

Ophelia is opening and closing the built-in cupboards in the hall. 'Lots of room for all my things, Mummy,' she calls out.

'There's a huge amount of storage,' Craig adds. 'You'll never run out of space.'

'How much is it on the market for?' Valerie asks, adjusting her silk scarf.

Craig consults the spec. 'The guide price is eight hundred and seventy-four thousand. But I know the owner is looking for a quick sale so I may be able to barter her down to eight hundred and fifty if you can complete soon. You're not in a chain, are you?'

'Don't be ridiculous.'

Ophelia sits next to her mother. 'I've simply got to live here. I'll text Daddy. I love it,' she says, her eyes drifting around the room. 'Did you hear that those poor little children that live here haven't got a daddy which is why they're moving away?'

'Spare me the sob story. Have there been any offers so far?'

'So far,' Craig pauses, 'there have been four: a couple of low ones and two at eight hundred and forty-five which have been rejected. One big advantage you have over the other bidders is that Abigail said that she only wants to sell to somebody who'll really appreciate it and look after it - preferably a girl. That would definitely count in your favour.'

'I'd look after it so well. It's just so...' Ophelia spreads her arms, 'It's just so me.'

'It's a lot of money, darling.'

'It'd be a great investment,' Craig says. 'It's a buyer's market at the moment. You'd probably double your money in five to ten years.'

'See, Mummy. He knows what he's talking about.'

'I'll have to talk to my husband. We may be willing to make an offer, but I saw a television programme about your company a little while ago and rest assured that if at any point anything happens that we don't like, or if we sense that you're lying to us or trying to pull the wool over our eyes, then we'll walk away. Have I made myself clear?'

'Perfectly,' Craig says. 'Mrs Simpson, I can assure you that programme is not representative of how things work in my office. We are
extremely professional.' He smiles at Ophelia. 'Do you have any other
questions before you talk to your husband?'

Valerie takes a small notebook from her Gucci handbag and flicks
through to a page of hand-written questions. 'How much is the council
tax?'

'It's in band H,' Craig says.

'That means nothing to me. How much is it, per year?'

'I think it's about two thousand pounds.'

She makes a note. 'Are there any other hidden charges?'

'You do have to pay a small service charge which goes towards main-
taining the property. That's around five hundred pounds a year.'

'No doubt there'll be plenty of hidden charges from you.'

'No hidden charges. We're just like any other estate agent, Mrs
Simpson.'

'Do I get a car parking space?' Ophelia asks.

'Yes,' Craig confirms. 'There's one allocated per flat. Have you got
a car?'

'Yes, a Mini.'

'Same here,' he says. 'Mine's a company car though.'

Valerie stares out of the window at the dreary weather. 'Do you really
live here?' she asks Craig.

'Yes, of course.'

'Isn't it a bit expensive for you?'

'It's not cheap but for-'

'I don't believe you. Prove it.'

'*Mum!*' Ophelia exclaims.

'What do you mean?'

'Go and open up your flat then, if you really live here. It's on this
floor you said. I'll watch you from the door.'

'Mummy, this is ridiculous.'

'We'll find out whether he's trustworthy or not, won't we.'

'All right,' Craig says. 'I'll show you.'

Valerie re-emerges from the bedroom and puts her mobile phone in her
handbag. Craig is on the chaise longue next to Ophelia, who's laughing

at his stories about nights out he's had in Clapham.

'Did you speak to Daddy? What did he say?' Ophelia asks.

Her mother eyes the pair of them with suspicion. 'He's going to phone back in a couple of minutes. He said that if you're sure it's what you really want, he's willing to make an offer, but he wants to talk to you first. And he wants some assurances from you, as well,' she says, looking to Craig.

Ophelia jumps up and gives her mum a hug and kiss but she pushes her off and tells her not to get too excited.

'That's great,' Craig says, with a cheery grin. 'As soon as you decide a figure, I'll get the ball rolling. Brilliant.'

Valerie's mobile phone rings. 'It's Daddy. Can you leave us in private for a few minutes?' she asks Craig.

'Sure, call me when you're done.'

Ophelia gives Craig an excited smile as he slips into the children's bedroom, shutting the door behind him.

He stands in the middle of the room silently pumping his fists, then takes deep breaths to calm himself. 'Thank you, thank you, thank you,' he says, his eyes closed.

There's a small plastic *Winnie the Pooh* ball under the boy's bed. Craig rolls it out and starts doing keep-ups. He manages ten before the ball slides off his polished shoes. He starts again and gets to six before a heavy touch knocks the ball too far in front of him. He stretches out his left leg in an attempt to regain control but only succeeds in toe-poking it straight at a mug of blackcurrant cordial that has been left on the girl's bedside table. The ball clips the mug, toppling it, and the liquid cascades down onto the basket of clean washing.

'Oh shit, shit,' Craig hisses, frantically picking up some of the soaking garments. He takes the whole basket into the bathroom and runs the hot tap. As much as he rinses, everything is stained. He wrings the clothes out and piles them by the sink.

Ophelia calls out to him from the hallway. He tells her he's coming but decides to quickly give the clothes another run under the tap.

'Brilliant news,' Ophelia calls out. 'Daddy's agreed. He's going to phone you later to make an offer.'

'That's great,' Craig shouts back. 'I'll ring him in a minute and then I'll get on the phone to Abigail and we'll see how quickly we can push this through.'

'Are you OK in there, Craig?' Ophelia asks.

'Err... yes I'll be out in a second. I'm just in the bathroom.'

He's scrubbing away with soap but the stains won't budge. He finds a plastic bag under the sink and starts filling it with the wet garments when suddenly the bathroom door bursts open and Valerie stands there giving him an accusatory stare:

'What the hell are you doing?' she shrieks.

'I'd–'

'What have you got in that bag? Are you stealing?'

'No, I'm–'

'Give me that.' She lunges at the bag.

Craig grapples with her but she gets a hand inside it and, to her horror, pulls out a tiny pair of stained pants.

'It's not what it looks like,' Craig says, mortified.

'You animal,' she says, dropping the pants. 'I've read about people like you, stealing children's underwear. Paedophile!'

'N, No,' Craig stutters. 'It's a misunderstanding. I'm not stealing them, I swear.'

'I'm calling the police, you deviant.'

'Mummy, please, stop,' Ophelia pleads.

'Please don't get the police involved,' Craig begs, 'I can't go through that again.' He empties the stash of wet clothes on the floor.

'Don't you tell me what to do. You're going to prison.'

'No, Mrs Simpson, please. I spilt a drink over them in the bedroom. I was taking them home to wash. I swear. Please. Please.'

'I don't believe you.'

Craig looks to Ophelia for help.

'Mummy, please don't call the police. It's just a mistake. He was trying to help. He was telling me earlier how much he loves the kids and how he plays with them.'

'Bragging about your perversions?'

'Not like that,' Craig says. 'Please, you must believe me.'

'You should be locked up,' Valerie says, dialling 999.

Craig snatches the phone out of her hand and runs into the hall.

'Give me that back you pervert!' she screams, chasing him with her arms swinging wildly. Craig cowers in a corner as she thrashes away at his head and upper body. Ophelia jumps on her mother's back and tries to wrestle her to the ground.

'Get off me! Get off me!' Valerie screams. 'He's a sex monster.'

'Calm down, calm down!' Ophelia battles to control her mother who's writhing on the floor so she slaps her and yanks her cardigan over her head until she stops struggling.

A police officer and a paramedic lead Valerie Simpson out. She has been sedated. Ophelia apologises to Craig and tells him to put some TCP on the scratches on his face. Craig says he's fine and sorry for causing a scene. He then says that if they still want to buy the flat, he could give her the owner's details if her parents refuse to deal with him or Cinq.

'Craig, that's so kind,' Ophelia says, giving him a hug. 'Can I take your mobile number?'

CHAPTER TWENTY-THREE

T he conductor announces that they will shortly be arriving in Norwich and reminds passengers to take all their belongings with them before alighting. The train slows as it passes storage warehouses and rows of dilapidated terraced houses. Carrow Road football ground is just visible through the mist. Craig rolls up his *GQ* and pushes it into his holdall as they pull into the station.

He jumps down onto the platform, zips up his jumper and weaves through the passengers, many of whom are students struggling to heave suitcases. It's cold and the wind swirls under the canopies overhead.

A girl with dreadlocks and a lip piercing barges past, almost tripping Craig up with her wheelie bag as a mother with two infants in matching raincoats hurries in the opposite direction through the station's atrium.

He stands outside the main entrance and scans the congested car park. Black cabs are lined up to his right and along from them is the bus stop where most of the students have congregated. Beyond the car park and the main road, a floating Chinese restaurant sits moored opposite the Riverside Hotel and traffic is queuing on the narrow humpback bridge which leads up to the city centre.

Craig is making a phone call when a new silver Ford Mondeo pulls up. He jogs over to the car.

'You haven't been waiting long have you?' asks Peter, Craig's dad, as his son gets in. He has a flat Yorkshire accent and is slim with a deeply lined forehead and short, wiry greying hair. He is dressed in a crew-neck jumper and jeans.

'I've only just got here. The train was a bit late.'

'That's OK then. I just popped into work and got caught up. How are you?' he asks, as they pull onto the main road.

'I'm fine. It was good not having to get up and go to work this morning.'

214

'Did you have to take a day's holiday?'

'Yep.'

'How was work this week?'

'Bad. Nobody's buying anything,' Craig says, staring out of the window as they pass the bars and takeaways along Prince of Wales Road.

'How's the job hunting going?'

'Even worse. I'm signed up with lots of agencies, but none of them have come up with any better alternatives.'

'Have you tried more estate agents?'

'Yes, but because the market's quiet, nobody is taking anyone on. And the fact I work for Cinq doesn't help much either. I'd rather forget work at the moment.'

They stop at traffic lights opposite Castle Mall shopping centre.

'What do you think of the new car?'

'It's all right,' Craig says.

'I did ask for one with a wooden house on the roof but they'd sold out,' Peter says.

Craig doesn't react.

They drive along Church Road, which is lined with large detached houses half-hidden by trees and hedges. Peter turns in between two overgrown conifers and parks in front of the garage. The Tennants' house is a modest three-bedroom 1930s property with a buttermilk exterior and racing green front door.

Peter stops to look at the flowerbeds under the front windows as Craig let himself in. The house smells of paint. He takes his bag upstairs and goes straight to his old room at the far end of the landing.

The bedroom is bare and an upright vacuum cleaner has been left in the middle of the floor. There is nothing on the freshly-painted peach walls and the new chest of drawers and wardrobe are empty. The lamp on the desk beside the double bed doesn't have a bulb in it. Craig puts his bag on the floor at the foot of a small bookcase containing leather-bound photo albums, and accidently kicks a polystyrene tray of paint pots and brushes. He stands at the window looking down onto the back garden and then checks under the bed where he finds a plastic storage box full of his old football medals and trophies.

A car pulls up outside and there is some muffled talking. Craig goes back downstairs and puts his shoes on.

The front door opens and he gives his mum a hug and a kiss on the cheek. Janet is a foot shorter than her son and has sandy hair tied in a bun. She has a thin face and a sagging double chin.

Craig carries the shopping bags from his mum's Renault Clio through to the farmhouse-style kitchen where she makes tea whilst his dad sits at the table reading *The Times*. He asks Craig what he thinks of his room. Craig wants to know what's happened to the rest of his stuff.

'Will you need picking up later? Janet asks, as she pulls up in the puddle-scarred car park.

'I'm not sure. I'll ring you.'

'Are you sure you'll be warm enough?' she says looking at Craig, who is wearing an old waterproof jacket over his jumper.

'It's not cold; it's just a bit wet. I'll be fine.'

'Say hello to Tony and Adam from us.'

'Will do.'

He kisses his mum on the cheek, closes the car door behind him and walks across into the Dereham Athletic clubhouse. It is a wide, single-storey brick building with a brass plaque by the door marking its reopening in May 2007.

The bar is warm and homely with a red patterned carpet, framed shirts on the walls and a trophy cabinet full of silverware. Five tubby old men dressed in red and yellow club ties stand talking and supping ale. Away from the bar, a group of children sit at tables with colouring books and soft drinks, supervised by two mothers.

Tony has already bought Craig a pint from the girl behind the bar. They sit on stools looking out to the pitch where the two teams are warming up. It's beginning to rain. The Lakenham Town manager is shouting instructions from underneath a golf umbrella as his team jog across the width of the pitch. Adam, wearing a club tracksuit and white boots, is chatting to a Dereham teammate and sucking on an energy drink as he goes through a series of stretches. He's grown a beard since he visited Craig in London.

Craig looks up at the collection of team photographs that hang over the bar. 'I'm trying to think of the last time I came here,' he says. 'I don't think it was last season.'

'Were you not here for the Norfolk Vase semi last year?'

'No, I was working.'

Tony sips his beer and then orders a packet of cheese and onion crisps. 'Have you thought about playing in London?' he asks Craig.

'I don't really have time, mate. I'd like to but I couldn't go training and I couldn't play most Saturdays.'

'Why don't you play on Sundays then?'

Craig flicks at the zip on his jacket. 'I suppose I could, but Sunday's the only day I get a lie in. If I was playing, I couldn't drink that much on a Saturday night and don't get much of a chance to go out, and I'm useless with a hangover. Also I wouldn't know where to join. I don't think anyone at work plays and I don't really want to just turn up somewhere on my own.'

'There must be loads of teams you could play for though.'

'Yeah, but it's not like being up here. I haven't seen that many sports clubs, it's more park football. People seem to prefer going to the gym, or running on their own.'

As the players amble back to the changing rooms to get ready for kick-off, a groundsman in a cagoule spikes the pitch with a fork.

Craig is accosted by a barrel-chested man in a Pringle jumper who asks him if he's going to come back and play this season.

The rain stops just before kick-off but the pitch is saturated, making it difficult for both teams to play with any fluidity. Adam takes several heavy tackles from the lumbering Lakenham centre-back who is marking him.

It is 0-0 at half-time and neither side has had a shot on target. Some of the Lakenham players look jaded as they leave the pitch in their mud-splattered kit, which has turned from white to grey in the wet.

Craig and Tony go back to the bar. Craig pays for the beers and glances up at the team photograph from the 2005/6 season. He is in the front row, second from the left. They take their drinks outside and squelch around the perimeter of the pitch, stopping between the two dug-outs.

Dereham take the lead from a corner when Lakenham's goalkeeper drops the ball at the feet of Dereham's right-back who taps in from two yards. Neither Tony nor Craig recognise him. Their second goal comes from a penalty after a handball, and Adam scores the third. He is put clean through, shoots straight at the 'keeper but knocks in the rebound after the ball holds up in a puddle.

The Lion is a traditional, intimate pub on the corner of two quiet residential streets. Its high ceiling and large windows make it feel spacious but drinkers are crammed around small tables and those standing have to constantly move as people jostle to get served. The sound of chat and laughter drowns out the juke box.

Some of the Dereham team are playing pool in an alcove to the right of the bar. They are drunk and keep sinking the cue ball by mistake.

Adam and Tony are at a table near the door, underneath an old photograph of three farm workers on a combine harvester. Outside, rain is hammering down from the black sky. A drenched young woman enters and shakes herself off in the doorway.

Craig pushes his way through the bar carrying a jug of lager and places it carefully on the table. Tony makes to pick it up but Adam stops him.

'Does it seem a bit boring coming back here?' Adam asks Craig.

'No, not at all. It's different. I miss it a bit to be honest.'

'It's cheaper,' Tony says.

'Home's home isn't it,' Craig says.

'Did you not invite Mark up for the weekend?' Adam asks.

Craig smiles. 'Ha, no. I don't think watching you play football and a few drinks in here is his idea of fun.'

'Where is he tonight?' Adam asks. 'Some posh nightclub throwing his money around?'

'I don't know actually. He's been really quiet for the last couple of weeks. He broke up with his girlfriend.'

'He had a girlfriend?' says Tony. 'Who was she?'

'I didn't know anything about her,' Craig says. 'She just turned up one morning at the flat.'

'What did she look like? Please don't tell me she was fit,' Adam says.

Craig laughs. 'No. She was big. Taller than you. No wonder he kept quiet about her. He was bringing other girls back to our place anyway, so it's not like it was ever going to last.'

'I was going to ask how you put up with him, but I suppose he's a constant source of entertainment,' Adam says.

'He's not always been like that, though. He was just showing off when you came down. He was pretty quiet at uni. He's changed since he started his job and now has a bit of money. He didn't really have anything to be full of himself about when I first knew him. He's an OK bloke if you can see past the bullshit.'

'Money wouldn't change me,' Tony says.

'No, you'd still be an idiot,' Adam says. 'What's happening with you and that girl from work, Craig? The one that blew us out. Anna was it?'

'No, Hannah. She didn't blow us out, she had to go home. There's nothing happening anyway, and I'm pretty sure nothing's going to happen.'

'Why?'

'Because she's fit?' Tony says.

'She's not that fit,' Adam says.

'She is,' Craig snaps back.

'Yeah, but she's gettable. Don't build her up too much otherwise you'll never ask her out.'

'It might make things difficult at work anyway.'

'Forget work. If she's as nice as you say she is, and she's single, and you get on, she'll probably go out for a drink with you even just out of politeness. Don't come on too strong or act mental and you've always got a chance. Back yourself.'

'That's the problem.'

'Mate, if you don't do it someone else will.'

'Cheers, but it just doesn't feel right at the moment though. And I haven't got any money to take her anywhere.'

'Don't worry about that. Just don't wait for something to happen because if you do that you'll never get anywhere.'

*

Peter and Janet have booked a table with a view of the river at The Duke's Head for Sunday lunch. Two swans are floating serenely near the water's edge despite the rain. Craig's eyes are red and puffy and Tony keeps yawning. Adam is the last to arrive.

During lunch, the subject of the boys' weekend in London comes up and Craig kicks Tony under the table when he starts talking about the bar bill in Mankini. Peter looks disapprovingly at Craig but he convinces his dad that Mark paid for it all.

Adam asks Craig's parents how the business is going, tactfully changing the subject. Peter says that one of their major competitors went bust last week, so they've been able to pick up some extra orders on the back of that, but everyone is holding their breath.

*

'What time train are you getting?' Peter asks as he joins his son in the living room.

'I'll have a look on the internet,' Craig says. 'I'll probably go around seven. Is that all right?'

'That's fine.'

Craig has his feet up on the sofa and is watching the Wigan v Man City match on the television, which sits inside an oak cabinet. Either side of the unit are bookshelves full of hardback sports autobiographies and antiques and gardening reference books.

Peter sits down in an armchair and flicks through a Cotton Traders catalogue that comes with *The Sunday Times*. He is dressed almost identically to the male model on the cover, wearing chinos and green check shirt. He closes the catalogue and drops it into a magazine holder beside his chair.

'Any chances?' he asks.

'They've only been playing ten minutes,' Craig says.

Janet knocks on the patio doors and waves her muddy trowel. Peter waves back. Craig cranes his neck and smiles.

'A letter came for you the other day,' Peter says. 'From HSBC. Mum opened it by mistake.'

Craig doesn't say anything.

The back door closes and Janet is humming to herself in the kitchen.

'Don't you want to know what it said?'

'It was probably just about my account wasn't it?'

'No. It wasn't. It was turning down your application to have your credit card limit increased.' Peter pauses. 'Is there anything you'd like to tell me?'

Craig turns to his dad and sits up. 'I've just been a bit short recently. I just needed some money to get me through until the end of the month.'

'Why didn't you come to me?'

'I don't want to keep borrowing money off you, Dad.'

'Craig, it's better you borrow from me than borrow from the bank. How much is your overdraft at the moment?'

He looks out into the garden. 'Six thousand,' he mumbles.

'*What?* And you're up to the limit?'

'Yes, just about.'

'How much interest are you paying a month?'

'About eighty pounds.'

'Bloody hell, Craig! That's just throwing money down the drain. What are you spending the money on?'

'Rent and bills... and petrol.'

'How much is the rent on the new place?'

'It's working out at over a thousand a month.'

'Craig, that's an obscene amount for someone on your salary.'

'I know, I know, but when we moved in I'd had a few good months and it seemed affordable. But since then the market's slowed I've not made the commission.'

'But you've still got your basic salary though.'

'That doesn't go anywhere.'

'Is it still seventeen thousand?'

'No. They've changed the pay structure to put more emphasis on sales. It seemed good at the time. I was taking home a lot more, for a while.'

'What is your basic then?'

Craig sighs. 'Four thousand five hundred.'

Peter shuffles forward in his chair, his brow furrowed. 'You're working for a basic of four thousand pounds a year? Craig, what were you thinking? The boy who comes in at the weekend to help clean the lorries gets more than that!'

Janet enters the living room carrying a pot of tea. 'What's wrong?'

'Do you know how much work are paying him?' Peter says. 'Four thousand a year! It's bloody slave labour.'

Janet puts the tray down. 'Now, don't get angry,' she says, seemingly not taking in what he was saying.

'Did you choose to go on this commission structure or did they make you?'

'I chose. It seemed like the best thing to do.'

Peter shakes his head. 'And no doubt they encouraged you?'

'Yes.'

'Craig, why didn't you talk to me you daft sod?'

'Peter, don't talk to him like that.'

'It's obvious why they did it. They can get away with paying you nothing whilst you work all hours because you're desperate for the money because the market's slumping.'

'It's meant to pick up soon.'

'How long will that take? Months? Years? All the while you're racking up thousands of pounds of debt.'

'It's not like that.'

'Well what is it like? How much money have you got on credit cards?'

'A fair bit.'

'How much? Exactly. And tell me the truth.'

Craig glances up at his mum who is standing beside him and then looks across to his dad. 'About ten thousand,' he murmurs, 'over four cards. I'm sorry. And I borrowed two thousand from Atlantic Finance.' He coughs and bites on his thumb.

'Jesus Christ, Craig!' Peter shouts.

'Oh, love.' Janet sits next to her son and put her arm around him. Craig leans forward, his head dangling towards the floor.

'It's hardly the time for sympathy, Janet.'

'Why didn't you tell us?' she asks.

'Sorry. I'm sorry.'

'I was always against you moving to London and you know that,' she says.

'Janet, please, that's not the issue here,' Peter says.

'If he was still here with us, he wouldn't be in this mess.'

'Janet, he's twenty-five. You can't keep him locked up. The problem is the bloody job and the rent. How many credit cards did you say you had?'

'Four,' Craig sighs, closing his eyes.

'We knew something was up when that letter came through, but bloody hell, Craig.'

'I needed the money,' Craig says. 'I had to do something to pay the rent. I didn't want to keep asking you. Dad, I was trying to be independent, I hate having to keep asking you for everything. I feel like a child.'

'Where's the money gone you saved when you were here?'

'I used it.'

'Drinking?' his mum asks.

'He's paying a thousand pounds a month in rent, Janet. I'm surprised he can eat, let alone go out.'

'Couldn't you have found somewhere cheaper?'

'I thought I could afford it at the time,' Craig says.

'Pushed into it by Mark no doubt,' Peter says.

'No, we both agreed. I knew it was a lot but I just had to make sure I kept the money coming in. It's work. Nothing's happening.' Craig picks at a fingernail to avoid his dad's gaze.

'What are the others at work doing? They can't be taking home anything either,' Peter says.

'No, they're not. Quite a few of them have left.'

'Are you still looking for other jobs?'

'Yes, when I get the time. But I'm working so much. It's difficult.'

'Have you been to more recruitment agencies?'

'Yes, a couple but whatever I'm interested in they just tell me that I haven't got the experience or the qualifications.'

'But you've got a degree,' Janet says.

'So has everyone else, and from better universities than me. It counts for nothing.'

Peter sips his tea and sits back in his chair, exasperated. 'Do you owe anyone else money?' His tone is now calmer and more controlled.

'Like who?'

'Anyone. People at work, loan sharks?'

'No, of course I don't. Dad you know I wouldn't do that.'

'Don't be silly, Peter.'

'I don't think I'm the silly one here. I was just checking. If you are in any other kind of trouble, now's the time to tell us.'

'No, there's nothing. I'm hardly spending anything. The train ticket back here is the most expensive thing I've bought this month.'

'What are you eating?' Janet asks.

'I go to Asda late at night and pick up the discounted stuff before they throw it away.'

Janet hugs her son and kisses him on the side of the head. 'Craig, I could cry hearing you talk like this.'

Peter takes a pad and pen from the walnut bureau and hands it to Craig:

'Write down absolutely everything you owe and don't leave anything out.'

'OK.'

'Have you paid this month's rent yet?'

'Yes.'

'Well at least that's something,' Peter says, taking out his pocket calculator. 'Look Craig, you might not want our help but you're going to get it whether you bloody like it or not.'

CHAPTER TWENTY-FOUR

L ambeth Council have sent Craig a letter informing him that his 'name and facial image' have been published on a website of drug users in Brixton. It also warns him that they withhold the right to use his image on any future anti-drugs poster and/or television campaign. The web address where Craig can see himself is underlined at the bottom of the letter. Also enclosed is a leaflet for 'Crack Up', an independent drug counselling service based in Stockwell.

Craig tears the letter and leaflet in half and throws them in the bin. He changes out of his work suit into shorts and a sweatshirt and goes into the kitchen to make dinner.

It's dark when Mark gets home. He tosses his rucksack into his room and gets a bottle of Evian from the fridge. His cheeks are flushed and his hair is unstyled.

Craig is lying on the sofa with Mark's MacBook on his stomach. He asks Mark where he's been.

'Gym,' he answers.

'What gym?'

'A new one's opened near work. I've got a corporate membership.'

'What is it, Fitness First?'

'No, it's a Pump House. They're a new chain aimed at blokes. It's mainly weight training and boxing. There's no pool, or yoga classes or anything bent like that.'

'What did you do tonight?' Craig asks, uninterested.

'Just did a bit of circuit training and then worked on my delts.'

Craig watches as Mark, whose suit trousers don't appear as tight as usual, puts a family-sized Marks and Spencer chicken arrabbiata in the microwave and stands flexing his biceps and rubbing his shoulders.

The microwave pings and Mark scoops the smouldering pasta into a bowl and sits at the table, using an old *FHM* as a placemat. He stops once he's eaten half of it and forks the remains into a Tupperware container which he leaves by the fridge. He briefly flicks through the magazine his bowl was resting on and then stares at the blank television screen. Craig is tapping away on the laptop.

'Why haven't you pulled the blinds?' Mark asks.

'It's only just got dark.'

'We should keep them closed at night. You never know who's watching.'

'I know who's watching,' Craig says. 'Nobody.'

'That's what you'd like to think. People would try to nick our TV if they knew it was here.'

'They wouldn't get very far. It'd take ten blokes to carry it.'

'A gang might steal it.' Mark closes the magazine. 'Sell any houses today?'

'What do you think?'

'Never mind. We can't all be good at our jobs.'

'Fuck off, Mark,' Craig says flatly.

'I was only joking. There's always tomorrow,' he says. 'What are you doing anyway?'

'I'm on Facebook.'

'Stalking Hannah again?'

'No.'

'Have you seen the photos of her holiday?'

'No,' he says, looking up at Mark's grinning face. 'Which holiday?'

'Thailand. The one she's just come back from.'

'How do you know...? How have you seen them?'

'They're on her friend's page.'

'You're not even friends with Hannah are you?'

'Yes.'

Craig frowns and picks at a small scab on his knee. He then goes back to Hannah's Facebook profile and searches in vain for the photographs before shutting the MacBook and lowering it onto the floor.

'Couldn't you find them?' Mark asks.

'I wasn't looking.'

'Would you like to see them? I could show you... but if you're not that bothered...'

Craig looks at the wall. 'Show me then,' he says, irritated. 'You're clearly dying to.'

He sits up and Mark shuffles along next to him. Mark logs onto Facebook, making sure that Craig can't see his password, and finds the profile of Emily Ferley, a pretty girl with pink sparkling lips.

'Who's she?' Craig asks.

'A friend of Hannah's. I did some detective work: I saw that she'd written something on Hannah's wall about Thailand so I clicked on her and there was a whole album of holiday photos. She just hasn't tagged them yet.'

Craig sits forward as Mark opens the album. There are forty-two thumbnail photos, initially of Hannah, Emma Ferley and another, unnamed girl in a hotel room. Mark clicks through to the second page.

'Here's what you want to see,' he says.

He selects a photo of Hannah sunbathing on a beach in Koh Samui. She is smiling and wearing a white bikini and large, square sunglasses. Craig studies it and takes control. He slowly scrolls through shots of palm tree lined beaches, an elephant trek, the chaotic streets of Bangkok, and then stops on one of Hannah posing on the back of a boat off the coast of the Phi Phi Islands. She is holding a snorkel and squinting in the sun. The next photo shows her in the sea, her wet hair pasted to her head and droplets of water glistening on her tanned shoulders.

'You probably want to stop there, mate,' Mark says.

'There's only a few left-'

'You've seen the good ones. Seriously, can I have it back now, I need to email-'

'I'll be two seconds.'

The next photo is tagged as 'Full Moon party'. There's a dark, crowded, fire-lit beach and the three girls are only wearing shorts and bikini tops. Their bodies are covered in luminous handprints and they have yellow and orange dots and squiggles over their faces. Hannah is holding a pink bucket that their other friend is drinking out of. The next shot has a tall, deeply tanned man wearing a fluorescent green headband with his arms around Hannah and Emma. In the next photo he's painting something on Hannah's chest and she's laughing. In the final photo, they are kissing.

Mark looks at Craig and goes to speak but stops. Craig doesn't look away from the screen and logs Mark out.

'I tried to warn you,' Mark says.

'Cheers,' Craig says, deflated.

'Mate, everyone pulls on holiday.'

'I don't.'

'That's because you never go on holiday. What are you so upset about anyway? You whacked it on that girl from the *Addams Family* right in front of Hannah the other week.'

'I was smashed. I didn't know what I was doing.'

'At least the bloke Hannah's with is good-looking.'

'Is that meant to make me feel better?'

Mark checks his BlackBerry. 'You've not even pulled Hannah though have you?'

'You know I haven't.'

'And you never will unless you actually try.'

'I have tried, sort of.'

'What do you mean, "sort of"?'

Craig gets up and walks to the kitchen. Mark follows him.

'Don't ignore the question,' Mark says.

'Do you want a drink? I'm having a beer.'

'Err, yeah OK. Stop ignoring the question.'

Craig takes two bottles of Carlsberg from the fridge.

'Well?' Mark says.

'Well what?'

'What do you mean you've "sort of" tried to pull Hannah?'

Craig opens the beers and sits on the worktop. 'I asked her if she wanted to go to the cinema last weekend but she said she was going home for her sister's birthday.'

Mark laughs. 'So?'

'So, she turned me down.'

'No she didn't. She had something else on.'

'It sounded like an excuse.'

'What made you think she wasn't telling the truth?'

'I don't know. It was just the way she said it I suppose.'

'Why, did she take ages to answer?'

'No, but-'

'Have you spoken to her since?'

'Not much.'

'You know she's probably wondering why you're ignoring her.'

'I doubt it.' Craig shrugs and places his beer between his legs.

'Mate, if you like her so much, why don't you do something about it?'

'I tried to.'

'You were hardly going to win her over with two tickets to *X-Men* and a Pizza Express. Cinema dates are for teenagers anyway. You need to get her in a situation where it's not just the two of you so it's not awkward, and where she's very drunk. Fire Bombs is really the ideal place. Does she go there a lot?'

'No. Hardly ever.'

'Umm.' Mark clicks his fingers. 'I'm just trying to think of somewhere you could go together where it wouldn't be weird for you to ask her.'

'She's quite sporty.'

'Craig, what are you going to do? Take her to a Norwich game?'

'No, I was just trying to think of something we have in common, apart from work.'

'Well perhaps work is the angle you should use. Why don't you send round an email in your office on Friday asking if anyone wants to go down the pub? If Hannah fancies a drink, she'll go, if she doesn't you can send her a jokey email saying that you're disappointed she's not coming.'

'Won't that look weird?'

'Only if you start acting weird.'

'But I don't like anyone else in the office – I don't even know half of them – and if Christian comes, which he definitely would, he'd stick to her like glue all night.'

'I thought she didn't like him?'

'She doesn't.'

'Well that's perfect then; you've got a mutual enemy. You should take every opportunity to take the piss out of him in front of her and then, when she lets her guard down, you should suggest going for a drink.'

'I'm not sure that would work.'

'You'll never find out if you don't try.'

'I suppose so. It's just, I'm not sure that she thinks about me in that way. Perhaps I'd be better off just trying to become better friends with her first.'

'No. That's the worst idea ever. Guys who try to worm their way in with girls by being friends always leave empty-handed. Once you start being friends with a girl, you can kiss any chance of sleeping with them goodbye. One minute you're going shoe shopping with them, the next minute they're telling you about a guy they've sucked off outside a nightclub.'

'Hannah's not like that.'

'You've got to be a bit clever. No girls want a bloke who's going to follow them around like a lovesick puppy. It's boring. How often do you see a girl with a bloke who looks like an arrogant twat?'

'All the time.'

'Exactly. The blokes may be twats, but because they act like they're something special, girls start to think there's something special about them, even when there isn't.'

'What are you suggesting I do then?'

'Just don't act like a drip. Actually pulling that girl in Fire Bombs might turn out to be a good thing, even though she was rabid. It showed Hannah that you can pull, probably making her jealous, and that you're not that bothered about her.'

'But I am.'

'Yes, we know that, but as soon as she knows, she'll lose interest, if she has any in the first place. How did seeing that photo of Hannah kissing that bloke make you feel?'

'If I'm honest... a bit sad.'

'Craig, that's a loser's mentality. It should make you feel more determined. If you don't make a move on her soon, it could end up being too late.'

'Yeah, I know, but it's never the right time.'

'You've got to make it the right time. Take the initiative for once. Can we go and sit down please, I think the wrestling's on.'

The pair go back into the living room and Craig passes Mark the four remote controls it takes to operate the television and surround sound. On the screen, a woman with fake breasts hits a huge oily man over the head with a fold-up chair in an underground car park. Mark turns the sound up. The wrestling cuts to a car advert and he turns the volume back down.

'When did Hannah break up with her boyfriend?' Mark asks.

'A while ago now.' Craig is stretched out with his hands behind his head.

'Who was he?'

'Some bloke who she'd been with since she was sixteen.'

'What did he do?'

'He worked for some Japanese bank. I think he had lots of money.'

'Not necessarily.'

'He'd still have more money than me. They went on holiday to Barbados just before they broke up so he can't be penniless. Why are you suddenly trying to be helpful anyway?'

'It's all those endorphins being released after exercise; they put me in a good mood. And I'm bored of seeing you looking miserable. I thought you might benefit from my advice.'

'I was forgetting what an expert with women you are.'

'I pulled more girls than you did at uni.'

'You pulled more rank girls.'

'I would never discriminate against a girl just because of what she looks like. I'm an equal opportunities puller.'

Craig smiles. 'You've got that right.'

Mark turns the volume back up and flicks over to *Shameless*. 'I'm not here tomorrow night, by the way.'

'OK.'

'I'm going to dinner with Amy.'

'You've been out with her a lot recently, haven't you?'

'Yeah, but only because we've both got client hospitality budgets to spend. If you spend less than two grand a month on entertaining, Justin starts asking questions.'

'Aren't you meant to take clients?'

'Yes, but he never checks who you're with.'

'Where are you going?'

'I suggested Nando's but Amy has booked us a table at Manger Sans Yeux - the place where you eat in the dark.'

Craig looks across at Mark. 'You eat in the dark? What's the point in that?'

'It's meant to improve your other senses so you appreciate the flavours of the food more.'

'And you sit there in the pitch black?'

'Yep.'

'How do you order?'

'You order before you go in.'

'How expensive is it?'

'I'm not sure. It's French cuisine though so it won't be cheap.'

'And you sit there in complete darkness and you're expected to eat and drink?'

'*Yes.*'

'How would you know what you're eating if you can't see it?'

'By tasting it, obviously.'

'How about if it's undercooked? It's not like the waiters would know. How do they even know they're bringing the food to the right table?'

'I'm not sure,' Mark replies, getting annoyed.

'They must use night vision goggles or something.'

'Craig, it's a restaurant, not *Silence of the Lambs*.'

Mark goes to his room with his laptop and Craig grabs the remote controls. There is the sound of a printer in action. Mark emerges holding a printed sheet and sneaks into Craig's bedroom without him noticing. He's only in there a few seconds and then goes back and sits with him.

'You know what we should do?' Mark says.

'No. What?'

'Have a party. Here.'

'Why?'

'To get Hannah and other girls over here of course. It'd be perfect. We'd get loads of booze, music and get smashed.'

'Umm, who'd pay for it?'

'It'd cost hardly anything. People would bring drinks.'

'What other girls could we invite?'

'Girls we've pulled. There are loads of girls who'd come over.'

'Name some.'

'Amy. All the girls from my work. And your new best mate down the hall and her friends.'

Craig looks sceptical. 'I'm not sure it's the best idea.'

'Why? You'll never get a better chance to impress Hannah. If we can throw a great party, it'll make you look cool.'

'People might come in off the street and steal our stuff like you always say they will.'

'I'll hire doormen. We'd invite people from work, the old uni boys, and our other mates. Think about how good it'd be. We could get a DJ and put lights up everywhere. Make it like a club.'

'I literally can't afford to pay for anything though,' Craig says.

'It won't be expensive.'

'And I don't think the neighbours would be pleased.'

'We'll invite them, they'd love it. I'll put an event on Facebook,' Mark insists. 'When can we have it?'

'I don't know, Mark. It's your party; you're in charge of organisation.'

'We should have it soon so we can use the terrace before it gets too cold. How about next weekend?'

'Too soon. People need some notice. And I need to check Hannah can come.'

'The weekend after? I'm not doing anything.'

'That's still pretty short notice though.' Craig takes his phone out of his pocket and checks the calendar. 'How about the weekend after that? The 4th?'

'Sorted. Mate, if people know that we're having a party, *everyone* will come. Trust me.'

'I'll take your word for it,' Craig says, yawning. 'Not that you'll ever get around to arranging it. I think I might go to bed.'

'OK, night. Start making a list of party guests.'

'What, in my sleep? I'll do it tomorrow.'

Craig makes a mug of cocoa and wanders to his room. Above his headboard, Mark has blu-taked an A4 colour print out of Hannah kissing the guy at the Full Moon party.

'Cock,' Craig mutters, tearing the picture off the wall.

CHAPTER TWENTY-FIVE

There are only five people waiting on the eastbound Central line platform at Bank; four Australian backpackers and Mark, who is standing in front of a Maximuscle poster with his iPod headphones in his ears.

The tube rumbles into the station and the doors open. Mark sits down opposite a man with long greasy hair who has a guitar case between his legs. Next to Mark, an Indian man with a droopy moustache folds up a copy of the *Metro* and drops it over his shoulder into the narrow gap between his head and the window. The tube arrives at Liverpool Street and jolts to a stop.

Mark taps his Oyster card on the reader and proceeds up the steps onto the overland station's bright, busy concourse. A suited man on crutches is limping his way towards Platform 17 through the fast-moving flow of commuters. Nobody is queuing in the thirty-bay ticket office. Above Mark's head the giant electronic board displays the departure times of trains to Stansted Airport, Cambridge, Great Yarmouth and Norwich.

He queues at the cash machines at the foot of the stairs leading up to ground level and stares up at the parade of shops that overlook the concourse: Marks and Spencer, Tie Rack, Supercuts, Vodafone, and, directly ahead of him, McDonald's and Pret A Manger. Mark withdraws £20, checks his watch and treats himself to a strawberry and granola breakfast pot in Pret.

A crowd of office workers have gathered outside The Broker, the pub on the corner of Liverpool Street and Old Broad Street. There's a lot of shoulder shrugging and glum expressions. Mark watches as the doors are unbolted and they file in. He looks at his watch again. It is 11 a.m. 'Someone's celebrating,' he says to himself as he licks his plastic spoon clean.

In a quiet corner of Starbucks, a woman in a long coat is crying into her mobile phone. Her mascara is running. Mark orders a venti white chocolate mocha to take away and wanders around the corner to his office.

There are four television crews outside filming ashen-faced MenDax employees leaving the building, carrying their possessions in filing boxes. A bald man with a fawn trench coat slung over his arm pushes a TV cameraman out of his path. The woman who follows him out of the revolving doors doesn't say a word when a reporter asks her what the atmosphere is like inside. A bemused-looking graduate is telling ITN that this was meant to be his first day.

A microphone is thrust under Mark's nose and he is asked for his reaction to the news. He knocks it out of the way and points to his earphones. He pushes his way inside against the tide of departing staff, swipes his ID card and waits by the lifts.

The doors on the far left roll back and its passengers spill out into the reception. Two tubby men are arguing. Mark gets into the empty lift and selects the twelfth floor.

The Scandinavian markets department is deserted. The computers are off and it's silent. Mark pulls his headphones out. Amy's handbag is on her desk next to an uneaten croissant. A scarf is draped over the back of her chair. He plugs his dead BlackBerry into the charger on his desk and turns on his PC, sipping his coffee as the computer boots up.

Amy walks in through the glass doors. Her eyes are streaming and she's holding a packet of tissues.

'I thought you might have been here earlier,' she says to Mark, dabbing her nose.

'I had a meeting.'

'With Runoff?'

'No. One of my clients.'

'How much did they have invested?' Amy asks, taking another tissue from the packet.

'Not much at the moment,' Mark says focussing on his computer screen. 'I was trying to get them to put in another ten million.' Suddenly he stops. 'WOOHW WOOHW WOOHW WOOHW WOOHW! WHAT THE FUCK IS THIS?!' he shouts.

He turns his computer screen to Amy. *MenDax Wealth Management collapses* is the top story on the BBC Business website. He rocks back in his seat with his mouth wide open.

'Christ, Mark. Please tell me you're joking. Where have you been? Haven't you read the emails? It was even on the news.'

'I've had meetings.'

'Don't talk crap, Mark. Why do you think there are television cameras outside? Why do you think everyone downstairs is clearing their desks and going home? Why do you think there's nobody here and I've been crying? Are you really that fucking unobservant?'

'Don't swear at me, Amy. I thought you were upset about something.'

'I am upset, Mark. I'm upset because I haven't got a job. And if I haven't got a job, I can't pay my mortgage.' Amy starts crying again.

'I'm too busy to watch the news.'

'Busy? Busy doing what? No wonder this company has gone bust with clowns like you working here.'

'What do you mean gone bust? And I'm not a clown.'

'What bit about going bust don't you understand?'

'It can't be. We've got loads of money.'

'Not any more. Anyway we never had money. It all belonged to other people.'

'But surely we've got something.'

'Loansbanki collapsed over the weekend.'

'What?'

'Loansbanki went into receivership. It's now owned by the Icelandic government. How can you not have seen that anywhere?'

'So? Surely we'll get all the money back.'

'No. We probably won't get any of it back.'

'But not all of our money was in Loansbanki was it?'

'No, Mark. Not all of it, just ninety-six per cent.'

'What, this can't be right. There must be something we can do.'

'What do you mean?'

'Well, don't we need to have a meeting with Justin or something?'

'Mark, MenDax has shut down. It no longer exists. We don't have jobs. There's no company to have a meeting about, you idiot.'

Mark closes the webpage. 'Where are the others? Justin must be gutted. Hasn't he just bought a new house?'

'Forget Justin, Mark. He sensed this was coming.'

'What? How?'

'He's already got a new job.'

'What do you mean he's got a new job? Where?'

'He's working for Runoff Investment Securities.'

'Who?'

'They're American. A private wealth management company. They're based in New York, but they're opening a London office which Justin is going to be running. Have you heard of Reggie Runoff? Big American financier.'

'Yes, of course. How do you know this?'

'Ian told me. He came in earlier to pick up his stuff.' Amy sniffs.

'How did he know?'

'Him and Julia are going to work there as well.'

'What?' Mark's jaw drops even further and his eyes narrow until they are tiny slits.

'Justin's taking them with him. This must have been going on for months. I thought the three of them kept disappearing together for meetings. They were probably having interviews. I thought you'd be with them actually.'

'Why, because I was Justin's number two?'

'No, because you were out of the office so much.'

Mark turns on his BlackBerry and reads the emails confirming what Amy has told him. 'Have you phoned Justin?'

'What would I want to talk to him for?'

'I'm going to call him. This can't be right. He wouldn't do this. We must be going there as well. We were best mates.'

Mark calls his former boss and leaves a message asking him to call him when he has a moment.

'He wasn't your mate, Mark,' Amy says.

'Yes he was. Think of all the nights out we went on. We *are* mates.'

'Those were just to keep you sweet.'

'No they weren't. He used to tell me I'd be his successor. He said I'd have fifty staff under me by Christmas.'

'Is that why he gave you the smallest bonus in the department?'

'What? That's not true. I got more than you did. And anyway my bonus was only that size because my salary was going to treble when we bought those other companies.'

237

'What other companies?' Amy says, shaking her head.

'I'm not sure, Justin didn't say.'

'Mark, go and look in Justin's office.'

'Why?'

'Because he's left the bonus structure on his desk, just in case we don't get the message that he doesn't want us.'

'How do you know they're right?'

'My bonus is right. It's the second smallest.'

'But it wasn't that much was it?'

'Go and look for yourself.'

Mark rushes into Justin's office. All of the personal items - the framed certificates, the family photographs, the portrait, the putter, even the coat stand - have gone. In the middle of the desk is a single sheet of A4 with the names of the five department members and their 2008 bonus payments. Mark falls forward onto the desk, propping himself up with his outstretched arms. His head hangs and his eyes are closed.

After several minutes he pushes himself up and walks back to Amy at a funereal pace. His face is colourless.

'I feel sick,' he says, falling onto his chair. 'This is my 9/11.'

'I'm sorry, Mark. I don't want you to think I'm rubbing it in.'

Mark shakes his head. 'Sixty-five grand for Ian. *Ian*. That sap.'

'He was trying to get me to buy shares as well. He must have hated me.' Amy wipes her eyes.

'He gave you forty grand though. He told me I'd got one of the biggest. I think I'm going to be sick.'

Mark drags his fingers down his face, temporarily deforming his features, and then pulls his bin under his mouth and dry wretches. Amy watches in mild disgust.

'I think your phone's buzzing,' she says.

Mark's mobile is next to his keyboard. 'It's a text from Justin.'

'What does it say?'

He reads the message and then holds it up for Amy. It says: *MenDax has closed. Your unemployed, you twat. Good luck in life.*

'Little shitbag,' she says. 'And he's used the wrong you're. It should be apostrophe R E. Just about sums him up.'

Mark and Amy sit in silence. Mark opens his email inbox and deletes everything apart from an email from Mankini, which he forwards to his private account.

Amy is going through her desk drawers, throwing old bits of stationery and MenDax promotional material in the bin. She takes down the family photograph she has pinned to the right of her computer and slips it inside a Louise Bagshawe novel she has never started. She places the small make-up bag and mirror she kept at work into her handbag and offers Mark her croissant. Her desk is completely clear. There is no sign of her ever having been there.

'What are you going to do about your laptop?' she asks.

'I haven't thought about it. I don't want it. I've got a better one at home. I might just leave it on a train for somebody else to have.'

'Like the first two you had? I think I might take mine home.'

'You can't, can you?'

'Why not?'

'It's stealing.'

'I couldn't care less. What are they going to do? Sack me? If they want it back, they can come and get it.'

Mark shuts down his computer and throws the empty file on his desk in the bin. His desk drawers contain one copy of the *Metro* from November 2007 and a brochure from Porsche, both of which he disposes of.

'Why didn't someone stop this happening?' Mark asks, glumly tapping a pencil on the desk.

'Like who?'

'The directors.'

'The directors are the ones who have got us into this mess.'

'It's not their fault really though is it?'

'Mark, of course it's their fault. We had virtually all our money invested in one bank. Our fortunes were inexorably linked to Loansbanki. If they failed we failed. They're a bunch of selfish, brainless morons.'

'Come on, they're not morons are they? They're rich and successful businessmen.'

'Rich and successful? Mark, why are you defending these people? It's because of them we've lost our jobs. All of our investors have lost their money. They've milked this company for every penny. Do you know how much the board paid themselves in bonuses last year?'

'Um, no.'

'Over five hundred million. Five hundred million! For running a company that was completely reliant on the success of one corrupt bank.

It's madness.'

'Yeah, but they deserved that money then.'

'Why?' Amy's scowling.

'Because they did. It's how money works. You have to take risks.'

'They didn't take a risk. What they did was plain fucking stupidity.'

'No it wasn't. The investors knew the risks.'

'Mark, people came to us thinking that their money would be safe. Not that we'd just stick the whole lot in one high interest bank account and hope for the best.'

'They were taking a chance. Anyway, how about the hundreds of people working downstairs? I thought it was just us who used Loansbanki?'

'It was initially. But the returns were so good the senior management eventually channelled all of the incoming money there. Money that wasn't there originally, they had transferred.'

Mark stares out of the window. Every few seconds another person carrying a brown box crosses the road and disappears into Liverpool Street. There are a crowd of people drinking on the street outside The Broker. Mark's mobile phone is buzzing. It's Uncle John. He ignores it.

'Shall we go for a drink?' Amy suggests.

'OK. I've got time for one,' Mark says, with no hint of irony.

They push their chairs under their desks and take in the deserted office. Amy sighs despondently and puts her coat on.

'Don't worry about it,' Mark says. 'We'll get new jobs, no problem.'

He turns the lights off and they head out through the glass doors for the last time.

Outside, a smug BBC reporter asks the pair for the reaction to the collapse. Mark says he doesn't work for MenDax and carries on past.

The pub is packed. Some people are already drunk. A loud, bearded man in his fifties is drinking champagne with a group of indistinguishable male financiers who go outside in ones and twos to smoke. In one corner sit members of the MenDax post room team. They're all wearing company polo shirts and looking miserable.

Mark orders a Magners and buys Amy a vodka and orange. Amy talks about how, even when Lehman Brothers fell, she never thought they were vulnerable. She says that there are so many people unemployed now that competition for jobs is enormous. Mark tells her to stop being so depressing.

She asks Mark what he is going to do. He says that he'll either get a job somewhere else through one of his contacts or go on holiday for a while. She finishes her drink and says she's going. Mark asks her to stay longer, but she says she needs to update her CV. Mark downs the rest of his cider and follows her out of the door and across to the tube station. She tells Mark that she wants to be on her own, says she'll call him and leaves him standing at the ticket barriers.

He wanders in shock along Bishopsgate and up Threadneedle Street, towards Bank. He then purchases a sandwich and a Mars bar from Boots and sits on a bench outside the Royal Exchange, by the statue of Wellington. When he finishes his lunch he remains there, eyes fixed on the Bank of England, for almost an hour.

A clock chimes to signal two o'clock and Mark strides off down Poultry. He goes into Austin Reed, buys himself a new shirt and tie on his MenDax American Express card and gets on the Northern line back to Clapham.

*

The International Bank of Scotland's City branch is so vast and ornate that it takes Mark several minutes to locate the customer services desk. Once there, he tells Shelley – who is around forty and has a monotone voice - he wants to meet whoever is in charge of small business loans. She asks if he has an appointment. He says that he didn't think he'd need one. She asks him to take a seat.

Mark sits and places his red 'Business' folder on the table next to him. Shelley knocks on a giant arched door at the other end of the bank and goes in.

Mark reads over his business plan once again and avoids looking at the stream of stern-faced suit-wearers who file past. A cashier is trying to explain to a confused old lady that this isn't NatWest.

Shelley paces back over to Mark and tells him that someone can see him, but he'll have to wait an hour. To her surprise, he says that's fine.

Fred, a slim, confident Scot with short grey hair and a narrow, joyless face, shakes Mark's hand and welcomes him into his office. The walls are covered with gilt-framed John Constable landscapes and behind the antique mahogany desk is a tartan-covered gold throne. A set of skis are resting in the corner next to a full-size stuffed tiger. There is no computer.

Mark is invited to take a seat and offered a glass of mineral water. Fred settles down on his throne and apologises for keeping Mark so long.

'That doesn't matter,' Mark says.

'Shelley didn't really explain why you wanted to see me, so perhaps you could tell me a little about yourself and how you think we can be of assistance.'

Mark has a drink and clears his throat. 'Basically, I'm a young entrepreneur looking for a backer. My background is in high finance and I've got a degree in business and I want to borrow a small amount of money to help launch my next venture.'

'OK,' Fred says. 'What is your business?'

'I'm going to open a chain of luxury ice cream parlours around London and in all other major cities in Europe: Paris, Madrid, Barcelona, Berlin, Amsterdam, Los Angeles, Las Vegas.'

'Right,' says Fred, with a wry smile. 'That's certainly very ambitious.'

'Obviously not all at once though. I want to launch in London and then build from there.'

'What's your interest in ice cream? Do you have any experience of the ice cream trade?'

'I have conducted extensive market research and there's a gaping hole in the market to be exploited. Everyone loves ice cream, but at the moment the only places you can buy ice creams from are corner shops or those vans run by pikeys. People don't want to have to walk the streets eating their ice creams, and the USP of my business is that not only will we sell amazing ice cream - the real luxury stuff in thousands of flavours - we'll give the customer somewhere luxurious to sit and enjoy it. Think of it as being like a luxury ice cream restaurant.'

'I think I understand the concept,' Fred says. 'What market research have you done?'

'I carried out a survey in some of the most popular areas of London and the results were almost unanimous. I went to places like Clapham Common, Battersea Park, Hyde Park and I asked people if they like ice cream and everyone said "yes".'

'But that's not a basis for starting a business, that's just a straw poll. What research have you done into the ice cream market?'

'Lots. Do you know how many places there are exclusively selling upmarket ice cream in London?'

'No.'

'I'll tell you – none.'

'But why do you think that is? What proof have you got of the demand for an upmarket ice cream parlour?'

'The sales of ice cream are going up and up every year in shops and supermarkets. The average person in Britain consumes one hundred litres of ice cream a year yet there is no shop or restaurant that caters exclusively for ice cream lovers.'

Fred purses his lips. 'One hundred litres? That sounds like a lot.'

'It is a lot. If I can attract just a fraction of that custom I'd have a massively profitable business. Also, two hundred million rich tourists visit London every year. I'd absolutely clean up in the summer. I aim to make my chain an iconic luxury brand. I'm not selling them ice cream; I'm selling them a lifestyle. It's a lifestyle brand. If you buy one of my ice creams, it says something about you as a person.'

'What is your target market?'

'The rich. That's why I've already decided where I'm going to launch my first outlet.'

'Where?'

'On the King's Road, in that row of shops between Sloane Square and the Saatchi Gallery. It's one of the richest streets in the world. People who shop there have lots of money, and a lot of them have children, and children love ice cream.'

'Shop rents on the King's Road are very expensive.'

'Three hundred and fifty thousand a year.'

'How are you going to get these people into your shop?'

'By being a luxury brand that rich people would want to be associated with. It's essential that the business attracts the right sort of customer which is why I'd place my products right at the top end of the market. I'm not going to be selling cones for a pound, I'll be selling the best ice cream money can buy at prices only a select number of people can afford.'

'But aren't you limiting your market that way, if only a fraction of people can afford to buy your product?'

'No, I don't think so. If I made it too cheap, my shops would be overrun by teenagers and people with nowhere else to go. I want to make it look and feel more like a Bond Street jewellers. I want people to think twice before coming in.'

'How much are you planning to charge for your ice creams?'

'A cone would be at least ten pounds. A bowl of ice cream and a seat at a table would start at around twenty-five pounds per head.'

'And you think people would pay that?'

'Yes, definitely. My target customer is the woman who has just spent three grand on a handbag, or the man who's just bought himself a new Jacob Perville suit in Peter Jones and needs to take the kids somewhere for a treat. If people will pay three grand for a handbag, or two hundred grand for a car, they'll pay a tenner for an ice cream.'

'What makes you so sure?'

'I know how the rich think.'

Fred links his hands and brings his index fingers to his chin. 'Would you just sell ice cream? Do you think that people would buy ice cream in the middle of winter?'

'Ah, I've already thought of that. You know how in the summer Starbucks sell iced coffee, frappuccinos and other cold drinks? Well, I'd serve ice cream warm.'

'Warm, how would that work? Surely by its very nature it's a cold dish?'

'No, warm ice cream would be a huge seller. It would obviously still be cold to an extent, but I'd create new flavours which would warm people up, using brandy and other ingredients. Think of dry white wine. Wine is wet, but it can be dry at the same time. My ice cream would work to a similar theory. We'd have a designated winter range. People would love the innovation and the novelty. I'd also serve drinks of course: coffee, lemonade, tea, whatever people wanted depending on the time of year. Another factor is global warming. Scientists predict that in five years' time the average temperature will increase by around three degrees per year and when the weather gets hotter, people want to eat something that cools them down.'

Fred clicks his gold pen. 'Who's actually going to supply the product?'

'I'm in negotiations with several suppliers at the moment. One in Manchester and another based in Cornwall who makes bespoke flavours.'

'And how far have you got with negotiations with them?'

'I'm in the process of drawing up contracts.'

'So you already have some financial backing?'

'Yes. I have two private investors who have put in three hundred thousand each.'

'And who are they, may I ask?'

'My uncle and his business partner.'

Fred writes that down on his pad and then scribbles something else out. He looks intensely at Mark. 'You said you were an entrepreneur, Mark, but what actual experience have you got of running a business?'

'Yes,' Mark says and drinks some more water.

'Can you tell me what exactly?'

'At the moment I'm a junior director at Runoff Investment Securities.'

'Yes, but that's not *your* business is it?'

'No, that's my nine-to-five job. I've worked there since university to get experience in a corporate environment as I thought that was vital to my development as a businessman, but I also have another company that I run in my spare time. I'm a property developer.'

'And how long have you been doing that?'

'For a couple of years. I buy properties, mostly abroad, renovate them and then sell them on.'

'And you do that on your own?'

'No, with a business partner, Craig Tennant, he looks after the business on a day-to-day basis. I'm the majority shareholder and make all the big decisions.'

'And has your property business been making a profit?'

'Err, yes, we turned over £1.34 million last financial year.'

'That's a lot for a two-person operation.'

'But we have a team of contractors employed almost twelve months a year, so it's far more than just the two of us.'

'And you posted a profit?'

'Yes. Last year it was five hundred thousand.'

'You made a five hundred thousand pound profit on a £1.34 million turnover? And I would be able to see the accounts of this business would I?'

'Err, yes, I'll bring them in one day.'

Fred pauses. 'You seem very young to have had such a successful career so far. How old are you?'

'Twenty-six.'

'That is young.'

'Yes, but look at Alan Sugar or Richard Branson, they were much younger than me when they were millionaires.'

'Perhaps. So I take it that you have already invested heavily in this new idea?'

'Yes. Thousands.'

'And you want the bank to invest some extra capital just to push you over the line?'

'Exactly.'

'Can I see your business plan?'

'Yes, of course.' Mark opens his folder and hands Fred a single sheet with a single paragraph printed followed by a short column of figures.

Fred reads. 'Mark, this isn't a business plan.'

'That's the simplified version. The long plan runs to over ten pages.'

'That would have been what I wanted to see.' Fred glances back down at the sheet. 'It says here that your running costs would be over one million pounds a year. You'd have to sell a lot of ice creams to make that back.'

'Yeah, but I've factored that in, haven't I, in the figures.'

'Yes, you estimate you'll sell, on average, one thousand ice creams a day at an average price of twelve pounds.'

'Yes, that gives me an income of four million three hundred and twenty thousand per outlet per year. That's a massive profit.'

'Mark, experience tells me that people just won't buy any kind of luxury product at that price in that quantity.'

'They will. Think about how much money people spend on alcohol.'

'Yes, but having a drink is all part of socialising. People will not sit in your ice cream parlour all night and have ten ice creams.'

'They will when I build it. You wouldn't have thought people would sit around drinking coffee or eating pizza or fish and chips but they're all successful markets.'

'Yes, but a pizza or fish and chips is a substantial meal at a far cheaper price. Also I think there's the health aspect to consider. People are very health conscious these days. They won't want to be seen to be pumping themselves and their children full of ice cream.'

'The average person in Britain is morbidly obese. I don't know if you've been to an Asda or Lidl recently. Those people would lap up my idea.'

'But the average Asda or Lidl customer isn't your target consumer, or am I wrong?'

'No, that's the genius. They would aspire to eat at one of my parlours. They'd save up and go there as a special treat. Once they were inside, they'd be so blown away by what was on offer they wouldn't be able to help themselves.'

'Mark, I'm finding your pitch very confusing. I simply cannot see how this would be a viable business.'

'How about Starbucks then? Do you not think that's a viable business either?'

'Starbucks would not sell many coffees if they were in excess of ten pounds each.'

'You don't know that. They have a loyal customer base that would go there whatever it cost. People in the City who queue up at Starbucks every morning haven't got a clue how much it costs, they just hand over the cash.'

'Mark, I think you're underestimating the consumer,' Fred says, shaking his head. 'Members of the general public would not spend small fortunes on ice cream, particularly in a country where the weather is primarily cold and wet.'

'I don't agree. It would all be about marketing. If you can give me a small amount of financial backing, I'd get the first place up and running and it would be a huge hit. I'd make ice cream sexy. I'd have the waitresses they have in the best nightclubs dressed up in skimpy outfits. It would give the place a touch of class and elegance.'

'I don't think a few girls in skimpy outfits is the difference between a successful business and a failure. How much of an investment are you looking for?'

'Only seven hundred thousand,' Mark says.

Fred laughs. 'That's completely out of the question.'

'But I read that you were meant to be helping new businesses, to kick-start the economy.'

'We loan the average small business around twenty thousand pounds.

Tom Canty

Seven hundred thousand pounds is an incredible amount of money. In fact I have never been asked for anywhere near that amount from a start-up in the entire time I've worked for IBS.'

'But I could repay that within two years.'

'Mark you have not presented me with any evidence that you could repay it. Your business plan is pure fantasy and I'm astonished that you even think we'd consider loaning you any money when you take such an amateurish approach.'

'I am not an amateur. I know about money and business. You can't spot a good investment.'

'Mark, the International Bank of Scotland has a responsibility to its shareholders. We are a business. We don't just hand out great big lumps of cash to everyone who walks through our doors and asks for it. I have to make a judgement. If someone comes in with a sound business plan, asking for a level of investment that I deem suitable then we will offer support. However, this is not the case with you. If I gave you what is frankly a staggering amount of money I would be hauled up in front of the board. We have to make sure that when we do invest, we do so to people we feel would make good use of the money. There is no evidence to suggest that your business would succeed, particularly in such an uncertain climate, so I'm afraid we won't be able to help.'

'I can't believe this,' Mark says, snatching back his business plan. 'I've offered you a golden opportunity to support a young, gifted entrepreneur and you're not interested. No wonder the economy is in trouble.'

'Mark, please don't be angry. If you expand your business plan and do some more research into the market and downgrade your demands, particularly if you're going to continue to look for support from the banks, you may find that in the long run someone may want to invest.'

'They will. You'll see.'

'Well, I hope they do. I can see you've got a lot of passion for the business.' Fred gets up from his seat, tweaks his gold watch and offers his hand to Mark, who takes it fleetingly. 'Oh and Mark, one last thing you may like to consider; I'd think about changing the company's name. I don't think Fatman Scoops really sets the right tone.'

'I was going to change that anyway,' Mark says, tucking his folder under his arm. 'I'm going to called it Licked Out.'

Clapham Lights

Craig is watching Sky Sports News when Mark gets home.

'You look knackered. Tough day?' Craig asks.

'You could say that.' Mark chucks his folder into his room and gets an apple from the fridge. 'You haven't seen the news today have you?'

'No. Why, what's happened?'

CHAPTER TWENTY-SIX

I t's a bright Saturday morning. Craig has opened one of the French doors and is in the kitchen eating peanut butter on toast. On the television, a footballer dressed like a gangster rapper on *Soccer A.M.* is laughing about how he slept with his teammate's wife before the Carling Cup final.

Craig kicks on his trainers and shouts to Mark - who is in bed reading *Nuts* - that he's off to get his hair cut and will be back to go shopping in about an hour. He suggests that Mark might want to start tidying the flat. Mark says he is going to.

There is a letter from MenDax and a statement from ING Direct for Mark in their post box. The ING envelope has come unstuck and Craig reads the contents. Mark's balance, which was once £26,455, is now £1514. Craig puts the envelope back, gets his sunglasses from his car and strolls up Wall Street.

Lavender Hill Bob is squeezed in between Ladbrokes and El Gringos Mexican cantina, just down from the Cinq Estates office. Inside, the salon is blindingly bright. The chairs, sinks, and walls are brilliant white and there are lightbulbs around each mirror. Even the hairdressers are dressed head-to-toe in white.

Craig waits on a bench in the window and, after flicking through an old *Esquire*, watches the row of four hairdressers snipping at the hair of their female clients.

Brian, Craig's hairdresser, appears from behind a door at the back of the salon. His white vest shows off his big tattooed arms and he has clipped brown hair flecked with grey, a beard, and a studded earring in each ear. He walks with his shoulders hunched and has scars on the bridge of his nose and forehead.

He has a gravelly south London accent and apologises for making Craig wait. Craig, holding a copy of *Heat* magazine, sits in the barber's chair. He says he hasn't had his hair cut in months and wants it a lot shorter. He's seen a picture in a magazine of a style he likes and wonders if Brian could do something similar.

'I'm a hairdresser, not a plastic surgeon mate,' Brian says, laughing at the photo of Brad Pitt that Craig shows him.

'I'm not expecting to look like him, I like his hair. It's choppy but smart. Can you do that?'

Brian slaps a rubber cutting collar around Craig's neck and says that he'll start by taking a lot of the length off.

'It's good to have a bit of sunshine,' he says as he starts trimming. 'The summer was awful.'

'Yeah,' Craig says.

'I was going to stay here but business was really slow, so I ended up heading off to Ibiza for a couple of weeks. Did you go away anywhere?'

'No, I wanted to, but I couldn't get the time off, or afford it. I just stayed here and worked.'

'Who do you work for?' Brian asks, concentrating on the back of Craig's head.

'An estate agent.'

'Oh yeah, which one?'

'Cinq Estates,' Craig says, managing to sound both depressed and embarrassed.

Brian stops cutting and looks at Craig in the mirror. 'You don't do you? I'm sure that's not what you told me last time.'

'I don't think it came up.'

'But you seem like a nice bloke. What are you doing working for that bunch of crooks?'

'I've been trying to leave for months.'

'Good.' Brian starts cutting again. 'You know, I sold my flat through you lot a couple of years ago and it was a fucking nightmare.' The woman in the next seat along glances across and he apologises for swearing. 'They were trying to rip me off every step of the way. Charging me fees for everything imaginable and telling me to drop the asking price all the time.

'I had a place just off Northcote Road, and they were telling me it was worth about thirty thousand more than the other agents, and initially I believed them. I started off dealing with this girl, Karen I think she was called, but then she left and I had this greasy bloke Christian D'Souza dealing with me. Do you know him?'

'Yeah. He's now the boss.'

'You're joking? He was the most dishonest bloke I've ever come across, and that's saying something. Stuff always went missing from my flat after he'd been there.'

'Like what?'

'Nothing major, just CDs mainly, and some cash once. I confronted him and of course he denied everything.' Brian closes the scissors with a snap. 'I wish I'd beaten some sense into him.'

'Um, yeah.'

'The housing market's gone down the pan recently hasn't it?' Brian says, moving round to start on Craig's fringe.

'A little bit.'

'It's going to be a tough few months for everyone they were saying on the news last night. I suppose that's one of the good things about hairdressing; people will always need their hair cut. I wouldn't like to be one of those poor mugs in the City who turn up to find the office has shut down. Although I don't feel sorry for them, greedy bastards most of them.'

'Umm.'

A tubby man in his forties with a mop of blond hair saunters into the salon. He helps himself to an iced tea and then wanders over to Brian and kisses him on the lips before heading into the back room. Craig looks bemused.

'That's my partner, Clive. We set this place up together after I got out in 1997.'

'Got out of where?'

'Prison.'

'You were in prison? Oh, right. What were you in for?' Craig asks quietly.

Brian stops cutting and glares at him. 'Don't ever ask someone what they're in for.'

'Sorry, I'm really sorry.'

'I'm only messing with you, you big girl,' he says, laughing. 'It was drugs and ABH. It was the best thing that ever happened to me though, being put away. I learnt how to cut hair when I was inside and when I got out I thought I'd try and make a go of it. It's kept me on the straight and narrow.'

Brian trims Craig's neck with clippers, assesses the cut from all angles and then holds a mirror up to the back of Craig's head.

'That's brilliant, thanks,' Craig says.

'You still look nothing like Brad Pitt though.'

Craig stands up and removes his gown whilst Brian brushes hair from his collar.

'That's twenty-two pounds fifty,' Brian says, going behind reception and opening the till.

Craig's smile sags and he digs around in his pocket for change. 'I'm really sorry but I've only got nineteen pounds in cash and I've left my cards at home. I'm sure it was less last time.' He looks worried. 'Can I drop the rest in later? I'm really sorry.'

'Don't worry about it mate,' Brian says. 'We put the prices up a couple of weeks ago. Give it to me next time.'

'Cheers, that's really good of you. I really appreciate it.'

'No worries, have a good weekend,' Brian says, slamming the till shut.

Outside, Craig checks his phone. He has four missed calls and a text message from Christian. The text tells him to cancel his plans and come to the office. Craig texts him back saying '*Impossible*'. Christian phones him incessantly for the next five minutes. Hannah texts saying Christian's going ballistic because five people have phoned in sick.

He gets another text from Christian telling him to '*gt bac to office NOW!*' so he turns his phone off.

He walks home via NatWest and tries to take £20 out of a cash machine but a message flashes up on the screen that the bank cannot authorise the transaction due to insufficient funds. He tries for £10 and gets the same response. Craig swears to himself and stands motionless as the machine beeps at him to retrieve his card.

By the time he gets back to the flat, Mark has rearranged the living room. The sofas and table are flat against the walls and he has moved the new television and the dining table's chairs into his room. The old television is back in its corner and the floor has been vacuumed.

'What the cock have you done to your hair?' Mark says as he throws newspapers into a recycling bag.

'I thought I'd go for a new look. You've done well,' Craig says, taking in Mark's handiwork.

'Yeah I thought I'd move the old TV back in. I didn't want someone spilling drink over the new-y. Are we going shopping in a minute?'

Craig pauses. 'Mark, I've had a bit of a nightmare and I need to ask you a favour.'

'It depends what it is.'

'The cash machine swallowed my card. I can't get any money out.'

'Is that all? I'll lend you whatever you need, mate. Christ, I thought it was something serious for a minute.'

'Cheers, you're a life-saver.'

'No worries. Let's get to Whole Foods. I've written a list of what we need.'

Mark loads the four funky house CDs he's bought into the stereo. *It Just Won't Do* blares out and he quickly turns down the volume. He switches off the main lights and admires the flat.

Rows of fairy lights zigzag across the ceiling creating a pearly canopy. Mark has also wound a set of multi-coloured garden lights around the railings on the terrace and lit sixty tea candles which glow against the night sky.

On the kitchen worktops there are over a hundred cans and bottles of lager and cider, a crate of Guinness, a crate of white and red wine, five bottles of vodka, and bottles of Jack Daniels, Gordon's gin, Coca-Cola, lemonade and tonic water.

Mark transfers the lager and cider into three plastic barrels they've bought from Homebase and covers them with ice. He then carries two of the barrels, with great difficulty, into the living room, placing them either side of the table where he's placed bowls of Doritos, cocktail sausages and chicken nuggets.

Craig - wet and dressed only in a towel - is tidying his bedroom, which Mark has nominated as the cloakroom and toilet. He hides his iPod in a cupboard and stashes all of his letters and bank statements in a bedside drawer. He selects a short-sleeved pink shirt and dark jeans to go with his white belt and canvas shoes.

He stands in front of his bathroom mirror and perfects his new hair. He uses *Harry Potter and Half-Blood Prince* as a door stop and goes into the living room where Mark is on the floor picking out DVDs from a shoe box.

'I can't believe it, mate,' Craig says, looking up and out onto the terrace. 'It looks amazing.'

'I told you it would look good. I'm going to put on some old retro DVDs. I saw it done in a bar in Old Street. They had old episodes of *The A-Team* and *Fall Guy* playing. It looked quality.'

'What are you going to put on?'

'A few old Wrestlemanias. I won't put the sound on.'

Craig smiles and opens a Corona. 'We're never going to drink all this.'

'We will, trust me. When it's free people drink twice as much.'

Craig has a new text message.

'Someone dropped out?' Mark asks.

'No, it's just Hannah asking what time she should come over.'

'Make sure she doesn't come too early, and don't get drunk before she gets here. What are you going to tell her?'

Daft Punk is booming through the crowded flat and a serious dent has been made in the alcohol stock. Craig drops more bottles of Heineken into the barrels of icy water, eats a sausage and goes back into the kitchen where Danny and two other male Cinq employees - whom Craig doesn't seem to know - are drinking WKD.

'You've got a cool place,' Danny says.

'Yeah, cool,' the boy to Danny's right wearing a long gold chain says. 'What's the rent on this?'

'Too much,' Craig says, mixing a strong vodka and orange.

He takes the drink to Amy, who has just arrived. She is wearing a short-sleeved black sequin t-shirt and has dark, smoky eye shadow on.

'I hope that's not too strong,' Craig says.

'That's fine, thanks,' she says, her whitened teeth shining. 'I need a strong drink. Crap week.'

'We've got tons so drink as much as you can. I don't think anyone else from your work is here yet, I'm not sure where Mark-'

Mark comes up behind them and drapes his arms over their shoulders. He's wearing a blue muscle-fit Hollister t-shirt with a black collar and his hug makes Amy spill some of her drink.

'I'm glad you've made it,' he says to Amy. 'Craig, your Norwich mates were wondering where you were. They're outside.'

Craig leaves them.

'I didn't think you were going to come,' Mark says, leaning against Craig's bedroom door. There is a queue developing for the toilet.

'I'm sorry about the whole bonus thing,' Amy says.

'It's OK, I'm over it. Have you done something different to your hair?'

'I had it done yesterday. I had an interview.'

'An interview?' Mark says, taken aback. 'With who?'

'Salingers.'

'How did you get that?'

'Through an agency.'

'Oh. How did it go?'

'Not very well. What have you been doing?'

'Umm, not much really. Been going to the gym a lot. I thought about signing up with a few recruitment places, but I thought I'd try using my contacts first.'

'Have you got anywhere?'

'No, not really. I might go on holiday. I need to take a bit of time out to think.'

'I can't afford to take time out with a mortgage to pay. I've got enough money to survive a few weeks but after that... I don't really want to think about it.'

'Amy, don't be negative. You'll be fine. This is just a minor setback. By Christmas everything will be back to normal and people will be fighting over the likes of us.'

'Mark, are you sure you're OK?'

'Why?'

'Well, you're carrying on like nothing's happened.'

'Not much has happened.'

'Mark, it's not healthy.'

'Yeah, well.' He shrugs.

'You know you can always talk to me.'

'Thanks. Come on, don't be miserable. Let's get hammered, forget about things. Oh, and don't say anything about MenDax to Craig, he doesn't know.'

Craig is on the terrace with Adam, Tony and three more of their old school friends. Adam, wearing a tight v-neck jumper without a t-shirt, is orchestrating a game of fives. Tony has lost four times in a row and been made to down a shot of vodka each time.

'Are we going on anywhere?' Adam asks Craig.

'I'm not sure. I'll see what Mark says.'

Adam loses and pours himself a double shot. 'We should head to a nightclub. Tony's up for it.'

'Yeah, yeah. Well up for it,' he says, leaning on Craig. 'Is that Hannah girl here yet?'

'She just got here.'

'Is she wearing a short leather jacket? Dark hair,' Adam asks.

'Yes, why?'

'She just walked out here mate. Don't turn round too quickly or it'll be obvious we've been talking about her.'

Craig leaves it a couple of seconds and turns, taking a couple of steps away from his friends. Hannah waves and walks towards him. She's wearing heels with jeans and holding a glass of white wine. They smile at each other but don't hug.

'You're here,' he says.

'I said I was coming. Sorry I took ages getting ready.' Her diamond earrings twinkle in the candlelight.

'You look amazing.'

'You're not drunk already are you?' Hannah says, smiling.

'No.'

'Well aren't you going to introduce me to your friends?'

Matthew, a university friend of Mark and Craig's, taps Mark on the shoulder. He has curly hair, glasses and a mature, confident demeanour. He tells Mark he loves the flat and says it's good to see him doing well. Then the subject of MenDax crops up and Mark says luckily he left just in time.

'Where are you working now then?' Matthew asks.

'Another place in the City, doing pretty much the same thing. Are you still with Emma?'

'Yes, we've just bought a flat together, in Fulham.'

'You'll be getting married soon, won't you?' Mark moves out of the way to let Tony get some water from the tap.

'She's putting the pressure on, but I haven't buckled yet. Are you coming to Simon's?'

'Simon's getting married?'

'Yes. In a few weeks,' Matthew says, looking surprised that Mark doesn't know.

'Who to?'

'Sophie, the tall blonde girl he used to work with.'

'I've not met her. They can't have been going out very long.'

'A couple of years at least. This is what happens when you fall out of the loop, mate. When did you last see him?'

'I can't remember to be honest. I'll have to send him an email. When's his stag weekend? I'd be up for that.'

Matthew drinks more beer. 'Too late mate, it was a few weeks ago. We went to Riga. It was awesome. We got lashed for three days and shot AK-47s. I expected to see you.'

Mark goes quiet. 'No, I didn't get the email. Perhaps it was sent to my old address.'

'Yes, possibly.'

'Who went?'

'Most of the university lot were there and some of his mates from home.'

'Craig didn't go, did he?'

'No, he dropped out at the last minute. Said he didn't have enough money. Anyway, Jim's here somewhere as well, he said he hadn't seen you for a while. Where's the toilet by the way?'

Mark directs Matthew to Craig's room, pours himself a JD and Coke and downs it. He then quarter-fills a pint glass with gin, tops it up with lemonade and stands against the sink looking sullen. A drunk girl asks him who he is.

Craig tells Christian not to smoke inside so he puts the cigarette out on the floor and asks Craig why he didn't reply to his messages. Craig says that he had too much to organise for the party.

Christian is sweating and his nose is running. He talks over the music about the need for everyone to be committed to the company and that if he feels that anyone isn't committed they're no use to him. He is only an inch away from Craig's face and tells him about how when he first sold a

258

house in Clapham he had the owners pay ten thousand pounds over to a holding company that would clear any money that he wanted to be kept safe for a short amount of time and that how without him doing that, the deal wouldn't have gone through and unless everyone takes that attitude to selling houses then they'll never make enough sales to justify having the amount of staff that are needed to run a decent agency and that makes him angry that people can't see the potential that their office has for being one of the biggest in the country if only they had better staff and more experienced people to be taking a more aggressive approach to sales and then they'll be able to turn things around but if people won't listen then it will be their fault because he's warned them. Craig asks Christian if he's on drugs. Christian tells him that's none of his business and warns him to stay away from Hannah as well because she's getting over her boyfriend and the two of them have a special bond. Craig asks him if he's on drugs again and Christian tells him to fuck off and pushes to the other side of the room and invades Danny's conversation, leaving Craig standing in front of Lex Luger v Yokozuna at SummerSlam '93 as Klaxons' *It's Not Over Yet* fills the flat at wall-shuddering volume.

'I had a chat with Anna earlier,' Tony slurs as he leans against the wall on the terrace. He has a huge red wine stain down his shirt.

'You mean Hannah,' Craig says, drinking white wine from the bottle.

'Yeah, the fit one. Adam was talking to her, so I went over there and told him that he shouldn't be doing that because you fancy her and that you'd told him not to.'

'Cheers mate, that's really helpful.' Craig rolls his eyes.

'She seemed to think it was quite funny.'

'What did Adam do?'

'Nothing. She was kind of ignoring him.' Tony burps. 'He's pulled someone anyway.'

'Who?'

Tony points around the corner to where Adam, who has his back to them, is joined at the face to Ophelia. Craig creeps up beside them and tiptoes back to Tony.

'That's one of the neighbours. She's quite pretty,' Craig says.

'Yeah, I think she bought a couple of mates along. I tried to talk to one of them but she said I was pissed.'

'You are pissed. Why are you so wet as well?'

'One of the girls said that white wine gets out red wine so she poured a glass of wine over me and then Adam said he thought it was beer that did that so he threw his pint over me.'

Craig smiles. 'Mate, borrow a shirt from my wardrobe. You'll never get in anywhere like that.'

'I think it looks good. I look like Terry Butcher.'

Tony wanders off and Craig gazes out over south London. As he goes to drink, his wine bottle slips out of his hand and over the railings, landing in shrubbery just inches from Mark's Audi.

It's one forty-five and the living room is packed. *That's Not My Name* is booming out and there's a *ThunderCats* DVD on the TV. Amy and Mark are talking in the corner of the room and sharing a bottle of Prosecco. Craig is getting a new shirt for Tony and Hannah is talking to a friend of Ophelia's outside Craig's door.

Adam and Tony and some of the old UEEC football team are in the kitchen downing double shots of gin. One of them is completely naked and is pretending to fry his testicles in Mark's pan. Three girls who are friends of Adam's from teacher training are out on the terrace, smoking, along with Danny and the other Cinq boys.

Suddenly the music stops and people boo. Mark, happily drunk, wobbles up onto the table:

'MY NAME IS MARK AND WE'VE MOVING THE PARTY TO FIRE BOMBS,' he shouts. Everyone cheers. 'I'VE BOOKED TAXIS FOR ALL OF US AND THEY'RE LEAVING IN FIVE MINUTES.'

A glass smashes on the kitchen floor and there are more cheers. He tells everyone to drink as much as possible and start moving downstairs. He switches the music back on at a lower volume and turns on the spotlights, making some people blink.

The guests down their drinks and retrieve coats from Craig's room. Some of the boys fill their pockets with bottles for the short journey.

Mark is the last one out and checks that the doors are locked and nothing is left on. As he gets out of the lift he spots Craig and Hannah standing together in the car park.

Fire Bombs' resident DJ is playing the theme tune to *Baywatch* and the dance floor is heaving. Hannah leads Craig away from the masses to the red glow of a booth where there are empty bottles of VK and spilt drink all over the table and large wet patches on the plasticky seat cushions.

'I hate this song,' Hannah shouts over the music. She sits down and draws Craig close to her. He is drunker than her.

Craig has a couple of mouthfuls of beer and points across to Mark who's jumping up and down in the middle of the throng, bellowing the lyrics. He shakes his head.

'What did you want to say to me?' Hannah leans into Craig so they are almost touching.

He tilts his head, and starts to say something before stopping himself. 'Um, I'm going to resign. I'm leaving Cinq.'

'Why? Sorry, stupid question. When?'

'This week I think.'

'Have you got another job?'

'No. I'm going to move home for a while, until I sort myself out.'

'To Norwich?'

'Yes. I have to.'

Hannah puts her hand on his thigh. 'You're doing the right thing.'

Craig half-smiles. 'Am I?'

'Will you miss seeing me every day?'

'You know I will.'

'How much?'

They edge closer until their lips are touching and they kiss, gently tumbling together into the padded wall.

Hannah runs her hand down his chest and pulls away. She whispers something in his ear and he opens his eyes.

He smiles. 'Thanks.'

Hannah laughs.

'Sorry, I didn't mean "thanks", I-'

'It's OK. It's sweet.' She takes his hand they get up. 'Come on. Let's go to the bar.'

*

Mark rolls out of bed and onto the floor. He crawls to the bathroom and kneels by the toilet bowl but it's already splattered with somebody else's sick so he turns away. There's a large yellow spot on his left shoulder and last night's t-shirt is screwed up on the bathmat. He struggles to his feet, rinses his mouth with Listerine and washes his face with cold water.

Back in his room, he pulls on his boxer shorts and sneezes, waking up Amy. She flicks her hair away from her eyes and lifts her head.

'How are you feeling?' she asks.

'Terrible,' Mark says, putting on a t-shirt. He opens a window.

'What time did we get in?'

'I don't know. I can't remember anything.'

He collapses back onto the bed, holding his head.

'Mark, can you see my underwear anywhere?' she asks coyly.

He tries to get up, but can't. 'Sorry. I can't move.'

'I'm going to get up, OK? So don't look.'

'OK.'

Amy puts her arm over her breasts and tiptoes around the edge of the bed. Her knickers are on the floor next to a beer can. She picks them up and slips them on.

'Mark, can I borrow a jumper? I'm cold.'

'Open the right of the wardrobe. There's a pile of them.'

The wardrobe is chaotic with clothes all over the place. Amy pulls a blue sweater from a stack and Mark watches as she slips it over her head.

'Mark! I said don't look.'

'Oh shit,' he says, breathlessly. He shoots up from the bed, bullocks into the en suite and throws himself at the toilet. A torrent of sick explodes from his mouth. 'Sorry, I'm sorry. UUUUUUuuugh, UUUUUUuuugh,' he groans as he wretches.

Amy stands behind him, rubbing his back. 'It's OK. You'll feel better afterwards.'

'UUUUurrrrrgh. UUUurrrrrgh,' Sweat pours from his forehead and more yellow bile gushes into the bowl.

The sun is pouring in through the living room windows and there is someone wrapped in a duvet on the floor outside Craig's room. He steps over them, shutting the door behind him, and surveys the aftermath. Danny and one of the other Cinq boys are asleep on a bed made of sofa cushions, and beyond them three sets of feet are poking out from under a double duvet on the sofa bed which is sagging precariously.

There's broken glass and squashed food on the floor and every surface is covered with discarded plastic cups and empty cans and bottles. Most of the spirits have been left with their tops off and there are only a dozen beers left in the barrels of melted ice. The doors to the terrace are open and the curtains occasionally billow.

Craig's flip-flops stick to the floor as he steps into the kitchen. He puts the kettle on and eats a couple of custard creams as he waits for it to boil.

Hannah is awake and has put her bra back on when Craig brings in the tea. She sits up with her legs crossed under the duvet.

'I made you a cup a tea,' he says, giving her his Norwich City mug.

'Thanks.' She combs her dishevelled hair with her fingers. 'My mouth's really dry.'

Craig goes into his bathroom and brushes his teeth. Hannah is fully dressed and putting her heels on when he comes out.

'You're going?' he says.

'I should go home.'

'OK.' Craig stands, sipping his tea. 'Do you want me to walk you back?'

'No, I'll be fine. Thanks though. You can sleep off your hangover.'

'Han, are you doing anything later?'

'I'm going for lunch with a friend and then I think we're going to the cinema. I won't be back until late.'

'Oh, right.' Craig passes her bag. 'Shall I text you later?'

'Yeah, sure.'

'OK. Perhaps we could do something one night next week, if you're not busy. Go for a drink or… if you want to.'

Hannah puts on her jacket. 'Are you going to be at work tomorrow?'

'Yep.'

'Good. You can buy me a coffee,' she says, smiling.

'Do you know how to get home?'

'Craig, of course I know how to get home. The office is only up the road.'

'Oh, yes. Sorry, I'm being stupid.'

She kisses Craig on the cheek and leaves, shutting the front door with a delicate click.

Adam and Craig are sitting on his bed together watching a repeat of last night's *Match of the Day*.

'I couldn't believe it,' Adam says. 'When we got the taxi back she dragged me to her place. I tried to leave earlier but she dived under the covers and begged me to stay.'

Craig laughs. 'You know that's the girl whose mum attacked me.'

'Yeah, she said. There are obviously a few defective genes in that family. She told me to go back round there later.'

'Are you going to?'

'No way, I'm too tired. And I need to get back soon.'

'Have you seen the other boys?'

'Some of the other lads are cuddled up in Ophelia's lounge but I haven't seen Tony.'

'Why are they at her place?'

'They tried to get in here, but the door was locked and you weren't answering. I might go outside and get some air.'

Craig follows Adam through the scattered bodies and they stand out on the terrace, sharing a bottle of Coke. The bottom half of a red sleeping bag is poking out from under a garden chair and the pair approach the cocoon. There is a pile of mashed pizza vomit by the head end of the bag and Adam loosens the head flap. It's Tony.

Adam kicks him gently. There is no response. Craig bends down and shakes him whilst Adam pokes his face.

'He's stone cold,' Adam says, looking to Craig. 'Do you think he's dead?'

Tony rolls over into the wall. 'Stop shouting you twat. I wish I was dead. My head's banging.'

'Jesus, mate, have you been out here all night?' Craig asks.

'Of course I haven't.'

'Do you want some Coke mate,' Adam says, putting the bottle by Tony's head. 'I'm glad you're not dead. There's no way I was carrying your body home.'

The boys stay out on the terrace until Tony drags himself up. He has tile print pressed into his cheek. Craig tells him to clean the sick up and the trio amble back inside to get a bucket of water.

'Who's under there,' Adam asks, pointing to the mound on the sofa bed.

'No idea,' Craig says. 'Leave them.'

Adam has a mischievous grin on his face and jerks back the duvet to reveal three huge naked men all face down. One is bulky and muscular; the other two are fat and covered in hair.

'What the fuck?' Craig says.

Adam and Tony burst out laughing.

One of the men turns his head and opens his eyes.

'Brian, what are you doing here?' Craig says.

'We got a taxi from Fire Bombs don't you remember? Your flatmate said we should come back for a drink.' He has a graze on his knuckles.

'Who are they?' Craig asks, pointing to the other snoring bodies.

'That's Clive,' Brian says.

'Well who's the other bloke?'

'That's Harry. He said he's a friend of Mark's.'

CHAPTER TWENTY-SEVEN

I t is six fifteen in the morning and dark when Craig leaves the flat. He drives to the BP petrol station at Wandsworth Bridge and puts his car through the car wash – which company policy dictates he isn't allowed to. He reads the sport section of *The Daily Telegraph* as the rotating brushes run over the Mini and when the fans finish, he edges out of the hangar and gets out to check the roof. There are two inches of water in the wooden house. He tries to flick it out with his palm but this makes his sleeve wet so he gives up.

He drives back along York Road, past the monstrous new-build apartments of Battersea Beach and the Livingstone estate. On Plough Road he gets stuck behind a 295 bus and follows it all the way to Clapham Junction.

By ten to seven, Craig is in the office. After switching on the lights, he sits at his computer and deletes his inbox. Once he's done this, he browses the BBC Sport website and checks his Hotmail as the sun slowly rises outside.

He is still on his own at seven twenty so he makes a cup of tea and drifts around aimlessly. He sits on one of the customer sofas in reception and flicks through the latest issue of *Maison d'Etre*, and then checks the sales board in Christian's office. It's the second week of October and he's joint top with Ahmed, on one sale. The other ten names have nothing beneath them.

A girl in a yellow puffa jacket enters the building. Craig jumps up from his chair.

'Sorry, we're not open yet,' he says.

'I work here, dickhead,' she replies, tilting her head and kissing her teeth. She puts her fake Prada handbag down in front of a computer and picks at her oily hair.

'How was your weekend?' Craig asks, amused.

266

'Why do you want to know?'

Christian turns up wearing sunglasses and a woolly cap pulled down over his ears. He hurries into his office without acknowledging anyone and shuts the door.

Craig stands outside and hesitates before knocking. There is no response so he knocks again. Christian shouts for him to wait and then the door opens. His left eye is black, he has a raw graze covering his nose and left cheekbone, and one of his bottom front teeth is broken.

Craig stares at his face. 'What happened?'

'I fell over on Saturday night,' Christian says, going back behind his desk.

'You look like you've been beaten up.'

'No, no, I was just a bit out of it. I fell over on the pavement outside Chernobyl.' He looks away and coughs.

'How come you went to Chernobyl?'

'I tried to get into Fire Bombs but the queue was too long so I went there instead.'

'Who did you go with?'

'I had a few mates in there. I remember being in the toilets and then suddenly I was outside and had blood all over my face.'

'Did anyone call an ambulance or anything?'

'No, I just went home.' He touches his eye and winces. 'I might go to the dentist later. Get my tooth fixed. And my nose is a bit bashed up. Good party though. Do you know where Hannah got to?'

'She was in Fire Bombs.'

'I text her yesterday and she didn't reply. She didn't pull that mate of yours did she?'

'No.'

'Good.' Christian rolls his tongue across the chip in his teeth. 'Why are you here so early, anyway? Catching up on stuff you should have done last week?'

'No, not exactly. There's something I want to talk to you about.'

'Yeah, what's that then?' he asks, his attention focussed on his computer.

'I'm resigning.'

'Hang on.' Christian types away on his keyboard. 'Typed the wrong password. What did you say?' he says turning to Craig.

'I'm resigning, Christian. Leaving.'

'No you're not.'

'I am. Sorry.'

'Craig, you aren't leaving because I'm not letting you. You've got targets to hit. Once you've hit your sales targets then I might consider letting you resign. But until then, no chance. It's not happening.'

'I'm afraid it is.'

'Craig. I'm the boss. I decide whether you work here or not, not you. You leave when I want you to and not before.'

'I'm leaving now.'

'You can leave if you want to but it's gonna cost you.'

'What do you mean?'

'The only way for you to leave before your contract expires is to buy your way out.'

'I'm not buying my way out. I'm leaving. This isn't the army.'

'Craig, check your contract. If you leave voluntarily within the first four years of employment, you have to pay a five thousand pound get-out charge. I suggest you go back to your desk, forget these stupid ideas you've got and go sell some houses.'

'I would have checked my contract, Christian, but I never actually signed one.'

'You would have done. You've probably lost it.'

'No, I never signed one because when I joined you said it was company policy to have an informal agreement rather than a contract... so you can get rid of people more easily.' Craig shuffles in his chair.

'No, Craig. It's not so we can get rid of people. We have a gentlemen's agreement with the staff because that's how we expect them to behave. A gentleman doesn't just walk into his boss's office one morning and tell him he's resigning.'

'It makes no difference.'

'Well it does because the terms of this gentlemen's agreement are binding. You'll have to pay the five grand whether you like it or not. We've invested thousands in your training and development. We can't just watch that investment walk out the door.'

'What training?'

'What do you mean "what training"? All the expertise that I've passed on to you. You wouldn't have made a penny without my guidance.'

Clapham Lights

Blood starts to trickle from Christian's left nostril. Craig tells him and he stuffs it with tissue.

'And that's not all,' Christian continues.

Craig sighs. 'What else is there?'

'You've gotta pay three hundred pounds for us to process and release your P45. And a one thousand pound damage charge for your car.'

'There's no damage to my car.'

'There is. The wear and tear from driving alone will cost us more than that. And you have to pay back your clothing allowance.'

'I've never had a clothing allowance.'

'You did. It was built into your salary. Thirty pounds a month for twenty-odd months. That all adds up. Then there's the cost of advertising for new staff which will have to be paid for as you're leaving us one salesman short and there'll be the shortfall in revenue. All in all, you're looking at about fifteen grand.'

'Christian, I haven't got any money. That's why I'm leaving.'

'Craig, do you not understand what I'm telling you? If you want to leave then you can pay up. If you're really that desperate to go you should get out there and sell some houses. Once you've made the commission you can pay us what you owe and you'll be free to go. If you work hard you can be out by March next year.'

Craig shakes his head. 'No. I'm leaving as soon as I can. I'll give you a week's notice.'

Christian leans forward onto the desk. 'I'm fucked off, Craig. You've been like a son to me. I've sacked hundreds of better sales people than you and I could have got rid of you, but I didn't because I thought you might develop. I even let you use the saw. But now you stab me in the back.'

'How have I stabbed you in the back?'

'You're selfish.'

'Why?'

'You're leaving here because you can't hack it and you'd rather leave the hard work to others. You're spineless.'

'No I'm not.'

'If you had any guts you'd stay and tough things out, like I have to.'

'I'm leaving because I make less than the minimum wage.'

'Because you're not making the sales.'

'Because nobody is buying houses.'

'Because you aren't trying hard enough!'

'I've tried everything.'

Christian slams his fist on the desk. 'No you haven't. If you'd tried everything you'd have a board full of sales. You know I've just bought an apartment in Battersea Beach, don't you?'

'I know, you've told me.'

'I've got a huge mortgage and do you know how I pay the mortgage?'

'Money?' Craig says sarcastically.

'Yes, money. Money I earn from working here. Money I earn from managing a team who are meant to hit their targets by selling houses.'

'And.'

'And Craig, how am I meant to pay for my flat if my most experienced salesman comes into my office on a Monday morning and tells me he's jacking it in?'

'Christian, that's not my fault.'

'YES IT IS YOUR FAULT!' he shouts. 'What am I meant to tell my bank? Sorry but I can't pay the mortgage this month because Craig Tennant didn't want to do any work?'

Craig shrugs.

'Don't shrug your shoulders at me, Craig. After all I've done for you. You've got a responsibility to me and a responsibility to this company. You were more than happy to work here when you were raking the money in.'

'I was never raking any money in. I took a pay cut to work here because I believed all the lies I was told.'

'The only liar around here is you.'

'I haven't lied about anything.'

'Yes you have. If you weren't such a liar you would've told me you were planning to leave months ago.'

'I wasn't planning to leave months ago.'

'You must have been.'

There's a knock at the door. Christian's fists are clenched and he is taking short, angry breaths.

'COME IN,' he shouts.

It's Hannah. She has her glasses on and looks shocked at Christian's appearance. She asks if they are having a team meeting. Christian says he'll be out in five minutes. Hannah smiles at Craig as she leaves.

'And whatever childish playground flirting is going on between the two of you stops now,' Christian says.

'Why?'

'If it doesn't, I'll suspend you.'

'Can you suspend me permanently?'

'Don't push me.'

Craig laughs. 'Jealous are you?'

Christian clenches his jaw and a vein in his neck throbs. 'You did something with her, on Saturday night, didn't you?'

'It's got nothing to do with you.'

'You did, didn't you? I knew it. I wondered why I hadn't seen her leave the house on Sunday morning. And that's why when she came back she was wearing the same clothes she had on the night before.'

'How do you know that? Shit, are you stalking her?' Craig says, astonished.

'Get outside. You're dead to me, Tennant.'

Christian shoots up from his chair and tears open the door, slamming it against the wall. 'RIGHT, TEAM MEETING, NOW,' he yells. 'You too Hannah.'

The eight sales staff who have turned up exchange concerned glances and roll chairs into a semi-circle at the back of the office. Christian stands next to a flip chart with his arms folded, glaring into the distance.

'What happened to your face, boss?' Danny asks.

'I'll tell you what happened to my face when you sell some houses Danny, you little prick,' Christian says, throwing a topless felt-tip pen which hits Danny on the chest and marks his suit.

Craig loiters at the side of the group. Hannah sits two seats away.

'Right, everyone here?' Christian growls.

'Yep,' Danny says, turning his shaved head left and right to check.

'Good.' Blood starts to trickle from Christian's right nostril. It reaches his lips and he licks it, and then he wipes his nose with his sleeve, making a red smudge on his shirt and across his face. 'I'll do all the target stuff later. Firstly I'd like to announce that unfortunately two members of the team, Craig and Hannah, have been sacked.'

'*What?*' Hannah says.

'You've been sacked. You and him,' Christian says, pointing at Craig.

'Sacked for what?' she asks.

'Gross misconduct.'

'But I haven't done anything!' Hannah says angrily.

'Yes you have. You know exactly what you've done.'

'Christian, I've not done anything.'

'You slept together,' Christian says through gritted teeth.

There are embarrassed smiles from the staff. Danny cheers and gives Craig a thumbs-up.

'SHUT UP DANNY!' Christian shouts.

'I haven't slept with anyone,' Hannah says. 'And even if I had, you can't sack me for it.'

She gives Craig a fleeting, angry look as the rest of the staff turn back to Christian:

'I can do whatever I like. You're members of my team. It's unprofessional and I'm not letting it happen. I can't trust you, Hannah. Get out and take him with you.'

'You can't do this,' Craig says. 'I'm leaving. Hannah's not.'

'You're both leaving.'

'You're pathetic, Christian. Just because I turned you down. Is this what it's about?' Hannah says.

'YOU NEVER TURNED ME DOWN. CLEAR YOUR DESK!'

Hannah stands up and Craig starts to follow her but she ignores him and heads to the toilets. Craig's face drops.

'Aren't you going to chase your girlfriend, Craig?' Christian asks, smirking with blood running down the side of his mouth.

Craig glares at him, chucks his car keys at Christian's feet and walks out.

Craig sits in Café Nero at Clapham Junction until midday. He texts Hannah to apologise and swears that he told Christian nothing, but she doesn't reply. After a cheese roll from Greggs, he walks back to the flat and watches the *Hollyoaks* omnibus on E4 with an expression of numb sorrow.

*

Three days later, Craig is on Lavender Hill to get passport photographs taken. On his way home he passes the Cinq office on the opposite side of the road. A boy with a crew cut is getting into his old car and there is nobody behind reception.

He goes into HSBC to pay in £50 that his mum has sent him. As he folds his receipt into his pocket and moves towards the doors, Hannah appears at one of the cashpoints in the entrance foyer. She is dressed for work and has a Mulberry handbag over her shoulder. Craig stops and waits as she slips her debit card into her purse and takes her cash. She glances left and sees him.

'Craig, hello,' she says, turning to face him.

He wanders over as she puts her purse into her bag and takes out her glasses, accidently dropping them on the floor. She starts to bend down but Craig retrieves them for her.

'I'd just come to pay some money in. I saw you,' he says in a hushed voice.

'Sorry I haven't replied to your messages.'

'That's OK.'

'No, it's not. I shouldn't have ignored you. I was angry and everything came as such a shock.'

'You know I didn't say anything to Christian don't you? He told me to stay away from you. I wasn't showing off. I'd never do anything to embarrass you like that.'

'I know you wouldn't.'

'You look… really smart. Have you got another job?'

'No,' Hannah says, checking her watch. 'I'm back at the office. I got my job back.'

'Oh.'

'I'm not staying there though.'

'What did Christian say?'

'Christian's been sacked.'

'Really? How?'

'He didn't come in on Tuesday and the Fulham branch manager told us he'd been fired and that he'd be managing both branches for the time being. There had been a lot of complaints apparently, and money going missing. Someone said he'd been arrested although I don't know if that's true. There's been a rumour about the whole branch being shut down.'

'Do you think that's true?'

'I don't know. There have been meetings going on with senior managers for the last couple of days. I've started looking for a new job.' Hannah fiddles with her glasses. 'Have you been OK?'

'Yeah, yeah, I'm fine,' Craig says, sounding more upbeat. 'Just been trying to sort everything out. It's been weird not having much to do.'

'Have you been out enjoying yourself?'

'No, not really. I've barely left the flat. I'm just relieved to be away from Cinq to be honest. I wish I'd left there twelve months ago. It was only seeing you that kept making me go back.'

Hannah smiles. 'I'm sure you don't mean that.'

'I do mean it, Han. I certainly wasn't doing it for the money.'

They walk out into the autumn sunshine and stop to face each other on the pavement.

'Craig, I should get back to the office.'

'OK, I don't want to hold you up. Han, I just want to say... I didn't want to make such a mess of things, and I didn't want us to say goodbye on bad terms.'

'You haven't made a mess of things. And who said anything about saying goodbye. You told me you were only going home for a few weeks.'

'Yes, I am.'

Hannah reaches out for his hands. 'We can see each other when you come down then. You're better off away from there and at least you've got a job with your dad to go back to, even if it is a long way away. I could be unemployed next week.'

'Even if the office does shut, you won't be unemployed for long.'

'You don't know that.'

'Yes I do, because you're clever and beautiful. You could walk into any office in London and they'd offer you a job.'

Hannah smiles. 'I wish.' She looks at her watch again. 'Craig, you're making me late.'

'Sorry.'

'It's OK.' She pauses. 'Are you doing anything the weekend after next?'

'Umm, I'm not sure, why?'

'Are you going to be in London?'

'I don't know. I can be. Why's that?'

'I've got two tickets for *Jersey Boys* and I've got nobody to go with so I thought you might like to come, if you're down here. I was meant to go with Marcus but obviously...'

'Of course I'll come.'

'Definitely? You don't have to if-'

'Yes. Definitely.'

'Text me and let me know how everything's going, you promise me.'

'Yes, I promise.'

'You better not stand me up.'

'I won't. Of course I won't.'

'Good.'

They hug and Hannah hurries off along Lavender Hill. Craig waits for the lights to change at the crossing and when he looks back up the road she has gone.

CHAPTER TWENTY-EIGHT

T he bus stops at Clapham Common tube station and Craig steps off onto the leaf-splattered pavement. It's late Sunday evening. He stands under a streetlight to loosen the shoulder straps on his rucksack and weaves his way across the road through two queues of buses and cars. He buys himself a bottle of water and a Mars bar from a convenience store and eats the chocolate as he walks along the south side of the common. A lone teenager on a bike and a man in tight jeans walking a poodle pass Craig in the opposite direction. He looks across the road into the blackness of the trees and then at the building site to his left which is supposedly Lambeth College.

The only person at the tables outside The Whore on the Common is a man in a thick coat, having a cigarette. Inside, the pub is quiet and there's nobody at the bar. A middle-aged man and a woman in a rugby shirt are drinking red wine at a table by the fireplace, and there is a thin, bearded pensioner in a tatty sports jacket sitting on his own reading *The Independent*.

Craig orders a pint of orange and lemonade and calls Mark, but it goes straight to voicemail. He takes his drink and has a look around the corner in the restaurant.

Mark is the only person in there, sitting side-on to Craig at a table on the far left with his back against the wall. He's wearing a navy polo shirt with a long-sleeved white t-shirt underneath, and he's got thick stubble. He's clutching a full pint of cider to his chest and there are two Bulmers' bottles, an empty pint glass and the *News of the World* on the table. He doesn't notice Craig approaching.

'Mark,' Craig says, resting his rucksack against a leg of the table.

Mark gives Craig a troubled, distant look and asks him if he wants a drink. He sounds tired.

'How long have you been here?' Craig asks, taking a seat on the opposite corner.

'Since lunchtime.'

'Have you been here on your own?'

'No, no. Amy was here. But she had to go. What's the time?' he asks trying to sit up.

'It's nine fifty-four,' Craig says, checking his phone. 'How much have you had to drink?'

'I'm not sure. Not that much. Just a few ciders, and some wine with lunch.'

'Are you drunk?'

'I've been trying to get drunk, but it's not worked.'

'What time did Amy go?'

'About three.'

'Three? Mate you've been sitting here for almost seven hours on your own?'

'It doesn't seem that long. I've had a lot of thinking to do. Anyway, that's why I phoned you. I hoped you'd keep me company. Where have you been?'

'Just back at the flat. I was sorting my stuff out.' Craig glances down at his bag. 'Mate, I'm going home for a few days, to Norwich.'

'When?'

'Tonight.'

'Tonight? But it's late. Have a beer. Go back in the morning.'

'I can't. I'm getting the last train. I won't get in until one thirty.'

'When will you be back?'

'I'm not sure.'

'What do you mean you're not sure?'

'I'm not sure how long I'm going back for.'

'I thought we could go out and watch the Champions League games somewhere on Wednesday. Will you be back for that?'

'No... I won't, I don't think.'

'Will you be back at the weekend?'

'Probably. I'll need to pick some more of my things up.'

Mark sits motionless, staring at the table. 'You're moving out?' he says, barely moving his lips.

'No. I don't know,' Craig corrects himself. He scratches his ear lobe. 'I'm going to work for my dad, hopefully. Just for a few weeks, to earn some money in the short-term.'

Mark doesn't say anything.

'Sorry. I was going to tell you,' Craig says.

'What about job hunting? How are you going to do that when you're up there?'

'I can do it online. I'm only a train ride away if anything comes up.'

'But why don't you just stay down here? I don't understand.'

'I haven't got any money, mate. Literally none. In fact, a lot less than none. I don't want to go back, but I have to. My dad's paid off most of my overdraft and loans and I've got to start paying him back.'

Mark puts his glass down. 'Are you sure you have to? There must be some other way. I thought you liked it down here.'

'I don't have a choice.'

Mark doesn't react and starts reading the cider bottle.

'Mark, I need to earn some money, quickly.'

'But you can get a new job.'

'I've been trying. Estate agents are closing down, not taking people on.'

'Do something else.'

'Like what?'

'Can't you get your old job back?'

'No. I hated it. That was the reason I was getting further and further into debt. I've got less money now than I had at uni. I just can't afford to live here at the moment.' He pinches his bottom lip. 'I'm sorry.'

'Can't you get your parents to give you a loan? I don't see how moving back is going to help.'

'My dad's already given me a massive loan. He's paid off all my cards. I've got to work to pay it off, that's what I'm trying to say. They're not going to pay for me to stay down here when I owe them thousands and I'm unemployed.'

'But can't you say you're job hunting and just stay down here with me. You'll get another job won't you?'

'I don't know where. The recruitment people I've met have all been useless. One of the agencies I was with shut down last Friday.' Craig taps the rim of his glass with his finger. 'And the job market's going to get worse apparently.'

'You can't believe the newspapers.'

'I read the other day that this is the worst crash in something like a hundred years. Getting another job could take months.'

'They're just scare-mongering, to frighten people.'

'Mate, everything you read is about the credit crunch and recession and places closing. I don't feel like I've got a chance down here at the moment to be honest.' Craig takes three small sips of his drink.

'But you can't just run off.'

'I'm not running off. I'm going back to sort everything out.' Craig watches as Mark makes small tears in a beer mat. 'What are you going to do?' he asks tentatively.

'About what?'

'About work.'

'Work's fine,' Mark says. He swishes the cider around in his glass.

'Mark. *I know.*'

'Know what?'

'About MenDax.'

'I don't work for MenDax any more.'

'I know. Nobody does.'

Mark slumps forward, rests his chin on his hand, and gazes down into his pint. There is a long pause. 'I was going to tell you.'

'It must have been a shock.'

'Yeah,' Mark says. He sighs and looks everywhere apart from at Craig. 'Sorry I didn't say anything. I wasn't hiding it from you. I was just a bit, I don't know, embarrassed I suppose. I didn't want-'

'It's OK. I understand.'

Mark closes his eyes for a couple of seconds and puffs out his cheeks. 'How did you find out?'

'It was something Amy said at the party. And someone had written on her Facebook wall saying that they were sorry about her job, so I googled it.'

'Was there much on it?'

'A few reports. I was going to ask you about it, but, but I've not really seen you. And I didn't think you'd want to talk about it.'

'No.'

'I thought I'd see you one day but you'd always gone by the time I was up. What have you been doing? Going to recruitment places?'

'I was going to, but I've just been killing time most days. Trying to clear my head and decide what I'm going to do. I've been everywhere just to avoid sitting at home: museums, London Zoo. I even went on an open top bus.'

'What was that like?'

'Shit - it rained,' he says with weary laughter. 'I passed my driving test though.'

'Well done,' Craig says. 'I thought I hadn't seen your car.'

'That's because I've sent it back. It was only leased. Such a waste of money. Do you want another drink?'

'Mate, I really should go in a minute.'

'Come on, just one drink before you go. You've just told me you're leaving me. You can at least stay for a beer.'

Mark gives Craig some change and asks him to go to the bar because the Aussie barman has refused to serve him. Craig orders a pint of Fosters and a cider and brings them back over to the table. Mark sends him back to get some crisps.

'What are you going to do then, mate?' Craig asks, dropping down two bags of McCoy's.

Mark throws his hands in the air. 'To be honest, I don't know.'

'Have you told your parents?'

'I've spoken to my mum, but my dad's not talking to me because I've been spending my inheritance money.'

'I'm sure he'll be all right when he's calmed down. There must be other jobs doing what you were doing aren't there?'

'I don't know. Hopefully.'

'What have the other people in your department done?'

'Justin took Ian and Julia with him to his new place. Amy got another job last week.'

'I thought you got on well with Justin? Couldn't he help you?'

'No. He could have helped me, but he didn't. I wouldn't work for him anyway.'

'I didn't like him. He said all estate agents were wankers. How did Amy get her new job?'

'Through an agency.'

'Why don't you register with some agencies this week? You never know, there might be something perfect, well not perfect, but something you'd be good at.'

'I doubt it somehow. Amy's given me the numbers of some people to contact, but I'm not sure they'd be able to help.'

'Why?'

'I don't know. I don't feel like they would. I've got pretty simple requirements. All I want is a job that pays loads where I have no responsibility and can choose my own hours.'

'I can give your CV to my dad if you want.'

'Will I have to move to Norwich?'

'You can commute. It's two hours on the train.'

'What's he like as a boss?'

'He won't ever take you to a strip club, put it that way.'

'I'm not interested then,' Mark says, managing a sad smile. 'You know I was thinking about starting my own company.'

'Doing what, finance?'

'No, ice cream.'

'What do you know about ice cream, apart from how to eat it?'

'Nothing. But I had a good idea. I was going to start a designer ice cream brand. Guess what it was called?'

'I don't know.'

'Licked Out.'

Craig starts choking on his beer and apologises. 'How far have you got with this?'

'I went to a bank and asked them for some money to start up.'

'What did they say?'

'The guy I met didn't think it was a very good idea.'

'How much money did you ask for?'

'Seven hundred grand.'

'Is that all? You should have asked for more,' he says dryly. 'No wonder he didn't like it. I can't really imagine you as a Mr Whippy.'

'It wasn't going to be like that. It was going to be like a posh Starbucks, but for ice cream.'

'But people only eat ice cream in the summer.'

'Yes, I was going to serve it warm in the winter.'

'That's the worst idea I've ever heard.'

'Mate, when there's a Licked Out on every street in Britain and I'm a billionaire, you'll eat your words. If you're lucky I might hire you to wash the dishes.'

'Cheers,' Craig says helping himself to the crisps Mark has been hogging. 'I've got a choice between working for my dad or working for you washing dishes.'

'Or being an estate agent.'

'Yes, or being an estate agent. I think I'd prefer a long prison sentence to working somewhere like Cinq again.'

Mark takes a large handful of crisps. 'If you want a long prison sentence you could kill Justin for me. I'd pay you. Not that I can afford much at the moment. Perhaps we could start a business as hitmen? I could do the planning and you could do the hits.'

'Why would I have to do the hits?'

'I don't like blood.'

'Nor do I.'

'I *really* hate it. I wouldn't want there to be loads of blood anyway. That's how amateurs do it. I'd be a poisoner or strangler.' Mark burps and opens the other crisps. 'I wouldn't attack anyone with a hammer or anything like that, far too messy.'

'Are you sure you're not pissed?'

'No,' Mark says taking another gulp. 'When we've killed Justin we could take some photos and use that on all of our marketing.'

'Marketing?'

'Every company needs marketing. We'd have to advertise. Make sure we're getting the best jobs. We'd have a website and take out double-page spreads in the Sunday newspapers.'

Craig laughs. 'You've lost the plot. Are you going to take this idea to the bank?'

'I might do.'

'I'd love to hear what they say.'

'I'll start writing a business plan. How much do guns and stuff cost?'

'I don't know.'

'And we'd need some balaclavas.'

They both chuckle. Mark takes his iPhone out of his pocket and taps away. 'It's Amy. She's checking I'm not still here.' Mark is struggling to focus on the screen. 'I'm telling her I'm with you.'

'What's going on between you two?'

'Nothing. We're just... friends, I suppose,' he replies, still trying to compose a message.

'Friends who sleep together?'

'She told me that was a mistake.' He puts the phone down in front of him. 'The thing is, I think Amy... I don't know. I think she feels sorry for me. She's being so kind and so helpful, she makes me feel like a stupid little kid sometimes.'

'She's trying to help you because she likes you.'

'I'm like a challenge for her though. I think that's what she gets out of it. She's very positive and determined, and honest with me. There's no need to pretend I'm something I'm not because she sees straight through me. I feel different around her.'

'What do you mean?'

'I don't know, just different. She's always giving me loads of encouragement and tells me I can do whatever I want with my life, but somehow that just makes me feel worse because I don't know what I want to do. I'd rather not think about it.'

'You can't just ignore everything though, mate. It makes things worse. I should know.'

'Yeah, I know you're right. You're both right.' Mark sighs. 'I told Amy I love her the other night.'

'You said you loved her? Do you?'

'I don't know. I'd had quite a lot of wine.'

'What did she say?'

'She said that I should stop drinking so much.'

'What did you do?'

'I fell asleep on the sofa watching TV. She put a blanket over me.'

'Did she say anything the next morning?'

'No. I didn't mention it either. I don't know why I said it. I just made myself look stupid.'

'I'm sure she understands.'

'Yeah I know. She could find someone... better. I don't blame her.'

'I sure that's not what she's thinking.'

'I just... I just think... I don't know. I don't know what I think about a lot of stuff at the moment.' Mark pats his stomach. 'She keeps telling me to look forward rather than back. And that in six months I'll probably have an amazing job-'

'You probably will. And I'll still be hanging out in Norwich with my mum and dad.'

'You don't have to go back. The economy *must* pick up soon. We've just got to ride out this blip and try not to top ourselves in the meantime.'

Craig downs the last third of his pint.

'You're not going are you?' Mark asks.

The bell rings for last orders.

'I better go in a minute, mate. My train's at eleven thirty.'

'OK.' Mark nods but his mouth is turned down at the corners. 'What are we doing about the flat?'

'My dad's going to cover the rent for the next few months.'

'What all of it?'

Craig smiles, briefly. 'No, just my half. Text me when we get any bills and I'll transfer the money.'

'Haven't we got some kind of release clause?'

'We did, but only after six months, so we have to pay until the contract is up now. Don't you want to stay there?'

'Yeah, but it's not cheap is it. And it's a bit big to live in on my own.'

'Mate, if there's anyone you want to move in for a few weeks, you can.'

'I don't want anyone to move in. I don't want you to leave. I don't want to go back there on my own. It's depressing.'

'I'm sorry mate. I've really got to go.' Craig gets up and puts his bag on his chair.

Mark stumbles around the table. 'Well,' he says. There are tears in his eyes. 'I hope everything is OK at home.' He lunges forward and wraps Craig in his arms, burying his head into his shoulder.

'Cheers mate,' Craig says, gently patting Mark's back. 'I'm probably coming back at the weekend.'

'I look forward to it, mate,' Mark says, stepping back. He's left a damp patch on Craig's sweatshirt. 'I don't really want to go back to the flat without you. You're my best friend down here. Who else am I going to take shopping and watch football with?' Mark dries his eyes on his sleeves. 'Sorry. I'm being embarrassing. Good job there's no one here.'

'Don't worry. It's the drink talking.' Craig lifts his rucksack onto his back.

'No, it's not.'

'Sorry, I've really got to go. But I'll text you when I'm coming back down. OK?'

'Yeah. Sure,' Mark says, clearing his throat. 'Go. Go on. I'll text you.'

'Take it easy, mate. Don't have anything else to drink.'

'I might as well get smashed. It's not like I've got to get up early. Craig, just one last thing: you're not... you're not leaving because of me are you?'

'Don't be ridiculous, why would I leave because of you?'

'Because I've been a bad mate and you hate me?'

'I don't hate you, I don't hate anyone. But I've got to go. I'll see you soon, take care.'

Craig walks out the pub, turns right towards Clapham South tube and fades away into the night. Mark drops onto his seat, almost toppling backwards, and pours the last of his cider. The Australian barman strides across, takes Mark's glass and says it's time to go. Mark asks for two more minutes and when his request is refused, tells the barman he should be deported for being a fucking bellend. The barman grabs Mark by the collar, marches him outside and bolts the door behind him.

Mark is sitting beneath the pub's giant lantern, looking out through the trees towards the main road. It's cold and he rubs his forearms. An empty double-decker bus trundles past on its way to Clapham Junction and he jumps up and runs four paces, but it's too far gone, so he shuffles back to the table and lays his head down, using his arms as a pillow.

'Are you all right?' a young woman asks.

'I'm fine,' Mark says, his eyes closed.

The girl crouches down to check his face.

'I'm fine,' Mark repeats, his words half-muted.

'You don't look fine,' she says, standing over him. She has long dark hair and is wearing a grey woollen poncho done up to the neck. She sits down next to him and asks if he wants a cigarette.

Mark lifts his head. 'Yeah, thanks,' he says, his eyes shimmering.

The girl takes a packet of Marlboro Lights from her handbag and hands him one.

'I don't normally smoke,' he says.

'I can see that.'

He holds the cigarette away from his face. 'You work here don't you? Behind the bar.'

'Yes. I saw you were a bit upset inside. Sorry about you getting thrown out.'

'It's OK. I'm just a bit tired.'

'Pissed, you mean.'

Mark inhales and coughs. 'Yep. Pissed. And tired. Sorry.'

'That's OK.'

'My best mate just told me he's moving home.'

'Was that the guy with the rucksack?'

'Yep. He quit his job and says he can't afford to live down here any more so he's gone back to Norwich.'

She has a long drag on her cigarette. 'Is it just the two of you?'

'Yes, we've got a place off Lavender Hill. Do you live around here?'

'St John's Hill.' Her cigarette goes out so she re-lights it. 'Shouldn't you be getting home? Haven't you got work in the morning?'

'No. My company shut down. A bank collapsed so I lost my job.'

'What did you used to do?'

'I was a fund manager for an investment company in the City.'

'That sounds important.'

'Not really,' Mark says, flicking ash onto the ground. He rubs his arms again. 'What's your name?'

'Annabel.'

'I'm Mark.' They shake hands and Annabel blows smoke into the air. 'How long have you worked here for?'

'Four months. Since I left uni. I've got two jobs at the moment.'

'What else do you do?'

'I'm on a six-month internship at an experiential marketing company in Soho.'

'What's that like?'

'Not great. I'm basically free labour. The only people who do any work are the ones who aren't getting paid.'

'Sounds shit.' Mark coughs. 'Where did you go to uni?'

'You wouldn't have heard of it: UEEC.'

Mark coughs again and smiles.

'It's a shithole,' she says.

'I know. I went there.'

'Really? When?'

'I graduated in 2005.'

She looks at him disbelievingly. '*Really?*'

'Why would anyone lie about going there?'

'Fair point.' She smiles. 'I bet it was easier to get a job then.'

'My uncle got me my old job, so I don't know really.'

'I wish someone would help me. I didn't go to uni for three years to work in a pub. It makes you wonder what the point in having a degree is.'

'Huh. There is no point. That's the only thing they don't teach you. You know, if your job's really that bad and you don't want to work in a pub, you should leave. Go home, go travelling or something. Is there a job at the end of the internship?'

'Probably not.'

'Then quit. Seriously. When you've done your time, they'll say thanks very much, we're really sorry but we can't take anyone on at the moment and let you go, and the next day they'll have another work experience girl come and take your place.'

'I know.'

'The worst thing you can do is carry on because it's the easy option.'

The lights in the main bar are switched off as two police cars speed towards Balham followed by an ambulance. There is a long silence.

Annabel puts her cigarette out and gets up. 'Thanks for the advice. Will you be OK getting home?'

'How are you getting back?'

'Walking. I've not got enough money for a cab.'

Mark twists his legs out from under the table and rubs his eyes. 'Would you mind if I walked with you, please? I'll keep you company. I don't want to go home on my own. We're going in the same direction.'

CHAPTER TWENTY-NINE

J anet knocks on Craig's half-open bedroom door and pokes her head in:

'Dad said not to worry about going into work.'

'Oh. OK. Why?' Craig's tie hangs undone around his collar and he's holding a pair of cufflinks.

His mum has her coat on. 'He says he wants to talk to you later.'

'Has he gone already?'

'Yes, he left at seven.'

'Why did he leave so early?

'He's got a meeting in Cambridge.'

'Oh, right. But couldn't he do with some help? I'm sure there's something I could be doing.'

'You'll have to ask him.'

'But what am I meant to do here?'

'You can help me with the garden after lunch.'

'But he definitely doesn't want me to go into the office? I might ring him and-'

'He's not had any time to plan anything yet, love. He'll explain everything later. I don't think he wants you to be bored and don't-'

'But I'm meant to be working to pay you back.'

'Yes, I know love, but it might not be quite as simple as that.'

'But I can't repay you if I'm not working? And what am I meant to do here?'

'Craig, Dad will talk it all through with you later, don't start getting in a tizzy. We thought you might need a couple of days to relax anyway.'

'Thanks, but I'd rather just get on.'

'We know why you want to do it love, but perhaps it would be better for you just to take things easy for a day or so. Get some fresh air and catch up with your friends.'

'They're all at work.'

'Go into town and have a look around the shops then.'

'I can't even pay the bus fare, so I'm not going to go window shopping.'

'Take this,' Janet says. She hands him a £20 note from her purse which he reluctantly accepts. 'You don't have to spend it but if you want to go and watch a film or get yourself a coffee, you can.'

'Thanks Mum.'

'I don't want you worrying about money all the time; it's not good for you. Now I'm going to be out until after lunch as I've got a few people to see but if you need anything just ring me, I've got my mobile. Come on,' she says, giving him a hug, 'cheer up. It's not all bad.'

Craig waits for the front door to close, hangs his shirt and trousers back up, and falls asleep on his bed.

Craig is watching BBC *Look East* when his dad's car pulls up on the drive. It's almost seven o'clock. He turns the television off and heads into the kitchen where his mum is cooking. There is a shepherd's pie in the oven, a bowl of salad on the worktop and three places laid at the kitchen table. He offers to help but Janet doesn't need any, so he asks if she wants a cup of tea.

The front door slams and Peter goes straight upstairs. Craig is standing by the kettle whilst his mum flicks through a *River Cottage* recipe book.

'What's wrong with Dad?' Craig whispers.

'Nothing as far as I know.'

'Why did he run upstairs then?'

The bathroom toilet flushes and Peter comes down into the kitchen. He's taken his tie off and put a jumper over his work shirt. Craig says hello and quickly turns back to watching the kettle boil.

'I was desperate for the loo,' Peter says. 'I thought I wouldn't make it back to the house at one point.'

He pecks Janet on the cheek and mouths 'Is he all right?' at her, pointing at Craig. She nods.

Craig pours the tea, passes it over and disappears into the living room.

'Are you sure he's all right?' Peter says, keeping his voice down.

'He's been a bit quiet. I think he's worried.'

'About us or about work or what?'

'A bit of both. I think he was expecting to go to work with you this morning.'

'I didn't expect him to come back here at that time last night. I should have said something then. I-'

Craig comes back into the kitchen, avoiding his parents' gaze, and sits at the table with the *Eastern Daily Press*.

'Craig,' Peter says. He looks up from the newspaper. 'Would you like a glass of wine? I'm going to have one.'

'I'm fine thanks.'

Peter brings his drink to the table. 'What's happening in the world?' he asks.

Craig's reading a story about a robbery at a Fakenham Post Office. 'Not much,' he replies.

'What have you done to your hair?'

'I had it cut.'

Peter frowns. 'We were a bit surprised to see you last night. You should have called rather than getting a taxi.'

'I didn't get a taxi, I walked. I thought you'd be asleep. Anyway, I thought you wanted me at work this morning.'

Peter clears his throat. 'Craig, it's not going to be quite as simple as that. We need to have a little chat about things. I don't know if Mum told you but Cuthbert's Kitchen Warehouse have gone under.'

'No, she didn't. Did they owe you any money?'

'Fortunately not a lot, but obviously losing their account is a bit of a hole to fill and we're going to have to be very careful over the next few months.'

'OK.'

'I think we'll be able to get by without making anyone redundant, but equally we won't be taking anyone on.'

'What do you mean?'

'I mean that I won't be able to take you on, in the short-term.'

Craig pushes away the newspaper. 'Dad, but I thought you wanted me to come back to work for you?'

'That was just a suggestion but I've thought things through and there's really nothing you could do for me. I can't just create a job that

290

doesn't need doing to pay you so you can pay me back. In effect I'd be taking money out of the company and paying it into my own bank account, so there's no way I'm doing that.'

'And there's definitely no one looking to leave or you could let go?'

'Craig,' Peter snaps, 'don't be so bloody selfish or I will get angry.'

'Sorry, sorry, sorry. That came out wrong. I didn't mean that.'

'I should hope not.'

'Peter, no need to shout,' Janet chips in.

'But how am I meant to pay you back then? If I can't work for you, I'm not sure what else I'll be able to do, unless I take a job in a pub or restaurant, which I'll do if you want me to.'

'Craig, I think we should put the issue of your debt to one side for a minute. A lot of this depends on you. In an ideal world would you really want to move back here and go back to your old job?'

'If you want to move back, you can,' Janet says, checking the oven.

'Craig, we both love having you here, but we want what's best for you. And I don't think living here and working for us again is necessarily what's best.'

'But I want to pay you back.'

'We know you want to pay us back and we're happy you do, but if you'd have enjoyed working here and living here so much, you wouldn't have gone down to London in the first place. I know you like it here, but I don't want you to spend the next two or three years paying us back and then suddenly finding yourself approaching thirty stuck in a career you're not interested in.'

'It's not that I wasn't interested, it's just that after university, coming back here and working for you again seemed a bit... It was like I had nothing to look forward to any more.'

'We understand that.'

'But I preferred it to being in London with no money.'

'But did you though? You've had plenty of opportunities to come home before now.'

'I know. But I couldn't carry on getting further and further in debt.'

'Nobody likes having no money, Craig. You might think you were trying to be responsible and independent, but you've got to be mature enough to know when to ask for help. The problem wasn't going to go away.'

'I know. I'm sorry.'

'You don't have to keep apologising, we feel responsible as well. I never wanted you to feel you couldn't talk to us.'

'It's not your fault.'

Janet puts her oven gloves on and brings the shepherd's pie to the table.

'Me and your mum are both in agreement that you can stay here if you want to, but if you want to go back down to London, we'll support you.'

'Thank you. But it's not really an option, is it. What would I do?' he says with a shrug. 'I'm the one who's made a mess of everything. I don't want it to end up costing you even more to get me back on my feet.'

'But you'll never be able to pay us back on Norwich bar job wages, that's my point.'

'And it's better you owe money to us than to banks or credit companies,' Janet says. 'Love, we just don't want to see you getting yourself into problems.'

'Look, we know you've not done any of this deliberately but it's important that you learn to ask for help rather than trying to do everything on your own, because you're not on your own.'

'We just don't want you to be unhappy,' Janet says.

'I know, I know.' Craig has a tear in his eye but swiftly wipes it away.

'It's time to draw a line under what's happened and work out what you're going to do next,' Peter says, taking the salad servers from Janet. 'To be perfectly honest, I'm not happy with you living here when we're paying for a room in a flat in London which nobody's using. Do you know anyone who'd want to move in?'

'No. Nobody.'

'I'm not surprised at that price,' Janet adds.

'What does Mark think about all this? He doesn't want to live on his own does he surely?'

'Mark's lost his job.'

Peter puts his fork down. 'Since when? You didn't tell us.'

'It happened a few days ago. His company shut down.'

'Christ almighty,' Peter says, exasperated. 'So he's up the creek as well? What's he going to do?'

'I don't know. He's taken it pretty badly. I think he's got enough money to last him for a while though.'

'Has he got anything else lined up?'

'Not as far as I know.'

'Poor lad,' says Janet. 'It can't be good for him. No job and sitting there on his own all the time.'

'You two could both do with getting out of that place as soon as possible.'

'Our lease has another six months.'

'If I was you I'd go through that contract with a fine-tooth comb. They treated you bloody awfully so I wouldn't have any qualms about trying it on with them. Have you got a copy of what you signed?'

'Yes, it's in my file upstairs.'

'Would you mind if I have a look at it? If they're as disorganised and dishonest as you say they are, you can almost guarantee that the contract won't be worth a penny.'

*

It's Wednesday night and the family are in the living room watching a repeat of *Midsomer Murders*.

'Craig, would you be against going back down to London?' Peter asks unexpectedly, getting a glace from Janet for talking over the TV.

'Not until I can afford to.'

'How about if we covered you, initially? If the economy goes the way it looks like it's going to, I think you'll be better off down there than you are here.'

'You think?'

'I can't imagine there are going to be many opportunities in Norwich, unless you want to work in insurance.'

Peter coughs and asks Janet to pass him the *Radio Times* before looking back to Craig:

'Look, I hope you don't think I'm interfering, but I made a few phone calls this afternoon to some of my contacts and dropped into conversation that you may be looking for work.'

'Of course I don't mind.'

'I was a bit concerned that you'd think I was trying to get rid of you or push you into something you didn't want to do.'

'And we're not trying to get rid of you, love, we're just trying to think of what's practical,' Janet says.

'I'll do anything. I don't mind what it is,' Craig says.

'I had a word with Phil Symonds just before I left the office, do you know the name?'

'No.'

'His company lease office furniture. It's a very successful business. I was talking to him and he said there's a possibility that he might want to take on another account manager.'

'Right. Where's that?'

'I think he's based in Wimbledon. That's not too far from you, is it?'

'No. A few stops on the tube.'

'Now this is no guarantee of anything, but he said that if you were interested, you should give him a ring.'

'And what did you say?'

'I said I'd ask you.'

'Do you know anything else about it?'

'You'll have to talk to him yourself. I've told you as much as he told me, but Phil's a good man, he wouldn't have you doing any old rubbish. So you'll speak to him will you?'

'Definitely.'

'Good. I've got to ring him tomorrow about something else anyway, so I'll tell him that you'd like to talk to him and I'll arrange a time for you to call him. How does that sound?'

'Great. Thank you.'

'Good,' Peter says.

Janet leans across the sofa, checks her husband isn't looking and says quietly:

'Love, you know you can always stay here with us, don't you?'

*

It's three o'clock on a cold, grey afternoon and Mark is in the City, sitting in the garden of St Boltoph-without-Bishopsgate Church. He hasn't shaved but is dressed in a suit and tie.

The church is surrounded by high-rise glass-panelled office blocks and dwarfed by the steel skeleton of another new tower being constructed across the road. There are two other people on the row of benches; a cycle courier who takes regular sucks on a water bottle, and a podgyfaced woman reading a chick lit novel.

Mark shivers and stuffs his Pret bag into an overflowing rubbish bin by a tree. A pigeon swoops down and pecks at a discarded sandwich crust at his feet. He straightens himself up and turns left out of the church along Bishopsgate. He looks at the 'Three free shirts with every suit over £130' offer in the window of Taylors the Tailors, and then wanders down towards Liverpool Street station. 'UK ON BRINK OF RECESSION' is the headline on the *Evening Standard* boards.

Mark stops outside The Broker, which is virtually empty, and then takes a left down Old Broad Street. There are 'Office Space To Let' signs hanging in the former MenDax offices, and all evidence of the company has been removed from the reception. Mark gazes up at the building and is being watched by a security guard when his phone rings.

'Hello, Mark Hunter,' he says, monotone.

'Yes that's me.' He clears his throat, scurries down a narrow passageway away from the noise of the road and stands in the doorway of a newsagent.

'Yes that's right.

'Which headhunting firm did you say you were from?

'OK. Can you give me a few more details about the job?

'No, I'm massively interested. I've got the experience and I was looking at moving into that kind of area anyway. Where's it based?

'And would I have to travel to Dubai?

'How often would that be?

'No, not a problem at all. I've travelled a lot with work so-

'And how much money are we talking?

'Good. And what's their bonus structure like?

Mark starts smiling. 'No, but obviously if they're really interested in me I'd negotiate with them.

'Of course, of course.

'Could you send me all the details on an email? Cheers. Yes, use the one on my contact details.

'Sorry you cut out, could you say that again?'

Mark swallows. 'Yes they did close. But I was leaving anyway because I had an offer from-

'Oh yes of course I know, I'll send you an updated one. I've not had the chance to update my details because I've been so busy on-

Tom Canty

'Where am I working at the moment?

'I'm working for... I'm consulting for... I have my own private consultancy, I've been doing consultancy for...' he looks through the newsagent's window. 'Tango.' He clenches his teeth and silently admonishes himself. 'I mean... on their investment account and, um, at the moment I'm working for...'

'No, not strictly. I'm a consultant.

'Self-employed then I suppose you'd say.

'Am I registered? Um, yes of course.

'No, just me.

'*Why?* Um, I've been using my contacts to build a portfolio for-'

'No, that was deliberate. I didn't want to commit myself to one company but I am looking to-

'No, I'd stop that, or I could do it on the side as I'm... I'm always looking for opportunities.

'Technically no, but-

'I've explained that-

'No, no, no. Hang on, but I'd be perfect, I've been waiting for-

'But headhunters are meant to find people jobs-

'No, I'm not wasting your time, you called me. I've got all the-

'No I am not unemployed! I can prove-'

'I've turned down five jobs already this week.

'No, turned down, not been turned down.

'You can't put the phone down! No, wait! I'm the-'

Mark mutters 'prick' and stands staring at his feet until the shopkeeper calls out for him to stop blocking the doorway. He then gets a text from Craig saying that he's coming back on Friday for an interview.

For the next hour, Mark wanders the streets of the City as the light fades, gazing glumly through the windows of busy offices. He then sits by the ruins of London Wall and calls all twelve restaurants in his phonebook to reserve tables under the name Justin Fortesque, telling each one that he'll be coming in at eight and would like the most expensive bottle of red on the wine list to be opened and allowed to breathe for half an hour before he arrives.

After more aimless wandering, he finds himself outside St Paul's Cathedral. He tries to go in but is put off by the £13 entry fee which he attempts to avoid by claiming he just wants to pray.

CHAPTER THIRTY

S ymonds' Furniture Leasing is based on the second floor of a red brick building with mirrored windows near Wimbledon station. Phil Symonds, a genial, slightly overweight man in his late forties with greying hair, greets Craig in reception and takes him up in the lift. Unlike Craig, who's in a suit and tie, Phil is casually dressed in sand-coloured chinos and a red open-neck shirt.

Initially Craig looks pensive but starts to relax as Phil gives him a brief history of the company – which he set up in 2002 having worked for another leasing firm – and shows him into the roomy office which overlooks a shopping centre.

There are only three other employees – each with their own desk and leather chair – and the business appears very well organised, with no piles of stray folders or loose sheets of paper anywhere. The computers, photocopier, and coffee machine are all brand new and a 2008 day planner and a note-covered whiteboard take up most of the back wall. A young man a similar age to Craig gives Phil a friendly nod as he walks in and there are two young women having a conversation in the kitchen area.

Craig waits in the glass-walled meeting room as Phil gets him a coffee. He takes a copy of his CV from his bag and places it on the table, then makes sure his mobile is on silent.

'I was on the phone to your dad again earlier,' Phil says handing Craig his drink. 'We're kitting out an entire office block in Manchester next month and he's doing all of the transportation for us. I like dealing with your dad, he's very straightforward. Never promises anything he can't deliver.'

'He's always been like that. He says that if you mess people around they stop trusting you, and if they stop trusting you, you lose their business, so it's better to just be honest from the start.'

'Very true,' Phil says. 'So Craig, he was saying that you're looking for a new job at the moment.'

'Yes.'

'And before you were working as an estate agent.'

'Yes, I was a sales negotiator at Cinq Estates. It's all on my CV, if you look-,' Craig pushes the page across the table but Phil only takes a brief glance at it before moving it to one side. 'Thanks, I'll have a look at that later. There was a programme about them on recently wasn't there?'

'Umm, yes. Some BBC reporters went undercover at a couple of branches and exposed some of the tactics they use. The company came out of it very badly apparently.'

'They were breaking the law a lot of the time weren't they?'

'I think so. Some of the things people were encouraged to do were... illegal.' Craig coughs into his hand.

'I'm not going to start questioning you about it, don't worry. I know that's how some businesses operate and that if you're working there it's very difficult because nobody wants to rock the boat. Was it as bad as it was made to look though?'

'I didn't actually see the programme, but we were all told to lie if it would help us push through a sale, and to try to steal customers from other agencies. The branch I worked for wasn't organised enough to do what some of the others were doing.'

'Like forging documents?'

'Yes, like that. I never liked lying to the customers and that's why I didn't get on with my boss. He would do or say literally anything to make a sale.'

'Did you have to drive one of those cars with the house on the roof?' Phil asks, smiling.

'Everyone had to. It was embarrassing at the start but you soon got used to the funny looks. If you passed a certain sales target you got to drive an unbranded car, so it was meant to motivate you to sell more, but the target was so high that nobody ever achieved it.'

'So why did you end up staying there as long as you did?'

'I was looking for other jobs when I was there but the right thing never came up, and also part of me wanted to try to make it work. I didn't want to go back to my mum and dad's after a few months, I wanted to prove to everyone that I could do things on my own, and I wanted to stay in London.'

'Well at least you stuck at it I suppose, and I don't blame you for wanting to stay down here. When I moved to London from Banbury, where my parents were, I worked for a builder's merchants in north London, which I didn't enjoy, but it seemed a better option than moving home, and I stayed there for five years in the end. It easily happens.' Phil has a sip of his coffee. 'Now Craig, how much has your dad told you about the job?'

'Not very much.'

'OK, fine. Basically we're looking for another account manager because at the moment we're getting more enquiries and having more requests from our current clients than we can deal with.'

'OK.'

'You know what we do, don't you? I probably should have explained that.'

'You rent out office furniture.'

'Yes. Exactly. We own the products and then lease them out to businesses that need desks and chairs and whatever else but don't want to buy them outright. If you're a new business, kitting out an office is expensive and with the financial situation not looking too rosy at the moment we're a far more cost-effective option. And they have the option to buy the stuff at the end of the contract anyway.'

'Right,' Craig says, nodding.

'So what we need is another person to help us deal with the workload.'

'Right.'

'Your dad said you did a similar type of job for him?'

'Yes, I was an account handler there, so I was responsible for a number of our clients and had to make sure they were getting their produce and products delivered on time to the right places. But I'd also deal with the new business as well. So people would ring up saying they need this transported there by Friday and I'd have to agree contracts and prices and everything with them.'

'Great, because that's pretty much exactly what I'd want you to do here. The most important thing is to understand precisely what the client wants, so that usually means going out and visiting their premises and matching their requirements to their budget, which can be a bit tricky sometimes. But you've obviously got plenty of experience about price negotiation from your estate agent days so that won't be a problem. So do you think this is something that you'd be happy doing?'

'Yes, definitely. I'm used to travelling around and meeting people and discussing prices. And I enjoyed the work I was doing for my dad far more than trying to convince people to buy houses.'

'Excellent. This isn't a sales role, so you won't be ringing people trying to talk them into buying furniture. The clients come to us.'

'Good. I don't particularly enjoy cold-calling people.'

'Does anyone? You won't be doing any of that here. Did you have to do that a lot at Cinq?'

'Yes, and most people just put the phone down.'

Phil chuckles and thinks for a moment. 'Your dad said you've got a business degree, is that right?'

'Yes. Business and sociology from UEEC in Cambridge.

'I'm sure that will come in useful along the line. Out of interest, do you know anything about the office furniture market?'

'Umm, not really...'

'Oh, it doesn't matter at all if you don't; it's more to help me train you. You'll pick everything up in no time, it's just a case of familiarising yourself with the products and the pricing. So when can you start?'

'When can I start?' Craig repeats the question as if he's misheard it.

'Yes.'

'Err, Monday?'

'Good, is everything OK? You look a bit shocked.'

'Um, yes,' Craig says, 'it's just... Is that the whole interview?'

'Unless there's anything else you want to ask me?'

'Not that I can think of.'

'Good then. I'm happy if you are. What were you expecting, a five-hour interrogation?'

'I'm not sure what I was expecting. I'm happy though, great. Actually I do have a question: What's the, um, salary?'

'Oh yes, money. The salary is twenty-eight thousand with a ten per cent bonus as long as we hit our company target. I know that's probably a bit less than you were on, but you get thirty days' holiday and you have a pay review once a year. How does that sound?'

'Excellent, thanks. Really good.' Craig smiles and all of the tension disappears from his face.

'We also have a team meal once a month and I think you'll really like the rest of the team, they're a friendly bunch.'

'Excellent.'

'Good. Well then, Craig.' Phil stands up, Craig follows, and they shake hands. 'Let me introduce you to everyone else.'

CHAPTER THIRTY-ONE

' Turn right out of the station and take the road running up the left-hand side of the green. You'll pass a pub on your left called The White Horse, walk to the end and my house is facing you. It's number two-one-one and it's flat three. Ring the bell.'

Amy leaves her BlackBerry on the coffee table, straightens up the throw on the sofa and pours some crisps into a bowl. The living room of her one-bedroom flat is small and cosy with a view of Parsons Green. A framed print of the Paris skyline and a blown-up photograph of Amy and friends at their Durham University graduation ball hang side by side on the wall. She quickly checks herself in the mirror and applies some lip balm.

The entry system buzzes. Amy remotely unlocks the front door and then opens the door to her flat.

Craig apologises for being late and explains that he had to drop into the office on the way over. He's wearing a yellow scarf and has a brown satchel across his body. Amy kisses him on the cheek and says that she's only just got back from work anyway. She makes a pot of tea and they go through to the living room.

Amy sits with her legs tucked under her on the sofa whilst Craig plants himself on the matching single-seater.

'How's work at the moment?' he asks.

'Tiring. I have to get in for seven thirty and this is the first night I've left before nine this week. A whole team have just been made redundant and everyone's nervous about losing their jobs. The woman who used to sit opposite me has been signed off on sick leave because her hair started falling out. I think she must be having some form of breakdown.'

'So not good then.'

'The only positive thing I can say about it is that it's better than being unemployed. I think the problem now is that because the job market's so terrible, even companies that haven't been affected that much by the credit crunch are using it as an excuse to get rid of people and work everyone else harder. They know nobody will complain because they can't afford to. Everyone's keeping their heads down.'

'Is what you're doing now similar to your old job?'

'There are far less client meetings. The majority of the time I'm looking at data and compiling reports. At MenDax, there was no monitoring at all whereas at my new place, you feel like you're being watched every minute you're there.'

'What's the company called?'

'Hades Asset Management. The office is by Monument tube. How's your job going?'

'Yeah, really good. It's actually taken me a while to get used to not working at the weekend. Just doing normal hours and getting home at seven, I have so much more free time. And I'm not on commission so I'm not always fretting about not having enough money at the end of the month.'

'You do look a lot happier. And more relaxed.'

'Do I? I definitely feel more relaxed. I'm getting a lot more sleep. I've only been there ten weeks but it feels a lot longer.'

'It's only quite a small firm isn't it?'

'There are six of us now, and we've got a temp at the moment.'

'I wish I worked somewhere smaller sometimes... but once you get on the corporate treadmill, it's hard to get off.'

'I suppose so.'

Craig takes a handful of crisps. The red light on Amy's BlackBerry is flashing and she checks her emails.

'How's everything going with Hannah?' she asks.

'Pretty good, I think. We're just seeing each other a couple of times a week and taking it all slowly. I don't want her to feel like I'm pressurising her into anything so I'm just happy to see where things go. Her new job's going well, so she's happy.'

'What's she doing now?'

'She's got a marketing assistant job for the Olympic delivery people.'

'Wow, that sounds good.'

'Yeah, it does. It's what her degree's in, and she's sporty so it's perfect really. Although I suppose anything would be a perfect job after working on the reception at Cinq.'

'Working on reception was probably the best job there.'

'I can almost guarantee she got paid more than me.' Craig pauses. 'I'm thinking about asking her to go on holiday.'

'With you?'

'Yes, with me. What do you think?'

'Where were you thinking about going?' Amy asks, adjusting her sitting position.

'I'm not sure. Do you know I haven't been on holiday in five years?' Craig says, glancing at the art on the wall. 'I was thinking about going to New York but it's pretty expensive and I think I'd rather go to a beach somewhere and just chill rather than sightsee. I might even ask Mark if Hannah isn't interested.'

'He needs a job, not a holiday. What's he been like this week?'

'Exactly the same. He goes to the gym every morning when I go to work and when I get home he's either on the internet or playing on the Xbox. He's lost a lot of weight.'

'Yes, I know. Is he eating properly?'

'I think so.'

'Has he had a shave yet?'

'Yes, he has. He's still not got his hair cut though.'

Amy huffs. 'Well done for getting out of the contract on the flat, by the way. Mark text me yesterday.'

Craig smiles mischievously. 'It was quite easy in the end. I was expecting a lot of problems but one of the guys I used to work with is still there and he helped me out. He found the original copies of our contract and shredded them. I then emailed him to say that our lease was up, he emailed back to say he couldn't find our documents and I replied saying that wasn't our problem and that we were moving out, and that was that. That office was so disorganised by the time my old boss left that the new guy has come to expect this sort of thing apparently so there were no questions asked. I even got our full deposit back.'

'Don't people normally get their deposits back?'

'It's Cinq policy to never refund the full deposit. Even if the tenants had been perfect, we were always told to keep at least twenty-five per cent. Some agents used to go round to houses and deliberately break tiles and stain carpets so they could blame the occupiers and keep the money.'

'What bastards.'

'That's what happened,' Craig says with a shrug.

'When do you move into the new flat?'

'Two weeks on Friday. I've taken a day off work and hired a van. It shouldn't be too difficult.'

'Where is it, near Putney Bridge?'

'Yes, it's in a block next to the river. It's a lot smaller than Clapham, less than half the size probably, but it's all modern inside and it's got a balcony. Mark won't be able to spread his mess everywhere.'

'Mark said your boss owns it.'

'He asked me if I had any friends who were looking for somewhere because his tenants were moving so I said that we'd take it. He's given us a good deal on the rent – it's just about half of what we're paying at the moment – and I think it's a better area. I took Mark to see it last week and we had a couple of beers by the river afterwards. It all seemed a bit more chilled than Clapham.'

'Do you think you'll miss Clapham?'

'No.'

'Why's that?'

'I'm not sure really. It was fun to start with, and I'd probably go back there for a night out, but it's overpriced for what it is and although the common's nice when it's sunny, it's not that great a place to live. It always feels crowded and there are a lot of posers.'

'It's the type of place you shouldn't stay for too long. You can move there straight after university and then suddenly ten years later you're still living like a student. I could have seen Mark falling into that trap.'

'I don't know, I think he would have got bored of it eventually. I can understand why people do it, but it's just not for me. I prefer somewhere a bit... quieter.'

'Like Norwich?'

'No, not Norwich; that's the Las Vegas of East Anglia.'

'At least it shows he's got a vivid imagination,' Amy says. They've finished their takeaway pizza and are now sitting together on the sofa in front of Craig's laptop which is perched on the edge of the coffee table.

'Apart from his name and date of birth, he's not written a single thing which isn't either made up or a big exaggeration.'

They are reading Mark's CV, which Craig emailed himself from Mark's MacBook.

'Are you sure this is the most recent copy?' Amy asks. 'This can't be what he's been sending people.'

'I found this hidden away in a folder in his documents; he hadn't left it on his screen for me to see. There was only one other CV but that was from a couple of years ago.'

'I thought there at least might be some parts of this we could use, but we're going to have to start from scratch. Make up a new document,' Amy tells Craig. 'We can keep the format.'

Craig copies the CV and deletes everything apart from the contact information and section headings.

'The profile just makes him sound like an idiot.' Amy reads, '*Mark Hunter is a fearless financier and entrepreneur. He acts as a consultant to no less than six FTSE 100 companies (unnamed for legal reasons) and has business interests that are predicted to have a turnover of £50m by 2020. He has won a host of awards including 'City A.M. Fund Manager of the Year 2007 (under-30 category)' and was described in the comments section of an article on the Financial Times website as 'one of the sharpest young brains in Britain'. International business leaders consider this an accurate assessment of his abilities.*'

Craig is laughing.

'It's so stupid it makes me feel sad,' Amy says. 'I hope for his sake he's never actually sent this to anyone.'

'It's just so obvious that it's all bollocks. But it's not like he's never had a job or doesn't have any qualifications.'

'No, according to this he got a 2.1 in economics from King's College, Cambridge and an MBA from the University of California.'

Craig chuckles. 'You know we said he'd lied about everything apart from his name and date of birth, he *has* lied about his date of birth. He's made himself a year older. He was born in 1982, not 1981.'

'For goodness sake. Change it then. I suppose otherwise the dates wouldn't add up, although it wouldn't surprise me if he claimed to have taken his A-levels when he was seventeen.'

Craig scans down the document. 'Yep, we need to move all his education forward a year.'

They are still working on Mark's CV at half past midnight. Amy makes notes on a pad and dictates sentences to Craig. They decide to award Mark a 2.1 from UEEC, a grade higher than he got, which Craig is uneasy about but Amy insists they should put ethics to one side for the moment and reasons that he'll be competing against people with lies on their CVs and that nobody ever checks degree certificates anyway. Craig agrees this is probably true.

Neither of them can think of a term to describe Mark's current work situation. Craig suggests it could say Mark's been travelling but Amy dismisses this as a lie that could easily trip him up in an interview. They settle on calling him a 'Freelance Financial Analyst' and Amy says she'll be one of his referees and will say that Mark's been working for her if it comes to that.

'What *are* Mark's interests?' Craig says, placing the cursor below the only heading with nothing written beneath it.

'The gym, I suppose is one now.'

'We can't really put drinking and playing on the Xbox. He reads all those business autobiographies, so we can put that.'

'And I suppose he likes sport as well.'

'Most of the things he liked at university he seems to have lost interest in. He used to go and see bands and I think he played rugby and tennis when he was at school, but he doesn't do any of that any more.'

'I've been trying to encourage him to take up some hobbies to keep his mind active. I'm worried that all he does is sit at home all day making himself depressed.'

'I think he feels like he was doing so well and that it's so unfair that it's all been taken away from him.'

Amy shrugs. 'He feels foolish because I warned him time and time again about getting too close to Justin. Justin and Julia and Ian weren't his friends; they didn't care about him and they didn't care about MenDax, but he wouldn't listen. Also, Mark wasn't doing that well. He always wanted to believe that a massive pay day or promotion was just around the corner, whereas in reality it never was. The whole company was a complete sham by the end and relied on people like Mark who never questioned what was happening.

'I wasn't blameless either and I never expected things to end as suddenly as they did but it taught me to be careful. If you work for a big corporate and you have any loyalty to them *at all*, then you're deluded, because they will get rid of you without giving it a second thought. That was the problem with Mark; he actually thought that Justin and the other bosses at MenDax had his best interests at heart. All they were doing was making as much money for themselves as possible. Once the money stopped coming in, people like me and Mark were dispensable. It sounds harsh but it's true. Do you think that the MenDax board – the people who were taking millions and millions out of the company year after year – gave a shit about people like me?' Amy shrugs. 'Sorry, I should stop going on about it.'

'It's OK.'

'That's why I want to help Mark. I'm not going to watch him go into a downward spiral whilst a lot of the people who were responsible for MenDax going bust carry on as normal.'

Craig types in some of Mark's interests and Amy tells him that a couple of lines is enough. He adds himself and Amy as referees and says that he'll pretend to have worked with Mark at MenDax if anyone calls him. He asks Amy to email him with a few lines about MenDax so he'll be able to lie competently if required.

She says she'll send his details to the recruitment agencies she used when she was job hunting and asks Craig to set up a new Mark Hunter LinkedIn profile, and, if possible, find out his password and delete the current one.

Craig runs a spellcheck and emails the document to Amy. By the time he shuts his laptop, it's twenty past one.

'Do you think this will work?' he asks.

'It can't do any harm. We have to do *something*. He can't just carry on like he is. I hate seeing him look so sad, and he sounds miserable.'

'It's like he's lost all of his energy. He used to go out all the time but now, apart from going to the gym, he barely leaves the flat. Most of the time when I'm there he's either sitting in silence or asleep. Even when you talk to him he barely says anything. It's like he's there but he's not there, do you know what I mean?'

Amy nods.

'When I took him to the see the new flat, he hardly said anything. The old Mark would have been telling me it was too small or he didn't like the bedrooms, or that he hated being by the river or something…

but he was just drifting from room to room, and expecting me to take the lead all the time.'

'I think he's lonely, and he said that if he was you, he wouldn't want to be mates.'

'When did he say that?'

'Last week. He hadn't seen you for a couple of days and was getting a bit upset.'

Craig frowns and picks at his chin. 'He was a complete dick at times. I just wanted him to be more like he was at uni, more normal, less like your old boss. It didn't suit him.'

'I said that I didn't think you'd be moving into a new flat if you didn't want to be friends.'

'However much he annoyed me, I don't like seeing him like this.'

CHAPTER THIRTY-TWO

C raig has a two-minute shower and pulls on jeans and a hoody. He bangs on Mark's door, tells him to get up, and says he's off to get the van.

When he returns an hour later, Mark's bedroom door is still shut. Craig mutters swear words, knocks twice and when there is no answer, goes in.

All of Mark's clothes and possessions are boxed and labelled. The bed has been stripped, there's nothing on the walls, and the bathroom has been cleaned. The wardrobe doors are open, as are the windows.

'Meant to do this on my own, am I?' Craig says to himself. He sends Mark a text and walks out to the kitchen.

All the kitchenware is packed up, the cupboards have been emptied, and the fridge and oven are spotless. Craig searches through the boxes, finds a glass wrapped in newspaper and has a drink of water.

Mark has left a note on the table: *Gone to Tower Bridge. Go on without me as I may be some time - I know you're strong enough. Take care of my stuff. Sorry for doing this to you. I'll make it up to you in another life. M*

'Oh my fucking god, what's he...' Craig says, starting to panic. He stands holding the note and reads it back to himself again and again before stuffing it into his pocket and grabbing the van keys.

He gets behind the wheel of the rented Volkswagen and leaves Amy a message asking her to call him straight away as he hurtles up to Lavender Hill. It's a gloomy, overcast morning and the roads through Clapham are relatively clear. He gets a call as he reaches Battersea.

'AMY,' he shouts, switching the phone to speaker and placing it on the passenger seat. 'CAN YOU HEAR ME? IT'S MARK.'

'Mark? Craig? What about Mark? I'm on my way to a meeting.'

'Shit,' he says, just making it through a red light.

'Craig, are you driving? I can't hear you very well, the reception's awful.'

'AMY, I THINK MARK'S GONE TO THROW HIMSELF OFF A BRIDGE.'

'What? What do you mean?' she asks calmly.

'WE WERE MEANT TO BE MOVING OUT THIS MORNING BUT HE'S DISAPPEARED AND HE'S LEFT ME A NOTE SAYING HE'S SORRY ABOUT EVERYTHING AND THAT HE'LL SEE ME IN ANOTHER LIFE.'

'Craig I can't really hear you. Are you sure? I can't imagine Mark-'

'HE'S LEFT ME A NOTE SAYING HE'S GOING TO TOWER BRIDGE,' he shouts louder. 'WHERE'S TOWER BRIDGE?'

'Where are you?'

'BATTERSEA.'

'You need to go towards the City. Craig, are you sure he's there?' she says, sounding increasingly anxious.

'YES! YES, I'M SURE. I'M VERY SURE. HIS PHONE'S SWITCHED OFF AND HE'S CLEARED HIS ROOM OUT. AMY, I NEED YOU TO MEET ME THERE.'

'OK, OK. I'm in Kings Cross, but I'll leave now. Craig, don't panic. And be careful. Ring me as soon as you're there. I'll keep trying his phone.'

Craig speeds across Battersea Bridge and turns right onto Chelsea Embankment narrowly missing a taxi whose driver slams on the brakes and beeps furiously as Craig accelerates away. He follows the signs for Central London but gets held up at the traffic lights by Albert Bridge. Once they turn green, he powers along the tree-lined road, the Thames on his right and Battersea Power Station rapidly approaching in the distance.

'Where the hell's this?' he says as he passes Chelsea Bridge and drives down into Pimlico. He reaches the junction of Millbank and Vauxhall Bridge Road and goes straight ahead, but there are roadworks and he ends up tailgating a Mercedes people carrier.

He continues past rows of Georgian mansions and uses the drop-off area outside the Tate Gallery to overtake the Mercedes and a Royal Mail van.

As he approaches Westminster, the traffic is heavy and he's stuck behind a lorry loaded with timber. The roads around Parliament Square are slow and Craig tells himself to stay calm. His hands are sweating on the steering wheel. He tries Mark's mobile again at traffic lights on the Victoria Embankment but the call cuts out without ringing.

Amy calls as he passes Temple underground station, but he accidently cancels it as he grabs at his phone and it drops between the passenger seat and handbrake. He leaves it and concentrates on the road as he flies down into Blackfriars underpass.

Craig reaches the City, where offices and commercial buildings block his view of the river. He mutters, 'Fucking hell, how many bridges are there?' as he passes Southwark Bridge Road and repeatedly thumps his fist on the dashboard along Lower Thames Street as he's boxed in by courier vans, taxis and motorcycles.

The Tower of London and Tower Bridge dominate the horizon as he crawls past All Hallows Church. He tails a bus and takes a right onto Tower Bridge Approach then swings left down St Katherine's Way, a side road running parallel to the bridge. He brakes sharply and parks on double-yellow lines in the shadow of the Tower Hotel.

He retrieves his phone, locks the van and runs down the cobbled street to the water's edge.

There is a police boat and a black motorised dingy bobbing on the river less than a hundred feet away. A police helicopter hovers high above and a crowd has formed on the bridge at the base of the north tower.

Craig sprints up the steps and shoves his way through the onlookers, who are mainly tourists. Some of them are filming the search operation. He hangs over the ramparts and looks down into the water. A police diver on board the dingy is relaying a message to the pilot of the boat.

'What happened?' Craig demands to know from an elderly man in a baseball cap.

'Someone jumped in,' says the American.

'Who jumped in?'

'A woman. I saw it all. I was just walking across the bridge and then all of a sudden this lady – tall, smart lady in a suit – takes her shoes off and climbs up on the barrier by that lamppost there,' he points over Craig's shoulder, 'and throws herself in. It was all over in seconds. Just like that. Boom. Straight in. We all looked down there but she just disappeared in the water.'

'Definitely a woman?'

'Yes. A tall, thin lady. She jumped straight down. No hesitation. Are you feeling OK, son? Do you need to sit down?'

'I'm fine, I'm fine,' Craig says, swaying into the woman behind him.

He turns away from the edge, pushes his way through the pack and staggers back in the direction of the van, barely looking where he's going. He stumbles down the steps and makes it to a bench overlooking the river. It takes a couple of minutes for him to stop panting as he sits staring vacantly at the rescue boats.

Two police frogmen resurface. There are stunned faces and a couple of camera flashes on the bridge as the divers pull a body from the water.

Craig walks to the railings on the water's edge. There are beads of sweat on his forehead and he shivers. After several minutes of gazing down into the water, some colour returns to his face and he wanders along the river, away from the bridge, past the reception of the hotel.

Amy calls.

'Amy.' His voice is strained.

'Thank fuck for that.' He sits on a low brick wall facing the river by a statue of a sundial. He leans forward with elbows on knees and apologises for swearing.

'Where is he?

'I'm by the river.

'Why didn't he ring me? I left so many messages.

'I got here and police divers were looking for someone in the river. They've just pulled a body out, I think. They're still out there now. When I got here and saw that I-

'No, it was a woman. I ran up onto the bridge and I saw all that happening and couldn't help thinking the worst. God I was-

'Well he better be. I feel like I've had a heart attack.

'No, I'm OK.

'OK.

'Sorry, I didn't mean to worry you, but I'll show you the note...

'When I got here and saw all the people looking into the water, part of me was just waiting for them to find him. I-

'No, it's fine. I might just go and get a coffee and something to eat first, then I'll go and find him.

'It's my fault.

'Thanks. I just need to sit down, my heart's still racing. All I was thinking about was how was I going to tell people, and what I would tell people. I don't know why but I felt like I'd caused it.

'When I was driving here I was thinking about everything he'd said in the last few days and wondering if he'd been trying to tell me something which I'd ignored or not picked up on. And then the note this morning...

'No, don't worry I won't. I'm not angry, I'm just glad he hasn't done something stupid.

'No. Are you sure?

'Text me where you are and I'll–

'OK. I just need to sit on my own for a minute and cool down though. I think I'm still in shock. I'll ring you if I can't find him.

'Call me when you get to Tower Hill.'

Craig wipes his forehead and watches as the rescue boats disappear down river. The crowd on Tower Bridge has dispersed. He gets to his feet and crosses the lock into St Katherine Docks.

The marina – bordered by the back of the Tower Hotel and a Victorian-era warehouse which has been converted into shops and offices – is teeming with multi-million pound yachts. Beyond them are two larger docks full of equally expensive vessels, surrounded by modern apartments and a decked piazza of shops and restaurants. Facing Craig across the cobbles is the Sir Frances Drake, a timber-framed pub with verandas overlooking the marina. After stopping to admire the boats, he starts to walk towards Starbucks but then heads to the pub instead. As he approaches the entrance, something catches his attention in the window: Mark, drinking a pint.

Mark does a double-take and grabs *The Daily Telegraph* from the next table as Craig bounds up the steps. Craig turns the corner to see him, arms outstretched, trying to hide behind the newspaper.

Craig walks up to him and stands there.

Mark brings the paper closer to his face.

'Put the paper down, Mark.' Nothing happens. 'Mark, stop being a prick,' Craig says grabbing *The Telegraph* out of his hands.

'Sorry mate,' he says sheepishly. He's had his hair cut and is wearing a smart suit and tie. 'I swear I was only having one pint and I was coming straight back. Please don't go mental at me.'

Craig sits down. His face is red and he's clenching his jaw. 'What are you doing here? And why are you dressed like that? Have you–'

'I've had a job interview.'

'What? Really?' Craig is instantly less agitated.

'Yes. Sorry. I was hoping it wouldn't last that long so I could come back and help, but it overran and then they called me back for psychometric testing. I didn't want to tell you in case nothing came of it. I did leave you a note.'

'Yes, I know,' Craig says, tugging it out of his pocket. 'Do you know what I've done this morning?'

'Got angry and come looking for me?'

'I wasn't *angry* mate. I, I thought you'd thrown yourself in the river.'

'*What?*' Mark says, dumbfounded. 'Why did you think that?'

'Look at what the note says.' Craig flicks it over to him.

Mark reads it. 'What made you think I'd thrown myself in the river?' he says half-laughing.

'*Gone to Tower Bridge.*'

'I had gone to Tower Bridge.'

'Yes, but why didn't you write, *Gone for an interview near Tower Bridge*? This makes it sound like you're standing *on* the bridge.'

'Mate, I meant the Tower Bridge area, why did you take it so literally? And what made you think I was going to throw myself off?' Mark says open-mouthed.

'*Go on without me. I may be some time.*'

'I didn't want you to be sitting around waiting, that's all. I didn't know what time I was going to be back. I hoped I'd be back quickly; I was just warning you.'

'Yes, but *I may be some time* was what that explorer said before he walked off into an Arctic storm to die.'

'What explorer? When was this?'

'I can't think of his name, but it's a famous quote. It was probably about a hundred years ago. He thought he was slowing the team down, so to give the others a better chance of surviving, he killed himself.'

'Really? I've never heard that before.'

'It's a famous story. Google it. Anyway, how about all this about me being strong and *take care of my stuff*?'

'I was talking about carrying boxes! Some of my stuff's a bit delicate. I didn't want you chucking it around and breaking it. Not that you'd do that, but I just wanted to tell you.'

Craig shakes his head. 'And *sorry for doing this to you.*'

'I am sorry, genuinely. I didn't want to leave you to carry everything on your own. That's why I did as much as I could before I left.'

'Yes, I know but that just made me even more worried because it was so tidy, it was totally unlike you. It was like you were packing everything away and saying goodbye.'

'That's what I *was* doing. We're moving out! What did you expect my room to look like?'

'A tip as usual! But I... but you said you'd make it up to me in another life. Who says that? Why not write, *I'll buy you a beer* or something like that?'

'That's just one of those sayings,' Mark says, trying to play it down. 'Anyway I won't make it up to you in another life; I'll make it up to you today. Do you want a beer?'

Craig ignores the question. 'Do you realise I almost caused about four accidents driving over here and I've probably been done for speeding. And when I arrived they were pulling someone out of the river!'

'Really?'

'Yes,' Craig snaps. 'I thought it might have been you. I thought I was going to have to identify your body and call your mum and dad to tell them that you're dead!'

Mark starts laughing.

'It's not funny Mark. I was going mad.'

'OK, OK, I'm sorry, I'm sorry. I just never thought you'd jump to such a mental conclusion. I'm really sorry. I never meant to cause all this fuss. Honestly.' He looks out towards the water. 'Who was in the river?'

'A woman,' Craig says, calming down.

'How old was she?'

'Not that old I don't think.'

There's a long, reflective silence.

'I still don't understand though mate, why did you think I'd want to *kill myself?*' Mark asks, lowering his voice towards the end of the sentence. 'I'm a bit... hurt to be honest.'

Craig sighs. 'I don't know. Because of how you've been recently I suppose.'

'What do you mean? I've not been that bad mate.'

'Mate, since you stopped working, you've been like a different person, like a ghost.'

'I thought you'd think that was a good thing.'

Craig shakes his head. 'No, not completely. I was worried. And Amy was. I didn't actually think you'd kill yourself, at least I hoped not, but think of it from my point of view. You've seemed so down for the last couple of months, you've barely spoken to me, and apart from seeing Amy or going to the gym you've just been in the house all day. You've not been yourself and then when I saw the note, my mind just went into overdrive.'

Mark frowns. 'Sorry,' he says eventually.

'And I know when people feel a bit depressed they can do things that are completely out of character.'

'I suppose so.' Mark reaches for his glass and huffs. 'I understand. I've not been depressed though. It's just... the last couple of months have been a bit of a shock. It's all been a bit... confusing. You know? Everything was going really well and then suddenly... nothing. I wasn't sure what to do. I had loads of ideas, obviously, but...'

'I know how it feels.'

Craig goes to the bar to get an orange juice. Mark looks deep in thought when he returns.

'I remember how I felt all the time I was at Cinq,' Craig says. 'Not having any money, not being able to get another job. I felt so anxious all the time. I could have a few beers to forget about it, but the feeling always came back the next morning.'

'At least you had work to keep your mind occupied though.'

'But work was the problem. I couldn't escape it.'

The boys sit quietly with their drinks, barely talking, until Amy arrives. Her cheeks are bright red and her hair has been blown about in the wind. Mark stands up to greet her but she sits down next to Craig and asks if he's OK.

'I'm better now,' Craig says.

'*You* didn't think I'd done anything crazy did you?' Mark asks her.

'You shouldn't have just gone off like that,' Amy says bluntly.

Mark's smile fades. 'I did leave a note.'

'Yeah and look what it says.' Craig shows it to Amy.

'Bloody hell, Mark. You could have chosen your words a bit more carefully.' She tuts and passes it back.

'Look, I'm sorry, OK? I really didn't mean for both of you to get in such a panic. I thought I'd be out and back quickly and everything would be fine.'

'Yeah but it wasn't fine was it,' Craig says.

'I've said sorry about a hundred times now. What more can I do? Anyway why has nobody asked me how the interview went?'

'How did it go then?' Amy asks. 'You look smart. Your hair looks better.'

'Thanks. It went well.'

'What's it for?' Craig asks.

'It's a corporate partnership manager role.'

'For who?'

'The Royal Military Trust. They're a charity that raises money for wounded soldiers and their families. They want someone with financial experience to deal with their corporate donors and, if possible, wring more money out of them.'

Craig looks at Amy. 'That's–'

'That sounds great,' Amy says, kicking Craig under the table. 'When did you apply for that?'

'I didn't. I got a phone call from a recruitment agent who'd seen my LinkedIn profile and he arranged an interview.'

'Did you have to send your CV in?'

'He said he already had it.'

'Where did he get it from?'

'I think I applied for something through him a while ago. He must have had it on file.'

'Yeah, probably,' Craig says. 'Did they ask you any tough questions in the interview?'

'Not really but I had a bit of a panic before I went in.'

'What about?'

'Well, I suddenly realised that I didn't know which version of my CV they had, and I couldn't remember what I'd said on what version.'

'What did you do then?'

'I took a risk: I just told them the truth.'

Craig and Amy glance at each other.

'What did that feel like?' Craig asks.

'It was easier than I thought it would be. I didn't have to remember anything; I just told them more or less what I'd been doing. I only slipped up on one bit, which was the year I left school. I went through a spell of making it a year earlier on my CV and I'd stuck to that for so long that I confused myself about when it actually was.'

'How did you get out of it?'

'I said I'd got concussion from a bang on the head playing rugby at the weekend so I was a bit confused about dates.'

'So you lied,' Amy says.

'Yes, but I could hardly tell them the truth could I?'

'I suppose not. When do you find out if you've got it or not?'

'Oh, I've found out already. That's why I was in here having a beer. They've offered it to me.'

'Well done mate,' Craig says.

'That's brilliant. I'm really happy for you,' Amy says.

'Thanks,' Mark says, 'but I'm not sure if I'm going to take it.'

'*Why not*? Are you serious?' Amy says.

'Well I'm not sure if it's the right job for me. The bonus scheme isn't that good and I've got my business interests-'

'What business interests?' Craig says.

'Mark, if you turn this job down, you're an even bigger fool that I thought you were,' Amy says. 'You're in no position to be picky. How are you going to pay your rent? Your parents aren't going to help you.'

'They're not even talking to me.'

'Why not?' Craig asks.

'They found out about me spending the inheritance money.'

'Oh.'

'There are other jobs out there though, I don't want to commit-'

'How many other interviews have you got lined up?' Amy asks.

'Um, well, none at the moment, but I'm getting a few calls from recruitment people but...'

'But what?'

'I just want to take time and consider all my options.'

'Mark, you've had the last three months to consider your options.'

'I know, but like I said, I'm pretty sure there could be something better out there.'

'Like what? Don't you realise that if you don't take this job it could be six months or a year before you get another one.'

'Don't be dramatic,' Mark says. 'I think we'll probably be sitting here in a couple of years, in 2010, and we'll look back at this so-called crash and we'll wonder what all the fuss was about.'

'Well, you're in a minority of one,' Amy says. 'And I'm not being dramatic. You need money, quickly, and who knows what state the job market might be in in a few months.'

'And I can't pay your rent mate,' Craig says.

'Craig, you'd never need to pay my rent and I know some doom-mongers are saying the economy's ruined but let's just wait and see–'

'No Mark, let's not just wait and see. I'm actually getting angry now,' Amy says, 'We've been busting a gut trying to help you.'

'How?'

'How? Are you being serious? Who wrote your LinkedIn profile, Mark? Who's been sending your CV to recruitment agents? Who's been applying for jobs for you?'

'I did LinkedIn, ages ago, and all the job–'

'We've been doing it you *idiot*,' Amy snaps. 'Why do you think you've been getting phone calls and emails about jobs?'

'I just thought–'

'Just thought that if you did nothing, the jobs would come to you?'

'No but–'

'We spent ages rewriting your CV, and Amy has been doing all these covering letters and application forms for you,' says Craig.

'You don't realise how bad the job situation is because you haven't been trying to get one,' Amy says. 'You're not immune from this, Mark. You're not some special case.'

Mark is visibly shaken by Amy's retort and doesn't say anything for a few seconds. 'But I don't understand,' he says finally. 'Why would you do all this for me?'

'Because we care, Mark. Why else do you think we'd do it?' Amy says. 'The longer you're out of a job, the harder it will be to get one, and we're not going to let you fall by the wayside. And Craig needs a flatmate who can pay half the bills.'

'Do you both think I'm that useless that I couldn't get a job by myself?'

'No, mate,' Craig says. 'But we just thought you might need a little push in the right direction.'

'Well thanks, but today that was me, not you. It was me on my own in the interview and it was my experience and my qualifications and my personality. It wasn't anyone else.'

'We never said it was anyone else,' Amy says.

'And they thought I was the best person for the job. They seemed to like me.'

'But why wouldn't they like you, Mark? What's wrong with you just being Mark rather than feeling you have to act up to this stupid City idiot persona all the time? Everyone would like *this* Mark; you've just chosen to keep him hidden. We're not interested in what car you've got or what nightclubs you've been to-'

'Or where you're going skiing,' Craig chips in.

'We'd rather you just tried a bit less hard at trying to be someone you're not and tried a bit harder with the people who care about you, like us two, and your family. Nobody is interested in the bullshit; not us, not your employers, not anyone.'

Mark gives Amy a sulky glance and his head drops. A waiter asks him if he's finished with his glass. He drinks the remaining inch of his pint and hands it over.

He sniffs and says, 'So you both think I'd be stupid to turn this job down?'

'*Yes*,' Craig and Amy say emphatically.

'Perhaps you're right,' Mark says with a shrug. 'I'm not ungrateful. I knew that somebody must have been doing something. I haven't got to let the Trust know until Monday but I'll ring later and tell them I'll take it. I know I shouldn't go on hoping something better will come up.'

'That's the first sensible thing you've said since I've known you,' Amy says.

Mark half-smiles. 'That's a bit of an exaggeration. I'm not a complete moron,' he says, leaning back in his chair.

'You're not a moron, Mark, just a bit... misguided. But at least you won't be unemployed. And I bet you it'll be a better place to work than where I am at the moment.'

'I'd hope so. But the bonus-'

'Will you stop going on about the bonus, it's like you've been brainwashed,' Amy says.

'I've never had a bonus, from any job,' Craig says.

'OK, sorry. I know a good bonus isn't everything and if I don't like it I suppose I can just get another job somewhere else.'

Amy rolls her eyes. 'Why don't you give the new job a few weeks before you start thinking about your next move?'

'I suppose it's better to be working than sitting in watching Sky all day isn't it?' Mark says, sounding slightly more upbeat. 'And I'll have more money again.'

'Probably more than you had before now you're not paying an astronomical rent.'

'I hadn't thought about that. There are some positives.'

'There are lots of positives,' Amy says, 'I can't believe it's taken you so long to realise it.'

'I do realise, honestly.' Mark gets to his feet and gets his wallet out. 'We should have a celebration drink.'

'Mate, um, I don't want to be a spoilsport,' Craig says, 'but I've got the van and we need to move our stuff this afternoon. We shouldn't really-'

Mark shakes his head. 'Craig, forget the van; I'll sort that out later.'

'But-'

'Come on, don't be boring. Amy, call work and tell them you're not coming back this afternoon, and Craig, call Hannah and get her down here as well. Let's have a drink; I owe you.'

'Yes, but you don't have to do it right now,' Craig says. 'We've got the whole weekend-'

'We've got the whole weekend to move. Please, have a drink with me. I'll sort everything out, I promise.'

'Mark, I've got a meeting this afternoon,' Amy says.

'Make up an excuse and cancel it, please, just for me, I'm not taking no for an answer. We're celebrating, come on. I've read about loads of entrepreneurs who've had things go wrong and lost all their money and come back stronger. That's what I'll do. This is the second coming of Mark Hunter. Now suddenly everything's making sense. That must be worth a drink surely? Someone get me a wine list. They'll do champagne here, won't they? They must do, I'll ask the barman. Can I borrow one of your credit cards?'

Acknowledgements

Thanks to Morwenna Monk; Terry and Sandra Canty; Humfrey Hunter, Robert Dinsdale, Laura Sherlock; Toby Lovatt, Richard Goldthorpe, Oliver Pearson, Rebecca Canty; Josh Monk, Chris Perry, John Scott.